PRONUNCIATION GUIDE

Jeru – JEH roo

Meshara – Meh SHAH ruh

Lark – Lahrk

Tiras – TEER us

Boojohni – Boo JAH nee

Degn – Dane

Corvyn – COHR vin

Zoltev – ZOHL tehv

Volgar – VOLH gahr

Kjell – Kel

Kilmorda – Kil MOHR da

Bin Dar – BIN Dahr

Drue – Droo

Firi – FEAR ee

Bilwick – BIL wik

Enoch – EE nuk

Quondoon – qwahn DOON

Janda – JAHN da

Jyraen – jeh RAE un

Jeruvian – jeh ROO vee un

Nivea – NI vee uh

the

BIRD

and the

SWORD

New York Times Bestselling Author

AMY HARMON

Library of Congress Cataloging-in-Publication Data

Harmon, Amy
The Bird and the Sword — 1st edition
ISBN-13: 978-1533134134 | ISBN-10: 1533134138

THE LAND OF JERU

PLASSE
2016

WILLA

DENDDOU

PORTA

THE JYRAEN SEA

CORWYNN

KILMORDA

FIRIN

DRUE FOREST

BINDAR

DEGN

JERU

Nivea

Ancient Seabed

QUONDOON

BILWICK

GAUL

IANDA

WENOCH

For the word is quick and powerful,
Sharper than any two-edged sword,
Piercing, even to the dividing asunder
Of soul and spirit,
Of joints and marrow.
It is a discerner of the thoughts
And intents of the heart.

PROLOGUE

S he was so small. The only thing large about her were her eyes, and they filled her face, grey and solemn like the fog on the moors. At five summers, she was the size of children two summers younger, and she was slight in a way that caused me concern. Not unhealthy, exactly. In truth, she'd never been ill. Not even once. But she was delicate, almost fragile, like a tiny bird. Little bones and small features, a pointy chin and elfin ears. Her pale brown hair, heavy and soft, felt like feathers brushing my face when I held her close, furthering the comparison.

She was my little lark. The name had entered my mind the moment I laid eyes on her, and I accepted it, acknowledging it from the Father of all Words, trusting the name was meant to be.

"What are you doing, Lark?" My voice was sharp, as I intended it to be, but my daughter wasn't afraid, not even a little bit, though she'd been caught in a place where she shouldn't be. I was worried she would prick her fingers on the sharp spindle of the spinning wheel or fall from the high, open windows overlooking the courtyard. This was my special room, and I loved it here, especially when she was with me. But she'd disobeyed me in entering alone.

"I'm making poppets," she answered, her husky voice a comical contrast to her tiny frame. Her pink tongue peeked out between pursed lips, indicating great focus. She wrapped a length of string around the wadded piece of cloth in her hands, creating a head, though a misshapen one. She'd already made its legs and arms and had three more poppets, already constructed, lying next to her on the floor.

"Lark, you know you can't be here alone. It's not safe for such a little girl. And you can't use your words when I am not with you," I reproached.

"But you were gone so long," she said, raising woeful eyes to mine.

"Don't look at me like that. That is no excuse for disobedience."

She bowed her head and her shoulders fell.

"I'm sorry, Mother."

"Promise me you will remember and obey."

"I promise I will remember . . . and obey."

I waited, letting the promise settle on both of us, etching it into the air so she was bound by her words.

"Now . . . tell me about your poppets."

"This one loves to dance. She pointed at the lumpy doll to her left. "And this one loves to climb—"

"Like a certain little lark I know," I interrupted tenderly.

"Yes. Like me. And this one loves jumping." She held up the smallest one.

"And this one?" I pointed to the poppet she'd just finished.

"This one is a prince."

"Oh?"

"Yes. The Prince of Poppets. And he can fly."

"Without wings?"

"Yes. You don't need wings to fly," she chirped, repeating something I'd told her.

"What do you need, Daughter?" I asked, quizzing her.

"Words," she answered, her big, grey eyes alight with knowledge.

"Tell me," I whispered.

She picked up the poppet nearest her and pressed her lips to the place on the poppet's chest where its heart would be.

"Dance," Lark whispered, believing it could. She set it down on the floor and we watched together. The little, cloth doll began to twirl and raise its ill-formed arms and legs, leaping and turning across the room. I laughed softly. Little Lark picked up another.

"Jump," she urged, pressing the word into the poppet's breast. It leaped from her hand and bounced soundlessly behind the dancing doll.

She repeated the action, giving a word to the remaining poppets, and we watched in fascination as one doll scrambled up the curtains and the Prince of Poppets flew into the air, arms outstretched like lumpy wings, and darted and dived like a happy bird.

She clapped her tiny hands and danced and jumped with her new friends, and I danced with her. We were so delighted and so lost in the experience that I failed to hear the boots in the hall outside the door until it was almost too late. I'd been foolish—carelessly so. That wasn't like me.

"Lark, take the words away!" I cried, running to lock the door.

Lark grasped the dancing doll and took its word away, the way I'd taught her, breathing the word into its chest, backward.

"*Ecnad,*" she said, swallowing it back into herself. The hopping poppet was scampering around her feet, and she scooped it up and whispered "*Pmuj.*"

There was a pounding at the door, and my servant Boojohni called to me, his voice urgent.

"Lady Meshara! The king is here. Lord Corvyn says ye must come now."

I caught the climbing poppet as it scaled the rock wall near the heavy door. I tossed it to Lark, and she removed the word as she'd done the others.

"Where is the flyer?" I hissed, searching with frantic eyes, peering up at the high beams and the dark crevices. Then, from the corner of my eye, I spotted it. It had flown through the open window and was flitting like a handkerchief in the breeze. But there was no wind.

"Lady Meshara!" Boojohni was as frantic as we, but for a very different reason.

"Come, Lark. It will be all right. It is too high for others to see. Stay behind me, understand?"

She nodded, and I could see I'd frightened her. There was reason to be afraid. A visit from the king was never welcome. I opened the door and greeted Boojohni demurely. He turned and strode away, knowing I would follow.

Twenty riders were gathered in the wide courtyard of the keep, and my husband was bowing and genuflecting when I arrived with Lark trailing behind my skirts. For one so disdainful of the king, my lord was quick to kiss the king's boots. Fear made weaklings of us all.

"Lady Meshara!" the king boomed, and my husband rose and turned to me, relief in his face.

I curtsied deeply, as was required, and Lark mimicked my salutation, catching the king's eye.

"What have we here? Your daughter, Meshara?"

I nodded once, but didn't offer her name. Names had power and I didn't want him to have hers. There had been a time when I'd considered vying for the king's attention—I was the grand-daughter of the Lord of Enoch and of noble birth, and I'd been drawn to the handsome King Zoltev of Degn. That was before I saw him cut off the hands of an old woman caught spinning wheat into long ribbons of gold. I'd begged my father to arrange a marriage with Lord Corvyn instead. Corvyn was weak, but he wasn't evil, though I wondered if weakness wasn't just as dangerous. The weak allowed evil to flourish.

"No sons, Corvyn?" King Degn asked mildly.

My husband shook his head in shame, as if embarrassed by the fact, and I felt a flash of fury.

"I am showing my son his kingdom. All of this will one day be his." King Zoltev indicated the keep, the mountains, even the people kneeling in homage, as if he owned the very sky above our heads and the air we breathed.

"Prince Tiras, let your people see you." The king turned in his saddle, beckoning his son forward.

The King's Guard parted, opening the way for a boy on a huge, black stallion to amble to his father's side. The boy was lanky and lean, all elbows and shoulders and knees and feet, perched on the cusp of a growth spurt. His hair and eyes were dark, almost as black as the horse beneath him, and his skin was as warm as the Spinner's gold. His mother, the late queen, was not of Jeru, but of a southern country known for their darker complexions and skill with the sword. He rode the horse comfortably, but warriors surrounded him in a loose circle, as if to protect him. He didn't wear a royal crest across his chest, and his charger was draped in solid green, like every member of the guard, but that could have been for his safety. Being the son of an unpopular king—or a popular one, for that matter—made you a target for kidnapping and revenge.

I curtsied deeply once more, and Lark darted around me and raised her hand to touch the prince's horse, unafraid as always. She looked like a fairy child next to the enormous animal, and the prince slid down from his mount and extended his hand to her in greeting, introducing her to his horse. Lark giggled in delight, tucking her tiny hand in his, and he smiled as she placed a kiss on his knuckles. I thought I heard her whisper as her mouth touched his skin, and I stepped forward to draw her away, suddenly fearful that she'd bestowed one of her innocent gifts. But no one was looking at her or the prince.

A gasp had risen from the assemblage, and I raised my eyes to the fluttering white poppet dancing in the air. For a heartbeat there was silence as both man and beast watched the silly creation dip and dive like an oddly-shaped dove. Like a child drawn to its mother's side, the poppet had returned to its creator.

"Father, look!" It was the prince, and he was charmed by the funny flying object. "It's magic!"

"The Prince of Poppets followed us, Mother," Lark whispered timidly, and she stretched her hand toward the doll she'd imbued with a single word. *Fly.* So harmless. So innocent. So deadly.

I plucked the flyer from the air and shoved my fist behind my back where Lark now cowered. I could feel her little hands pulling desperately on my skirt, but I dared not draw attention to her.

"Magic!" the king's soldiers hissed, and suddenly the spell was broken. Horses reared and swords were unsheathed. The prince looked on in horror, trying to calm the horse that had been docile only moments before.

"Witch," the king breathed. "Witch!" he shouted, extending his sword toward the heavens as if calling on an entirely different kind of power. His horse reared, and his eyes gleamed.

"Confess, Lady Meshara," he roared. "Kneel and confess, and I will kill you quickly."

"If you kill me, you will lose your soul and your son to the sky," I warned, my eyes straying briefly to his young son who met my gaze, his hands clinging to the mane of his enormous horse.

"Kneel!" Zoltev commanded again, righteous outrage ringing in the air.

"You are a monster, and Jeru will see you for what you are. I will not kneel for your slaughter, nor will I confess as if you are my God."

Lark whimpered, and she pressed her lips to the poppet in my fist.

"*Ylf*," I heard her whisper, and the squirming poppet went limp as the king swung his sword in final judgment. Someone screamed, and the sound continued without ceasing as if the king had rent the sky in two and horror dripped out. I fell to the earth, covering my little girl, the poppet still clenched in my fist.

There was no pain. Just pressure. Pressure and sorrow. Incredible sorrow. My daughter would be alone with her enormous gift. I would not be able to protect her. I felt my blood flowing from my body over hers, and I pressed my lips to her ear and called on the words that limned every living thing.

"Swallow Daughter, pull them in, those words that sit upon your lips. Lock them deep inside your soul, hide them 'til they've time to grow. Close your mouth upon the power, curse not, cure not, 'til the hour. You won't speak and you won't tell, you won't call on heav'n or hell. You will learn and you will thrive. Silence, daughter. Stay alive."

I heard someone shouting, pleading for mercy, and realized Boojohni had thrown himself over me, doing his best to shield me from another blow. But another blow would be needless.

Corvyn knelt beside me, moaning in horror, and I lifted my head from Lark's ear to find his stunned grey eyes, wet with fear. I had to make him strong, make him believe, if only for his own survival. I concentrated on what must be said. My power to tell was spilling out onto the cobblestones.

"Hide her words, Corvyn. Because if she dies . . . if she is even harmed, you will share the very same fate."

His eyes widened as mine closed, and the words and the world grew quiet.

ONE

In the beginning was the Word,
and the Word was with God, and the Word was God.

I can't make words. I can't make a sound. I have thoughts and feelings. I have pictures and colors. They are all bottled up inside of me because I can't make words.

But I can hear them.

The world is alive with words. The animals, the trees, the grass, and the birds hum with their own words.

"Life," they say.

"Air," they breathe.

"Heat," they hum. The birds call "Fly, fly!" and the leaves wave them onward, uncurling as they whisper "grow, grow."

I love these words. There is no deception or confusion. The words are simple. The birds feel joy. The trees feel it too. They feel joy in their creation. They feel joy because they ARE. Every living thing has a word, and I hear them all.

But I can't make them.

My mother told me with words, God created worlds. With words He created light and dark, water and air, plants and trees, birds and beasts, and from the dust and the dirt of those worlds, He created children, two sons and two daughters, forming them in his image and breathing life into their bodies of clay.

In the beginning, He gave each child a word, a powerful word, which called down a special ability, a precious gift to guide them in their journey through their world. One daughter was given the word *spin*, for she could spin all manner of things into gold. The grass, the leaves, a strand of her hair. One son was given the word *change,* which gifted him the ability to transform himself into the beasts of the forest or the creatures of the air. The word *heal* was given to another son, to cure illness and injury among his brothers and sisters. One daughter was given the word *tell*, and she could predict what was to come. Some said she could even shape the future with the power of her words.

The Spinner, The Changer, The Healer, and The Teller lived long and had many children of their own, but even with blessed words and magnificent abilities, life in the world was dangerous and difficult. Often-times, grass was more useful than gold. Man was more desirable than a beast. Chance was more seductive than knowledge, and eternal life was completely meaningless without love.

The Healer could heal his siblings when they grew ill, but he couldn't save them from themselves. He watched as his brother, The Changer, spent so much time as a beast—surrounded by them—that he became one himself. The Spinner, who loved The Changer, was so crazed with grief, she spun and spun, round and round, until she'd spun herself into gold, a statue of sorrow next to the well of the world she'd climbed up from. The Teller, realizing she'd predicted it all, swore to never speak again, and The

Healer, alone without them, died of a broken heart he refused to heal.

Their children spread across the land, and years became decades and decades became centuries. Their numbers grew great, and there were many with the power of words or the ability to change or heal or spin. But the power was diluted and altered by the mixing of the gifts. New gifts emerged and some gifts were lost all together. Some used their gifts to harm.

A descendant of The Changer, a king who could transform into a dragon, ravaged the countryside, destroying the land with fire and killing the people who opposed him. A powerful warrior who wanted to be king slayed the dragon and garnered the gratitude of a terrified people. He claimed that everyone should have the same gifts. He said those who could spin or tell or change or heal shouldn't be able to use their gifts because it gave them an advantage over other men. People had grown both jealous and afraid, and many agreed with the ambitious warrior, though some did not. A woman whose son was saved by a healer argued that the gifts *did* benefit all. A man whose crop was saved by a teller who predicted a terrible storm and warned him to harvest early, agreed with her.

But the voices of fear and discontent are always loudest, and one by one, the Tellers, the Healers, the Changers, and the Spinners were destroyed. They burned the Tellers at the stake. They cut off the Spinners' hands. They hunted the Changers like the animals they resembled and stoned the Healers in the village squares, until those with special gifts—any gift—were afraid of their abilities and hid their talents from each other.

The warrior became king and his son reigned after him. Generation after generation of warrior kings held the throne, vigilant in removing the Gifted from the population, convinced that equality could only be realized if no one was special, and the power of the words was eradicated.

My mother made words. She was a Teller, and her words were magic. She spoke and the words became life. Reality. Truth. My father knew it, and he was afraid. Words can be terrible when the truth is unwelcome.

My mother was careful with her words, so careful that she made them soundless when she died. Now they swarm silently all around me, like quiet watchers waiting for someone to speak them into being.

But as I walked, the forest was thick with sound.

The night whispered to me, words layered over one another. The owl cried *who,* but he didn't want to know the answer. He already knew, and he watched without trepidation. The moon was huge above me, the ground soft beneath my feet, and I relished the sense of belonging among other silent creatures. We were the same. We lived, but no one really noticed us. I brushed my fingertips against the rough bark and felt an answering greeting, though it was more a feeling than a word. The world was sleeping. The forest was sleeping too, though not as deeply. There was a world coming awake here, and I leaned against the tree that felt like a friend and let the peace wash over me.

A sudden shrieking bled through the leaves and pierced the calm, making the tree retreat into itself, and the words that hovered around me quieted instantly, leaving only one. *Danger. Danger*, the forest rumbled, but instead of running away, I turned toward the sound.

Something was in terrible pain.

I don't know why I ran toward it. But I did. I ran toward the cry that rent the darkness and made the hair on my skin stand up in warning. The scream quieted briefly only to rise again, a death call, and I stumbled into a clearing and drew up short. There, bathed in moonlight, was the biggest bird I'd ever seen. It lay in a heap, an arrow protruding from its chest. Feathers quivered as it drew breath, labored, gasping, and I approached carefully, one softly placed step at a time.

I couldn't soothe it the way a mother soothes a child, but human sounds rarely soothed animals unless the animal was a beloved pet or a faithful horse. This was neither. The bird raised its glossy white head, eyes black and trained on my face, and watched me in wary desperation. Its wings shuddered with the impulse to fly, but there was no strength behind the movement.

It was an eagle, the kind you only see from a distance, if at all. It was magnificent with its regal, white head and sooty black feathers, the very tips tinged a blood red. I didn't dare touch it, not for my own sake, but for the eagle's. My touch would alarm, not comfort, and the bird would struggle to fly, which would only cause pain. I crouched nearby and studied it, trying to ascertain what could be done, if anything, to alleviate his suffering.

I reached out and placed a hand on the fan of the wing nearest me. Closing my eyes, I pushed a word toward him, silent energy encompassed in thought. It was the way the animals shared their essence with me, and it seemed to work in varying degrees when I wanted to get my way.

Safe, I told him silently. *Safe*.

His wing stopped shuddering beneath my hand. I opened my eyes and regarded him gratefully. *Safe*, I promised again. He was still, perfectly so, but his eyes clung to my face, and his breaths were more shallow.

He was going to die.

The arrow was buried deep in his chest, and pulling it out would kill him more quickly. I worried more about his pain and the animals that might find him and make a meal of him before he was dead.

Then there was the matter of the arrow itself. Where was the shooter?

I listened intently, pushing my senses outward, hearing the conversation of the trees, the hum of the nightlife, and the rustle of the wind. I couldn't feel danger or fear, and I didn't sense pursuit or hear the approach of human thought. Maybe the eagle had been able to fly a distance before he fell, escaping the archer.

Light. I felt the word rise up from the bird. *Light.* I wondered if his yearning was for the day, as if it would save him from his fate, as if the night was responsible for his death. Or maybe the bird saw the radiance of a shiny forever beckoning him to fly into endless skies among the Gods.

Light.

I could stay until then. I could stay until dawn, if he lasted that long. I would keep the predators at bay as he left one world to fly into the next. I relaxed beside him, moving my hand to the silken feathers of his breast.

I kept my touch light and my intentions heavy, pressing the power of my intent into his pained breaths.

Relief, I told him. *Comfort. Quiet. Peace.* The words were only a balm, not a cure. I was not a Healer, after all. But I urged wellness on him too, though it was only a wish. He was so resplendent, and I hated to see him die.

Boojohni would come looking for me. He would grumble and bellyache and groan about his sore feet and knobby knees, but he would come because he loved me and would worry if I didn't return soon. My father had tied me to him when I was young. Tied, like an unruly dog. My father was so afraid something would happen to me, he had never left me unguarded. It was Boojohni's job to make sure nothing happened to me. We were about the same height then, making us appear like two naughty children being harshly disciplined wherever we went. Boojohni hated it even more than I did. But he was compensated for his trouble and humiliation. My humiliation was not considered.

Boojohni was a troll, more closely resembling a monkey than a grown man, with a flat, rubbery nose above an impressive beard that matched the wild hair that started low on his forehead and continued down his back. He was only four feet tall, fully grown, but he wore clothing, walked on two legs, and was as wise as any man, though Boojohni was the first to disown the human race.

I was much taller than Boojohni now, but he was still my protector, though I'd outgrown the leash. I would not be caged, though my father tried. If his concern had come from love, it would have been easier to endure. But it came from self-preservation, from fear, and the resentment between us had grown deeper and deeper since my mother had died.

I sighed softly, just a huff of breath, but the eagle raised its eyes and regarded me.

Light. The word rose up from him again. Urgent. Questioning.

Soon, I soothed, stroking his head. I lied. There would be no light. Dawn was hours away. But I would stay, and Boojohni would just have to grumble. He had a nose like my father's hunting dogs. He would find me easily enough if he insisted upon it.

I eased myself into a more comfortable position, wrapping my gown around my legs to ward off the slight chill and pulling my cloak around me. The growing time was fast approaching, and the snow was gone from the ground, thankfully. The trees were clothed in green, and the grass was thick beneath me. I curled myself in a half-moon around the bird, laying my head on my arm, and I kept my other hand soothing and stroking, urging healing with my thoughts.

I proved myself a poor protector.

I concentrated so hard, with such intent, pouring my energy into communicating peace and rest to the poor bird, that I fell fast asleep, lulled by my own mental suggestions.

TWO

I awoke to Boojohni's fat little hands patting my cheeks and dawn weaving its way through the trees from the east, golden tendrils tickling my lids. I was stiff and cold, my left arm numb, and in my right hand I clutched a long, black feather, tinged in red.

The eagle was gone. There was blood and a few feathers and little else left behind. Had he died? I shot to my feet, startling Boojohni, who had known better than to walk through the forest calling my name. It did him no good to call when I couldn't answer. He'd used his nose and his knowledge of my favorite places, but he looked tired and relieved when he grasped my hand, pulling my attention down to him.

"What?" he asked, noting my alarm.

I pointed at the blood and the feathers. *Eagle. Injured.*

I made a sloppy sign with my hand. I didn't know if he felt the words I pressed upon him or if he understood my hand gestures. Maybe it was the language of long-time companions or all those things combined, but Boojohni and I had our own language, and primitive as it was, we managed to communicate.

"It's gone. Looks like something dragged it off," he grunted simply. I bowed my head in regret. But I hadn't heard anything! I would have heard something, I was sure. Unless the eagle had died, and the wolf was stealthy.

He squatted down low and followed the path of broken twigs and disturbed fauna, leading away from the blood and feathers.

Wolf?

"No," he grunted, like I'd spoken out loud. He did that often. "Not a wolf. A man." He pointed at a partial heel print in the earth. "That's not an animal."

Arrow.

He looked up at me. I tapped my heart and drew back my arms like I was shooting a bow. The archer had found his prey after all, it seemed. I was lucky he only wanted the bird. I'd been extremely vulnerable.

Boojohni scowled at me, obviously thinking the same thing. He stood and put his hands on his hips, abandoning his tracking.

"Yer soft heart is spreading to yer brain and turning it to mush. Ye could have been killed, Bird. Or worse."

I inclined my head, acknowledging his words. But it didn't change anything. It *wouldn't* change anything. I would do what I was going to do, and he knew it. I stayed still a moment longer, searching for the bird, for his imprint in the air, but found no trace of him. He was gone. I sighed in defeat and settled the hood of my cloak over my hair. The fat braid that circled my head felt like a crown of thorns and probably looked like one too. I'd already removed a leaf and a downy bit of a feather. I was not vain, but I did not want to draw attention when I returned to the keep.

"Please, please, for the love of trolls and other blessed creatures, stop wandering around in the forest like yer a bat instead of a wee lady!" Boojohni was building up to some serious grumbling. He spoke harshly, but the word that rose from him was *love*. I didn't hear people's thoughts the way they came out of their mouths. I heard single words, the dominant word. The way I heard the governing words of every living thing. The dominant word from Boojohni was always love, and I could endure his chastisement knowing that.

I sighed and continued walking. He hurried to get in front of me, extending his stubby arms to halt me. I side-stepped him. I wasn't trying to be difficult, but I couldn't argue, and I could listen and walk at the same time. Boojohni could not. His mouth and legs had difficulty running simultaneously. He tugged on my arm.

"There is a war going on only miles from here! A war! Hundreds of violent men and beasts with no scruples about dragging a woman off by her hair! Especially one sleeping in the woods like a gift from the fairies!"

I nodded, letting him know I understood. It didn't pacify him.

"Your father would cut off me beard if he knew how often ye slip away to commune with the forest! Do you not want poor Boojohni to find true love and happiness? What troll would have me without my beard?" He shuddered in horror. I tugged on it affectionately and started walking again.

He seemed momentarily lost in the horrified speculation of his possible beardlessness, and I allowed my mind to skip to the war in Jeru, the war my father and his advisors kept a close eye on. The king himself was camped on my father's lands near the front lines of the latest skirmish. Carrying on his father's legacy, the young king spent more time killing on horseback than sitting on his throne. This time, however, the creatures coming against him were even more terrible than he was.

Rumors of the Volgar were probably exaggerated, but the rumors were truly terrifying. Some said they killed only to drink blood and eat flesh, believing life force was transferable. Their leader, known only as Liege, had wings like a vulture and razor-sharp talons. He flew above his armies and directed them from above.

Liege wanted the Land of Jeru, believing there was power to be consumed, though the King of Jeru, King Tiras's father, had purged the population of magic. Liege wanted the lands of Jeru and Dendar and Porta and Willa. He'd taken Porta. Then Dendar. And he'd left nothing in his wake.

Now he was on the border of Jeru, in the valley of Kilmorda, and King Tiras and his warriors were assembled against him. My father was caught between hope and loyalty. He was a lord of Jeru, and he needed Liege and the Volgar to be defeated. But he also wanted to be King. Preferably, King Tiras would die *after* he defeated the Volgar Liege and his swarms of miscreants. That way my father wouldn't have to contend with marauding monsters when he ascended the throne.

My mother had told the old king he would sell his soul and lose his son to the sky. It hadn't all come to pass—King Zoltev was gone, his soul still in question, and his son was very much alive—but my father was banking his future on the fact that it would. He was next in line for the throne. He wanted to be king, and I just wanted to be free of him. My mother told my father I wouldn't speak again, and she told him if I died, he would die too. He had not doubted her, and I had spent the last fifteen years caged and cornered. My father watched me anxiously for signs of health and hated me because his fate was tied to mine.

When my father looked at me, I almost always heard the same word. I heard my mother's name. *Meshara*. He looked at me, and he was reminded of her warning. I would hear my mother's name in his voice, then he would turn away. Always.

He didn't turn away because I looked like her. My mother was beautiful. I was not. My eyes were a flat grey. Not blue like the sky or green like the sea. Grey. My skin was pale, my hair a light brown—ash, my mother had called it. Not rich. Not dark. Just a quiet brown like the little brown mouse that huddled in the corner and waited for me to sleep so he could steal the crumbs beneath my table. My coloring was as timid and unassuming as I was. Pale. Insipid. So reticent that it had never fully materialized. I was a slight, grey ghost.

"Ye aren't as invisible as ye think, Bird," Boojohni huffed, as if he'd heard my internal musings. "I wasn't the only one who took note that you were missing this mornin'. Strange things are afoot. Mertin, one of the stable hands, was found naked as a wee baby lying in the hay just after dawn. One of the horses was gone too—yer father's favorite grey. Then Bethe comes screeching down to the kitchens claiming yer room is empty and yer bed wasn't slept in. I made her swear to be quiet about it until I could sniff ye out, which I obviously did."

I shook my head and sighed. Bethe was my maid. She was prone to fits of alarm, but the theft of the grey was upsetting. She was a good horse, and I hated that she'd been taken.

I touched my eyes and asked a question with my hands. Boojohni answered immediately, understanding.

"No one saw anything . . . except poor Mertin's ass when he ran from the stables." Boojohni snickered.

I indicated my clothing from head to toe. *Everything?*

"Yeah. All of it. Boots, breeches, shirt, and cloak, to be sure. I don't think Mertin bothers with underthings."

I winced, not liking the thought of Mertin's underthings. He was a big man with a surly attitude and enough hair on his body to weave a small hearth rug. But he was good with the horses and not a man to mess with. I wondered that someone had stolen his things without waking him.

"Mertin thought he'd been pranked until he noticed the horse was gone. He's not laughing now. He'll be getting a handful of lashes fer drinking on his watch. He claims he wasn't drinking—at least not enough to pass out. He has a huge knot on his head, so I'm inclined to think someone clocked him."

That made more sense, and I nodded.

"Your father isn't happy. He's already on edge with the battle on the borders. We won't mention that ye slept in the woods last night with thieves about."

We hurried in silence, skirting the road and cutting through the trees, though it wasn't the most direct route. Boojohni seemed to understand that I would like to avoid the eyes of the early risers, already about their business. I had no reason to be out and about at this hour, rumpled and hooded, looking like I'd spent a night rolling in the hay with Mertin.

My father's keep sat on a rise with several small villages making a half-circle around it in the south, fields and forest ringing it from the north. The only road to the keep was steep with stiff drops off the craggy mountains that rimmed the upper valley of Corvyn. It was fertile land, beautiful and breathtaking, and well-fortified by the natural landscape. But the Volgar were winged men. Cliffs and climbs would do little to deter them if the army at the border failed to hold them off. We were a mere twenty miles from the front in the valley of Kilmorda, and my father, though worried and constantly in talks with his advisors, had not sent a single warrior from Corvyn to help King Tiras defeat the Volgar.

The keep itself was like a small city—two forges, a butcher, a mill, an apothecary, a printer, a clothier, bakers and weavers and makers and healers—all of the very un-magical sort. Skills were acceptable. Mystical gifts were not. Everyone was quick to show how staid and useful they were, and as a result, my only desire as I grew was to be valuable too.

I was never taught to read or write. My father wouldn't allow it. He was afraid to give me words, in any form, and because I couldn't speak, people often forgot that I still understood, and they talked freely in front of me. I learned a great deal that way, listening and watching. I had spent time with the old women of our keep, women who'd never been to school but who were educated in hundreds of other ways. From them I learned to heal with herbs and soothe with my touch. I learned wisdom and wariness, and I learned to patiently accept and quietly wait. For what, I wasn't sure, but in my heart I was always waiting, as if the hour my mother spoke of would someday arrive.

"We thought you'd been carried away by a birdman!" Bethe shrieked as Boojohni and I entered the kitchens from the rear of the keep, my hood still high, my eyes averted. I sighed. I had hoped I would make it up the back stairs without anyone seeing me, but Madame Pattersley, the housekeeper, and my maid had clearly been watching for us.

"What would one of the Volgar want with little Lark, eh?" Boojohni huffed. "She's on the scrawny side. He'd need to carry you off too, Bethe. But that would be a bit difficult." Boojohni winked and slapped Bethe on her very ample behind. She swatted back at him and forgot about me completely, which was what Boojohni intended, but I didn't get by my father's housekeeper quite as easily. She swooped in and jerked the hood from my head. She gasped at the sight of my hair.

"Milady! Where have you been?"

Not being able to answer was a relief, and I shrugged and began unwrapping my hair from around my head, releasing the twigs and leaves caught in the coils.

"You've been with a man!" Bethe squealed. "You've spent the night in the woods with a man."

"She did no such thing," Boojohni growled, offended. I patted his head, gratefully.

"Your father will have to be told, Lark. You know how he worries. I can't keep this from him," Madame Pattersley said righteously. Madame Pattersley had spent the fifteen years since my mother's death trying to win my father's affections. We were alike in that regard, though I'd given up years ago. She told him everything. Maybe that made up for the fact that I could tell him nothing.

"Keep what from me?" My father stood in the doorway.

"Lark was out all night, milord," Madame Pattersley declared, her proclamation bouncing off the pots and pans hanging overhead, her glee echoing the din.

I raised my eyes to my father, willing him to look back at me, but he looked at Boojohni instead. I could see myself in the grey of his eyes and the fine bones of his face. He was elegant without being feminine, tall without being gangly, thin without being gaunt. But he was also shrewd instead of wise, mannerly instead of kind, and ambitious instead of strong.

"I hold you all responsible," my father said quietly. "She must be watched at all times. You know this."

The women dropped deep curtsies and Boojohni bowed, but I could feel his empathy. It permeated the space between us. My father turned and left the kitchen without another word.

THREE

The chattering squirrels didn't like our presence. They wanted us to leave. A snake coiled in the bush to my left, and I felt him taste the air. His life force pulsed, emitting the word *enemy* and then *wait*. It wouldn't strike, but it was poised and watching. A toad belched to my right, completely unconcerned with the company. He hardly noticed us at all, and he felt no fear. He belched again, reminding me of my father slumped against the dinner table, the dogs at his feet, waiting for him to leave the table so they could fight over what he left behind. Whispers and clicks and buzzes and hums, slithering across the forest floor and sliding up my skin and into my head. Sound everywhere, yet my companion didn't seem to notice it.

I dismissed the babbling creatures the way they dismissed me and began filling my apron with the sweet berries hidden by the brambles. A bee fled with one goal in mind. *Home. Home.* Then he was gone. It had been three days since I'd discovered the wounded eagle in the woods. I'd come back every day, as if I would find him again, or he would find me. Or maybe I thought I

would find the archer who brought him down and break his arrows one by one. It was not against the law to hunt, and I did not
judge a man for feeding his family from the forest, but I was
filled with helpless fury when I thought of the eagle. My agita-
tion must have shown.

"You'll prick your fingers, Milady." I raised my eyes and
met Lohdi's gaze. Boojohni had been needed elsewhere, and
young Lohdi—a clumsy youth of sixteen who couldn't hold his
tongue for five seconds—had been assigned to shadow me. I preferred my own company but was rarely given that option, and it
was beyond infuriating. I lifted a shoulder, dismissing his concern.

"Your father said I can't let you harm yourself."

I ignored him with clenched teeth and kept picking. I had
almost twenty-one summers. Most women my age had several
children of their own, and I did not need a nursemaid, especially
one younger and decidedly less capable than I.

Lohdi shifted nervously and looked at the skies, as if the
patches of blue we could make out above the trees would soon
turn to stormy grey.

"We need to go. They will be here soon."

I raised my gaze from the berry bush once more, questioning
him.

"Your father didn't tell you?" Lohdi asked in surprise.

I shook my head. No. My father didn't tell me anything. He
didn't talk to me because I couldn't answer him.

"He is expecting visitors. Important men. Maybe even the
king."

I stiffened, the news making me drop my skirts and lose the
berries I was collecting in my shawl. My stomach clenched pain-
fully as Lohdi chattered on in excitement. If the king was coming, I didn't want to be caught in the woods. I wanted to be safe-

ly away, tucked in my mother's old tower room where he couldn't find me. Or harm me.

I started immediately for home, Lohdi falling into step behind me, expressing gratitude for my hasty return. When we heard the pounding hooves we started to run, Lohdi in anticipation, me in terror. I flew through the trees, skirts in hand, my hair streaming behind me. My maid complained that my hair was like corn silk. She couldn't get it to curl or stay or conform to the exotic shapes and styles that were fashionable among the women of Jeru, and I'd stopped trying to tame it, brushing it and leaving it loose more often than not.

"Milady! Stop!" I heard Lohdi call out behind me, but it wasn't my fault he was slow. I was many things, but slow wasn't one of them, and I picked up speed, hearing the thundering of the horses and feeling the energy in the air. I broke out of the trees seconds before two dozen riders came over the rise from the nearest village, flags waving and bugles screaming. Green and gold, the colors of the kingdom, adorned each horse and every rider. They were almost upon me, and I stared in horror as they slowed reluctantly, the horses resisting their reins, their eagerness to *run, run, run*, coming off them in waves. Horses had very few words. *Run. Eat. Home. Fear.*

But I was the only one afraid now, because I was too late.

I stepped back, intending to turn and run back into the forest and hide in the shadows until the king's party left, even if it drew my father's ire, but at that moment, Lohdi barreled out from the dense tree line onto the hard-packed road, and collided with my back. I fell to my hands and knees directly in the path of the procession. I heard several horses whinny in panic, stomping and sidestepping, and someone cried out. I felt a foot in my back, and I fell to my stomach on the hard-packed dirt. I realized Lohdi hadn't just knocked me down, he was trampling me.

"Halt!" someone roared, and I scrambled to my feet, narrowly avoiding a rearing, sweating stallion with bared teeth.

Lohdi cried out as he also tried to rise. I reached to assist him, not wanting to see him harmed, though at that moment I could have killed him myself. Someone beat me to it, catching the back of his shirt and hauling him to his feet. The King had dismounted, and he stood towering above the wriggling Lohdi.

"King Tiras," Lohdi gasped and fell back to his knees in subservience before being yanked to his feet again.

"Stand up, lad," he commanded.

"Yes, Majesty! So sorry, Your Highness." Lohdi bobbed and genuflected. The king released his arm and turned to me, pinning me with eyes so dark they appeared black in a face that was arresting rather than beautiful, formidable rather than cold. Warm skin covered sharp edges and well-formed features, and I was certain he was accustomed to bows and obeisance though I gave him neither.

His hair was completely white against his bronzed skin, like a man well on in years, though he couldn't yet be thirty summers. His hair had been black when I'd last seen him, but he looked very little like the boy I remembered, and I was certain he didn't remember me. I'd been five years old when my mother was brought down by his father's sword. He'd been older than I, but I doubted that day had made the same kind of impression on him as it had on me.

"Are you injured?" he asked. I wondered if I looked as disheveled as I felt. My hair was a wild tangle and my face felt flushed. My palms stung and my skirt was torn, but I didn't allow myself to smooth my tresses or straighten my clothing. I didn't care about his opinion and stared back at him stonily.

"She doesn't talk. She's a mute," Lohdi rushed to explain. His eyes shot sideways in apology. "Sorry, Milady."

"Milady?" the king questioned, his eyes still on me. I held his gaze without expression.

"Lord Corvyn's daughter, Your Majesty," Lohdi rushed to explain.

King Tiras shared a weighted look with the man to his left—a dark-haired, broad-shouldered warrior in the king's coat of arms who had also dismounted—then returned his attention to me.

"So if I ask you if your father awaits, you won't be able to answer?" he asked me, though it didn't sound like a question.

"She's not stupid, Your Highness. She understands pretty well. She just can't talk," Lohdi provided. I wished he would shut up. I did not require an interpreter.

"I see," the king inclined his head, still taking my measure. "Lead the way then, Milady. I have business with your father." He mounted his horse smoothly as I turned to obey.

I should not have given him my back. It was foolish. But King Tiras had given me no warning of what he intended. I was suddenly swooped off my feet and settled in front of him on his enormous horse. I arched my body in alarm and swung an elbow back, connecting with his breastplate. I only succeeded in hurting myself. His arm simply tightened around my body until I could barely draw breath.

"You will sit here during negotiations. If your father doesn't want to see you harmed—if *you* don't want to be harmed—you will both cooperate. I would rather not tie you up and drag you behind my horse. But I will. Be still." His voice was harsh in my ear, his hair tickling my face, and I did as he commanded. I wondered if he could see my pulse pounding in my throat. Lohdi stood, gaping at the sudden turn of events. His eyes clung to the king, and his face was a horrified mask.

"Tell your master the king is here, boy," the man named Kjell demanded, and Lohdi was off like a shot, stumbling again amidst the laughter of the guard who followed in a protective formation around their king. My father would be alarmed that I'd been taken hostage, but not for the reason the king hoped.

Someone had already alerted my father and the rest of the keep that the king's procession was *en route*, and he stood in the courtyard amongst a growing group of onlookers, a striking figure in the colors of his keep—brilliant blue and silver. He'd assembled a small group of his guard, but none of them were foolish enough to draw their swords. This was the king after all, and if the king wanted to take the daughter of a nobleman in his own kingdom, no one would stop him. They looked more stunned than anything, their eyes lingering on me in confusion. I was not exactly a prize.

"Corvyn," King Tiras greeted coldly. His words stirred my hair and made the flesh rise on my neck. He disliked my father. His disdain was a frigid breeze, and it made me wince and long to wiggle free. I was clearly broadcasting my distress, and the king's horse whinnied and danced at my discomfort. I bade it *be still*, a hand in his mane, and he seemed to understand.

"King Tiras. What is the meaning of this?" My father's voice was surprisingly firm. He didn't look at me.

"Your loyalty has come into question, Corvyn. Your men never arrived at Kilmorda. Lord Bin Dar sent three hundred men. Lord Gaul sent two hundred men. Lord Janda sent at least that many. I received men from every province and every region. Thousands of men from all over my kingdom were sent to respond to the attack on our northern border. But no men ever arrived from Corvyn." King Tiras's voice was curious. Conversational. I shivered against him, completely unconvinced. His arm tightened.

"I sent men, Your Highness. Hundreds of men," my father stammered. The lie made a yellow halo around my father's neck, a noose of his own making.

"Be very careful, Corvyn," King Tiras warned softly, and he pressed his gloved hand to my chest. "Your daughter's heart is pounding beneath my fist. She knows you lie. I know you lie."

"She knows nothing. She is . . . simple. Like a child. She has not spoken a single word since her mother was murdered before her eyes. Your father killed my wife. Will you now kill my daughter too?"

I felt the king stiffen at my back, and I knew he remembered her. I could feel her name in his mind, *Meshara*. Her name winked out like he'd flung it away. There then gone.

Suddenly, Boojohni pushed through the crowd, shoving people aside, tunneling through legs and skirts. My heart rose to my throat as he fell to his knees on the cobblestones in front of the king.

"I am the servant of the lady, Your Majesty," he cried, breathless. "Please! Don't harm her. Take me instead."

Laughter rose up among the king's guard, and I shook my head adamantly. Boojohni growled at my denial and repeated his request.

"Take me instead!"

"Why?" the king asked, his eyes on Boojohni. "Why should I take you?"

"I have no loyalty to Lord Corvyn. My loyalty is to her. Only to her."

"Your loyalty should be to your king, Troll," Kjell barked, and Boojohni touched his forehead to the dirt in total surrender.

"I am at His Majesty's service," he said humbly. I felt tears prick my eyes. His fear for me was palpable, and my love for him had me shaking my head once more.

"The lady does not want you to do this," the king said, taking note of my refusal.

"The lady is more concerned for me than she is for herself," Boojohni rejoined.

"You hold no value to me, Troll, though I admire your courage," King Tiras replied, then added, "I remember you." I felt my mother's name flicker in the air again, a whisper from the king's thoughts that only I could hear. I wanted to hate him for it, but instead it gave me hope.

Boojohni's eyes found mine, and his expression was desperate.

"Then let me come with her. Take me too," he implored.

The king was silent for a heartbeat, considering. "So be it," he acquiesced suddenly, and called out to someone in the back of the procession.

"Jerick! The troll will ride with you."

A warrior rode forward and pulled Boojohni up behind him. Boojohni looked equal parts relieved and distraught. He had never been able to ride without getting motion sickness. The trip did not bode well for my little friend. I predicted he would be running alongside the warrior before long.

"Your daughter will be returned when the enemy is defeated, Corvyn. But if I die, she dies."

I almost laughed. How ironic. I was convinced if the king knew the curse my mother had lain on my father's head, he would make me suffer terribly.

"None of this is necessary, Majesty," my father protested weakly. "I give you my word." He'd taken on a grey pallor, as though he believed his days were numbered.

"And I will take it, and your daughter," the king replied smoothly. "Just so I am assured of your fealty." He took up the reins and Kjell raised his arm, signaling their retreat.

"I left an army at the border of Kilmorda. We've beaten back the Volgar. For now. But I will expect you to send five hundred men to assist."

"Five hundred?" my father gasped.

"You are welcome to send more. The sooner the Volgar are destroyed, the sooner your daughter returns to Corvyn. It is all up to you, Milord."

FOUR

We rode toward Jeru City for three hours at a steady pace, and I held myself stiff and straight, refusing to touch the man at my back. The bony ridge of the stallion's spine was impossible to avoid, and though he seemed impervious to my weight, an occasional word escaped his master's thoughts, letting me know he wasn't entirely comfortable either. He yanked me against him once and barked that I was going to fall if I didn't relax.

I gritted my teeth and held firm, ignoring the ache in my hips and the burning down my spine. If spite was the only weapon at my disposal, I would continue to wield it. Boojohni, just like I'd predicted, had grown ill after the first hour and pled to be let down. The man named Jerick had refused. We were moving too quickly, and Boojohni could not keep pace with the horses for miles on end. Boojohni had lost the contents of his stomach and was now moaning miserably from his perch. He'd been tied to Jerick to keep him from tumbling off when he vomited, and Jerick looked as peevish as I felt.

Darkness was falling when the rear watch warned of Volgar in the skies. A murmur rose in the ranks and the king called a halt as Kjell peeled away from the formation to confer with the watchmen. He was back within seconds.

"King Tiras! Volgar approaching from the rear. Hundreds of them," he cried.

We were in a wide clearing with open fields to the right and to the left and a wooded grove a ways ahead. It was the only cover available, and the king directed his men to head for the trees. I was instructed to hold on, and I obeyed, abandoning the perch of a noblewoman for my safety, kicking my left leg over the stallion and lying flat against his neck, my fingers twisted in his mane. I felt the king pressed against my back, his gloved hands tightening over the reins, leaning into the stallion, into me, urging haste. We flew across the clearing, eyes clinging to the cluster of trees. I turned my head, peering up at the sky, unable to resist the lure of the lurid. I wanted to see what was coming.

I heard them before I saw them.

Horses scream. Men scream too, though they never admit it. But the Volgar shrieked, a cross between man and gull, amplified by ten, and the sound was piercing, ear-splitting, and I almost fell in my desperation to cover my ears.

Then there was no more separation, no more distance between earth and sky, and the birdmen began to drop, plucking warriors from their mounts with curled talons and powerful legs. They rose, straight up, clutching their dangling prey only to release them to plummet to their deaths.

King Tiras slid from his horse, pulling me with him, dragging me back as he swung his sword at a birdman with tattered wings, pointed ears, and skin the color of dead grass. The king shoved me beneath the low branches of a huge evergreen, the trunk at my back, and lunged into the fray, his blade already wet and dripping. I could only watch as death descended in droves.

The now rider-less horses screamed and reared, trampling a felled warrior and creating a stampede in the midst of the melee.

Through the branches and the crush of man and beast, I saw Boojohni running toward me, his legs pumping and his eyes wide with terror. A shadow swooped over him and dropped, claws extended, to carry him away.

I didn't stop to think. I only ran, scooping up the hilt of the trampled warrior's enormous sword as I raced toward my only friend. Boojohni screamed, his back arching in panic and protest as the claws of the Volgar latched in his tunic, lifting him off the ground. I wouldn't reach him in time to do anything but watch him rise. The sword wobbled in my arms, too heavy to throw, too awkward to swing.

Release him! My head shrieked, my frozen voice trapped in my throat.

RELEASE HIM!

The birdman paused mid-air, his eyes locked on mine, and like a chastised child, his claws snapped open and Boojohni fell from his grasp, falling to the earth in a scrambling heap. Boojohni had hardly touched down before he was up again, running, screaming my name. The birdman retreated dizzily, as if he'd forgotten how to fly. An arrow slid through his chest, and he cartwheeled toward the earth, slain.

"Run!" Boojohni screeched, grabbing at my arm. I still clung to the useless sword, unwilling to let it go. Another birdman descended nearby, sinking his talons into Kjell, who, with both hands, swung his sword over his head, sinking the blade into the breast of the winged beast. The birdman shrieked in outrage and tried to fly away, pulling Kjell a foot off the ground before the warrior twisted his blade, and they both landed in a tangle of blood and grey feathers. Kjell rolled out from beneath the dying creature and yanked his sword from its shuddering chest, only to stagger to his feet to fight again.

There were so many. I stumbled forward, still dragging the sword, as Boojohni called out a desperate warning. I spun in fright, gripping the sword in both hands. With momentum and sheer luck, I managed to cut down another Volgar, whose blood was vivid green on an all-too-human chest. He staggered back and crumpled, his wings twitching as he died. I retched at the gaping wound I'd inflicted and mentally begged the horrific creatures to retreat, hating them, but hating the carnage even more.

Fly. Leave, I urged the birdmen that kept coming. *Go. Leave now. Live.*

I saw a few wing for the sky, as if heeding my pleas.

"Lark!" Boojohni urged, pulling me forward, "Run!"

I threw myself beneath the branches of the evergreen where King Tiras had bade me stay and peered out at the swarming Volgar, at the taloned feet and hands, the sharp horns, the razor-sharp wings sprouting from human trunks. King Tiras and Kjell stood back to back in the midst of it all, swords swinging, a dozen beasts encircling them. Neither hesitated nor faltered, but their clothes were slick with blood, and a dozen fallen guards lay strewn like abandoned poppets at their feet.

We were all going to die.

I resisted the thought, pushing it away, fearful of the very suggestion, and turned the voice outward on the flying horde.

Fly before you die.

Fly before you die.

Fly before you die.

They weren't listening. I was too afraid. My fear made the words tremble and break before I could release them. I watched as another warrior plummeted to the earth and King Tiras sank his sword knuckle-deep into a Volgar's belly. Two more took its place before the king could free his sword. One of his guards threw himself in front of the king only to be swept off the ground. I closed my eyes to shut out the terror and the certainty of defeat.

Fly before you die.
Fly before you die.
Fly before you die.

I made the words a roar in my head, filling up the black space behind my closed eyes, making me tremble and my ears pop. I heard Boojohni shouting, but I didn't open my eyes. I didn't dare.

Then I couldn't hear anything but my own thoughts, echoing like I'd fallen down a well and found my voice at last, only to scream for rescue.

Fly before you die. Fly before you die. Fly before you die.
Before you die.
You die.
Die.

Pain bloomed hot and sharp across my face. The words clanging in my skull faltered and broke, leaving a dull ache between my eyes and a metallic taste in my mouth. Boojohni's beard tickled my nose and his sour breath singed my eyebrows. I turned my head to find fresh air and forced my eyelids open, my hand going to my stinging cheek. Someone had slapped me. Hard.

"She's awake. She's awake!" Boojohni chortled, his relief making him giggle. I glowered up at him, noting that night had fallen while the battle raged. Of course I was awake. He helped me sit up and gave me a measure of space. He must have pulled me out from under the evergreen at some point. I swayed, and a hand shot out to steady me. I met the black eyes of King Tiras who was crouched above me. Even in the light of the fat, full moon he was filthy with gore, but he appeared uninjured. The same could not be said for more than half of his men. Bodies of the Volgar were intermingled with the dead and dying members of the king's guard.

"They've gone, Lark!" Boojohni reported. "The beasts have gone. They just suddenly retreated."

The king rose to his feet and turned away, dismissing me for weightier concerns. Those who were able were piling the bodies of the birdmen and tending to their own wounded and dead. The stench of blood and death clung to my every breath, but I rose to my feet as well, determined to assist where I could.

"We will send men back for the dead," the king commanded, "but we leave now, while we still can." His eyes rose to the skies as if expecting the Volgar to return. "They could have killed us all. Their retreat makes no sense."

"The horses have scattered," Kjell said in defeat. "And we have wounded who can't walk."

I took three steps on shaking legs and tugged at the king's sleeve. I pointed through the trees.

He raised a black eyebrow. I tried to make my hand resemble a fleeing horse and looked to Boojohni for help.

"Lady Corvyn has a way with animals, Your Majesty," he offered feebly.

"There are no animals left, Milady," the King responded wearily. He knelt to check the pulse of a fallen guard. I could have told him the man was dead. His soul had flown, leaving him wordless and lifeless.

I pointed through the trees once more. I felt the fear of the horses and called them back. Horses were easy to sense. Their emotions were like great beacons, glowing in the dark. They'd run in fear, but they'd run in a circle, leaving a loud, red stream of desperation behind them. They weren't far.

"If Lady Corvyn says the horses went that way, then the horses went that way," Boojohni said simply. He sniffed the air and winced. "I will be able to get their scent once we put some distance between us and this place."

"We can't go anywhere. We can't leave these men, and we can't carry them," Kjell argued.

The king nodded, his eyes on my face.

"Are they close?" he asked.

I nodded. They would be soon. I could feel their thundering hearts slowing as their fear cooled. They wanted to go home. *Home. Home. Home.*

"Show me," he insisted quietly and wrapped his hand around my upper arm. Boojohni trotted along behind us, and the king didn't protest, though Kjell had demanded to come as well and was denied.

"You can't go off alone, Tiras," Kjell argued. I'd noticed the familiarity between the two men. Unlike the rest of the guard, Kjell called the king by his given name, and he didn't hesitate to voice his opinions.

"I won't be far, Kjell. And we won't be long. Stand watch."

We walked in silence, and oddly, though the king gripped my upper arm, keeping me close, he let me lead. I was grateful for his hand; my rubbery legs and my ringing ears made each step treacherous.

I wanted someone to fill in the blanks for me, to tell me how long my eyes had been closed, how many had died while I'd tried to use my words. I wondered if I'd made the Volgar retreat, then felt silly and small at my wistful thought. I'd simply closed my eyes and wished while others fought. Once I'd made a poppet fly, but the Volgar? No. It was impossible.

I stumbled and the king's grip tightened.

"We don't have time to wander," he murmured. His voice wasn't harsh, but I could feel his impatience, his worry, and his doubt. The doubt made me stumble again.

I stopped and pulled my arm free. His words were too loud, and I couldn't feel the horses. He released me without protest, and Boojohni raised his little nose to the air and sniffed. He sniffed again and chortled with glee.

"There." He pointed directly in front of us. I couldn't see anything, but I heard them. I felt them.

Home. Home. Home.

The king whistled sharply, and his doubt dissipated with an audible pop as a branch snapped and then another, drawing our eyes to the darkest shadows that shifted and changed and became horses, chuffing and picking their way toward us.

"All of them," the king whispered, counting as the horses neared. Three dozen horses, led by the king's black stallion, and near the rear, my father's grey. The grey that had been taken from our stables.

"Shindoh," the king greeted his mount, and he extended his hand in welcome. The huge charger nuzzled his palm gratefully. *Home.*

I pulled away from the king and walked to the grey, greeting him with my own hand outstretched. When he whinnied and bumped me with his velvet nose, I looped my arms around his neck and rubbed my cheek against him. Then I turned and found the king watching me. I walked toward him, leading the grey, and when I reached him I thumped my chest.

Mine.

"The grey looks like a horse that was taken from Lord Corvyn's keep, Majesty," Boojohni explained. He knew full well it was the same horse but was wise enough to be judicious.

"Maybe it belonged to one of those soldiers your father sent, think you?" Tiras answered with a mocking twist of his lips. "We found him two days ago not far from Kilmorda."

"That must be it, Highness," Boojohni rushed to agree. I could only shake my head.

"You may ride the grey back home when your father fulfills his obligations," the king murmured, and even the grey scoffed.

FIVE

There was a horse for every man, even the dead and dying, but I still rode with the king. The fallen were tied to their mounts, and as the night deepened, we made our way down the road once more, descending into the lush, green valleys of Degn. We would reach the King's fortress by dawn if the Volgar did not return.

I fought exhaustion for as long as I could, but my limbs shook and my head bobbed. The king cursed as I swayed and pulled me back against his soiled breastplate, supporting my hips between his big legs. I tried not to relax against him, but it couldn't be helped, and when he swore again and tugged sharply on my hair, I bowed my head in defeat.

"Stubborn woman. Sleep."

I did for a while, cursing him even as I turned my face into his shoulder. But when the moaning of the wounded waned and the light crept over the Jeruvian hills to the east, I opened bleary eyes on the domed fortress that would be my home for the unforeseeable future. Black ramparts and parapets and a wall that extended as far as the eye could see gleamed in the early light, the dark stone threaded with Jeruvian ore and the precious nacre that lined the ancient sea bed to the west. The women of Corvyn wore the stone in their ears and around their necks—the black iridescence made beautiful jewelry. Clearly, it was so plentiful in Jeru City they built walls with it.

"Welcome to Jeru, Lady Corvyn," the king murmured, and pride rose from his pores like perfume. I pulled away from him and did my best not to breathe him in. The beauty of his city, of the king himself, was confusing to me. I doubt he noticed the stiff line of my back and the obstinate tilt of my chin; if he did he didn't care. His relief at being home rivaled that of the horses, and it reverberated around him as if we were trapped in a bell tower.

As we approached the wall, a trumpet sounded and a massive door lowered in a well-oiled greeting. It was just after dawn but the city was awake and shouts of welcome rose up from the guard beyond the wall.

"Hail the king!"

"King Tiras has returned!"

"We have injured and dead," the king called, his voice deep with fatigue. "See to them first. And alert their families."

The guard who were able slid from their tired mounts and assisted those who weren't. Kjell and King Tiras continued on through the wide street and climbed a tree and guard-lined hill to the domed fortress I'd glimpsed beyond the gates. When we neared the entrance, King Tiras swung off his horse and without fanfare, lifted me down behind him. My legs were like water, and they pooled beneath me. He swept me up again, much to my chagrin, and carried me across the courtyard, through palace doors that were opened for him with deep bows and stiff salutes, across a wide foyer and down a long hall which turned into the most enormous kitchen I'd ever seen. King Tiras plopped me unceremoniously on a kitchen stool and barked orders at the servants, who scurried from all corners.

"Feed her. Bathe her. Put her to bed."

A woman in a dress of crisp black stepped forward, bowing deeply. She looked older than the tittering maids who watched the king with awe and admiration, and she seemed to be in charge.

"Yes, Majesty. Welcome home, Sire," she said smoothly, eying me with equal parts disdain and curiosity. I had no doubt I resembled a skinned rat.

"And lock her in the north tower," he added as he left, not looking back to see if his orders were heeded.

After eating in the kitchen—a meal I was too tired to enjoy—I was escorted to the north tower, to a room so sumptuous it would have been a pleasure to be a prisoner if I'd cared about rose petals in my bathwater and sleeping on silk sheets. I didn't. I was grateful I would not be cold or uncomfortable, hungry or naked, but beyond that, I longed for Boojohni and news of his welfare. I needed the woods near my home and my room at my father's keep. I didn't know if I'd ever return.

I was bathed and dried in front of a roaring fire, though the day beyond the open windows wasn't especially cold. Lavender oil was brushed into my hair and massaged into my skin as if I were royalty instead of a captive from Corvyn. Three women attended me, and when their simple questions were met with my silence, they gave up trying to converse at all, sharing glances amongst themselves.

"Can you hear, Milady?" one asked, her voice sharp. They thought I was being quietly contemptuous.

I nodded.

"Do you understand us?"

I nodded again.

"Can you speak?" she snapped.

I shook my head, no.

She had the grace to look slightly chagrined, and the two other ladies-in-waiting tsked in shock.

"You don't speak Jeruvian or you don't speak at all?" the youngest of the three asked curiously.

I shook my head again. That was two questions with two different answers. But they seemed to understand when I touched my throat.

They murmured words of regret, and I knew they were bursting to discuss my ailment, if not with me, then with each other. The palace court would talk about me for a while, then they would forget about me all together. I had that effect on people. Silence was a close cousin to invisibility.

When they finally left me alone and locked the heavy door behind them as they'd been instructed, I crawled into the huge bed draped in white gauze and slipped between the downy covers, worrying again about Boojohni. I doubted he'd been given a second glance, not to mention a warm meal and a place to rest. But my final musings before succumbing to sleep were not of my faithful troll, but of the young king who reigned over Jeru. He was not what I had expected.

For three days I saw no one but the staff. I was fed. I was bathed. I was dressed in fine clothing. No one spoke to me, no one even made eye contact, and I stayed locked behind the heavy door. I spent most of my time on the huge balcony overlooking the city. I was kept in a tower so high, the people below were tiny poppets, just flashes of color and energy and life, far beyond my reach. I thought about finding a way to climb down, but there were guards stationed around the perimeter and I didn't think I could scale the palace walls, though I studied them carefully and looked for possibilities.

On the third night of my odd imprisonment, my covers were thrown off me, and I was dragged from my bed by a desperate Kjell. He didn't explain himself or tell me where I was going, but his grip was bruising and his expression tight. He hurried me through empty corridors and down winding stairs lit by blazing sconces until he stopped in front of a huge, metal door that made me think of dark dungeons and tortured souls. My toes curled against the cold stone floor, and my teeth began to chatter. I gritted them stubbornly and refused to cower when Kjell unlocked the door with a heavy ring of keys and shoved me inside.

"Help him," he commanded tersely. "Help him, and I'll help you."

I stared at him in confusion, but he said nothing more as he pulled the door closed between us and locked me inside. I yanked on the handle, testing what I already knew to be true, and listened as his footsteps retreated then stopped. He hadn't gone far. His desperation was audible, as if he stood shouting his concern through the echoing halls.

But it wasn't Kjell who called out from the shadowed corner. It was the king.

"I told you to go, Kjell. Get out!"

I took several steps forward, unable to see beyond the heavy table bolted to the floor and laid with a simple, untouched meal. A goblet brimming with burgundy wine had me clearing my suddenly parched throat. There were sconces lining the walls here as well, but only one was lit, and the flickering flame created dancing ghosts and warning whispers on my skin. The meal was fit for a king, but these weren't the king's quarters. Obviously. It was the kind of room where prisoners were housed, the kind of room I'd imagined myself being held in on the journey to the city.

"Kjell? You bloody bastard. Leave me!" the king bellowed, obviously sensing my presence, but unable to see me. I crept around the table and past the partial wall lined with bolts and shackles and a heavy chain that had clearly been there for some time.

He was pressed against the wall, crouched there, as if he were too weak to stand. Manacles circled his wrists and ankles, though each manacle was attached to a length of chain that should allow him a small range of motion. It seemed more to contain than to torture, though he was definitely suffering. His shirt was opened, and his skin gleamed slickly beneath, as if he was expending great effort not to fight against the restraints. His chest heaved and his body shook. He was a big man, his muscles bulging beneath breeches that clung to his crouching legs, but he was folded into himself, his hands fisted in his long white hair, his brawny back bent in what appeared to be distress. His body cried *help* though he demanded to be left alone.

He lifted his eyes and peered at me through the hair that shrouded his face. He didn't look surprised to see me, though his shoulders sagged in defeat.

"Are you a Healer?" His voice was soft. Pained.

I waited until he lifted his eyes again, and I shook my head. He groaned softly then asked, "If you aren't a Healer, why are you here?"

I couldn't answer, so I stepped closer.

"Stay back!"

I hesitated, frightened.

His body trembled, and his skin rippled as if the muscles of his back were caught in a violent spasm.

"Go!" he roared, the sound otherworldly, a lion or a beast given the gift of speech. "Leave!"

I couldn't go. I couldn't even scream. I couldn't beg or plead or barter for my life. Still, I scurried to the heavy door behind me, pounding against it.

"Kjell!" Tiras bellowed. "Get her out of here!"

The door remained closed.

"Kjell! I'll kill you!" he roared.

But apparently Kjell did not believe him, or maybe he intended for us both to die. I wondered if King Tiras was contagious, exposed to a deadly illness that would kill me when it finished him off. Why Kjell thought I could help him was beyond me.

I kept my back to the king for several minutes, not knowing what to do, not daring to go near him. He'd stopped shouting, but I could hear him panting in distress. I didn't want to feel sorry for him. I didn't want to feel compassion. He didn't deserve it. But I winced at his labored breathing and his obvious agony. It reminded me of the quiet suffering of the eagle in the forest.

I'd had compassion for a bird, surely I could show a shred of compassion for a man, even one I wanted to despise. I turned from the door and walked back toward him cautiously. His eyes rose—black, wounded, almost beseeching—but this time he didn't yell or tell me to go. Maybe he couldn't. He was shaking so hard the chains rattled against the floor.

I knelt beside him, so close he could have easily hurt me, but I found I was no longer afraid of him. I couldn't ask him where it hurt or what ailed him. I could only slip my hands inside his open shirt and press them to his chest, hoping I could help him find relief. It had worked with the bird. His skin was hot and slick, and we both flinched at the contact. I shut my eyes the way I had with the eagle.

Relief.

His breath hissed out. I concentrated harder.

Cool relief.

"What are you doing to me?" he whispered.

Breathe. Heal. Sleep.

Breathe, heal, sleep.

Breathe, heal, sleep.

I repeated the suggestions over and over, and he was motionless beneath my hands, not shoving me away, not demanding that I go. I pushed the words outward as hard as I could, and the harder I pushed, the more measured his breathing became.

"Are you a Healer?" he asked again, and his voice was faint, exhaustion making the question long and slow. I could only shake my head. I wasn't healing, I was telling. I was suggesting. Commanding his body to release the pain, to numb the agony. To heal itself. I had no idea if it was all in my head or if my words were escaping through my hands, but I kept my eyes closed and my palms pressed against his pounding heart.

"You're a witch," he moaned, but he leaned into my hands. I felt a surge of triumph and narrowed my focus further. I don't know how much time passed, but as his shaking quieted, mine began, and I felt my strength sputter and stop. I'd done it again, and just like in the woods, I'd emptied myself completely. Only this time, I felt the crash.

I could hardly keep my head from bobbing forward onto his shoulder. I tried to open my eyes and pull my hands from his skin, but I had nothing left, no strength remained to move myself away. My eyelids weighed a thousand pounds, my arms at least a ton. I swayed against him, powerless to stop myself. Then I was lying on the floor, the cool stones impossibly smooth against my face. I felt my hands fall from his body, and darkness consumed me, washing away all awareness.

SIX

When I awoke it was midday, and I was back in my tower room, stretched across my bed, a pillow beneath my head, a blanket over my shoulders. Sunlight streamed through the windows, and my stomach complained loudly. I sat up in confusion, wondering if the shackled king had been a bizarre dream. The bottom of my feet were filthy, and I'd slept half the day away. No. I shook my head, resisting the urge to pretend I hadn't been dragged to a chamber in the far recesses of the palace and locked inside, delivered like an offering to a violent god, the virgin sacrifice to the fiery dragon.

Although King Tiras had roared like a beast, he hadn't hurt me. He'd been the one in pain. Where was *he*? Had he survived the night? Had he survived . . . me? He'd called me a witch, yet he'd welcomed my touch. Now I was here, back in my room, like none of it had happened. It made no sense.

I started at the sound of the key scraping in the lock at my door and scrambled from the bed, my hands moving instinctively to the hair that hung down my back in heavy disarray. I expected Kjell or maybe even the king himself. But it was a maid who bustled in, the girl who brought my meals each day.

"You're awake!" Her voice was slightly sardonic, and the words *lazy girl* oozed from her thoughts.

I nodded. I had so many things to ask and no way to communicate.

"I brought breakfast hours ago, and you were so still I thought you'd died in your sleep. You must have been exhausted from doing nothing all day. Eat up. I'll send porters up with water for your bath, but there's water to wash your hands and face in the basin." She hardly looked at me as she prattled, and I clapped my hands to draw her eyes. I mimed the act of writing, and she looked at me blankly. I did it again, adamantly, and her face cleared.

"Oh, you want paper . . . and ink?"

I nodded gratefully.

She furrowed her brow as if troubled by the request. "I'll ask."

I was overjoyed when she returned with three books of blank, bound paper, along with paints, ink, and charcoal, muttering about excess and glut.

"A gift from the king," she said snidely, as if I'd done something scandalous to deserve it. "He informed Mistress Lorena that you may have whatever you desire, as long as you remain in this room."

I bathed quickly, eager to ask my questions before I was left alone again. As my hair was dried and dressed, I drew a quick likeness of Boojohni and showed the dour maid who attended me. She combed my damp hair with harsh tugs, impatient to be done with her duties, but she eyed my picture with reluctant curiosity.

"I haven't seen him, Milady," she shrugged. "He's a funny-looking little fellow. Don't see many trolls in Jeru City anymore. The late king was certain they sheltered the Gifted and had a bit of the magic in their own blood. He ran them all out. Good riddance, I say."

I quickly drew a picture of Tiras, a crown sitting on his pale hair. He'd never worn a crown in my presence, but I didn't have time to make a perfect likeness and needed her to understand.

"King Tiras?" she asked, as if I was daft.

I nodded emphatically.

"What about 'im?" she asked crossly.

I turned my palms out, hoping she understood that I was asking for his whereabouts.

"He doesn't report to me, Milady!" she sneered. "But I'll be sure to tell him you were askin' about him." She sighed and headed for the door, juggling the dishes from my meal, murmuring about "uppity ladies."

I wondered if she was rude because I couldn't rebuke her or if she enjoyed knowing I couldn't voice a complaint about her. Not that anyone would care what I thought. Still, one question had been answered. The king wasn't dead.

The next evening, King Tiras himself unlocked my door and strode into my room without warning, verifying that he was not only alive, but that he was in fine health. I'd been drawing all day at the table, enchanted with the variety of the supplies, anxious to keep busy after so many days of forced isolation, and when he had entered, I'd ignored the intrusion, thinking it was my dour attendant bringing me a meal I had no interest in. I didn't look up until he spoke, his tone wry, his voice soft.

"I see you received my peace offering."

I rose to my feet, eyeing him with wonder and not a little apprehension. He was clothed in a fine linen shirt and fitted breeches with tall boots. He vibrated with good health and vitality, looking completely recovered from whatever had ailed him, and I would have questioned my sanity—or at least my memory—had I any reason at all to doubt either. His thick, white hair was brushed back from his brown face, and he seemed even taller, even broader than before. Maybe it was that he stood towering over me, bearing little resemblance to the man who had been doubled over in agony on the dungeon floor.

"You have a Healer's touch," he said softly. His tone was nonthreatening, but I shook my head, denying his claim. I was not a Healer. I would not be accused of being one.

"Sit." He extended his hand toward the chair I'd just vacated and pulled out the one across from it, clearly settling in for further discussion on the matter. I did as I was told, my back stiff, my hands folded demurely in my lap. I eyed him warily, and he stared back with frank curiosity.

"What is your name, Lady Corvyn? Your given name?"

I touched my throat impatiently. He knew I couldn't respond. He seemed to have forgotten that.

"Write it." He shoved a blank sheet of paper toward me.

I shook my head and shrugged my shoulders, indicating I could not.

"You can't write?" his voice rose in incredulity. "How will I talk to you?"

I tugged at my ear. He could talk to me just as he was doing now. I could hear just fine.

"You can hear me, yes. But you can't respond."

I shrugged once more.

"What do I call you?" he asked, irritated. "I refuse to call you Milady forever."

I picked up a piece of charcoal and the paper he'd provided, and began to sketch rapidly.

"A bird?" He was confused.

I nodded and tapped the page then pointed to my chest.

"You're named after a bird?"

I nodded again, eagerly. I added details to the small bird, so he would recognize it.

"A lark?"

I nodded once more.

"Lark? That's not a name," he argued gently, almost as if he were offended on my behalf.

I lifted my eyes to his, because it *was* a name. It was my name.

He must have seen my affront and been amused by it, because his lips quirked infinitesimally.

"Why don't you know how to write? You are the daughter of a nobleman. You should know how to read and write. Why did no one teach you?"

I drew my father's face, crude but recognizable. I'd had practice drawing him. I tapped it. Tiras stared at it thoughtfully.

"Your father wouldn't allow it?"

I nodded. I turned to the paper again and drew a quick image of myself in chains. I set the charcoal back down.

"You were a prisoner?" he guessed hesitantly.

It was the most accurate response I could give, and he understood well enough. I was *still* a prisoner. I nodded at his question but raised a disdainful eyebrow, spreading my arms to indicate my surroundings.

"You are still a prisoner," he murmured, as if he'd plucked the words from my head.

I held his gaze and inclined my head, indicating that he was correct.

"But you are *my* prisoner now. Not your father's. And I want you to read. And write." He pursed his lips thoughtfully.

I pulled the paper toward myself and began to form the letters I'd been taught long ago. A, B, C, D and L for Lark. An old woman in the village had taught me L and told me my name began with that letter. My father had discovered I was being taught and sentenced her to twenty lashes in the village square. No one else had attempted to educate me after that.

"You know these?" he asked, his eyes on my ill-formed letters.

I nodded.

He took the charcoal from my hands and drew a straight line with another line laid above it. "This is a T. For Tiras." He wrote more letters and tapped them. "Tiras." He wrote an L and an A followed by shapes I didn't recognize. "Lark. This is the word Lark."

I couldn't pull my eyes away from my name. My name! I traced it reverently.

"Practice your name. Practice my name. I will be back tomorrow to teach you more."

I hurried to get in front of him, not wanting him to leave. He looked down at me in surprise. I grabbed his left hand in both of mine and pulled him back to the table. His hand was thick and warm and calloused and made me think of the bark on the trees near my home, but I pushed the awareness away and tapped the paper.

"I can't teach you everything now," he protested in surprise.

I tapped the letters I had made. A, B, C, D. I picked up the charcoal and urgently tapped the space after the D. What came next? I wanted all the letters. All the shapes. I wanted to write them all, to practice them all, so that when he came back I would recognize them.

"You want to know what follows?"

I nodded eagerly.

He took a quill from my supplies and dipped it carefully in the ink. Then using a fresh sheet of parchment, he started at A and continued on for several minutes, creating lines and squiggles and curved edges that looked both familiar and forbidden. I clapped gleefully, and he looked at me in surprise, a smile hovering around his lips. He put the quill down. I picked it up and handed it to him again, pushing it on him.

"All of them?"

I nodded so hard my jaw ached.

He laughed out loud this time, and the action made his black eyes crinkle at the edges and his lips turn up in a way that was terribly attractive and impossibly infuriating. I glared at him and tapped the paper insistently. It wasn't funny—*I* wasn't funny. He'd been given every word he needed, and every word had been stripped from me. I wanted them back. All of them.

He took the quill almost meekly, though his eyes gleamed with suppressed mirth. He continued for several more minutes, forming each letter in a strong line. I hoped he wasn't trying to fool me with symbols that meant nothing, simply so he could laugh at me when he returned.

When he finished, he laid down the quill and sprinkled the ink with a dusting of sand from a little corked vial, setting the ink. Then he looked up at me.

"This is every letter of the alphabet. Every word in our language is made from these letters."

I could hardly breathe. I clasped my hands against my chest to calm my heart and stared down at the beauty he'd created. Then I raised my eyes and it was my turn to smile. I couldn't hold it in. I wanted to. I didn't want to reveal my wonder and the thrill that coursed through my veins. But I couldn't hold it in. So I smiled at him and did my best not to cry happy tears.

He seemed almost stunned by my joy and rose slowly. He tipped his head to the side as if he couldn't quite figure me out. Without further comment, he turned and left the room.

SEVEN

realized after the king left that I hadn't asked about Boo-johni. I was ashamed of myself and waited eagerly for the king to return, like he'd said he would so I could draw him pictures and thereby demand answers. But he didn't return. Not the next day or the next.

My fingers grew black from practicing the characters he'd written out for me, copying them carefully. I found the letters in Lark and the letters in Tiras, but didn't know what they were called. They were simply shapes. Lines. Symbols that were completely meaningless. But I had a plan. When Tiras came back, I would have him write out the words for every object in my room on separate pieces of paper, naming each one. Chair. Table. Floor. Bed. Candle. I would put each paper in its proper place, and I would learn the words and decipher the sounds of each letter, every combination.

But Tiras didn't come back.

I tried to convince the maids to write the words they knew. I also showed them the picture of Boojohni, but they all shrugged and shook their heads. They didn't know much, and I didn't trust the one who seemed to dislike me more each day. The others called her Greta, and I got the feeling she didn't know how to read or write any better than I did, though she wouldn't admit it. She just stomped around and pushed me away when I tried to communicate. Then there was Kjell.

Four days after Tiras had shown me how to write my name, Kjell returned to drag me from my room in the middle of the night, just like before. I went with him willingly, eagerly, though his promise to help me had been a lie. I didn't do it for him. I didn't do it for the king, who'd lied to me too. I did it for the words he'd said he would teach me.

Kjell didn't take me into the bowels of the castle this time. We went to another tower, a tower directly opposite mine, and I marveled that the king had been so close all this time. I wondered if he'd seen me standing on my balcony, waiting for him to return. But when Kjell shoved me inside the chamber and slammed the door, locking it behind me, I found myself completely alone.

The king's bedcovers were tangled, his clothes discarded on the floor, but he was gone, and though I pounded on the door, Kjell did not return to explain what I was doing there and what was expected of me. Stepping out onto the balcony, I discovered the night was incredibly bright, the moon almost full, just like it had been the night I'd found the eagle in the forest. But there were no birds to save in Jeru City. Or kings, for that matter. I was lonelier than I'd ever been, and that was a feat in itself. I pulled my dressing gown around my body and returned to the richly appointed chamber.

There were books on the shelves and several lay open on a table not so different from the one in my room. My father kept the books at the keep locked in his study. I had never seen one up close. I turned the pages, studied the words, and tried to make sense of them, tracing the shape of each letter with my finger, the way I'd traced my name. I'd determined that the S at the end of Tiras looked and hissed like a snake. I studied the page and found all the words with an s in them. I'd also compared the R shape in our names and determined its sound. Of course the T made a tapping sound at the beginning of Tiras's name. T-T-T-T. I liked to focus on the sound, making it stutter in my mind like a woodpecker. I was going to take one of the books. When the king came back and found me in his room, I was going to fill my arms with books and refuse to give them back.

I kept the candles lit and pored over the pages until my eyes would no longer focus and my head began to droop. I curled up in a corner of the king's bed, trying not to notice how the covers smelled of fresh air and cedar. Then I slept, heavy and hard, dreaming of the shrieking of birdmen and the words that danced on the pages of the king's books. The letters shifted and re-formed, whispering their names in my mother's voice. I heard a cry, piercing, louder than that of the Volgar, and a desperate fluttering, like a dozen flags whipping in the wind. It was so close, so present, that I opened my eyes blearily, reluctant to abandon sleep so soon.

Dawn was breaking and grey light had just begun to spill through the open balcony doors and sneak across the king's chamber. The doors had been open when Kjell had pushed me into the room the night before, and it hadn't felt necessary or even right to close them, as if the king himself would use the balcony to reemerge from the night. But morning had returned without the king, and I blinked wearily, caught in that drowsy place where sleep and wakefulness become a strange blend of both.

The eagle from the woods, no sign of the arrow buried in his chest, perched on the balcony rail. I watched him through glazed eyes, my lids at half-mast, unalarmed and completely unconvinced that I wasn't still sleeping. He was aware of me, of that I was sure. He cocked his head and shrieked, as if warning me away.

The door of the king's chambers burst open, and Kjell erupted into the room, making me bolt upright, sleep abandoned, the eagle forgotten.

"Where is he?" Kjell growled, as if I'd spun the king into gold while he slept. I shook my head helplessly and extended my arms, indicating the empty chamber. He turned in place, his hands on his hips, frustration oozing from every pore. The word *hopeless* flitted in the air around him, and this time I didn't just hear the word, I saw it, recognizing the S—a pair of curling snakes that hissed with sound before disintegrating with his movement.

He grabbed for my arm, and I wriggled away, darting to the table where the king's books were spread. I grasped the first one I touched, scooping it up and clutching it to my chest.

"Put it down," he roared.

I danced away from him, flitting to the door he'd left gaping beyond him and dashing out into the wide hallway. I would return to my room, gladly. But I was taking a book.

I ran with the livid Kjell bellowing behind me, and when I finally stopped in front of my tower door, after easily navigating the corridors, he drew up abruptly, gasping for air, eyeing me like I was completely daft.

I thumped the book at my chest fiercely so he would understand why I had run. Then I pounded the door to the room where I'd been held for two long weeks. With a shake of his head and an impatient curse, he pushed me aside and unlocked my chamber door. I was shoved inside once more—an infuriating pattern emerging—with no explanation of what he'd expected from me and no enlightenment as to the king's whereabouts. But he didn't take the book.

Kjell was back less than an hour later. I was bathed and dressed, but my feet were bare, my hair lay in wet clumps down my back, and I hadn't broken my fast. When Kjell burst through the door, it was all I could do not to fling my goblet at him, and when he grabbed for my arm, his grip harsh and bruising as always, I shoved him back as hard as I could. He was as brawny as the king, and he only staggered because he was surprised, but I shook my finger at him in warning and lifted my chin. Then I turned and began walking for the door, indicating I would go where he wanted me to go, but I would not be manhandled. When he tried to grab me again, I smacked his hand and kicked at his legs.

"Fine. I won't touch you. The king requires your presence. Follow me."

I followed him docilely, my chin high, my hands folded, but when he made to shove me into the king's quarters, I shot him a look of such malevolence that he dropped his hands once again and bowed slightly, as if conceding.

"He asked for you. That is why you are here. The *only* reason you are here," he explained begrudgingly, and stepped aside, bidding me enter. But this time he didn't leave. He followed me inside and locked the door.

The king was not in shackles like the first time I'd been summoned, but his skin was flushed, and he trembled and thrashed on the bed. The bedclothes that weren't twisted around his body were pooled on the floor, and when I approached, he opened his eyes and tried to rise. He wore a pair of breeches that were soft and loosely gathered, and nothing else. I wondered if the breeches had been pulled on for my sake and mentally thanked the Gods for that. And where had he been all night?

I could not make him an elixir or blend the herbs for tea like I could have done at my father's keep, where I had my own supplies in my neatly organized bottles and vials. I had nothing here—nothing that would ease his pain or lower his fever. I couldn't even tell Kjell what I needed or send a summons to the kitchen. I thought about the words I'd pressed upon him when he was chained to the wall, the words that had brought comfort and relief. But I didn't dare touch him that way with Kjell looking on. I wouldn't survive the night.

Distrust tinged the air, and I dismissed Kjell with a sigh, turning my attention to the task at hand, to the mysterious king who exuded size and strength yet struggled with an ailment he was clearly hiding from his servants and his subjects.

Instead, I filled a basin from the pitcher on his dressing table and brought it to his bedside, soaking a cloth and wringing it out before running it over his arms and chest, repeating the action until the water in the basin was warm and I was soaked through. It didn't appear to be helping, and Tiras watched me with exhausted eyes, offering no complaint. But his agony pulsed like a drum beat. It was becoming deafening, and I wondered why I was the only one who could hear it. It had always been that way. *I* had always been that way, hearing the words nobody said.

I closed my eyes in defeat.

"Kjell." The king's voice was remarkably strong.

"Yes, Tiras?" Kjell was immediately at his bedside, his hand on the hilt of his sword, as if he could vanquish what ailed his king.

"Leave us."

Kjell eyed me, his eyebrows lowered dangerously, but he acquiesced without argument.

"I'll be right outside, Tiras." His warning glance told me he would be nearby should I attempt assassination. I would have laughed if the king weren't so sick.

The door closed softly, and I met the king's gaze. He looked as troubled as I felt. He wasn't writhing in horrible pain like he'd been the night he'd been shackled. He seemed more ill than wracked in pain, and I wondered again what was wrong.

"Put your hands on me," he instructed softly. "Like you did before."

I shook my head, stalling, wanting to understand. I pointed at his stomach and tilted my head in question. He shook his head. I placed my fingers on his throat and raised a brow. He shook his head once more. I touched his temples, his ears, his arms and his legs, and he finally spoke, answering my question.

"It hurts everywhere," he explained softly. "There is fire beneath my skin."

Suddenly there was fire beneath my skin too, and I felt the heat warm my cheeks and flood my chest. Last time he was hardly conscious. This time, his eyes clung to my face making the act terribly intimate. I was already sitting beside him on the bed, but I pressed my hands to his heart and closed my eyes. My hands were trembling, and he pressed his hands over them, weighing them down.

"You are afraid," he murmured. I nodded, not opening my eyes.

"Are you afraid of me?"

I nodded again. Yes, I was afraid of him. I was afraid that I wouldn't be able to help him, or worse, that I would, and I would mark myself a Healer. I would mark myself for death.

His breath caught and his back arched in agony, his question forgotten. I pressed him back to the bed, smoothing my hands over him, trying to focus.

Pain be gone, illness leave, skin is cool, sleep now, breathe, I instructed, pushing the words into his skin through my fingertips.

Fire is gone,
Fever leaves,
Health in the marrow,
Rest now, breathe

The words were like an incantation wafting in the air, and I liked the rhyme and rhythm. It made it easier for me to focus on the words, to release them into the air. It occurred to me suddenly that perhaps that was the reason witches created rhyming spells. The words had more substance. I'd never done such a thing before. My words were always singular. Simple. But I could feel Tiras's skin growing cool and damp beneath my hands as I silently chanted, telling his body to be well, inviting him to sleep.

And just like before, I put myself under in the process, curling at his side in a deathlike slumber. When I awoke many hours later, night had fallen once again. Someone had lit a sconce, and it threw wan bronze light around the dark chamber. I sat up in bleary confusion, shocked by the passage of so much time. The king slept on beside me, and when I touched his skin it was cool and dry beneath my tentative caress. I laid my head against his chest, listening to his heart, to his steady breathing, and almost fell asleep once more, so deep was my relief. When he spoke, his voice a rumble in the darkness, I jerked and hissed, the only sound I was actually capable of.

"You slept in my bed," he observed mildly, as if a great privilege had been bestowed on me. I peered down at his smirking face, our eyes adjusting to the tepid light. I eased away from him and rose with as much dignity as I could muster; I had slept like the dead and now felt like a corpse, shaky and weak and far too tired to spar with an arrogant king.

"Lark."

I paused on trembling legs, waiting for him to continue. I heard him rise as well, and he seemed much steadier than I. I watched as he walked to the table where a decanter of wine and a pitcher of water were set, along with a simple dinner. I wondered who had seen me in bed with the king and prayed it was only Kjell, who would know why I was there. Tiras poured himself a glass of water, drank it, and poured himself another. He drank the second glass, the column of his throat working eagerly. When he finished, he poured a glass of wine for himself and extended a glass to me as well. I took it and sipped at it gratefully, needing the warm comfort in my belly.

"You helped me," he said softly. "Now . . . what can I give you in return?"

He didn't explain what was wrong with him, what he suffered from, or what ailed him, but he seemed completely recovered once more.

"Draw me a picture, show me what you desire," he pressed.

I wondered if I drew a picture of my home would he allow me to return? It didn't matter, because I wouldn't make that request. I didn't want to return to Corvyn. I wanted to read.

I walked to the shelves laden with books and ran my hands reverently along their spines, but I didn't pull one from the shelf. There was one thing I wanted more than books. I turned back toward the king and fell to my knees. With my hands, I mimed the act of stroking an invisible beard. I needed to see Boojohni.

The king scowled in confusion at my pantomime, then his brow cleared, and he laughed out loud, making me jump and my heart shake in my chest. He was such a conundrum.

"The troll?" he asked, still laughing. "You want to see the troll?"

I nodded emphatically and rose to my feet.

"Done. What else?"

He would give me more? I bit my lip to contain my glee and turned back to the shelves. I pulled a book down, the fattest one of the bunch, and embraced it like a friend.

"I should have known." He crossed the distance between us and pulled the thick tome from my arms. "*The Art of War*?" he asked. "This is the book you want?"

I didn't care what the book was about, I just wanted to look at the words. I took it back from him adamantly. His chest was bare, and his breeches hung low about his hips, making him seem almost more indecent than if he wore nothing at all. I was not used to seeing men this way, but he seemed comfortable with his state of undress. I turned my face to the side, focusing my eyes on the door.

He observed me silently. I could feel his gaze on my face and the question in his thoughts.

"Would you like me to read it to you?"

My eyes shot back to his. I wanted that very much, and he knew it.

I walked to the foot of his bed and picked up the deep blue dressing gown that had been tossed aside and brought it back to him. I extended it toward him, my eyes averted, and he took it from my hand. Then without waiting for him to direct me, I sat on the curved settee in front of the enormous hearth, set my wine aside, and opened the book on my lap. He sat beside me and began to read, his voice low and warm, his hand smoothing the page between us.

"Lasting civilizations are forged on the blood of their citizens. Where there is life, there is conflict."

I stopped him immediately and pointed to the C shape that appeared several times. It didn't make a consistent sound. He said the words slowly, not understanding what I wanted.

"Civilization?"

I nodded, then pointed to the letter again in a different word.

"Conflict?"

I pointed to the first word again, and he repeated it. I held up two fingers and then pointed to the C shape in the two words.

"Two sounds?" he guessed.

I nodded.

"Many of the letters make more than one sound."

I stared at the words he'd said, trying not to cry in frustration. I would never learn to read.

"Shall I continue?" he said softly, as if he could sense my turmoil. I nodded but didn't look up from the page.

"But war, in all its forms and manifestations, is an art which the successful leader must master and utilize." He sighed. "Would you like to skip ahead to the chapter on disembowelment? This is a bit dry."

I brought my hand to the page and pointed at the words impatiently, and he sighed again. I ran a finger under each word so that I could match the sound to the letters, but I got lost almost immediately. He seemed to understand what I wanted, and he placed his hand over mine, moving my hand as he went, so that I stayed with him. He spoke slowly, clearly, unraveling words about life and death and conquering armies and ruthless kings, about blood and war and surrender. And despite the lurid instruction, I did my best to learn.

EIGHT

The king returned to my chambers with Boojohni in tow the very next morning, and I embarrassed myself by clinging to my friend with all the desperation of a lonely child. Boojohni stroked my hair and I wiped my wet eyes in his beard before pulling away and running my hands over his short arms and sturdy legs, my own way of asking him if he was okay.

He laughed and slapped gently at my hands.

"I'm fine, Bird."

I wanted details and specifics about his quarters and his keep and how he'd spent his time since we arrived in Jeru, but his eyes roamed my rooms as if reassuring himself that I too had been well cared for. The king stood back, letting us have a moment, but his presence made me uncomfortable, and he seemed unwilling to leave us alone.

I showed Boojohni the book and the letters the king had drawn, and carefully wrote my own name on a clean sheet so I could show him my name. I pointed to the word and pointed to myself in excitement.

"Lark? Is that how you write Lark?" Boojohni asked, smiling.

I nodded emphatically. He took the quill from my hands and wrote a B, one of the few letters I knew from before, and patted his chest. I knew there must be more to his name than just a B and beckoned to the king impatiently, tapping the letter.

"She wants ye to write my name, Yer Majesty," Boojohni offered, though the king seemed to understand perfectly well what I desired.

"Are you named for the lake in the Drue Forest, beyond Firi?"

Boojohni puffed his chest in pride. "I am. There are many creatures in the Drue Forest." He looked suddenly uncertain, as if the king might send soldiers to set the forest on fire, rooting out said creatures, but King Tiras simply nodded and began to form the word. I watched in fascination as the letters became two, then four, then eight. Boojohni had a magnificent name.

I focused on each letter, assigning a sound to each one, though I wasn't sure I did it correctly. I closed my eyes and the word trembled behind my lids, Boojohni's name set free.

"What?" Boojohni asked, and my eyes snapped open, making the word pop like a soap bubble.

Boojohni was looking at me oddly. Then he looked beyond me, to the door of my room. He waited, as if listening, and bowed to the king.

"I think I am being summoned, Majesty." He looked at me then, "I'll be back, Bird. I promise. I'll ask every day." He looked at the king almost fiercely, as if daring him to refute.

"You may come back," the king said, his tone mild. "But you will have to be accompanied by a guard, Troll. I don't want the little lark to fly."

Anger licked my skin and Boojohni bowed slightly, agreeing to the demand. Then he hurried away, and I watched him leave, fighting off despair. He'd only just arrived and now he was gone again.

"What do you want to learn today?" the king inquired softly, and I swallowed the emotion in my chest, willing the tears to slide back down my throat and extinguish the angry fire in my belly.

I turned determined eyes on him and touched my lips. His brow furrowed, creating black slashes over his narrowed gaze. I felt a surge of confusion and something else, something I couldn't name, lit the air between us.

I touched my lips again, adamantly, and pointed to the letters. His brow smoothed subtly.

"You want to know what they are called?"

I nodded and cupped my ear as if listening.

"Their sound? You want to know what sound each letter makes?"

I released my breath, my frustration easing. I nodded again.

Tiras spent an hour saying the name of the letters and repeating their sounds, his lips pursed and humming, my eyes trained on the shape of them and on the texture and the tones he created. I could only repeat the noises in my head, but I nodded and moved my mouth as he moved his, writing the letter as he said the name. He was patient, remarkably so, considering his gruff nature, and I wondered if he would be as patient if I could ask all the questions in my head. I couldn't, so he raced through the names and sounds, only pausing when I scowled or tapped at a letter insistently, making him repeat it more slowly. When he started to pace like a restless lion, I abandoned the table and the careful crafting of shapes and urged him with tugs and repeated pointing, to write the names of every item in the room. He abandoned the paper and began writing words in charcoal or paint over every surface.

"It is easy enough to wash off or paint over," he said with the unconcerned shrug of a man who has never cleaned up after himself, and I laughed silently, watching him as he filled my room with words, painting on the furniture and walls like a naughty child, drawing simple pictures so he could name things beyond my room—animals and trees and bushes and plants. I began to draw with him, as I was a good deal better at it than he was, and he labeled my drawings, saying the word and breaking up the sounds so I started to recognize them.

The maid gasped when she brought my supper, but the king looked at her with haughty dismissal, and she bowed and stuttered and left the room with great haste. She obviously told the rest of the servants, because no one scolded me or tried to wash our words away.

He spent the day with me, and when he left, I wandered from one word to the next, touching them, saying them in my mind. As I did, I was unable to stop the moisture that rose in my eyes and slipped down my cheeks. It was the happiest day of my life.

That night, just like before, the words filled my dream and spun in the air above my head. In my dream I could speak, my tongue was not tied, and my voice was not trapped in my throat. The words were mine to command and control, and I walked through King Tiras's castle unlocking doors and moving furniture, until I found myself back on my balcony with a longing to fly.

I plucked the word *fly* from my lips and pressed it to my breast, commanding myself to soar like the poppet from my most terrible memory, and as I rose in the sky, the Prince of Poppets, the poppet that caused my mother's death, appeared, beckoning to me. As we flew, the poppet became an enormous eagle with a white head and huge black wings, and I could not keep up with him, so I laid across his back, his feathers soft beneath me, my arms locked around his neck, and we flew until the light began to seep over the Jeruvian hills. Then he was gone, and I was falling and flailing, unable to remember the words to save myself.

The next day, Greta delivered a stack of books—all of them a good deal smaller and simpler than *The Art of War*—sneering that they were from the king, and I began to devour words, decoding them, uncovering them, losing all sense of time for the pursuit of language. I wanted to speak, if only by the written word, and I was insatiable. I was not a typical student. I was voracious. Determined.

When darkness fell, I burned a dozen candles to continue my studies, falling asleep among piles of books and waking to do it all again. The words I couldn't decipher, I copied in neverending lists that the king, upon his return, read and explained.

There were combinations of letters that made little sense and words that contradicted the things I thought I understood, but I committed each word to memory, and over the space of several weeks, my thoughts started to appear in written sentences behind my eyes, fully formed and complete. They were simple sentences with holes and probable misspellings, but sentences, and one night, half delirious, my eyes aching, I begged a candle to move closer. *Come here, candle.* The sentence trembled in the air like the text from a page.

And the candle obeyed.

Horrified, I gasped and leapt from my chair, making the candle I'd commanded topple over on my open book. The flame of the candle licked the page like a cat over spilled milk, and the book was almost instantly engulfed in fire.

One dusty book triggered the destruction of the next. The fire spread with an audible whoosh, enveloping the table completely. I ran for my wash basin and upended it over the blaze. It wasn't enough. The flames jumped to the chairs, and I tried to smother them with the heavy, braided rug from my floor. The rug proved ineffectual, or maybe it was my fear, but I retreated as the flames rose to the giant beams above my head. Smoke billowed around me, and I ran for the door, pounding desperately for someone to hear. The breeze from the open balcony doors pulled the flames toward the drapes, and they too were instantly engulfed, barring my only exit from the room. I tried to find the words to extinguish the flames, but I was terrified. Terror was not conducive to conjuring perfectly formed sentences.

I sunk to the cold, stone floor, trying to breathe, desperate to think.

Out, fire. Out.

I saw the words rise, and the fire in my chamber whooshed through the balcony doors, gone but not doused. That wasn't quite what I'd had in mind. I ran to the balcony doors, following the fiery banshee I'd created. It had fled my room and was climbing the tower wall like a living thing. The fire had simply spread outward. I heard shouting and realized someone had spotted the flame.

How did you spell disappear? I searched my memory, choking on the smoke still filling the room.

Die, fire. Disappear. This fire is no longer here, I commanded fiercely, the words bold and blue, cold and clear. I watched them fall on the flames, and the fire sputtered immediately.

I repeated the rhyme, more confident now. The words shot from my mind, and the flames disappeared completely. A pale ribbon of smoke rose from the blackened wall, the clinging soot the only remnant of the blaze.

I tried to instruct the soot to disappear too, but it stubbornly remained, proving that I could put out the fire, but I couldn't yet save myself from the natural consequences of my mistakes.

The door to my room slammed open, and I found myself face to face with a livid Tiras, who waved at the smoke and scooped me into his arms.

"Are you trying to kill yourself? Or are you trying to create a diversion for escape? It's a long way down, even for a lark."

The room suddenly filled with scurrying servants, and I was rushed from the smoky room, disheveled and terrified, clinging to the king who promptly dumped me in another chamber—right next to his own—and barked at me that burning alive was a terrible way to die.

I curled my hands around the silk-covered arms of the chair I'd been tossed into and seethed at his manhandling.

You are an ass! I thought to myself, the words *ass* and *Tiras* becoming almost one in my head.

"You think I'm an ass?" he asked, outrage making him hoarse.

My head shot up and our eyes clung.

You look like a god but you act like an ogre.

"An ogre?" His voice was beyond incredulous. "A god?"

I bolted to my feet, my chair barking against the floor with my sudden ejection. First the candle. Now the king.

Stop that.

His eyes were as wide as mine, and he approached me slowly.

"Stop that?" he whispered, his eyes on my mouth as if expecting them to move.

Impossible.

He nodded, agreeing. Then he shook his head as if to clear it. "Do it again," he ordered brusquely.

It was my turn to shake my head.

"Do it," he repeated. I sat back down in the chair—collapsed—my legs suddenly so weak I couldn't stand.

"Lark," he demanded, waiting, his eyes still trained on my mouth.

I wasn't sure what I was doing. But I pushed a word at him, the way I often did with Boojohni. It was a random word, the first thing that popped into my head. I seemed to have a penchant for words with a double S.

Kiss.

"Kiss?" he hissed.

My face was suddenly hot, and my hands rose to my cheeks.

Stop looking at my mouth.

"I'm looking at your mouth because I can hear you. But you aren't speaking." His voice was hushed with wonder, and he leaned over me, caging me in the ornate chair, and lifted my chin with the tips of his fingers so I was forced to meet his gaze.

"Again," he commanded.

Tiras.

"Tiras," he repeated.

Lark.

"Lark." His voice was awed.

Cage.

"Cage."

Afraid.

"Afraid?" His black eyes were suddenly fierce. His face was only inches from mine, and I couldn't bear it.

I closed my eyes, seeking the privacy I'd suddenly lost. I needed him to leave. I needed him to leave me alone.

Leave.

"Why?" he asked softly.

It hurts.

"It does?" His breath tickled my face. I couldn't sit back any farther in my chair, and he was everywhere. In my head and in my space, hovering over me like an avenging angel. I fought the panic that rose like a wave.

I pressed my hands to my chest. It suddenly hurt so much I could barely breathe. My heart was pounding, and my breaths felt like shards of glass.

"Tell me," he commanded.

I shook my head. *No. No. No.* I couldn't explain how it felt to converse with another human being. To actually *converse.* I had been reduced to sharing nothing of my innermost thoughts for most of my life. Reduced to throwing things when I was angry. Reduced to tears when I was sad. Reduced to the simplicity of nods and bows, of having people look away from me or become frustrated when they didn't know what I was trying to communicate.

I had been alone for so long with thousands of words I couldn't express. Now this man, this infuriating, beautiful, man—son of a murderous king—could suddenly hear me as if I spoke. A woman instead of a caged bird. A human being instead of a silent presence in the shadows.

And I didn't know how I felt about it.

Go, Tiras. Please go.

I didn't open my eyes, and I kept my mind muddled so no more words would escape. I felt him straighten, and the heat of his presence waned. Then his footsteps sounded, retreating. The door opened and closed again, and I heard his key scraping in the lock.

NINE

From the balcony of my new room I could see the king's guard, practicing their maneuvers and sparring in the jousting yard. Sometimes Tiras was with them—Kjell was there more often than not—and they seemed to take inordinate pleasure from knocking each other down and bloodying each other up.

But the king's duties extended beyond fighting and practicing with his men. Once a week the people made a long line around the castle, coming to the king with their problems, with their complaints, with their accusations. Greta explained that from dawn until dusk, one after another, the people were given a hearing. I wished I could watch and listen, but I could only observe the long lines of waiting citizens from my balcony and speculate about what they would say to the king. It would be exhausting to make one decision after another, to have people looking to you to be just and judicious.

The balcony also gave me a view of a well in the city square, where people gathered to visit and fill their buckets. Odd-

THE BIRD AND THE SWORD

ly, most people didn't fill pails with water. Instead, they leaned over the edge, one at a time, and seemed to peer down into the depths, almost like they were calling to someone or something below. It was strange. People lined up for their turn to look down in the well, and the line was almost as long as the one for the king on hearing day.

Public punishments were also carried out in the city square, following King Tiras's rulings. I saw a man dragged behind a horse, a woman put in the stocks, another lose her hand, another lose his tongue. I didn't know their crimes, but I could guess. Was it a Teller who lost his tongue? Was it a Spinner whose hand was hacked off? After I realized what was occurring, I huddled in my room and closed the balcony doors so I wouldn't hear the crowds and the horrific public displays.

I wondered about the punishment for starting a fire within the castle walls, the penalty for putting words in the king's head, for speaking without a voice, for moving things with one's mind, and I no longer felt certain of my innocence. I realized the harm I could do, and I was afraid. But my fear didn't stop the words from forming, the letters from assembling, my mind from spelling, and my thoughts from spinning.

New clothes were hung in the enormous wardrobe, clothes fit for a princess and rather ill-suited for a prisoner who never left her room. The king's servants washed the walls and replaced the heavy drapes over the balcony door in my old chamber. The pictures and words on my walls were gone, wiped away and painted over. But under the scent of paint and soap, I could still smell the smoke, a reminder of what I could do with a careless word. The books were gone too, and I wondered if Tiras would replace those or if I had become frightening to him, the way I frightened myself.

The fear didn't stop me from experimenting when I was alone. I tried commanding my voice to work, but it stayed frozen in my throat, unaffected by my demand. My words were not effective when I applied them to myself. I couldn't fly, I couldn't speak, I couldn't suddenly paint or sew or dance beyond my natural abilities. In fact I couldn't change myself at all, but beyond that, I discovered that when I spelled out a command, seeing the words in my mind before releasing them, they were highly effective. I was only limited by my ignorance, by my fear, and by my own sense of right and wrong.

I made my dresses dance around my chamber like headless ghosts at a royal ball. I made the furniture rise and reassemble on the ceiling. I commanded the lock to release on my door and stood in the hallway beyond my room, unsure of what to do or where to go now that I could easily escape.

I was free. I was powerful. I was terrified.

I returned to my room, re-engaged the lock with a simple spell, and huddled in my wardrobe in the dark. I felt no joy at my emerging power. I felt only dismay and disgust. And doubt. What was my purpose? What would be the price of this new-found power?

Tiras didn't leave me alone for long. A week after the fire, he was back, escorting me through the hallways and out into the sunshine, past the sentries and the servants, and into the busy town square, as if he was just one of the townspeople. I was a little surprised by his freedom of movement and his lack of concern, but when I looked closer, I noticed flashes of green and archers on the ramparts as well as guards trailing a ways behind us and a guard in every other alcove. The people bowed and bobbed, but most just went about their duties with a quick nod, obviously used to seeing him out and about.

We walked in silence, our postures identical, hands clasped behind our backs looking at the path in front of us. I kept my thoughts loose and formless, not allowing myself to create words that he might hear. As we neared the well I'd seen from my balcony, I stopped, one hand on the king's sleeve, one pointing toward the long line of those waiting to look down into the depths.

I didn't want to form the words, but he seemed to understand my question anyway.

"It's the Well of Words. Or some believe it is. Where the children of the God of Words climbed up from the lesser world. People stand around the well all day and take turns shouting into it. Their wishes, their desires. Wealth, health, love, eternal life."

I cocked my head and listened, trying to hear the things people were asking for.

"No one really knows if or when the wish will be granted. But sometimes they are. So people keep coming back."

I wanted to look down into the dark and write one of my words in the condensation on the wall. I would ask the well for my voice. But the line was long and I wouldn't know how to tell Tiras what I wanted without feeling incredibly foolish. He took my arm, and we turned back toward the castle, walking without conversation once more. Once inside the walls, we meandered through the courtyard and into a little garden off the great hall where Tiras heard the complaints of his citizenry. If I looked up I could see the balcony of my room.

"I only hear the words you give me, you know. It is your power. Not mine," Tiras offered suddenly, his voice mild, his eyes trained on the trees. I thought about that for a few minutes then took a tentative step, asking him a vain question that I could easily spell.

What does my voice sound like in your mind?

His eyes shot to mine and he smiled widely, as if I'd given him something of incredible value. He answered immediately, proving it wasn't a fluke or an illusion. We could actually converse.

"You have a low voice. It's warm. Feminine. But not overtly so. And it's slow, like you are searching for the words to say."

I *was* searching. I was spelling. He seemed suddenly uncomfortable and scratched the back of his neck like he'd been too expressive. I took a deep breath and asked a question that was much more pressing.

Are you going to kill me?

His head reared back like he was shocked, and he halted, grasping my arm so I was facing him. "Why would you ask me such a thing?"

I've seen what happens to the Gifted. I am strange. I have a . . . power. I used his word with a little push for emphasis. Power was something to fear and disown. He knew that well. I shouldn't have to explain it to him. His eyes narrowed, and I knew I'd made my point. When he spoke again, he chose his words carefully.

"It *is* strange. But how is it different from speaking? You use your head to speak. I use my mouth." He shrugged like it was a trifle. I suddenly wanted to slap him. He was being purposely obtuse.

Do you know anyone else who speaks with their mind?

"No."

I stared at him balefully, my point made.

"Do you know anyone who can wield a sword equally well in either hand?"

I raised an eyebrow disdainfully. I didn't. But I wasn't wildly impressed. He was an accomplished killer. Bravo.

Do you?

"As a matter of fact, I do." He smiled wickedly and my breath caught. He was beautiful and terrifying, and he knew it. I looked away, afraid the words would escape my head. But he didn't seem to hear me. Maybe he was right. Maybe he only heard the words I gave him.

"I can wield a sword with either hand. I know no one who can do it as well, if at all."

Yet no one has struck you down for your gift.

He pursed his lips and stepped back, considering my words. "It isn't a gift. It is a skill," he said softly and maybe a bit defensively. "And many have tried to kill me for it. Make no mistake."

And speaking to you with my mind is a skill . . . not a gift? It was semantics, and he had to know it.

He stared off in the distance for several long moments. He didn't answer, and I could almost hear his mind churning.

He turned abruptly and commanded me to remain where I was in the garden. I obeyed, though I wanted to take to the sky. How was it that I could make a dress dance but I couldn't make myself fly? A moment later Tiras was back with a maid, the young girl who brought my meals and occasionally dressed my hair. Trailing behind them was Kjell, sweat-soaked and breathless, like he'd been pulled from the training yard.

"Sit," Tiras commanded the girl. She sat on a nearby stone bench, looking fearfully from her king, to me, to the sweating warrior beyond.

"Ask Lark a question—something you don't know, something she could answer in a few words."

"Wh-wh-who is Lark?" she squeaked.

Something flashed in Tiras's eyes, and a word rose in the air, filling my mind. *Shame.* He felt shame. I didn't know why.

He looked at me solemnly, and the girl followed his gaze. "This is Lark," he said, looking at me, his voice strangely apologetic.

What is her name? I pressed the words into him.

"Uh. What is your name?" Tiras asked the girl, who was quaking in her seat. I wondered if Tiras knew any of his servants' names.

"Pia," she answered, her eyes so wide I worried she would strain herself.

"Are we going to have a visit in the garden with the ladies, then?" Kjell growled impatiently. "What the hell is going on, Tiras?"

Tiras spun on his heel and glowered at his friend. "I don't have to explain myself to you. Sit." He pointed at the bench. When Kjell was seated, filling the space with the smell of perspiration, horseflesh, and dust, Tiras spoke again, repeating the question.

"Ask Lark a question, Pia. This is not a test. You won't be punished or harmed. Ask her a question."

"Er . . . How do you do, Lady Lark?" she chirped nervously.

Kjell groaned like he was being tortured. "She's a *mute*. Not a lady. What in the bloody hell are we doing?"

"Enough!" Tiras roared, making us all jump. The word rose from him again. *Shame.*

"No, Pia. Something specific. Ask her what her mother's name was. What her favorite color is." Kjell swore under his breath, and Tiras shot him an outraged sneer.

"What is your mother's name, Lady Lark?" Pia repeated obediently.

I glanced up at Tiras, and he inclined his head, wanting me to answer the only way I could.

I thought of my mother's name, the letters, the syllables. *Meshara.* Then I focused my thoughts on the crinkled forehead of the confused servant and urged the word outward. The girl stared at me blankly, and shot a look back at the king.

"Do you hear her?" Tiras asked her.

"Wh-what?" the girl stammered, her eyes widening once more. "She's not even speaking, Highness."

Tiras looked at me as if I weren't concentrating hard enough. I gazed back steadily.

"Leave," Tiras commanded the girl, and she stood and fled from the garden without further prodding. I winced. I was sure

84

the rest of the castle was going to hear all about "Lady Lark" and the king's request.

"What is this, Tiras?" Kjell rumbled, his voice more measured.

He rose from the bench and stood next to Tiras, his arms folded suspiciously. He still didn't like me. I could feel the disdain coming off him in waves. No words necessary.

"Ask Lark a question, Kjell. Something you don't know the answer to. Something only she can provide."

I was having serious concerns about this experiment. I'd been relieved when Pia had been unable to hear me. I looked at Tiras and shook my head, entreating him.

If he can hear me it will only endanger my life.

"He can be trusted," Tiras said, arms folded, quartering no argument.

Says you. Could Pia be trusted? She's already telling your housekeeper that you are losing your mind.

Tiras's eyes widened in affront. "He can be trusted," he insisted stubbornly.

"Tiras!" Kjell hissed. His brows were lowered over his blue eyes, and his hand gripped his sword like he wanted to draw it. Tiras was staring at me, talking to me, and it appeared as if I wasn't responding.

"I can hear her, Kjell," Tiras explained, his gaze moving to his friend. "She can't speak aloud. But I hear her in my head."

"What?" Kjell roared. He couldn't have looked more stunned if Tiras had told him I was actually a lark and could lay eggs.

"Ask her a question," Tiras demanded.

I felt like a spectacle, a freakish novelty, but I kept my gaze steady on Kjell who was glaring at me like I'd scrambled his king's brains.

He drew his sword slowly, and Tiras sighed. "Kjell," he warned.

"I'll ask the little lark a question then," he hissed. "How about this? If I toss you over a cliff, will you fly or will you fall, because that is where you're going."

I clenched my teeth so hard, I felt something pop in my jaw. My words were as sharp as glass, and they could have cut through the hedge they were so loud in my head.

I am neither a bird nor a beast, so I would fall. But judging from the way you smell and the way you act, if I throw you in among the pigs you will be right at home.

There was a stunned silence for several heartbeats. Then Tiras started to laugh, his shoulders shaking with mirth at Kjell's outraged expression.

"I'm guessing you heard *that*, Pig Man," he hooted, gasping for breath.

Kjell extended his sword toward my throat.

"Are you Gifted?" he hissed.

"Kjell!" All the laughter fled Tiras's voice, and I heard him draw his sword as well, though I dared not move my eyes from the furious warrior before me. The word coming off his skin was *destroy*.

Destroy.

"Are you like your whore mother?" Kjell whispered, his eyes never leaving mine.

My mother was a Teller. Not a whore.

"A Teller," he whispered, confirming that he could, indeed, hear me loud and clear. The tip of his sword tapped the underside of my chin. I tried not to gasp when I felt the sharp nick, and in my mind I heard my mother whispering into my tiny ears before she closed her eyes for the last time.

Swallow, Daughter, pull them in, those words that sit upon your lips. Lock them deep inside your soul, hide them 'til they've time to grow. Close your mouth upon the power. Curse not, cure not, 'til the hour. You won't speak and you won't tell. You won't call on heav'n or hell. You will learn and you will thrive. Silence, daughter. Stay alive.

I hadn't hidden the words well enough. I hadn't stayed silent. Now I would die.

TEN

A drop of blood slid down my neck and between my breasts. Then another.

"Will you kill me too, Kjell?" Tiras asked, his voice a strained whisper. I didn't understand the question. Obviously, the king's life was not in danger at the moment.

Kjell looked to his king, his throat working, and I saw the horror and indecision in his face. He was afraid of me and afraid for Tiras.

"I would give my life for yours," Kjell told Tiras, and *truth* rose around him. I did not doubt him. He would save the king at all costs, and he wouldn't hesitate to run me through.

"You can't kill her, Kjell. Put down your sword," Tiras warned.

"But the law . . ." Kjell protested.

"You were willing to break the law when you thought she could heal me," Tiras interrupted.

"You said she couldn't," Kjell argued, his voice rising.

"She can't. Not the way we hoped."

I was bleeding, they were talking around me, and I didn't understand all the things they weren't saying.

"Put down your sword, Kjell," Tiras commanded again, and his voice harbored no argument.

Kjell lowered his weapon reluctantly, but he didn't sheath it. The blood continued to slide down my neck and pool between my breasts, but I didn't wipe it away or lower my gaze.

Why would he kill you? I asked the king. Kjell sneered at my bravado.

"The question is, what good are you to us? We are losing the king, just as your mother foretold. And you are unable to heal him."

"Kjell!" Tiras warned softly.

I'd forgotten my mother's curse. Suddenly, I could hear her voice the way it echoed across the courtyard of my father's keep, warning the king as he told her to kneel before him.

You will lose your soul and your son to the sky, she'd said.

Tiras was that son.

And there was something terribly wrong.

We were interrupted by a clattering of boots and shouts, and several of the king's guard burst into the garden, genuflecting even as one began to speak. The king stepped neatly in front of me, shielding me from their view.

"Your Highness. The members of the delegation are starting to arrive. The Lord of Corvyn and the Ambassador from Firi along with representatives from several other provinces and their entourages. Should we escort them individually?"

My father was in Jeru.

"How many men?" Kjell asked.

"Two score and ten, sir," someone answered.

"Allow them to enter," Tiras said calmly. "Escort them here and provide them room and refreshment. Make sure there is a guard detail on each member of the delegation, just as we discussed."

"Yes, Majesty," the men replied and left the garden as hastily as they'd arrived.

"Go to your room. I will send Boojohni to attend you," Tiras commanded me, throwing the words over his shoulder as he strode away, Kjell on his heels. I sank down to the bench, disregarding his command. My legs wouldn't hold me. I was trembling from the confrontation, from the sword at my throat, and from the strain of revelation, my own and the king's. I wasn't safe, the king was cursed, and the world was upside down. I wanted to use my words to right it, to fix it, but I couldn't. That much was abundantly clear.

And now my father was in Jeru. I had no doubt he'd come to demand my return. My stomach knotted and my hands shook, and I wiped at the trickle of blood that refused to congeal. The bodice of my dress was stained, and my hands were streaked with it.

I had three choices: I could go home, I could stay here, or I could run away. Far, far away. I could run to the forest of Drue. Boojohni said it was filled with creatures. The odd, the strange, the Gifted. Maybe I could build a life for myself among other outcasts now that I could speak. The thought brought me up short. I couldn't speak! I could put words in people's heads. I wasn't a creature. I was something else entirely.

They would kill me.

My father was the only one who had any incentive to keep me alive. I should return to Corvyn. I should go back home and hide in my father's keep and pretend the words hadn't come alive inside of me. I could pretend that all was as it had been before, and maybe in pretending, I would save myself. But pretending wouldn't save Tiras.

I heard a sniffling and a shuffling, and Boojohni appeared around the hedge, a smile of greeting peeking out from his shaggy beard.

"The king told me ye were in your chamber, but I could smell ye out here." His eyes narrowed on my neck, and his smile disappeared. "What happened, Bird?"

I pressed my hand to my throat and shook my head.

"Come with me. I'll take care of ye." He reached for my arm, but I shook him off. I didn't want to be taken care of. I wanted to run away from all the men who sought dominion over me, who thought they could own me, imprison me, use me, cut me. I wiped a furious hand at the blood on my neck and the tears on my cheeks that I hadn't realized I'd shed.

Can you hear me, Boojohni?

He hissed and stepped back, his eyes filled with horror.

I bowed my head in defeat, sorrow making my chest constrict and my eyes overflow. Boojohni could hear me, and he was afraid. I felt the air around him swell with revulsion and dismay. His breathing was harsh, and I tried again, my inner voice broken and sad even to my own ears.

Are you afraid of me, my friend?

I felt his hand touch my hair, just a tentative brush of his fingertips, but I didn't look up at him.

"Bird?" he whispered, as if he still wasn't sure about the voice in his head. "Bird, is that ye?"

Yes. It's me. I nodded as I spoke, and he gasped again, like he couldn't believe it. He reached toward my lips, and his hand fell away like he'd changed his mind at the last second. He took several steps back, and I rose on quaking legs and followed him, wanting to plead with him, needing to convince him of things I wasn't sure of myself.

I found my voice, I tried to explain. *At least . . . a piece of it.*

He nodded slowly, his eyes still impossibly wide, but the horror he had exuded was abating.

You can hear me now. I can talk to you.

"I have always been able to hear ye, Lark. But before it was a feeling. An instinct. Now I hear a voice . . . *your* voice. And it's going to take some getting used to."

I understand. I'm afraid too. I'm so afraid, Boojohni.

His mouth trembled, and his compassion sang sweetly in the air. It was like a salve to my soul. He wiped at his eyes and pointed to the wound on my neck.

"Did the king do that?"

I shook my head. *No.*

"Good. I don't want to hate him. He's different from what I expected. Different from his father."

I don't want to hate him either, I confessed, and Boojohni looked at me sharply. I don't know what he saw, but I allowed him to take my hand and lead me out of the garden and up the wide, winding staircase to my tower room. "You need to prepare yourself, Lark. Yer father is here, and there are rumors afoot," he whispered, his eyes darting right and left like there were ears and eyes everywhere.

Tell me.

"The king is young. The members of the Council of Lords think he is too lax on the Gifted."

My eyes shot to his, and he grabbed my hand, comforting me. He said no more until we were alone in my chamber.

He doctored the wound at my throat as he talked, his voice barely above a whisper.

"They blame him for the rise of the Volgar. They say he has encouraged revolution. He has led the Volgar to believe he is weak and lenient."

I thought of the way Tiras and Kjell had fought the terrifying bird people, hacking them out of the sky, and wondered at the delegation's definition of lenient.

The Volgar are not . . . Gifted. They are monsters.

"The council believes there is no difference," he said.

I winced, and Boojohni patted my hand again. It was what King Zoltev, Tiras's father, had believed. But my mother was not a monster. I was not a monster.

We continued with our conversation, my words slow and small as I did my best to assemble them in my head. Boojohni listened in wonder as I answered his tentative questions, and at one point, wiped his eyes and smiled at me tearfully.

"Ye sound like a nightingale, Bird. Yer voice is beautiful. Sweet. I could listen all day."

Before long, Greta and the maid I'd just learned was Pia brought steaming buckets of water to my room and pulled a gown from my wardrobe. Boojohni informed us all that he would be waiting outside my door to escort me to the Great Hall when I was ready.

He shot me a sheepish gaze as he excused himself, and I pressed a frantic question on his mind that he studiously ignored. He wasn't telling me all that the king had communicated.

Pia's eyes grew round at the blood on my dress, and Greta was less abrasive than usual as I was bathed and primped, then dressed in a silvery silk that made me feel like a raindrop—grey, small, and all but invisible. Pia wrapped a diamond choker around my neck to hide the thin slice Kjell had carved into my throat. They didn't ask about the wound, and I wondered if it was because I couldn't speak or because they regularly saw things in the king's employ that they were forced to ignore. Pia informed me the choker had belonged to the king's mother, Aurelia, and that it suited me. It didn't. But it was beautiful, and its weight gave me courage.

Pia brushed a drop of lavender oil into my heavy hair so it would shine and held the length back from my face with a thin band of braided silver studded with diamonds that matched the jewels at my neck. The lavender eased my nerves, and I tried to focus on the scent so I wouldn't think about the evening ahead as Greta lined my grey eyes with kohl, blackened my lashes, and stained my lips and cheeks with rose-colored face paint.

I had the distinct impression I was being prepared for something I was not at all ready for, and when Boojohni rapped on the door and urged us to hurry, the maids stepped back and admired their handiwork like I had been the ultimate challenge, and they had succeeded with their task.

When Boojohni saw me, he seemed proud and pleased, and I shot him a question I'd been saving throughout the long beauty session.

What is happening in the hall?

Boojohni winced and covered his ears, as if that could keep me out.

"Hellfire, Bird!" he whined. "Adjust your tone. Ye don't have to yell."

My mouth dropped open, and I halted in surprise. I hadn't realized I could control my volume. But it made sense. Just like a person could moderate their voice, I too could 'speak' quietly, even whisper, so only the person next to me could hear. That meant I could also raise my voice in a crowd and deliver a message to a group.

I repeated myself more carefully, and Boojohni nodded, indicating I had been successful.

"There is a feast for the dignitaries. Ye are attending to show your father that you are in good health. Ye are to nod and smile and sit near the king. Ye are to keep yer words to yourself."

I had no intention of revealing my gift, but Boojohni's instructions bothered me. *You are suddenly the king's messenger?*

"I have no loyalty to your father, Lark. I never have. My loyalty was to your mother and now to ye. I believe ye are better off here in Jeru."

ELEVEN

Preparations for the arrival of the lords had been occurring all week, and the chandeliers dripped with hundreds of candles, the flame flickering in the crystal drops that reflected rainbow light across the walls and domed ceiling of the hall. I'd only seen the hall from the garden, and daylight didn't do it justice.

Huge tables draped in royal blue were laden with roasted fowl and entire pigs, still rotating on spits. Cheeses and berries, melon and pears, and delicacies from every province were arranged in towers and teetering displays. Breads of every hue were braided, brushed with sweet butter, and sprinkled in herbs and spices, making the air smell like a bazaar. The hollow drum of my stomach began to growl.

I poked carefully at members of the assembly, testing the limits of my voice.

May I serve you, madam? I asked the beautiful ambassador to my left, and without raising her eyes, she declined.

"I have all I need, thank you," she responded easily. I bit my lip and ignored Tiras, who had also heard my question.

More wine, sir? I asked the man sitting next to her, my eyes trained on him only long enough to pose my query. He didn't raise his head either, and he didn't respond. I asked again, raising my mental volume.

The man next to him looked around in confusion, his glass raised for a topping off.

Tiras growled.

I ignored him and tested my ability on the three people to the left of Kjell, just across the table. None of them, except Kjell, responded or glanced up at all. Kjell scowled and shot a warning look at the king.

"Stop that," Tiras whispered.

Why do you think some people can hear me and some can't?

"You look quite beautiful this evening, Lady Lark. Have I told you lately how much I enjoy your silence?" he murmured, ignoring my musings.

Have I told you lately what an ass you are? I didn't think ass was the most accurate word for the king, but it was easy to spell. I tripped over my comeback a little and the king snorted softly, indicating he'd heard. I stopped talking to him—we were surrounded by curious eyes and ears—and I lapsed into quiet study of the people assembled at the long table. The king sat to my right, at the head, and Kjell sat directly across from me, though the distance across the table was at least six feet, providing some much needed distance between us.

The Ambassador from Firi was the only representative who was as youthful as the king, and her beauty rivaled his. Her skin was dark—darker than Tiras's—and her hair was a wild, curling mass, embedded with tiny, sparkling gems that twinkled as she moved her head. Her ears were slightly pointed, as if she'd descended from elves. She was tall and voluptuous, her breasts round, her waist small, her legs tapering to tiny feet wrapped in silvery slippers. Kjell watched her with equal parts distrust and fascination, and I wondered if he ever relaxed. He was the most irascible man I'd ever met, and his presence made me want to run from the hall. The Ambassador from Firi eyed him with pursed lips and laughing eyes, as if she knew he was intrigued. At one point, Tiras engaged her in cordial conversation, his eyes resting appreciatively on her face, and I felt a sting of something unwelcome and unwieldy pierce my breast. I didn't want him to like her.

Kjell wants to bed the beautiful ambassador, and he despises himself for it.

My silent observation zinged between us, and the king choked, grabbing for his empty goblet. I felt my face flush and didn't meet his eye. I couldn't believe I'd shared such a thing, and I doubted I'd spelled all the words correctly, but I'd gotten his attention. He put down his empty goblet with a grimace and reached beneath the table and pinched me, hard.

My father had grown more gaunt and grey in the weeks that I'd been away. Six weeks was insufficient to truly age, but age he had, and I felt a sliver of compassion for him before he met my gaze and immediately looked away. Why did he dislike me so much?

"There hasn't been an execution or even a banishment of the Gifted in Jeru City in a year." Lord Gaul spoke up from the far end of the long table, and the conversation immediately quieted.

"Why, Lord Gaul, do you enjoy such things so much?" Tiras answered easily.

"It is not a matter of what I enjoy, Majesty. It is what I expect. We must have order. Fairness. Equality. The Gifted are a threat to all of us. If we allow them to flourish, they will enslave us. It is what the Volgar are seeking to do. Their numbers have grown exponentially in the last thirty years. They are no longer content to stay in their own country. They want ours as well."

"We have had banishments. Executions. Imprisonments as well, Lord Gaul. Many of them. In fact, I grow weary each week meting out punishment. There is not one week that goes by that some Jeruvian isn't attempting to steal or harm or violate. And so far, none of them have been Gifted, though many of them are quite skilled. I am far more worried about those people who are actively committing offense than I am about rooting out the Gifted with swords and accusations and punishing them for things they might do. Someday. Possibly."

"How would you know what they have done? They could be spinning gold and selling it on the streets under your very nose. They could be healing citizens and claiming it is skill instead of sorcery. They could be transforming into wolves and attacking another man's sheep, or changing fates with a mere word!"

"Animals who attack other animals are killed. Changers who do such a thing will receive their just punishments. So far we've not killed a single animal who was a Changer in disguise."

"You are clearly resistant to enforcing the laws your father and the council put in place."

Tiras looked from one representative to the next, his expression bland but his eyes glittering.

"Tell me, why are you all here? It is not yet time for our bi-annual assembly. And I did not invite you . . . though I am happy to entertain you." The king's tone was so dry he had the entire delegation clearing their throats and chugging their wine to ease the drought. No one answered the king's question.

After several seconds of heavy drinking, Lord Gaul began to speak once more. Tiras cut him off with a wave of his hand.

"I've heard your opinions already, Lord Gaul."

Lord Bilwick, the ambassador from the province east of Corvyn, a close confidant of my father's and a man I'd known all my life, seemed eager to change the subject. He was jovial and corpulent, but his merry eyes didn't quite contain his quick temper. I'd seen him slap his wife when he lost at cards. His daughters cowered in the corners—not unlike me in that regard—and his oldest son was as bad as his father. My father had hoped for a betrothal between us. Thankfully, the son had laughed in his face. He considered me broken, and I was incredibly grateful for all my jagged pieces that kept him away.

"How do we fare in the battle against the Volgar, Highness?" Lord Bilwick asked with a burp and a self-deprecating smile. "That is the only reason I am here. And to offer my demand that you return Lord Corvyn's daughter." He took a giant bite from an apple he'd selected, and looked so much like the roasted pig laid out before him that I almost missed what he said. My father spoke up immediately, taking the opening.

"I have put men on the border, just as you requested, Your Majesty. I would like to bring my daughter home."

Tiras met my father's gaze, and there was speculation on his face. I could feel him considering, feel his questions and his distrust of my father. My father squirmed and looked away, and something cold slithered down the center of my back, and wrapped its tentacles around my waist. It contracted, and I felt sick. Odd. Breathless. My father was exuding a word that scared me, a word that was stronger than it had been before. *Death*. He was exuding death.

"I want her to stay," Tiras said suddenly.

The table grew oddly hushed and the tentacles tightened as everyone strained to look at me. I took little breaths, sipping the air, and locked down every emotion, every expression. I was ice. No one would know the havoc being waged under my skin.

My father's brow rose, and his face flushed, and Lord Gaul regarded me with raised brows. Lord Bilwick laughed out loud.

I commanded the apple in his hand to slam into his gaping mouth. It obeyed with ferocity, and the fat lord choked and pawed at the glistening red globe wedged between his horsey teeth. His wife gasped and began pounding at his back. The apple came free with a wash of spittle, and the lords and ladies around him turned away with disdain.

The king turned on me with narrowed eyes, but my father rose from his chair with regal affront.

"I have done as you demanded, Majesty. I have put all able men from Corvyn on the border, while the harvest ripens in the fields with only the women and children to see to it. I expect you to be true to your word."

"If you recall, I said your daughter would be returned when the Volgar had been destroyed. Not before. Plus, your daughter is a Jeruvian lady of noble birth. She is of age. She could be queen."

Kjell cursed, a low hiss that found its way to my ears and wormed into the ice I'd created around myself. I dared not look his way. I dared not look at my father. I dared not come out of my ice fortress at all, but I trembled behind the façade, my heart pounding, my blood thick and hot, threatening to melt my glacial control.

"But . . . she is . . . a mute!" my father stammered, clearly as stunned as I.

"Yes, she is." The king smiled around the words, and his tone was wry and laced with humor. "A wonderful quality in a woman. She will keep all my secrets."

The assembled lords and ladies laughed uncomfortably, and goblets were once again drained. The king reached for his newly re-filled glass as well, but didn't partake.

I do not want to be queen.

He turned his head, giving me a scant sweep of his black eyes as his lips barely moved over hushed words.

"You lie."

I want to go home.

"Another lie."

You can't hold me prisoner forever.

He looked me full in the face, and his eyes held mine as he murmured, "Your father's prison holds no books. No words. No conversation."

I had no answer to that, and gazed back at him helplessly, wishing I could read his thoughts like I was learning to read his books, that I could examine the words he didn't say, piece by piece, until they made sense. Instead, I felt only his indecision, a blank question behind his eyes.

I don't understand you.

"That makes us even, then," he said, reaching for his goblet. He seemed to reconsider his wine and took my goblet instead. He sipped it carefully then downed it as if his gullet was on fire. His hand shook as he released it, and he gripped the edge of the table to steady himself. My heart began to pound in my ears.

Are you ill?

"I want you to go back to your room. Now," he commanded harshly, and he stood, dismissing me, addressing the assembly with complete control. "Please excuse me for a moment. Continue to enjoy your meal."

My eyes swung to Kjell, who was once again staring at the beautiful ambassador.

Kjell! His head snapped to me and his eyes widened in outrage as if my voice was a violation of his privacy.

The king is not well.

Tiras had already turned away from the table, and Kjell was immediately at his side holding his arm and speaking urgently into his ear, as if something of utmost import had just arisen, and the king was needed elsewhere. Tiras walked swiftly, straight and tall, his head bowed toward Kjell. The assembly watched momentarily then relaxed back into their conversations and their drink, unconcerned.

The king collapsed in the doorway.

Kjell dragged Tiras from sight, and no one even raised their eyes from the feast in front of them. I was all but invisible, and suddenly I was grateful for the scant attention I was generally paid. I stood and stepped away from the table, moving sedately away from the banquet, my eyes fixed on the arched doorway where I'd last seen the king, but suddenly my father was there, halting my progress. He wrapped his hand around my elbow and tugged me in the opposite direction.

"Lark. Come with me, daughter."

I panicked briefly, resisting and digging in my heels. My father had grown gaunt over the years, but he towered above me, and there was desperation in his grasp and fear in his face. I could only stumble along beside him.

Let me go, Father.

I pushed words into his head, forming them carefully, trusting that his sense of self-preservation would force him to guard my abilities, but he didn't react at all. He didn't look around in confusion, trying to ascertain who was speaking. He simply walked, and he pulled me along with him.

Let go of me, Father. The words wailed in my thoughts, but I was the only one who winced. He didn't hear me. Like Pia, he was completely impervious.

He headed toward the archway at the far end of the hall, pulling me along with him as I pushed furious words against the concrete wall of his mind. I'd been rendered mute once more.

Two footmen from Corvyn stood at the base of the broad staircase that led to the guest quarters on the farthest wing of the castle. They straightened and greeted my father as he approached.

"Lock my daughter in my quarters. Prepare to depart, just as we planned. We leave within the hour. There are rumors of Volgar movement, and we are needed at home. I've been away too long," my father instructed smoothly.

I yanked my arm from his grasp, but as always, I was utterly ignored, completely dismissed, and I could do nothing to free myself from those who could easily subdue me.

Yet.

The thought gave me comfort, and I walked agreeably with the two footmen, my hands folded demurely, my eyes straight ahead, making a plan.

When the door to my father's quarters was shut behind me, I waited, listening for the scrape of the key and the retreat of the two footmen. But they stayed, talking quietly among themselves, guarding the door. I paced uneasily, and worry clawed in my chest. I told myself Tiras meant little to me, that his suffering was not my concern. He'd become an odd savior of sorts, opening my mind even as he kept me locked away. He'd become a friend, though I would never admit that to him. To anyone. But I was afraid, and my mother's prophecy rang in my head. Kjell held me accountable. I held *myself* accountable. My mother had been slaughtered by Tiras's father. But my mother had died because of me. I did not want to be the cause of Tiras's death. Impatient, I ran to the window and commanded it to open, flinging the words out desperately.

The window shattered, spraying glass in every direction.

I covered my face and fell to the ground as the door burst open behind me, the footmen crying out that we must be under some sort of attack. They ran to the jagged opening to peer up into the sky, cautiously navigating the broken glass. When they could see nothing that would cause further alarm, they helped me to my feet. I was covered with glass but mostly uninjured, and I shook myself gingerly, sprinkling shards from my dress and my hair, and surveyed my clumsy attempt at escape. I started fires and broke glass. I needed a great deal more practice or I was going to hurt myself.

They left once more and carefully locked the door behind them again, murmuring about what could have caused the window to shatter in such a way. This time they didn't remain, but hurried off down the corridor, leaving a trail of mumbled words in their wake. I sighed in relief and calmly, purposefully asked the lock to disengage.

It did so with an audible click, and I sent up a grateful prayer to the God of Words.

TWELVE

eased the door open and peeked down the hall. It had grown dark, and sconces had been lit on every floor. I would have to be certain to avoid the staff who were all aware that I should not be roaming the palace unattended. I'd never been in this wing, never negotiated these halls, and I didn't know how I would reach the king without being seen. My father would be returning as well, and I didn't want to attempt another command that could completely backfire.

Twenty minutes later, breathless and frazzled, I eased myself into the king's quarters and leaned heavily against the door. The room was dark, the king's clothes in a messy pile, boots toppled, sword and sheath abandoned, even his crown—something he rarely wore—sat atop his tunic, like he'd melted into the oak floor and left his clothes behind. There was an emptiness to the room, a melancholic abandonment in the crumpled clothing that had me calling out, as if I could make contact with his thoughts.

Tiras, where are you?

I called again, sending my words outward, flinging them into the darkness, shouting the only way I could. But there was no response. I paused in indecision, afraid to leave the room, uncertain of where to hide myself or what I should do. I walked to the balcony and stepped out into the darkness, my eyes searching the guards below for Kjell, for Boojohni, for something.

Kjell? I pushed the word out into the night air, and it vibrated like a gong in my head. The guard below me didn't raise his head. I slumped down onto the balcony, pressing my face against the iron rails, weary and uncertain. I could see my chambers across the way. My room was ablaze with light, which was odd, as it had not been night when I'd been escorted through the halls to the banquet and I doubted that the maids awaited me now. I could see the open balcony door and beyond that, a tall shadow loomed. There was someone in my room. Tiras had instructed me to go there, I remembered now. Why hadn't I gone there first?

I wished again for flight, that I could wing across the distance between the two balconies. I couldn't change into a bird, a little lark, and flutter up into the sky, but maybe I could still fly.

I retreated back into the king's chambers and pulled the silk sheet from his bed. Clutching it in my arms, I pressed it to my chest, eyes closed, concentrating on the words that would give it flight. When I was a child, I had pressed the words into inanimate objects with my lips, with sound. This was decidedly more difficult.

Up, away, into the sky
Lift me high and let me fly.

Nothing happened, and I realized I had to be specific. I had to imbue the sheet with a name, and direct it by that name. When the candle had moved, I had called to it specifically. When the fire died, I had done the same. When the glass broke, I had been precise about what I'd wanted. So precise that it had opened the only way it could, by breaking.

Coverlet. It was a coverlet. With the tip of my finger, I traced the word into the silk, focusing on the letters. Then, with not a little dread, I fisted it in my hands and demanded it rise.

Rise, coverlet, from the floor, through the window, to my door.

It rose, billowing, pulling me toward the balcony like it was being sucked into a wind storm. But though it would have flown, I was too heavy to fly with it, and it simply flapped like a sheet in the breeze, helpless against my grip. I clung to it, not sure what to do next, and I didn't hear the door open behind me.

"What are you doing?"

I started and jumped, almost losing my grip on the coverlet that whipped and tossed in my hands.

Tiras stood in the doorway of his room, clothed like he'd spent the last hour in the stables instead of writhing in pain like I'd envisioned. Kjell stood beside him, his eyes wide and his jaw slack. I gasped and immediately focused on the task at hand.

Coverlet, be still

Obey my will.

It was the first rhyme that came to my head, but the flapping ceased and the coverlet drooped from my fists, the flight removed from every corner.

"Witch," Kjell breathed. "You are a bloody witch."

"Kjell!" Tiras said. "Leave us."

Kjell ignored him. "Tell me, Teller. Did you poison the king's wine? Did you do your father's bidding? Does the little lark want to be Princess of Jeru?" He strode forward and ripped the coverlet from my hands. I stepped back, eyes on his, arms at my sides. Kjell was afraid of me. His fear billowed out like the coverlet had moments before, whipping in the air, making me afraid too.

I shook my head. *No. I came to help.*

He winced as if my voice in his head caused him pain. I looked at Tiras, who hadn't moved except to shut the door behind him.

"Kjell. Go. I am fine. Go back to the hall and see that all is in order."

"Tiras, by all the Gods! She is dangerous!"

"She is," Tiras agreed, nodding, his eyes on mine. "She is that. Now go, Kjell. And make sure Lord Corvyn doesn't slip away. Poison is more his style, I think. He had help though. I'm guessing certain members of the council are expecting news of my demise. I'll be down shortly to let them see that they have failed."

Kjell growled an expletive that made me blush and the king sigh, but he did as he was told, his hand on his sword, stomping to the door and pulling it shut with great force behind him.

"Show me." Tiras nodded toward the sheet in my hands.

I stayed still, not willing to condemn myself further, and I pled with him silently. *It is nothing.*

"Show me, Lark," he demanded. I bunched the sheet in my hands and turned to put it back on the bed. He walked toward me slowly. "Why are you in my chambers?" he asked, allowing me to believe, for a moment, that he was not going to insist on a demonstration.

I thought you were ill.

"And you came to finish me off?" There was a smile in his voice. I looked at him sharply. "The door was locked. How did you get inside?" he asked as he continued to move closer.

I hung my head, having forgotten that detail.

It was not locked.

"It was."

I wondered if he could feel the lie on me, the way I could feel falsehoods when others told them.

"You are a Teller. Did you tell the door to open?" He was so close I could feel his breath stir my hair. "Did you tell the apple to hit Bilwick in his fat mouth?" There was laughter in his voice, and I relaxed the smallest bit.

Yes.

"Show me." He walked back to the heavy door and slid the bolt home. I hesitated briefly. He looked at me expectantly, and I knew there was no hiding any of it from him.

Open lock, upon the door, I wish to leave the room once more.

The bolt immediately released. The king laughed, and wonder rose from the sound.

"You could have gone . . . any time. Yet you have stayed in my castle behind locked doors, playing the prisoner. Why?"

I shook my head in denial. *Not any time. I had to learn the words. You gave them to me.*

"I gave them to you?" he repeated, dumbfounded.

You taught me to read. You taught me to write.

"This power is new?" His voice lifted in surprise.

The power is not new. The words are new. My mother took the words away when she died. She took my voice away so I wouldn't hurt anyone else.

"Maybe she took the words away so no one would hurt you," he ventured, and his voice was kind. "It wasn't your mother who made the poppet fly, was it?"

Sorrow crashed over me, weighing me down, causing my bowed head to hit my chest in despair.

No.

"Does your father know what you can do?"

No.

I had no desire to lift my heavy head, and felt Tiras approach once more and stop in front of me. I kept my eyes on his boots until he touched my chin with one long finger, tipping my face to his. His eyes were soft, and I found myself wanting to tell him everything.

My father hates me.

"How can that be? He seems desperate to have you return to Corvyn."

He is afraid you are going to hurt me. He is afraid I'm going to die. And if I die, he dies. Another gift from my mother. She made sure that his own survival depended upon ensuring mine.

"Ah, I see. Such a clever Teller. Your mother was very wise."

I nodded.

"We are all caught in her snare. Your father. You. Me. Even my father was obsessed with her. Meshara," Tiras whispered.

I felt my eyes widen and my heart skitter. Tiras raised both hands to my face and cradled it thoughtfully, his fingers tracing the line of my cheek and the sharp edge of my jaw down to the point of my chin. I could hardly breathe, and I didn't know if it was his gentle touch or my mother's name lingering in the air. Or both.

"None of us were ever the same after that day. My father lost me, just like your mother foretold. And he died knowing it." His hands fell away suddenly, like he realized what he was doing and checked himself. He stepped back, but his eyes still held mine. I wondered what he saw when he gazed at me. Did he see my mother from that long ago day, the way I'd seen his father in him? I'd hated him for what his father had done. Did he hate me for the same reason? I shook myself and asked a tentative question.

He lost you?

"He was a monster, and that day, I saw him for what he was. I began to turn from him, to change. I am a far different king than I would have otherwise been."

Kjell says you are dying.

"I'm not dying."

But there is something wrong.

"Many things." He smiled, just a sad twist of his mouth. "There are many wrongs to be righted." He walked to the balcony and opened the doors wider, letting in the evening air. After a moment he turned back to me once more.

But . . . you aren't ill?

He shook his head slowly. "No. Not ill. Not dying. But I'm losing the battle."

Against the Volgar?

"Against all of Jeru's enemies." He paused, considering. His eyes were black and his mouth was bracketed with weariness. "Will you help me, Lark?"

How?

"Show me what you can do."

I thought of the broken window and the accidental fire. I didn't want to hurt anyone. But maybe if I was very careful, very exact, it would be okay. And I wanted to show him, to show someone, what I could do. The attention was intoxicating and completely foreign.

I said a simple rhyme, lifting the coverlet off the floor, asking it to float in the air like a little boat. It rose and hovered obediently. I shot a fearful look at Tiras, but he seemed intrigued.

"Something else."

I asked the coverlet to drift back to the floor. I told the chair to dance and it started to rock back and forth in a clumsy rhythm. Tiras laughed. I shrugged. Dancing chairs and floating coverlets wouldn't right any wrongs.

"Can you compel me to act?" he asked quietly, and my heartbeat quickened. "Can you make me dance like the chair or rise into the air?" he pressed. I bit my lip and reached out with tentative words.

Dance now, Tiras, up and down. Move your body all around.

He stared at me, eyebrows raised, lips quirked.

You aren't dancing.

"No. I'm not. And I feel no compulsion to do so."

I shrugged helplessly.

It doesn't seem to work on people. You have free will. It is but a suggestion with a little push behind it. Are you even tempted to dance? Even a little?

"No. I'm not," he snorted, and my lips twitched too. "So how do you heal me, if your power doesn't work on people?" he asked.

I don't heal you. Not really. I tell your body to heal itself. It wants to be healed, and it obeys. I think.

"You think?"

I shrugged again. *I am learning more every day.*

"And the Volgar? You told them to fly away. In the clearing after I took you from Corvyn. We all would have died. But suddenly they flew, and I could feel something repelling them. I could feel it."

The Volgar are closer to animals than they are to humans, and it takes a great deal more energy to influence them than it does to instruct an object. A great deal more energy to influence you—even just your body.

"That is why you fall asleep so deeply when you try to heal me?"

Yes. It's . . . exhausting . . . forcing my will on others.

"But not on objects?"

There is no resistance with inanimate things.

Tiras nodded, as if that made perfect sense, and I relaxed further, enjoying myself.

"I want you to try again, but don't let me hear. I want to see what you are capable of," he urged, and my joy became reluctance once more.

I was allowing him to hear my rhymes, the little spells I flung into the air. If I instructed him to act and kept it from him, could I actually influence him in some way? *Could I make him love me?* The thought whispered through my heart and mind unbidden, and I turned away, embarrassed and rather surprised at myself. I wouldn't want that.

"Try again," he demanded, as if he'd heard my inner monologue.

My heart pounded in my chest, and I shook my head. Compelling someone was repugnant to me.

I don't want that much power. I don't want to bend people to my will.

"I give you permission," he murmured. "Don't you want to know what you can do?"

Not knowing is so much easier. So much safer.

"Focus," he commanded, ignoring my misgivings. I wondered briefly if his power to compel wasn't a great deal stronger than mine. I always seemed to obey him.

"What do you want, Lark? What do you want me to do?" he pushed, waiting, his posture tense as if he expected me to send him careening into a wall. As if I *could.*

I closed my eyes to create some distance and, keeping my feelings in my belly rather than my head, pushed outward, urging Tiras without even knowing specifically what I asked of him. I was trying so hard to hide my words from him that the command was more a base desire than a neatly formed spell. I hardly knew what I was attempting, when suddenly Tiras was looming over me, pressing his mouth to mine. I froze and opened my eyes.

The brush of his chin was slightly rough, his mouth insistent, almost angry, as if he sought to conquer rather than convince. He held my face as he had before, fingers splayed into my hair, but when I failed to respond, he immediately pulled back, but not much. His eyes glittered, and his hands stayed buried in my hair.

"Why ask for something you don't want?" he whispered, the words tickling my lips.

I didn't ask. I would never, ever ask for something like that.

His eyes narrowed further, and his hands fell to his sides, releasing me as suddenly as he'd kissed me.

I hadn't asked . . . had I? I would never, ever ask, no matter how much I wanted something. Or someone. I'd thought about love. That was all. Then he'd kissed me. I didn't know how to kiss, and I had responded with all the ardor of a rock wall.

I didn't ask, I repeated.

Tiras looked puzzled for a moment, then contemplative. He folded his arms across his chest, and I could feel him listening intently, like he was trying to peel back my protestations and uncover all the things I wasn't saying.

"I'm going to kiss you again," he murmured finally. "Unless you tell me no."

My mind was a huge, white wall. No protestations. No thoughts. No words at all.

"Breathe," he whispered, and I obediently sipped the air. "Come here." Again. Immediate compliance.

He didn't reach for me or pull me to him, didn't crush me against his chest. He simply tipped my chin up and brought his mouth down.

Then he coaxed cooperation with gentle conviction.

Sweet rose from his consciousness, and wonder limned the word.

He wheedled entry, pulling my top lip between his, tugging and tasting, only to slide past it to seek my timid tongue, plying me and playing me, until I was matching the pressure of his lips and exploring the heat of his mouth with eager strokes and breathless wonder.

I heard his decision to cease before he pulled away, leaving me with my chest heaving and my lips wet. Bereft and immediately embarrassed, I couldn't meet his eyes, but could feel him considering me, even as a decision was reached. Then he spoke, drawing my gaze.

"Kjell is right. You *are* a dangerous little bird. But I think I will keep you."

THIRTEEN

T he king escorted me back to my chambers and put four guards at the door.

"For your protection, and for mine," Tiras explained.

I didn't respond, and I still couldn't look at him. My heart felt strange and my hands shook beneath the long drape of the bell-shaped sleeves. I could still taste him, heady and strong, and though I longed to run my tongue along the seam of my lips to relive the moment, I felt claimed without being wanted. It was a feeling I knew well. It was a feeling that made me long for Boojohni, the only soul on earth who loved me.

I waited up, trying to read, trying harder to listen, but the castle was quiet and when Pia and Greta came to attend me, removing my dress and brushing my hair, they seemed tired and irritable, but nothing seemed amiss, and they chattered over the evening's events and the work that still needed doing. I didn't know whether my father had crept away, fleeing to Corvyn without me, or if he, like the rest of the delegation, had retired to his chamber to plot again.

The castle was full of secrets and schemes, full of people hungry for power and afraid of magic. Much like me, the castle hadn't learned to speak. I listened to the walls and collected random words until the dawn crept in and the city awoke.

The following evening, I was primped and adorned and escorted to the hall once more, seated to the left of the king as if all was well. The delegation seemed slightly less travel-weary, and eyes were sharp and conversation stilted. My father hadn't left for Corvyn. His face was just as drawn, his gaze as fleeting, but the death that had hovered around him the day before had fled.

The king neither ate nor drank, but engaged the gathering in trivial conversation and mild discussion of the happenings in the kingdom. As the meal was consumed and the hour passed, Lord Gaul rose, and with a weighted look around the gathering, he addressed the king with false solemnity.

"There are ten provinces—Kilmorda, Corvyn, Bilwick, Bin Dar, Enoch, Quondoon, Janda, Gaul, Firi and of course, Degn." He inclined his head toward the king when he said Degn. Degn was the province of Tiras's family, the province that surrounded the capital, the province of kings. "There are five representatives here tonight." He counted them off on his fingers. "Firi, Corvyn, Bilwick, Bin Dar, and Gaul." He inclined his head again. "Six, if we count Degn. If we count you."

The king waited.

"The representatives from Janda, Quondoon and Enoch, to the south, don't feel as threatened by the Volgar as those of us farther north. They weren't interested in . . . attending . . . this summit."

"They weren't interested in a coup?" The king asked, his mild voice dripping with false calm. "And the rest of you?" Tiras moved his eyes around the table, lingering on every member of the council, one by one, demanding a response.

"If this is a coup, then I have no interest in it either," the lovely ambassador from Firi interrupted, rising from her chair. "I am here to support King Tiras in his efforts to push back the Volgar. I am here to commit my province to the defense of Jeru. All of Jeru."

The king rose to his feet, bowing slightly to the young ambassador. Kjell rose alongside him, his hand on his sword, his eyes on the woman. When the king started to speak once more, Kjell's eyes swung back to Tiras. I wanted to stand too. It would have been ridiculous. I was no one. But still, I wanted to stand. If there were sides, I did not want to be on the side of people like Bilwick and Gaul and the smug ruler of Bin Dar who even now, was rising at the far end of the long table. I did not want to be on the side of those who thought people like my mother, people like me, were the real enemy.

"Kilmorda is in ruins," Tiras said, pinning the gathering with his black gaze. "Lord Kilmorda and his family are dead. The Volgar have been pushed back, but they've left behind destruction. The people of Kilmorda have fled to Firi, some to Degn, a few to Corvyn, though it is harder to access due to the mountainous terrain. The valley stinks of rotting corpses, and the waters are tainted with death. Unless you want all of Jeru to share the same fate, you will leave your political machinations for another time."

"But Your Majesty, that is why we are here," Lord Gaul insisted with cloying sweetness. "I think I speak for Lord Corvyn, Lord Bilwick, Lord Bin Dar, as well as myself, when I say your leniency on the Gifted has given rise to these attacks. The Gifted have fled north, and they have bred with beasts, giving rise to the monsters that now attack Jeru."

"One would think that if I were truly lenient on the Gifted they would have no reason to flee. Wouldn't they just stay here if I am so welcoming?" Tiras snapped.

"They must be destroyed, Majesty. And you have failed to destroy them. Now they rise against us with the Volgar. Lord Bin Dar stood beside Lord Gaul. Slowly, one by one, every lord was standing, including my father. Those of us who had no influence or title remained seated. I fought the urge to stand once more.

"How do you know this, Lord Bin Dar?" The king leaned forward, his arms bracketing the plate of food he'd hardly touched. "I have been in Kilmorda fighting winged beasts, killing them by the hundreds, and I've never seen what you allege."

"We have questioned the Gifted, Your Majesty," Lord Bilwick shot out, his voice a self-satisfied sneer.

"What Gifted?" The king's voice was barely above a whisper.

"The Gifted we've captured, of course. The Gifted in our own provinces. Before they are put to death they are questioned. Extensively. They all tell us the same thing. They are in league with the Volgar," Lord Gaul supplied smoothly.

Satisfaction rose from Lord Gaul, Lord Bin Dar, and Lord Bilwick like the cheap scents the vendors sold at the weekly bazaars. Their line of attack had been clearly orchestrated. My father exuded greed, his avarice creating a stench almost as thick as the plotting of his fellow lords.

"You've captured and tortured people, your own citizens, until they confessed to your allegations," the king bit out.

Lord Bin Dar's oddly-shaped brows rose until they disappeared into the sweep of his black hair. It was a flat, bluish black, a color achieved through tonics and dyes, and it only succeeded in making his pale face look older and more lined.

"Your father, King Zoltev, struck down Corvyn's wife without a trial . . . over nothing more than a kerchief fluttering in the air!" His hand mimicked the fluttering with an effeminate wiggle of his fingers, and he sighed as if the memory pained him. "At least we allow the Gifted trials before we put them to death."

Deception. Blame. Power. Destruction.

The words made a thick soup in the air, and I wasn't sure which words belonged to whom. My head began to swim, memories of my mother, of her blood on the cobblestones, of her body pressing into mine as she breathed her warning into my ear. I closed my eyes and bowed my head. Lord Bin Dar's voice echoed oddly, like I was submerged in water.

"The people are losing confidence in you, Tiras. The council is losing confidence in you. If you will not protect Jeru from the Gifted then we must protect Jeru from you."

The king's eyes narrowed, and something dark skittered across his face. His jaw was granite, and his hands gripped the edge of the table so hard the ends of his fingers were white like talons.

"I see. And who will protect all of *you* from *me*?" the king hissed, his eyes glowing fire. Lord Bin Dar blanched, and there was a collective gasp around the table.

"We are simply concerned!" Lord Gaul huffed. "It is our responsibility, our duty as Council of Lords to see that Jeru does not fall into enemy hands."

"It is my duty as king to vanquish Jeru's enemies. Whoever they might be."

"We will reassemble in one month's time. If the Volgar have not been defeated, the lords from every province will ask you to relinquish the throne. Corvyn is next in line, so Corvyn will be king. You will be Lord of Degn, a member of the Council of Lords, but you will not be king," Lord Bin Dar shouted, and the protests and dissent, along with cheers and jeers, rose as well.

"Corvyn is in line for the throne upon my death, and only upon my death. Do you mean to kill me? So far your attempts—all of your attempts—have failed. You have sought to take my life."

"You have taken my daughter!" My father cried out, finding his courage amid the clamor.

"And I intend to keep her, Lord Corvyn," Tiras roared, and my father visibly quaked even as my insides trembled. "I intend to keep her close by, to keep her next to me at all times. She will drink from my cup and eat from my plate to protect me from your poisons. She will sleep beneath me and hover over me and never leave my side. In fact, I leave in three days for Kilmorda, and she is coming with me. She will ride in front of me, astride my horse, clinging to me as I go into battle, a human shield against those you send against me."

Heat rose in my cheeks, and flames licked at my breast. I spelled out the word I-C-E, focusing on the slick, cold shape of the word, building a frozen barrier between my heart and the roaring cauldron in my chest, willing myself not to flinch, not to care that I was a pawn in a very dangerous game.

"If I die, she dies," Tiras said, just like he'd said the day he took me from my father's keep. I'd confessed so easily. I'd told the king my secret, my father's secret, and he used it without compunction. I refused to release the words that bubbled inside me. The king would not have my words. He was no different from my father; neither loved me and both used me for their own purposes. I suddenly hated them both with a fury that blinded me. I didn't even need to close my eyes to keep them out.

When the king took my arm and rose from the table, I rose with him without resistance, but I kept my face blank and my eyes unfocused as he dismissed the gathering, dismissed the lords and their ladies who retreated obediently, quietly, their words blurred and their thoughts tangled. Lord Bin Dar and Lord Gaul were already plotting—I could feel their icy contempt and their intent to betray even as they bowed in obeisance. My father, who quivered in fear and doubt, his emotions bouncing off my icy façade like tiny bubbles, followed behind them, and he didn't look back.

Tiras took me to his chamber and left me with Pia, who helped me remove my gown and take down my hair. She was breathless and beaming as she pulled a pale white shift over my head, as if I were being given some sort of honor, sleeping in the king's room. She didn't know that I was simply a weapon. A tool. There were guards at the door once again, and I could feel their tired thoughts.

But I didn't try to escape. I had nowhere to go.

I lay on Tiras's giant bed, the bed where I had soothed his fevered skin and slept at his side once before, but he didn't return. I heard him arguing with Kjell in the hallway, but he never came inside. I'm sure they thought I couldn't hear, but words managed to find me, whether I wanted to hear them or not.

Kjell was against bringing me to Kilmorda, against my presence in the castle and my nearness to the king. "You should banish her. She's dangerous, and she can't be trusted," he argued.

"She can help us. When we fought the Volgar, I didn't know it was her, but I could feel her influence pounding at me. She told them to fly, and they obeyed," Tiras answered, his tone slightly awed. "You saw it too. It was her, Kjell."

"She is a Teller!" Kjell spit out, as if the word was bile.

"She is a Teller," the king confirmed. "An incredibly powerful one. If she tells them to die, to fall from the sky, to throw themselves into the Jyraen Sea, they will."

"And what if she turns that power on you, Highness? Will you become her puppet? Will I?"

"That is a risk we must take, Kjell. And so far, she's not used her power on you. Obviously." Tiras's tone was so dry it crackled with mirth.

"You are different with her. You are almost . . . gentle."
Kjell said the word gentle with hushed disdain. "It's . . . strange,
Tiras!"

"I can't help but be gentle with her, because she is gentle
with me." Tiras sounded embarrassed, and I felt the ice at my
heart begin to thaw, even as Kjell scoffed loudly.

"She isn't even beautiful, Tiras! She isn't tall and strong.
Bearing your sons will likely kill her."

"She is strong in a different way. And your definition of
beauty isn't mine," Tiras argued. I couldn't believe what I was
hearing. I sat up in the bed, my chest pounding.

"You don't like big breasts and full hips? You don't like
brown skin and thick, dark hair? Since when, Majesty? She is a
pale wisp of nothing."

I winced.

"She is of use to me, Kjell. Who else can boast the same? I
know no other woman who is of any use to me at all."

Kjell was silent, and my pounding heart slowed to a sad
slog. I cursed myself for listening in. It served me right. I thought
of the wishing well and the silly people who threw their voices
down into the murky depths, hoping the God of Words would
hear them and grant their desires on a whim. I had been foolish
too. I had given my words to a man who could use me. And use
me he had. Use me he would. Until I was no longer of use. *Silence daughter, stay alive.*

I told myself I should be grateful I knew the truth. I laid
back down on the big empty bed and I hugged the edge like a
sculpture formed from buffeting winds and constant rains, impenetrable and hard. I refused to make words or entertain
thought—to feel at all—until blessed sleep took me away on
downy wings.

For three days the castle walls rang with preparations, and the city beneath my balcony geared up for yet another battle. The sounds from the forge filled the air, and the clanging of weapons and the sharpening of swords seemed never-ending. Horses were shod and fitted, supplies gathered, and carts and carriages filled as soldiers flirted and wives prayed and the line to the wishing well doubled.

The air crackled, like a storm was approaching, and I felt it gathering even as I tried to ignore the flurry and scurry outside the king's chamber. I had nothing to prepare for, no duties to attend to, so I read and wrote and pretended that I was master of my fate instead of a virtual prisoner of war. I didn't see the king again, not even once, though I'd seemingly been permanently moved to his room. Some of my clothing and all of my books, as well as my paint and writing supplies, were neatly arranged in an empty boudoir.

The day before the army departed, a feast was laid out in the square, table after table laden with roasted meats, figs and fruits and breads and sweets, and the food kept coming as each family in Jeru city brought an offering, and all shared in the spoils. The people ate all day, singing and dancing as if they would never do so again. I observed the party from above, spinning a spell every once in a while, just to prove I could. A horse reared and pawed the air, and I sent him a calm command before he upended an apple cart. A growling dog lunged at a child, and I banned him from the square. He retreated obediently, his tail between his legs.

I watched as the colorful skirt of a pretty maid snagged on a sharp corner and ripped straight up the back. She heard it tear and looked around in horror only to breathe in relief when she found it undamaged. It took a word to repair it, and I smiled at my handiwork.

Objects were easy, animals almost as easy, but people were harder to influence. So I tried my hand at simple solutions and what I deemed "helpful acts." A man in silks strode through the square amid the tables groaning with food, taking and never giving in return. I watched him eat three sticky rolls from a woman selling bread, only to tell the woman they were barely edible and refuse to pay her. The money on his belt clanked as he walked, and the woman watched him strut away with helpless anger.

Rip and tear, Pay your share.

The man's money made a trail behind him as he walked, the coins streaming from his torn money pouch, falling silently onto the hard-packed dirt. The baker followed behind him and took the coins she was owed, leaving the rest to fall by the wayside for others to find. I felt a twinge of guilt, judging him so completely, and repaired the tear before he lost everything.

I saw Kjell in the square. Boojohni too. I called to him in my mind, and he glanced up, waved, and did a little dance that made me laugh. He seemed happy and free, and I was glad for him, even as I wished to walk beside him and see the festivities up close. I never saw the king—it was as if Kjell had assumed the responsibility for directing the arrangements for the upcoming departure—and I wondered if Tiras was shut away somewhere, dealing with the business of the kingdom, plotting a way to defeat the Volgar and the Council of Lords. Or maybe he was ill and had given up on my ability to heal him. I thought maybe he'd forgotten all about me, though a guard remained at the door at all times, and I never went without a meal or a bath.

When the sun went down, the party moved from the courtyard and into the dwellings of the townspeople, and a pervasive silence slipped over the city, a silence that warned of an early morning and a long journey. I sat in the dark on the king's balcony, listening for anyone or anything that might keep me company, desperate to escape, if only for a while. Before I came to Jeru City I'd had little freedom, but I'd stolen what I could. I would steal it again if I had too. I looked around for a solution to my problem and spotted a horse cart teeming with straw near the path to the stables. It was too far away to serve as a soft place to land, but I could remedy that.

Cart of straw, against the wall, move below me, catch my fall.

The cart began to move, slowly, as if it had been released at the top of a small hill and was rolling back to the bottom. It came to a teetering stop beneath the balcony, a stack of glorious gold forty feet below me. I laughed, my shoulders shaking and my hands pressed to my mouth, almost giddy with the opportunity I'd made for myself.

But it was so far. And what if someone saw me jump?

I peered over the edge, down, down, down to the cart of straw and quickly reconsidered. I needed to get closer, somehow. I would never dare make that leap. The castle walls were lined with smooth stone, not especially ideal for climbing . . . unless I created foot holds.

I didn't stop to question the wisdom of the plan but climbed up onto the balcony ledge, balancing on the edge with my hands against the castle wall. I touched a stone near my head and demanded it fall.

Smooth rock, beneath my palm,
Move so I can climb this wall.

The rock immediately loosened and fell, creating a perfect divot for my fingers to cling to. I tapped the wall with my toe and repeated the spell, to create an opening for my right foot. The rock obeyed, and I started my precarious descent, creating hand holds and ledges all the way down, until the cart was a mere handful of feet below me. Then I let go.

It was a fortunate thing I couldn't scream, because I would have given myself away. The cart wobbled and began to tip, and I scrambled for the side and catapulted over it, skirts twining around my legs, as the car teetered and groaned. Thank goodness I hadn't dropped from forty feet—the cart would be in pieces. *I* would be in pieces. I dusted myself off, heart pounding, nerves quaking, but I smiled too. Victory was awfully sweet, and the act of rebellion gave me a surge of self-confidence that had me stealing along the town square and into the quiet city, not at all sure of where I was going, caring only that I was free to go.

A dog with a missing tail and a mangled ear followed me for a bit before I made him stay. He sat on his ragged rump and watched me disappear. I felt his need, and the word *alone* was present in his whimper.

I know, I soothed. *I'm sorry.* But I had no home to give him, and I could only offer commiseration. I kept walking, darting from one dark street to the next, trying to enjoy my brief freedom and the night that held it, but the joy was already leaching from my skin, and I stopped at the edge of an orange grove, feeling foolish and lost.

A bird flew overhead and released a mournful shriek, a sound that before now I'd only heard in the distance, and it pierced my heart.

I am lonely too, pretty bird.

It circled above me in a graceful descent that narrowed until he came to a quivering stop on a low branch so close I could have reached out and stroked him. I smiled in recognition.

Look at you! Where did you come from?

I took a few steps forward and stopped again, tilting my head so I could study him further. He looked exactly like the bird in the forest near my father's keep in Corvyn, like the bird who'd perched on the balcony wall, the one I'd been sure was just a piece of a dream.

Home.

The word rose from the bird, a warm sensation, and my lips trembled in empathy. I didn't cry easily. It was a badge of honor, of toughness. I was a slip of a girl, a woman with little to offer and nothing to say, but I had my dignity, and tears were undignified.

Home, he said again, and I felt the urgency and the sorrow, as if he'd lost his and wanted me to know.

I don't have a home either, I said to the eagle, and closed my eyes to deny the wet that wanted to spill over.

I felt his distress echo mine, a shot of alarm that split the word *home* into a warning and a wail, and with a sudden flare of his wings, the eagle left the branch and landed softly on my shoulder. I staggered in surprise, and my eyes snapped open as I steadied myself against the tree I stood beside.

I was afraid to move, fearful that I would make him fly, and I didn't want him to leave. He was so big that if I turned my head, my cheek would brush his breast, perched the way he was. His wings were pinned back and they trailed along the length of my right arm, the very tips brushing my hand.

Home.

I cannot take you home, my friend. But I will stay with you for a while.

I didn't know if he understood, but he nudged me with a brief bob of his silky head and lifted off as suddenly as he'd landed. He flew a little ways, landed on another branch, and waited for me to come to him. I tipped my head in question and he mimicked the gesture.

Home.

We continued on this way. The eagle would lift off, fly a little ways—always within view—and flutter to a stop on a gable or a gate or another branch. He would wait for me, watching me walk toward him, then he'd do it all again. I followed him, enchanted, not knowing where I was going, traipsing along the shadowed paths and the forested outskirts of Jeru City, as if the world belonged to the two of us. I walked until I neared the western wall, at least two miles from the king's castle. When I heard the call of the night watchman, I hesitated and turned around, suddenly unsure and more than a little lost.

We weren't far from the road, but the houses had grown sparse and mostly disappeared. If not for the night watchman's call and the wall that rose up in the distance, I would have had no clue as to my whereabouts. I felt silly and small and started back in the direction I'd come, hoping I could find my way back to the castle.

The eagle soared above my head, so close that I felt a gust of air above me and the brush of his wings, drawing my eyes and demanding my attention once more. There, just among the trees, not far from the wall, was a little cottage with a thickly thatched roof and sturdy walls, nestled in the trees, almost blending with the landscape. It boasted a window with a real glass pane and a dark-colored door, the hue undecipherable in the shadows.

The eagle landed on the highest point of the steep roofline and waited for me to approach. The cottage was too tidy to be abandoned and too still to be occupied. I could feel no life seeping through the walls, no tangled thoughts or peaceful dreams. If someone lived here, they weren't home.

Home.

I felt the word again, and the bird dipped and plunged before extending his giant wings and lifting up and away, a silent stretch of black that disappeared into the dark, leaving me in front of the little cottage in the woods.

I tested the door brazenly, emboldened by the sense that the bird had brought me here for a purpose. It came open with the barest of groans and a waft of quiet welcome. I left the door ajar and took a step inside, my eyes sweeping the little room that contained a big hearth and a pot for cooking, a small wooden table, and a bed that was made but slightly rumpled, like someone had sat upon it to pull on their boots. It was comfortable and neat, lived in yet . . . not. It didn't possess the detritus of a family or the residue of an oft-used residence. It looked like a hideaway or a trysting spot, and my hands rose to my cheeks, embarrassed by the direction of my thoughts.

A lantern with a thick wick sat on the center of the table, but I had nothing to light it with. It didn't matter. I was tired. Weary and woe-begotten all at once. I sat gingerly on the bed, my eyes clinging to the quiet corners. I would stay here for a few hours. I would let the sun rise, and then I would decide what to do. Maybe I would go back to the castle. Maybe I wouldn't. Maybe Tiras and my father could find a new pawn, and Tiras could leave for

Kilmorda without me. I suddenly cared very little about what was to come.

I left the door open. I wasn't afraid of beasts or bugs, and the only person who might enter in the next few hours—the owner—wouldn't be dissuaded by a closed door. Sleeping in the one-room cottage without seeing what or who was coming, even at the very last moment, made me nervous, and I'd been cooped up behind closed doors long enough.

I curled up on the bed and stared out the open door into the forest, finding the twinkle of a few brave stars glimmering down through the foliage. I sent up a message, a prayer of sorts, a spell that was more a request than anything.

I see you, stars. Do you see me, peeking up through velvet leaves? Keep me safe from mice and men, invisible to all but friends.

So far my spells had been completely useless when I attempted them on myself. Still, I felt safe and see-through as I fell asleep on a borrowed bed, dreaming of my two friends—Boojohni and the black-winged bird, who'd perched on my shoulder and begged me to go home.

FIFTEEN

The cottage faced east, and as the sun rose and light seeped over the treetops, I began to wake, conscious of the murmuring trees and the caw and twitter of early risers. The eagle was back, perched on the stoop just beyond the open door, and I smiled drowsily and welcomed him with my thoughts. His wings shuddered and he hopped forward, entering the cottage like he owned the place.

He was a bird.

Then he was not.

Huge wings dissolved into broad shoulders and long arms attached to human hands and flexing fingers. Feathers dissipated into a torso that grew and elongated from the breast of a bird to the chest and abdomen of a man. He crouched over legs that simply uncurled beneath him, lifting him until he stood, head thrown back, body arching like he'd just awakened from a deep sleep. His palms turned up and his arms stretched wide, like he worshipped the sun that bathed him in light. Or maybe the sun worshipped him. Every inch of him was golden and warm—even his white hair reflected the burnished hue of sunrise.

He was completely unclothed and breathtakingly beautiful, and for a moment I could only stare, forgetting that the moment he turned, even slightly, he would see me, lying across the bed, watching him. As if I'd called his name, his head snapped toward me, and his arms fell to his sides. I watched as the black irises of pale avian eyes spread and became the narrowed, dark gaze of King Tiras.

I gazed at him, not even breathing, battling disbelief, and I watched as several emotions played across his face—doubt, shame, concern—before his supreme confidence won out, and he jutted out his chin and glared at me, ever the king, ever undeterred.

"You ran away." It was such a peculiar thing to say, delivered with such perfect condemnation that I rubbed at my incredulous eyes and remained in the darkness I'd created behind my hands, certain I was still asleep.

If you are not a dream, will you please clothe yourself?

"And if I *am* a dream, would you like me to remain as I am?" he said wryly, but I heard the sound of movement and the rustle of cloth.

I nodded, then shook my head, then nodded again, my hands sliding to my burning cheeks, to my tousled hair, then to the wall for support, as I rose, refusing to look at him at all. I breathed deeply—once, twice, three times—then tried to dart past him out the cottage door, needing space, desperate for air, but he stepped in front of me and held out a hand like he was calming his horse. His tone changed to one of quiet pleading, as he pushed the door closed behind him.

"Don't run away from me, Lark."

I was pleased to see that he now wore breeches. He held a tunic clutched in the hand not extended toward me, and when he seemed satisfied that I wasn't going to bolt, he pulled it over his head and tucked the billowing ends into his breeches. He then proceeded to pull woolen socks on his bare feet and shove them into a pair of boots I'd missed in the darkness. I could have sworn they were boots I'd seen before.

You're a bird.

"Sometimes."

You're a Changer.

"Yes."

Gifted.

"Yes."

Like me.

"Like you." He hesitated. "Do you see now? Do you understand?"

I stared at him blankly, lost in the maze of my unconnected thoughts. I didn't understand at all . . . but I knew one thing.

You were the eagle in the forest . . . in Corvyn.

"Yes."

You were injured. You had an . . . arrow . . . sticking out of your chest.

"The light helps me change, and change heals me. I just had to make it until dawn. When I changed from eagle to man, you were still lying there beside me."

A few things started clicking into place, and he seemed to follow the train of my thoughts.

"I stole the clothes from the stable boy and a horse from your father. I rode back to where the army was camped, realizing that I'd almost died. Had it not been for you, I would have. I came back to find you, convinced you could heal me. When I realized who you were, and that you were unable to speak, I simply reacted, killing two birds with one stone, as they say. Your father has been plotting my death for as long as I've been alive. It was sweet justice that his daughter could save me."

But I can't.

"No. You can't heal me from this. You comfort me. You help ease the agony, but you can't heal me."

I can't heal what isn't broken.

His eyes widened, and he took another step toward me. I wasn't sure where my sentiment originated, but it seemed to stun him.

"I *feel* broken," he confessed bleakly. Then he shook himself and squared his shoulders, readjusting his cloak of superiority.

"Changing used to be something I could control. I would feel it happening, and through will alone, I could beat it back. But in the last year it has become painful—resisting the change—and I give into it more than I used to. I don't feel as much pressure to change in the daylight hours, though I can whenever I need to. I can when I am poisoned by plotting lords."

I remembered him collapsing in the hallway. *When you don't resist . . . does it hurt?*

"There is some pain, but it is fleeting, like the stretching of stiff limbs or the flexing of sore muscles. The second time you came to help me, it was overpowering, and I changed before you arrived in my room. When dawn broke, I thought you would see me, that you would see me become a man again. But Kjell heard my call and intervened."

But you were sick . . . after.

Tiras nodded. "I had to fight to change back. For the first time ever, the sun rose and I didn't become a man again. When I finally did, I was sick."

Have you always been able to change? I'd never known anyone else who could change. Or maybe everyone just pretended to be normal.

"The night after your mother died, I changed for the first time. It was as if she recognized it in me. She knew."

You will lose your son to the sky.

136

The prediction took on a whole new significance, and Tiras nodded as if he heard the words echoing in my memory.

"For several years it was a rare occurrence, and I grew accustomed to it. I almost convinced myself I was dreaming, though that became impossible after a while. It happened so infrequently, I believed I could hide it . . . from everyone."

I couldn't believe he wasn't hiding it from me. He continued without pause.

"Kjell was the first to find out. Then my father. I hid myself here, in this cottage for a month, afraid of what he'd do. I'd seen firsthand how the Gifted were treated. I thought he would kill me. But my father died instead, not long after. And I became king."

Why are you telling me this?

My voice sounded sharp in my head, whistling between my ears, and I wasn't the only one to wince.

"I want you to understand, and I don't want you to feel alone." His voice was gruff, as if it made him uncomfortable to be kind.

And you want me to come with you to Kilmorda. You want me to help you. I thought of the conversation I'd overheard between him and Kjell.

He had the grace—or the arrogance—not to deny it.

"You can do so much more than move haystacks and scale walls."

My eyes snapped to his, and his mouth quirked. "I saw you. Being a bird has its advantages."

The thought made me sad, as if I'd been betrayed by a friend.

"If you run, Lark, I will bring you back. I need you," he said without apology. "Jeru needs you."

I need you. The words were so seductive. So tempting. I need you. No one had ever needed me before. So why did I feel so bereft that this king simply had need of me, nothing more?

I have always wanted to be of use, I admitted. He waited, clearly feeling the words I wasn't saying. But when I didn't give voice to them, he nodded, dismissing the questions in the air.

"Then you will come with me," he said, brooking no argument. I sighed, and he immediately tensed. But I nodded, giving in.

I will come with you.

True to his word, Tiras and his army left for Kilmorda that very day, and true to mine, I left with them. The lords and their retinues left as well, heading away from Jeru toward their own provinces, to await the news of his failure or success. Lady Ariel of Firi—her father, the Lord of Firi, who was too ill to travel and had sent her in his stead—rode with us for a full day, talking gaily to Kjell as if we were heading to a celebration instead of war. She watched me curiously, and I felt her questions but refused to expose my ability to answer them. Firi was west of Kilmorda, and the region had taken the brunt of the influx of refugees from the besieged province. Lady Firi and her guard would part ways with us at the fork, but she seemed to enjoy the protection of the army and the attention of Kjell and the king while it lasted.

Does she want to be queen? I asked Tiras, breaking the companionable silence between us.

He grunted in response, though the sound lifted on the end like he didn't know who I was talking about.

Lady Firi. Does she want to be queen?

"Most likely," he answered.

I almost laughed at his conceit, though I was certain he was right.

Kjell is in love with her.

"I doubt it is love. But he is taken with her," he admitted. "So she will never be queen."

She isn't of use to you?

"She isn't of use to me," he replied simply. "And Kjell is my only friend."

We traveled for four days, slowed by the carriages filled with supplies that brought up the rear. I grew sore and begged to walk, my tender flesh unused to hours on the back of a horse. Tiras acquiesced, but only because of my very real agony, and I walked each day for a little while, Tiras constantly doubling back to make sure I hadn't slipped off.

I have nowhere to go, I would reassure him.

"You have no reason to stay," he would shoot back.

Boojohni would roll his eyes and whistle pointedly, and Tiras would spur Shindoh back to the front. At night, I slept beneath the stars with the men. We wouldn't make camp or pitch our tents until we arrived in Kilmorda. It took too much time and effort when the goal was to move as quickly as possible. I had a pallet and Boojohni at my side, and I found I liked the open air.

The first night Tiras slept nearby on a pallet similar to my own. The next two nights he retreated at sundown, and I didn't see him at all the third day. When someone asked where Tiras was, Kjell would always answer as if Tiras was simply out of sight. "Up front," he'd say, or "in the rear," or "just ahead" or "over yonder." But that day, I rode Shindoh alone, Boojohni trotting alongside us, following the army at a small distance. On the fourth day, Tiras was asleep on his pallet at dawn, and there were shadows beneath his eyes when he woke. When he lifted me on Shindoh and climbed up behind me, the final leg of our journey ahead, I asked after his wellbeing.

Are you able to rest?

He was silent for a heartbeat, then answered, his lips near my ear as if he were afraid others would hear.

"Eagles aren't nocturnal birds. I am able to sleep if I find a safe spot. But we are nearing Kilmorda, and I flew ahead to see the lay of the land. Forces from the provinces retreated to the ridge above the valley and have kept them from gaining ground, but the Volgar have nested in the valley, in the abandoned village there. Their numbers have grown."

How many?

"There are thousands of them."

Thousands?

"They have drained the livestock of blood and cleared the wildlife from the forests. They are hungry, and they are starting to widen their attacks."

Where are they coming from? There were no such thing as Volgar when I was a child.

"Nobody knows. The first time I saw a Volgar was three years ago. Since then, they have become the biggest threat to Jeru. Some think they originated from an island in the Jyraen Sea. All I know is that their numbers continue to grow, and we're losing the battle."

What about the army on the border of the valley?

"They're being picked off, one at a time."

SIXTEEN

W

e arrived at the edge of the valley near noon on the fourth day, but we didn't pitch our tents. Tiras bade everyone eat and rest, and he and Kjell and the leaders of the existing army stole away to make battle plans. I could feel the Volgar the way I could always feel large numbers, and the awareness made me jittery and obliterated my appetite.

Like most creatures, their words were simple. *Fly, eat, mate.* They didn't worry or dread. They didn't seem to fear us, and they certainly weren't making war plans. They just instinctually existed—*eat, fly, mate. Kill.*

The difference between them and any other large herd was that they enjoyed the kill. They lived for it. Their instincts were basic . . . but they were also base. They were simple, but they weren't good. They were predators at the top of the food chain, and their numbers had become problematic.

They normally slept during the day and had much better night vision than a mere human, but Tiras thought if we could lure them in at dusk, when there was still some light and they were just waking, it might improve our odds at taking larger numbers of them down.

We rested a full day, giving the horses a chance to recuperate from the journey, but the collective unease of the camp made the day feel wasted. Shrieks and shouts filled the night as the Volgar picked off men in the dark, the way they'd been picking off soldiers on the border, and when the day dawned tepid and grey, it reflected the mood of every warrior. No one wanted to wait any longer.

The weather was advantageous. The dark skies and the wan light made it much more likely that the Volgar could be lured into a daytime hunt. Tiras said we needed them to come to us, and that was where I came in. By late afternoon, the entire army—save Boojohni, the wounded, and the cooks—were gathered in the trees at the edge of the valley just to the west of Kilmorda. "A mile as the eagle flies," Tiras said, and Kjell shot him a look.

Black clouds curled and tumbled in their haste to flee the lightning that sheared off sections of the sky and touched down on the cliffs and crags that shot up from the ground like Tiras's castle in Jeru city. He held me in front of him, his armored arm tight around my waist, and we galloped through the warrior throng, Tiras throwing out instructions and encouragement even as the horse beneath us trembled with fright. I tried to speak peace to Shindoh's mind and felt the red emotion of his fear begin to weaken my own control.

"Save your energy," Tiras commanded, his mouth close to my ear. "I need you whole. Shindoh is accustomed to battle. He won't fail me."

I obeyed, but my hand sneaked out to curl in the cropped mane of the black horse, and Tiras said no more. He'd slung a shirt of mail over the green tunic and breeches he'd demanded I wear, but I refused the helmet and the clanking armor he'd urged upon me. It was so heavy I wouldn't have been able to move, and Shindoh wouldn't have been able to run as swiftly beneath our combined weight.

Tiras wore a helmet, but he told me it was to hide his identity more than anything else. Killing the white-haired king would be the ultimate prize. My own hair hung in a long rope past my waist, and I feared my presence would only draw attention to him, a woman in the midst of battle.

"Call them, Lark. Urge them to come closer."

I reached out, feeling the sigh in the clouds, the threat of rain, the hum of life that rose up from the ground, and I sifted through tepid light.

There they were.

I could hear them and the simple bloodlust that pulsed from them. They lived to kill. Not for hate or power. But still, they killed. They killed because death meant food. Death meant life. Death meant that their blood pounded hotter in their veins, and their flesh grew thicker on their bones. They were simple monsters, but monsters all the same.

And they were hungry.

Their pangs were sharp, as if their diet had been limited or reduced. I spoke to that hunger, telling them to come, to eat.

Lift your heads into the wind,
Food aplenty 'round the bend.

I felt them stir and shudder, wanting to obey, but beneath the collective heartbeat of innocent instinct, however bloodthirsty, there was an undercurrent of intent that was more man than beast, and it was separate from them.

Someone or something was controlling them, and the intelligence that led them was not like they were. His voice was moist and guttural, clinging to the mind of each beast, manipulating and instructing.

And he was aware.

I drew back with a gasp, and my head thunked against Tiras's plated chest.

"Lark?"

The leader of the Volgar, Liege, is he man or Volgar?

Shindoh whinnied like he understood, though I knew better. He felt my fear.

"He is both."

Is he Gifted?

"Some say he is a Changer . . . like me. Man and bird."

What if Lord Bin Dar was right? What if the Gifted are behind the Volgar attacks?

"What difference does it make? I would rather destroy an evil man than an innocent beast. The Volgar destroy, so they must be destroyed, but Liege wants to conquer, he wants to take. If he is Gifted, it means little to me. He wants Jeru. He can't have her."

"Tiras! The men are anxious. If we don't move now we won't reach the Volgar until dark," Kjell interrupted, trotting up alongside us with barely suppressed frustration. His countenance reflected the sky, dark and heavy and ready to burst.

"Wait, Kjell. Hold. Let them come to us, just as I said."

Kjell nodded, but his blue gaze settled on my face briefly, and I knew he wanted to argue. He lowered the grill of his helmet and moved away once more, but he didn't go far. His horse paced like a panther, and Tiras lowered his lips to my ear.

"Make them come, Lark," Tiras repeated, his voice a rumbling murmur that lifted the tendrils on my cheeks. "It's time."

I released my words into the breeze like a siren's call, urging the Volgar to do the very thing they desired. *Fly, kill, eat.* I pulled at them with temptation-infused words, terrified that they would actually come, more afraid that they wouldn't. They wanted Jeru. They wanted Tiras. And I discovered I wasn't willing to part with either.

There was a thunderous cawing in my skull, a beast denied, and I winced in pain as the undercurrent of control I'd felt in the Volgar was suddenly weakened. I heard the sound of thousands of wings beating the air, beating back the words that urged restraint. His words.

They're coming, I warned.

Tiras roared, an echo of the beast in my head, and Shindoh shot forward as Tiras prepared the eager line of Jeruvian archers who hovered in the trees, arrows drawn, waiting to unleash hell on the winged enemy. The sky above us began to wriggle and shift and the light of day was completely obscured by a blanket of black.

"Make them land, Lark," Tiras ordered. I barely hesitated, flinging my gift with all the urgency of the damned and desperate.

You cannot fly,
So you will fall.
Leave the sky
One and all.

I saw the simple spell pierce the air above us, the words like fireballs in a pit of writhing snakes, and the Volgar began to drop, screaming toward the earth. Some hit the ground with such velocity that they died instantly, but others seemed more resistant to my suggestion and landed with a tumble, still flapping, stunned but unharmed.

"Attack!" Kjell cried, and the soldiers crouched in the long grass to the right of the archers left the cover of the trees and charged across the clearing, swords swinging, spears flying, falling on the dazed birdmen before they had a chance to bare their talons and wield their razor-sharp beaks.

Tiras spurred Shindoh forward, running a birdman through with his lance, even as he warned a soldier of an attack overhead.

"Keep them down, Lark!" Tiras shouted, "We cannot fight them in the air."

You cannot fly,
Your wings are bent.
You will never
Fly again.

Another layer of birdmen dropped from the sky even as the Volgar in the clearing shrieked and fought back. Very few took flight. They believed their wings were bent.

There were so many. Ten to one—twenty to one—and they just kept coming and coming as Tiras rounded the raging hoard, barking commands and using every weapon at his disposal. Again and again Tiras called on me, directing me, wielding me like a sword, and I clung to Shindoh, doing my king's bidding, watching as death multiplied around me—men of Jeru with gaping wounds and sightless eyes lay among the birdmen. I could not save them all, though I tried. I spun words and spells until my eyes felt raw and my mind began to fail.

There was gore in my hair and grit in my teeth, and Tiras was tireless at my back, shouting and pivoting and moving his men. I could feel my pulse in my temples, and it reverberated like a gong. I wretched and quaked, too weak to keep myself upright. I careened forward against Shindoh's neck, not caring that his mane was slick with sweat and blood. I felt myself slipping, unable to hold on any longer.

I watched Shindoh's hooves dancing around the wounded and dead when suddenly Tiras caught my braid, wrapping it around his hand as he pulled me upright. I slumped against him, and his mouth brushed my ear, gentle even as he demanded more.

"Make them fly, Lark. End it."

The sharp tug of his hand in my hair, and the quick burn of my scalp cleared my head enough to wield a final plea.

Go now, birdmen.
Fly away,
Live to see another day.

"Mightier than the sword," Tiras mused, and I wrapped myself in the relief that echoed in his voice. Tattered wings lifted from the ground, and I watched with the warriors of Jeru, my lids heavy and my breaths shallow, as the remaining Volgar retreated to the sky. I fought the pull of unconsciousness, my arms leaden and my thoughts thick. Then I was sliding again, slipping free from Shindoh and sound and the weight of my gift.

I thought I heard Kjell crow in victory, and all around there was grateful triumph, like feathers against my cheeks.

"Is she wounded?" someone asked, and I felt the tightening of steel bands around my body. I was moving through soldiers, floating.

"We did it, Majesty!" Someone pounded the king on his back and my face bobbed against his breast plate. Tiras was carrying me, and the bands were his arms.

I will walk.

"You will rest."

I will walk.

"Stubborn woman," he murmured. "Sleep."

And I slept.

SEVENTEEN

I awoke in a bed of grass to moaning and cursing and the raw stench of blood and flesh. Shindoh whinnied next to me, and I reached a hand to comfort him and soothe myself. A bladder of water sat near my head, and I drank gratefully and doused my hands and face. I could see men moving in the darkness, tending to the wounded and piling the dead.

The men took shifts, some sleeping among the trees, others watching the skies and tending to the wounded. I picked my way among them, needing privacy to relieve myself and maybe a place where I could wash. My hair stuck to my face, and the shirt of mail, though it had kept me warm, was rubbing me raw beneath my arms.

Clearly, the battle wasn't over, but paused, and I trembled at what the morrow would bring. No words hung in the wind. The forest creatures had gone deep or fled. Night sounds were muted, the trees silent. Even the leaves spoke in whispers or not at all. Death made the living things hide. I crept into the brush and took care of my most urgent need, praying no one was near. I thought

I smelled water and sniffed the air the way Boojohni did, pausing to listen, even as I caught a hint of damp earth and peat moss. It was the creek that ran deeper and wider upstream near the camp.

I moved toward the scent and the quiet tumble of water over rocks. Water drew the living, just as it drew me, so I approached carefully, peering through the rushes that lined the banks. The creek gleamed in the darkness, the stars reflected in water that pooled at the shallow edges, and all was still. I knelt on the bank, stones digging into my knees, water seeping through my breeches, and as I leaned close to the surface to wash my face, a shadow slipped over the moon.

I jerked upright and lifted my eyes to the sky, watching as one birdman after another flew silently overhead, as low as the trees. I dropped to my belly in the rushes, not daring to move or even breathe. I had not lured them in. They'd been sent, and we weren't ready.

Tiras! Tiras! The Volgar are here. The Volgar are here! I sent the message out in a wave of terror, not caring who might have the ability to hear.

As if the birdmen had heard my warning, the silence shattered in shrieks and screams, and I burst from the rushes and began to run, fearing I would be cut off from the warriors of Jeru with the Volgar between us.

I raced blindly, unable to conjure spells and weave words, *Volgar* the only thought in my head.

Birdmen descended around me, filling the air with the heavy flapping of powerful wings. I tripped and fell, narrowly missing the sharp talons of a diving beast. Thwarted, he screeched and ascended, even as a new attacker dipped low to make another attempt. I scrambled, half-crawling, half-running, and talons glanced off my shirt of mail only to tangle in my hair.

I pulled at my braid, trying to free myself, my mind blank in the horror of the moment. The birdman beat his powerful wings and rose back into the air, taking me with him, dangling by my hair. I slapped and grasped at the Volgar's clawed feet, more terrified of being taken away than falling. The birdman screeched once more, and his ascension sputtered, stalled by the Jeruvian lance buried in his chest.

Suddenly freed and temporarily weightless, the ground rose up and snatched my breath. I lay stunned, the wind forced from my lungs.

"Lark!" Tiras roared, his voice breaking through my stupor. "Run for the trees!"

The clash of swords, the shouts of men, and the pounding of hooves bore down upon me, and I covered my head and rolled to avoid being trampled. I had no sense of the forest or the stream, of left or right, of friend or foe. Everywhere I looked the battle raged, and I pulled my legs to my chest and closed my eyes, searching for my words.

Volgar wings, both big and small,
The higher you fly, the faster you fall.
Every beak that seeks to kill,
It's Volgar blood you want to spill.

I hurled the words into the air, catapulting them above the trees, making them swoop and tumble and dive into the Volgar overhead.

For a moment the battle continued, and I pushed harder, wrapping the Volgar in my web.

Then the sky began to whistle as bodies fell like cannon balls, colliding with the earth. Blood sprayed across my cheeks, and I was swept to the ground, pinned beneath a birdman's wing.

I pushed and heaved, freeing myself, only to scramble back for cover as another birdman fell.

"Lark!" Tiras shouted, "Where are you?"

I started to climb over bodies toward his voice.

Here. I am here.

I felt Shindoh's red fear streaking toward me, even as I found my feet and instinctively stretched out my arm. Then the king was there, swinging me up behind him, no armor, no helmet, no mail or gloves. Only a sword, which he brandished in his left hand, and a spiked flail which he swung with his right. We had been caught completely unaware. I wrapped my arms around his waist and gripped Shindoh's flanks between my knees, and the battle waged on.

Among the Volgar birdmen were those who seemed unaffected by my spells, those who dove and flew and carried men away, impervious to the susceptibility of their brothers. But the greater number tumbled from the sky when I wielded my words. Those who survived the fall turned on each other as I'd instructed them to do. Our vulnerability became superiority, even as Jeru's warriors fought off the surprise attack.

When a fresh wave of birdmen descended, I sent up spells to bring them down, and as dawn's timid light crept over the shivering trees, the Volgar who remained were dead or dying.

I laid my weary head on Tiras's back, welcoming the end of the second conflict, refusing to entertain the thought of more. His back bowed as if he too had reached his limit, and a tremor shook him, making me tighten my grip around his waist. His breath hissed, and his hand clamped down on my arm, repositioning it.

You're wounded.

"Not seriously. I need to change."

I pulled at his tunic and he hissed again, the wool tugging at his wound. His flesh was warm and sticky beneath my hands, and he shivered again.

"Leave it, woman. You're spent," Tiras commanded, but I pressed my palms to the long gash across his left side. Blood spilled over my hands and he cursed.

All the ills, the dirt and grime
Flee this wound and quicken time.
Gaping flesh and broken skin
Mend together, whole again.

Tiras sighed and relaxed, lifting his hand to cover mine, thanking me without speaking. I pictured his flesh repairing itself, the torn skin uncurling and binding together again.

Heal the wound beneath my hand, ease the pain inside this man.

It wasn't a well-crafted spell, but it was all I could conjure, and I pressed the words into his abdomen through the tips of my fingers, giving him the last of my strength.

My eyes were heavy, and my awareness hung on by the thinnest of threads, but I thought I heard him mutter.

"I think I will keep you."

When I awoke again, darkness had fallen, or maybe it had simply come and gone and come again. The sounds of revelry and laughter trickled into my tent, accompanied by the smell of meat and men, and all of it made my stomach turn. When I'd lost consciousness, I'd been surrounded by broken bodies and torn flesh, and the scent was still clinging to me.

I was warm, comfortable even, though I still wore the tunic and breeches the king had insisted I wear into battle. The shirt of mail was gone, along with the ill-fitting boots, and my hair was loose around my head. Tiras was gone too, though there were signs of him everywhere. The bed of piled furs covered in silk and the size of the tent, along with the richly appointed simplicity of my surroundings left little doubt that he had done as he vowed he would. He'd kept me near. I sat up slowly and stretched my body experimentally. I was among the living, but my heart ached, and I wanted to weep.

The smell of boar on a spit and something earthy, like yeasty bread, tickled my nose once more, and my stomach growled even as it revolted. I was filthy and thirsty and in desperate need of a chamber pot. I crawled from the corner pallet where I'd been laid, a simple coverlet spread over me, and flinched when the flap of the tent rustled and someone entered.

I would have felt Boojohni before I saw him had I not been so discombobulated. He was singing a little tune beneath his breath, and his beard was braided neatly with a little bow at the tip, as if he'd spent time being cared for and primped by nimble fingers. There was celebration in his step, and he smiled widely when he saw that I was awake.

"Ye slept so long! King Tiras told me ye saved everyone." He whispered the last part, and his eyes darted right and left as if he worried someone might hear. He should. No one but Tiras and Kjell and maybe, to some extent, Boojohni knew what part I had played. I was the king's pet. I'd heard the men refer to me that way.

I need to wash. I pulled on the boots near my pallet, ignoring Boojohni's congratulations.

Boojohni tilted his head and looked at me with pursed lips.

"Aren't ye glad, Bird?

I can't be glad when there is so much death. I don't want to hurt people. I don't want to hurt animals, or beasts, or even birdmen.

"But sometimes we must," he said softly.

I nodded, but I had a hard time looking him in the eye. I fumbled in my satchel and pulled out a gown, silky and smooth, and shook it out. It was too fine for the circumstances in which I found myself, but it would feel good against my skin once I was clean. Boojohni followed my lead, grabbing up a wedge of soap, a blanket, and a cloth for drying, and folding it all into a pouch that he balanced on his head. He led me from the king's tent and past the smaller shelters and groups of men toward the stream on the edge of camp.

Revelry abounded. There was nothing more raucous than men who'd faced death and lived to see another day. Men who'd killed to keep slaughter from their lands, men who still had gore on their weapons and blood on their clothes. They drank and laughed, and some crept off to be with the small band of women who followed the king's army whenever they traveled. It was understandable. But I wondered how those women felt embracing men with death on their skin. Maybe they were grateful.

I didn't know. But I couldn't celebrate. I couldn't laugh, or smile, or drink from the community flask and kick up my feet, though many smiled at me and even bowed when I passed, as if I'd gained a certain measure of celebrity. I kept my head high and my hands to my sides, and Boojohni hurried behind me, his eyes darting left and right at the celebration, and I saw him accept a cup brimming with something red. I pushed back my nausea and started down the little valley to the rushing water. I had to wash. If I didn't wash I would be sick, and if I was sick then I would cry. If I started crying I wouldn't stop.

The water was bracing, and I washed my hair twice, scrubbing at it until my brain was half-numb from the cold. Numb was good, numb was welcome. Once my hair was clean, I waded out into the middle of the creek until the water lapped against my chest. I slipped the soiled tunic from my shoulders and stepped out of the breeches as well; the water and the darkness were enough to hide me, and the clothing reeked of guilt and gore. I gathered it above my head and tossed it ashore.

I washed under the water, the coarse soap and the difficulty of the task demanding speed and attention. Boojohni stood nearby and kept his eyes pinned just beyond my head, giving me privacy and security at the same time. He drank from his cup, not trying to converse with me, and when I approached the shore, my hands crossed over my chest, he simply turned his back and held out the cloth for drying and the scratchy blanket that smelled of ale and horse. Still, it covered me from head to toe, and I pulled it around my shoulders gratefully as I blotted my hair with the cloth.

"Ye need to eat, Bird," he said quietly. "Ye slept for an entire day. You'll get sick if ye don't," he added.

I was already sick, but I nodded and pulled the blanket higher, creating a hood to shroud my face. Boojohni tottered behind me as I returned to the king's tent, his goblet emptied, his hands full of my wet, borrowed clothes and what was left of the soap.

While I dressed and braided my wet hair, Boojohni found me dinner and sat with me quietly while I did my best to show him my appreciation by eating as much as I could. He stayed until the king returned and the revelry outside quieted. Then he kissed my hand and patted my cheek and bowed to the king as he turned to go.

"Your mother would be proud of ye, Lark," he said before he stepped through the flap and let it fall behind him. I wondered if there was someone waiting for him, a woman who knew the worth of the little troll, and I said goodnight, the words sounding much like a spell. I pushed it outward and hoped he heard me, even as he walked away.

Sleep my friend, with peaceful dreams,
And never travel far from me.

EIGHTEEN

didn't attempt to converse with the king, but rolled into the blankets of my pallet and faced the wall, awkward and unsure of what to do with myself if I wasn't sleeping. I listened to him move about, pretending disinterest and feigning sleep, until he lowered the wick and settled on his furs. Restless energy hummed in the air, and I knew he was troubled. Or maybe I was confusing his emotions with my own. It was I who was troubled, and I certainly wasn't tired anymore. I listened as his movements stilled, and I thought he was asleep when he spoke, startling me.

"I know you're awake. Your mind is loud."

I wondered if I was keeping him awake too. It was strange that I could. But he was getting better and better at hearing me, even when I didn't intend for him to.

I'm sorry.

I tried to quiet it, and for a moment I thought I'd succeeded.

I heard him shift, his movement fluid, and remembered that he'd been hurt.

How is your wound?

"Gone. You stemmed the bleeding and eased the pain. Changing healed me completely."

Silence rose between us once more, but questions tiptoed around us.

I sat up, irritated and restless, and threw off my covers. I rose from my pallet and walked to the opening of the tent, needing to escape but not wanting to be alone. I heard him rise as well, though he kept his distance. After a moment, he began to speak.

"I remember when I killed a man for the first time. I was fifteen. He tried to abduct me and hold me for ransom. He was one of my father's advisors, and he was desperate. But I knew my father would let me die before he succumbed to blackmail or threats. He didn't negotiate with anyone."

King Zoltev, with his black eyes and his shining sword, rose in my memory, and I shuddered as Tiras continued.

"I knew I would have to save myself. I took the man's sword—he'd completely underestimated me—and I remember the way it felt to plunge the blade into his belly. There was very little resistance in his flesh . . . or maybe my fear gave me power." He paused. "But I saw the life leave his eyes, and it was absolutely terrifying. I wished I had let him kill me instead."

Why?

"Because in that moment, as I watched him die, I felt something leave me too. Like he'd taken part of my soul. The best part. I've never gotten it back. And I miss it."

I knew exactly what he meant. His innocence had been completely stripped away. Virtue had fled and left regret in its stead, even if the regret was only for what had been and could never be again.

"Where do you think he went?" he asked soberly, and I started, realizing he meant the man he'd killed. I struggled to offer possibilities.

Where does anyone go when they die? Back to the Creator of Words? Or maybe they dissipate and become part of the elements from which they were formed. I don't know. Maybe some simply cease to be. Maybe some have earned the right to exist somewhere else or to exist again. I hope the birdmen I killed today aren't waiting for me somewhere.

"Is that what's troubling you? Are you afraid of Volgar vengeance in another time and place?"

No. That isn't what troubles me.

He waited for me to offer more, but I was holding myself tightly, refusing to think at all, so I wouldn't share more than I wanted to.

"They would have killed us. All of us. You saved so many."

I killed so many. My inner voice snapped back at him, lashing out like a snake. He left his bed and came toward me. I turned and braced myself for his touch, but he stopped before he reached me.

"Yes. You did. It was like nothing I've ever seen before." His tone was frank. Admiring. I wanted to scream. My fingers curled into fists at my sides.

I am not a sword.

"What?" he asked, surprise coloring the word.

I am not a sword!

I squeezed my eyes shut against the hot tears that rose immediately. I didn't want to share any of this with him. But my thoughts were unruly, and he was listening intently.

I am not a weapon. I don't want to be a weapon!

"You are what you are. I am what I am. It matters little what we want."

I am not a weapon. The words were a cry in my mind, mournful and resistant. I felt him draw closer, but still he didn't touch me, and for that I was grateful. If he touched me I would break down.

"I never wanted to be king. But it is what I am. It matters little what we want," he repeated. I turned and stared up into his face, filled with an anguish that wouldn't abate.

You're wrong. It is the thing that matters most.

"Why?" he murmured, his eyes intense.

Because without desire, there is only duty. My lips trembled, and I bit down on them, bidding them to be still.

He pressed a thumb against my mouth, freeing my lower lip from the grip of my teeth. "Do you desire me?"

I jerked, resisting the coiled need that suddenly sprang from my belly and filled my chest. His eyes flared and his breath caught, and I wondered what word I'd given him. I could only guess. I stepped around him, but he caught me up, lifting me off the ground, one arm beneath my hips, one braced around my back. He walked back to the thick furs where he slept and laid me down on them.

This is not my duty. Or my desire.

"It is both," he responded, his arrogance setting my teeth on edge.

NO.

"Yes."

Lust is different from desire. There are women who will gladly assuage your lust. I will not.

"You want me. I heard it. I feel it."

It matters little what we want, I shot back, using his words against him. *I may be your weapon. But I am not your queen.*

He sat back on his haunches, his hands on his thighs, and he considered me.

"Do you want to be my queen?"

Why would I want that?

"Most women would."

I am not most women.

"You don't want power? Riches?"

Power only gets you killed.

He recoiled but rallied quickly. "What about adoration?"

Whose? Whose adoration?

He tipped his head, eyeing me with speculation.

"The adoration of a grateful people, of course."

Why would they be grateful? You don't intend to tell them I am Gifted, do you?

"No. It might frighten them," he admitted.

I shook my head wearily.

"What do you want, Lark?" he asked, his voice so soft I wanted to curl into it. Instead, I rolled away from him and closed my head and my heart. I would not give him that. What I wanted, my deepest desires, my dreams, they were mine. Only mine.

"You won't tell me?" I could hear the frustration in his voice. I resisted the question, mentally changing the subject.

I would give you this power. This gift of words. I would trade you for your ability to change, and I would become a real lark. A little bird. And I would fly away. I would make my nest high in a tree, and I would sing. Sing and fly. If I were a real bird people would lose the ability to disappoint me. I wouldn't consider them at all. I would have only four little words in my head. Sleep, eat, fly, sing. And that would be enough for me.

He had the audacity to laugh.

"You lie. That would not be enough for you." I felt him move up behind me, lying next to me on the thick furs. He moved so close I could feel his heat and the feel of his breath moving my hair. He propped himself above me, looking down at me.

"Your hair has a silvery sheen. It's strange because it's brown. But it isn't brown. Not really." Confusion rose from him. Confusion and something else. I listened, not believing the word that came to my mind.

Yearning.

Yearning? What did he yearn for? I was not foolish enough to think he yearned for me.

Ash. My mother said my hair was like ash.

"Ash." He stroked his hand over it, from top to tips, and his yearning became mine.

"What do you want, Lark?" He asked again, and his inner elegy was so deafening it pierced my walls. There was something he was hiding from me, something I had not figured out.

I want to be wanted.

He stiffened, and I realized I had let him hear. I had let him in. Just a bit. He was so close, and my need was loud.

"I want you," he said, his voice sharp.

You don't want me. You need me. I am of use. It isn't the same thing.

"I want you to be my queen."

I would be a terrible queen.

"I can teach you what you need to know. I can teach you how to please me." His voice was so low and soft the hair rose on my neck. I shivered and rose from the furs. I didn't have to lie there. I was angry at my response to him and angry that he felt I needed to be taught to please him.

He followed me. I turned, warding him off with an outstretched hand as he rose, stepping back to create distance between us. The upper part of his face was in shadows, but the light touched his mouth as if directing my gaze. I shivered again.

Why do I have to be taught?

"Because you just said you know nothing about being a queen. Because I am king. And because it *is* your duty to please me."

I laughed, and wished I could howl my frustration at the fat, lazy moon who looked on us through the flaps of the big tent like a drunken voyeur, too sauced to hide his riveted attention.

Why don't I please you as I am?

Tiras reached forward and without warning, lifted me off my feet, his hands encircling my waist and raising me up until our eyes were level.

His black eyes were unreadable, but frustration sang in the air between us.

Maybe I will teach you to please me, I taunted him, refusing to be intimidated, though he held me as though my weight were insignificant.

"What could a lark teach an eagle?" he dared, and I felt that challenge from the grip of his hands to the gleam in his black gaze.

An eagle can't sing. It was the only thing I could think of.

His lips twitched. "And my lark can't speak."

I am not your lark.

"You are." He brought my body against his, and I felt a charge zing from my toes to my heart before it flared in his eyes. He wrapped his arms around me, holding me in place against him as his fingers twisted in my hair.

"You are," he repeated, and his lips came down on mine so softly that I hardly realized he'd arrived. His mouth hovered there, tender and tentative, and completely at odds with the sharp ache at my scalp, where he gripped my hair in his fist.

Mine.

I didn't know if the word came from his kiss or from his thoughts, or maybe the word was mine alone, but I took it and swallowed it whole, planting it deep inside my belly where desire, need, and longing grew and flowered.

His kiss was warm and persuasive, and completely different from the first time he'd kissed me. He still took—demanded even—but laced with his power was something sweeter. Something I needed from him. Something I longed for. *Yearning.* There it was again. Suddenly yearning had a flavor. It tasted like a king, a beautiful, frightening, infuriating man who flew into my life and began to free my words.

He pulled at my hair again, tugging me back from his lips as if he needed to impart something of great importance.

"You will be my queen."

Do I please you? I mocked him even as I wished he would continue to kiss me.

He laughed, a harsh bark of disbelief. "You are not a lark. You are a great, shrieking harpy."

All the better to keep up with an eagle.

"You will be my queen," he insisted, setting me back on my feet, releasing me like the matter was settled. I felt almost bereft, until he tipped my chin up to meet his fierce gaze, forcing a response.

"Lark?"

I couldn't say no.

I wanted it too much. He was right. I lied. Being a mere lark would never be enough for me. He'd ruined me. He'd made me want to be an eagle. I bowed my head in acquiescence and kept my joy locked away, allowing myself to agree, but not allowing him to know the exaltation that sang through my soul.

Yes, Tiras. I will be your queen.

We remained camped near Kilmorda for two weeks, and we sought out the Volgar, pushing deeper into Kilmorda every day. I called to them, sitting in front of Tiras on Shindoh's back, wooing them, coaxing them to me in small groups, only to watch them take the lure and be slain. When I grieved for the beasts, Tiras would take me to a field strewn with bones or a village where only rats, fat from human remains, resided.

"They will kill if they are not destroyed," he would remind me, and I believed him, even as I suffered pangs of remorse for using my gift to lure them to their deaths.

Day after day we cleared the Volgar from the hills and valleys of Jeru's northernmost parts, though there were stretches, sometimes only hours, sometimes two days at a time, when Tiras disappeared into the sky.

Boojohni remarked on his absence in the second week as I rode on Shindoh, following Kjell as he circled the valley on a patrol of the areas already cleared. Boojohni trotted beside me, always the diligent servant, without ever seeming to tire.

"Where does he go, Bird?"

Who?

"The king, Goose! You know who I'm talking about. The man ye are always watchin' for, the man ye love," he growled, as if he had no patience for protestations.

I don't love him.

"Ye do."

He wants to make me queen.

Boojohni tripped over his own feet, surprise making him clumsy. Then he began to hoot and clap, drawing the attention of the warriors around us. Shindoh whinnied in irritation, and I reined him in, halting as Boojohni celebrated my announcement.

"The king is clearly a man of great wisdom," Boojohni chortled, and he did a little jig, making Shindoh toss his head.

I am of use to him.

"Ah, I see." Boojohni stopped dancing and cocked his head. "And is he of use to ye, Bird?"

The question caught me by surprise, and I had no response. Was Tiras of use to me?

"He has freed ye," Boojohni prodded gently. "Surely that is worth something to ye."

He kidnapped me!

"True. But he has freed ye too. Admit it, lass."

He taught me to read . . . and write.

"That he did. And he sees yer gifts."

He is using me.

"That seems to bother ye, Bird. Why? He doesn't have to make ye queen to use ye. He is king. He can take what he wants."

He could. And he often did.

"He knows your secrets . . . do you know his?" This time Boojohni wasn't smiling, and I remembered how the conversation began. I nodded slowly.

Yes. I know his secrets.

"Ye know where he goes?"

Yes. Do you?

"He is very careful. But I am very quiet. And curious."

And protective.

Boojohni nodded, admitting as much. "That I am."

Why do you ask if you already know?

"Because ye love him. And I needed to know if ye understand who . . . and what he is."

I didn't bother to argue with him. Boojohni was as stubborn as I, and he had convinced himself of my feelings.

"Are ye afraid of him, Bird?"

No.

It was Boojohni's turn to nod, and he began to walk again, as if the matter was settled. I urged Shindoh forward.

I agreed to be his queen, Boojohni.

"Of course ye did! He's a fine bit o' man flesh."

If I was capable of snorting, I would have done so, but Boojohni snorted enough for the both of us.

NINETEEN

We traveled back from Kilmorda the way we'd come, moving quickly, Tiras disappearing one full day and two of the four nights, only to ride through the next day like nothing was amiss. Though I hadn't admitted it to Boojohni, I worried at the amount of time he spent as a bird, the tale from my childhood seeping into my thoughts. The very first Changer had eventually become what he'd surrounded himself by; the more time spent as a beast, the harder it was to become a man again.

I tried to imagine how it would feel to be a bird, to fly above the ground, to surround myself with peace and air and freedom. I imagined it was particularly alluring to Tiras, who had so many people depending on him and looking to him for everything. Still, on the third day of our journey back to Jeru, I sought out Kjell, who stepped into Tiras's shoes whenever the king disappeared. I was riding Shindoh, my stamina increasing every day, my body adjusting to the rigors of riding for long hours at a time.

Kjell saw me coming, and his face tightened even as he slowed and waited for Shindoh to move into step beside his mount.

He is gone so much.

"Yes, he is," Kjell said sharply, and anger curled around him. I ignored it, as always. I had never been particularly good at making people like me.

Has it always been like this?

"It is far worse." He looked at me with such loathing that I gasped.

Why do you hate me?

"I hate what you are."

And what am I?

"You are Gifted." He said the words quietly, but he spat them out, the way he always did when he said "Gifted."

But you don't hate Tiras.

"Tiras isn't Gifted," he said simply.

I stared at him in stupefaction, and he shook his head in disgust, as if I were incredibly slow.

"It's not a gift. It's a bloody curse."

What's the difference?

"He was not born this way."

I wasn't sure what Kjell was trying to communicate. I was guessing most Gifted didn't fully-realize their abilities until they were older, though a few, like me, who had guidance from my mother, recognized their gifts earlier. Gifted or cursed, the result was exactly the same. Kjell seemed adamant about the distinction, as if one was internal and the other external.

"I was there the day your mother died. Do you know that?" Kjell said quietly, pulling me from my own thoughts.

I shook my head, stunned.

"I heard your mother curse King Zoltev. I saw him kill her."

My throat was so tight I couldn't swallow, and I stared ahead, unable to fathom why he would want to hurt me this way.

My mother did nothing wrong. She did not deserve to die.

"She damned an innocent boy! Tiras does not deserve to die either, but he is losing his life little by little."

King Zoltev damned himself and everything he touched. Fear is his legacy.

"My father was trying to protect his kingdom."

I looked at him sharply, and he scoffed.

Your father?

"Don't worry, Milady. I have no claim to the throne. I am a bastard son. You and your father can fight over it. I don't want it. But Tiras is still my brother, and I will do everything in my power to protect him. Even from you."

Tiras had not explained the relationship, but now that it had been pointed out, it was easy to see. Tiras and Kjell were each striking, though Tiras was darker skinned. Once his hair had been as black as Kjell's, making me wonder if his gift had been the cause of the whitening of his hair.

We rode in silence for several minutes, the anger between us zinging in a hot arc. I had asked for none of this, but Kjell had already made up his mind about me. It would do no good to attempt to change it.

"He told me he is going to make you queen. Queen Lark of Jeru. It's fitting really, isn't it? Tiras has always kept his friends close, and I see now he is keeping his enemies closer."

I didn't respond.

"Now your father will never be king. If something happens to Tiras, you will rule the remainder of your life. As long as you are living, you will be queen. If your father were to have you killed . . ."

He would die.

"Yes. Tiras told me that as well. He has outflanked your father, hasn't he?"

Again I was silent. When I pulled up, reining Shindoh around, Kjell met my gaze with a smirk. He was confident he had bested me.

Don't worry, Kjell. I will keep your secret.

His brow lowered and his mouth tightened. "And what secret would that be, Milady? My paternity is known by most."

It has come to my attention that I can only communicate with the Gifted . . . and animals. So you are either one or the other. You know my opinion on which it is.

Tiras wasted no time. The announcement was made the very night we returned to Jeru. Bells rang all over the city, and the royal crier stood on the wall and read the bans for two solid hours, repeating himself as people gathered and scattered, then gathered again, eager to spread the news.

"Lady Lark of Corvyn, daughter of the noble Lord Craig of Corvyn, will wed King Tiras of Degn. So it is written, so it will be done on the first day of Priapus, the month of fertility. May the God of Words and Creation seal their union for the good of Jeru," the crier shouted into the night, singing the words into my mind and heart and into the consciousness of every citizen of Jeru.

I stood on the balcony of my room, listening to the bans being read, still half shocked that it was the truth. In response, the cry went up again and again, "Hail, Queen of Jeru, Lady Degn," and I welcomed it, even as the words hung in the air like childish taunts and teasing truths.

I would be Queen of Jeru, Lady Degn. No longer Lark of Corvyn. No longer a daughter of a lord, but wife of a king. But only on the outside. On the inside I would still be little Lark, brittle bones and sharp feelings, certain that I would never be able to fulfill the duties before me. When the people learned I couldn't speak, they would talk, they would say all the words I couldn't say, and their words would follow me, mocking me, reminding me every day that I was not up to the task.

A message had been delivered to my father, conveyed by three members of the royal guard who'd gone directly from Kilmorda to my father's keep in Corvyn. A royal invitation would be sent to all the members of the Council of Lords in the days to come. I was not so foolish as to believe I'd been chosen for love, but I'd been chosen, and I reveled in that, even as I trembled in fear at what was to come.

When Tiras attempted to lock me in my tower upon our return, I warned him that I would not be a captive any longer, and he began to argue that it was for my safety. I reminded him that I could move haystacks and scale walls, not to mention open locks and control the minds of beasts.

He actually grinned at me, as if my abilities thrilled him, and promised I could come and go freely, as long as I had a member of the guard with me at all times. I found, for the most part, it was easier to stay in my room.

Tiras made sure I had books on Jeru's history, Jeru's laws, as well as Jeru's yearly crop yield and rainfall, and I read each tome with the commitment of the truly terrified. When Tiras could, he would read with me, allowing me to follow along with his hand over mine, tracing the words he was saying as I tried to take everything in. I was desperate to learn, and Tiras seemed desperate as well, spending long hours answering my questions and quizzing me on a thousand details that past queens of Jeru couldn't possibly have known.

My only reprieve was when he Changed, disappearing for a day or two or three. Then I would miss him—though his presence and attention always came with a price—and the respite would feel more like a punishment than a reward.

When I complained about the endless instruction, he grew stern and quiet, making me more nervous than I would have otherwise been. He showed little affection, beyond an occasional smile and a peck to my hand, and I grew stiffer and colder as the day of our marriage approached, wondering if the kisses he'd given me that night in Kilmorda were the last kisses I would receive, wondering for the umpteenth time why he seemed so intent on making me queen.

It was on one such afternoon, Tiras instructing me on Jeruvian trade laws, making me follow along as he droned on about the art of negotiation, when the late summer heat and the tedium of our studies threatened to drive me mad.

This book is a waste of parchment. I slapped it shut, narrowly missing Tiras's fingers and dropped it beside my chair. A burst of satisfaction echoed in my chest when it clapped heavily against the floor, followed by immediate remorse when a page fluttered free.

I can fix that, I offered meekly, but made no move to do so. Tiras sighed heavily, but rose to his feet, signaling we were through.

"Come," he said, surprising me, and took my hand in his, pulling me from my chair.

Where are we going?

"You need a break from words."

I practically skipped down the corridor from the library, and Tiras seemed equally as eager to escape.

"You've seen the watch tower, the siege tower, the arsenal tower, and the upper, middle and lower baileys. We've walked along the perimeter of the wall, inspected the ramparts and the parapets, and of course you've seen the dungeon," he listed, smirking slightly.

You've still not taught me to fence or joust.

"If the day comes when Jeru's survival hangs on her queen's ability to joust, we will already be doomed," he retorted dryly. "But if you'd like to spend some time in the yard, I can certainly arrange it."

I think I would rather visit Shindoh.

"Wise choice. We'll see the stables and the mews today."

We visited the stables first, the enormous enclosure housing hundreds of horses at a time. The royal horses included mounts for the guard and the city constables, though they were quartered in separate sections. The king's personal stables were connected to the main, providing easy access for trainers and breeders and stable hands. The scent of straw and earth and animal's well-cared for permeated the air, and the knot of disquiet in my chest eased considerably.

I walked along the rows, greeting the horses with words they could sense and handfuls of oats, and Tiras trailed behind me, giving me names and pedigrees, until we halted in front of Shindoh's stall.

"Shindoh is from a long line of Jeruvian Destriers. His sire was Perseus, whose sire was Mikiya," Tiras said, stepping inside the enclosure and greeting the charger, who seemed happy to see us both.

Something niggled in my memory.

Mikiya. I know that name.

"Mikiya was my horse when I was a boy. He was battle worn by the time I was big enough to handle him, but we were born only days apart. My mother named him. Mikiya means—"

Eagle.

"Yes," he said, surprised. Our eyes met over Shindoh's back, and my throat burned with a secret I couldn't quite remember.

"How did you know that? It is the language of my mother's people, not a language of Jeru."

I'm not sure. It is a word . . . and like every word, it has a meaning. I just . . . knew.

He handed me a brush and we worked without speaking for several long minutes. Shindoh radiated contentment, and it was contagious.

Maybe the secret to happiness is simplicity.

"There is a certain freedom in it," Tiras agreed, and I asked the question that I'd often pondered.

When you are a bird, are you ever tempted to . . . fly away and never return?

"When I am a bird, I still know that I am a man. I know who I am," he murmured, his hushed voice and the privacy of the stall making his answer seem more like a pained confession. Shindoh chuffed and butted him sympathetically.

Tiras knew who he was, but he was constantly being transformed into something else. I wished I hadn't asked.

That would make it especially difficult to eat mice and rabbits. I was trying to make him laugh, and he did.

"That is when I allow instinct to take over." He winced. "I surrender to the bird. In the beginning it was extremely difficult."

I couldn't imagine it.

"When I first began to change, I was . . . frightened," Tiras said, grimacing. "I didn't know what to do with myself or where to hide. I found shelter in the mews until I started to figure out how to . . . adjust. My father's falconer thought I'd been injured because I huddled in the rafters and wouldn't fly. He left me dead mice and bits of raw meat. I couldn't make myself eat them, even though I . . . wanted to. The eagle I'd become wanted to."

Did you hate her? I didn't specify who I was referring to, but Tiras knew.

"No," he said, and truth rang from his voice. "I wanted to. It would have been so much simpler to blame her." He looked at me. "I blamed my father."

"Come," he said, giving Shindoh a brisk pat. "The mews await."

I followed him eagerly. My father, like every lord, had falcons, though it was more a status symbol for him. He didn't enjoy the hunts or the birds themselves, saying the falcons were vicious. I had been forbidden to go anywhere near the mews in Corvyn.

Where the stables had been full of light and warm animals, the mews were shadowed and cool, the quiet interspersed by cooing, fluttering, and the occasional shriek. The main level housed the falcons and hawks and was so spacious and lofty, the birds, perched and leashed on stands that looked like inverted pyramids on posts, could fly around the interior.

Tiras explained that an upper level—accessible by steep stairs near the entrance—was for the pigeons, trained to carry messages all over the kingdom.

A man hurried forward, removing a falconer's glove as he walked. He was small and neat with a pointy grey beard that matched the color of his sharp eyes, eyes that made him look like the birds he trained. When he reached us, he bowed so low his forehead nearly touched his knees.

"This is Hashim. He is Master of the Mews," Tiras introduced. "Hashim, this is Lady Lark of Corvyn."

"Our future queen," Hashim marveled, rising and beaming.

The title made my neck hot, and without looking down, I knew a flush was climbing up my chest and pinking my cheeks. I breathed deeply, commanding it to cease, and extended a hand to the man.

He bowed again, kissing my hand with great flourish. "The birds are molting, my king. As you know, it makes them irritable. I've hooded many of the falcons, but I would keep a good distance," he warned, and Tiras nodded agreeably. Genuflecting,

Hashim retreated down the long aisle and through a tall door, leaving us to do what we wished.

We moved through the rows of captive birds, but my eyes kept moving to the heavy beams that supported the upper floor, to the drafty corners where an eagle, who was really a frightened boy, could huddle and hide.

"I still come here sometimes, when I change," Tiras said quietly. "Hashim is a good man. Gentle. He is always glad to see me. He believes he has tamed an eagle, and even gave me a name." We stopped near the stairs to the loft where the pigeons were kept and turned to retrace our steps.

Mikiya? The name was simply a nod to our earlier conversation, but the burning sensation rose in my throat again, and I wondered if I was growing ill. I touched it gingerly, but the discomfort was already beginning to ease.

"Mikiya," Tiras repeated, his voice a whisper. Then he shook his head. "No. Hashim calls me Stranger. More and more, that is what I'm becoming."

TWENTY

The day of the nuptials dawned crisp and clear, and the city came awake with a rush. For most of the day, I was prepped and buffed and smoothed and tweaked, and finally, wrapped in a dress of the most luxurious, pale blue silk I'd ever seen. When the preparations were complete, the women stood back and nodded gravely, like arrogant artisans. Their work was done. They retreated with instructions that I "not touch anything" until the guard arrived to escort me to the castle gates to begin my procession.

But no one came.

The bells began to chime, a signal for the start of the ceremonial march, and I debated leaving my room and descending the stairs on my own, impatient that I must always wait for men. I imagined myself beginning the slow walk to the cathedral through the gathering crowd without following the proper protocols. But ceremony was everything to Jeruvians, and I dismissed the thought immediately. Something was amiss.

Then the whispers began, floating up from the streets below through my balcony doors. I cursed the ability that drew the conversations to my consciousness, as if the words belonged to me. They swarmed my tower room and stung me like angry hornets.

There is not going to be a wedding.
The king has changed his mind.
Her father objects.
Lady Ariel from Firi should be queen. She is the most beautiful woman in all of Jeru.
The Lady from Corvyn doesn't even speak.
She's a mute, poor thing.
The king is missing . . . again.

Buzzing, buzzing, buzzing. The talk was incessant and painful. I shut the balcony doors and opened a book, replacing the gossip that whirred in my brain with something of my choosing, but I couldn't concentrate, and I was suddenly afraid. I heard boots in the hallway, and Kjell rapped on the door before entering alone.

He was decked out in his finest, his boots gleaming, his hair slicked back from his handsome face, but he looked especially grim.

"I can't find Tiras, Lady Corvyn."

I set my book aside and rose with as much calm as I could muster, and I stated the obvious.

He couldn't change.

He grimaced. He didn't like that I knew the truth, yet his relief warred with his fear. He'd borne the brunt of the king's secret for a very long time.

"I believe that is what has happened," he agreed softly.

Have you seen him?

His gaze lifted, and I knew he understood. I was asking if he'd seen the eagle.

"No."

It is not against Jeruvian law to kill such a bird. What if something happened to him?

Kjell swore and stomped to the balcony, flinging the doors wide as if begging Tiras to fly through.

"Can you call to him? The way you did to the Volgar?"

I was stunned that he knew and wondered how many of Tiras's warriors had heard me beckon the enemy in Kilmorda.

He is more man than an animal. The Volgar are simple. Tiras is not.

"He is not simple. But he is a bird as often as he is a man. Maybe more often," he murmured, and my heart grew heavier in my chest.

I walked to the open doors and raised my face to the sky. Then I closed my eyes and thought of the white-capped bird with the sooty black feathers. I saw the span of his wings with the fiery red tips, unlike any bird I'd ever seen, and I asked those wings to bring him to me.

I concentrated on the word he'd given me when I'd followed him from branch to branch, wall to wall, as we walked through the night to the cottage in the woods. *Home*, he'd said. *Home.*

Come home, Tiras, I urged. *Come home.*

But I felt nothing. No tendrils of connection, no whisper in the wind, no heartbeat. No warmth. The sun was beginning to sink toward the western hills, and wherever Tiras was, he was not within my reach.

I cannot feel him. If he is close by, he is not a bird.

Kjell swore, stepping back from the balcony doors and drawing me with him.

"The lords are insisting that the procession begin."

They know the king is unaccounted for?

"Yes. And they want to publicly humiliate him."

And me.

"They don't care about you, Milady."

Of course not.

"Their goal is to take down the king, by whatever means necessary, and tradition dictates that you must walk in order to be queen."

I don't understand.

"The bans have been read. The date set. The bells have tolled, the hour has come. You are to walk, before sunset, through the crowds and kneel at the altar in the cathedral and wait. If the king does not arrive, you will not be queen. Ever. It is a public statement that the king has . . . changed his mind."

And if I don't walk?

"It is an open declaration that you are refusing the king and his kingdom. The result is the same. You will never be queen."

But I will have some dignity.

"Yes." His mouth tightened. "And the king will be publicly rejected. This is what the council is hoping you will do."

My father will retain his position.

"Tiras will be shamed. You will never be queen, and therefore, your father is still next in line for the throne. Brilliant, really."

Frustration and futility beaded on his skin. The room was warm, and Kjell's tension made it warmer.

"What do you want to do, Lark?"

It was the first time Kjell had addressed me by my name, and the quiet desperation in his voice eased my own disquiet. He was asking me to make the decision.

I will walk. And I will wait at the altar.

"And if Tiras doesn't come?"

Then I will walk back.

179

His lips twitched at my simple response, and he relaxed into a deep breath.

"So be it," he agreed, bowing slightly. He held out his arm, and I took it, and together we made our descent.

At the castle gates we were greeted by members of the Council of Lords who were assembled to give their blessing before they began the procession. They'd come to Jeru City days before, bearing gifts and proper congratulations, but beneath the shiny veneer I felt the intrigue and collusions, the words they said to each other and sought to keep from the king.

My father immediately stepped forward and held out his bejeweled hand. Kjell bowed and stepped back, his eyes immediately scanning the skies.

"Daughter," my father greeted, his gaze glancing off mine and fixing just beyond my shoulder. He leaned in, as if to embrace me, but his mouth rested by my ear, and the words he spoke made the flesh rise on my neck. "I promised your mother I would keep you safe. Will you make me betray her?"

Will you betray me? I pressed, but he continued to talk, unable to hear me.

"The king is not what he seems, Daughter."

Then what a perfect pair we will be.

"I will take you back to Corvyn. You only have to make the walk, and it is over. The king will never arrive." His grip on my arm was bruising, his hoarse voice in my ear almost shrill, and *death* clung to his conscience once again.

What have you done, Father?

"Lord Corvyn, it is almost time. Let us give our good wishes to your fair daughter," Lord Bin Dar purred, suddenly at my father's shoulder, Lord Bilwick and Lord Gaul flanking him. My father stepped back obediently, and Lord Bin Dar bowed so low, his nose almost touched his knees, and his voice was thick with mockery.

"Soon you will be queen. I'm sure your father thought this day would never happen." His lips twisted, and he snapped his fingers to someone behind him.

"I've brought you a present, a gift for the queen-to-be." A servant stepped forward, staggering under the size and heft of the item he carried. With a dramatic flourish, Lord Bin Dar unsheathed a beautiful, gold birdcage. It was empty.

"I thought about giving you a songbird from Bin Dar, something colorful and sweet. But I thought you might want to make that decision. So the cage is my gift, Milady. The bird you choose is up to you." Dread curled in my belly. "We will be waiting for you in the cathedral, Lady Corvyn," he murmured, bowing again.

Lord Bilwick looked at my breasts and my hips and sneered even as he, too, bowed to my father and dabbed at the line of sweat collecting on his upper lip. Lord Gaul seemed pensive, and his thoughts were centered on the bell tower. The tolls had begun again, and he counted the chimes, the chant rising from his thoughts, even as he placed a cold kiss on my hand.

The remaining lords and ladies did not approach me at all, other than to bow with deference as they took their places in the line. Lord Firi was too ill to walk, and he'd sent his daughter once more. She was a brilliant rose amid thorns, standing with the eight lords of Jeru. The people would wonder again why she wasn't being crowned. Her presence made me square my shoulders and lift my chin. I would not draw pity. Yet.

The Council of Lords would walk first. I would follow at a distance, and Tiras would walk last, the bridegroom following his bride. Archers lined the walls, and the guards stood in full regalia, ready to accompany the procession.

The people of Jeru lined the long road leading from the cathedral to the castle, and I walked all the way, my back stiff, my eyes level, the long train of my pale blue dress trailing behind me for a full thirty feet. The people cheered and threw flower petals on my train, symbolizing the goodwill and wishes they wanted me to take with me on this new journey. White and pink and yellow and red, petals of every color imaginable, and so thick that my train was completely obscured and a few pounds heavier. I walked slowly, lifting my hands in regal greeting as I'd been instructed.

The people had already lined the path before me with the same flowers, protecting my bare feet—a representation of my vulnerability and humility as I walked among the people I would rule. My head was heavy with the jewels woven through my hip-length hair, but I didn't allow it to droop, and I didn't lower my eyes.

When I reached the cathedral on the hill, I was met by a veiled matron, the oldest woman in Jeru city, who knelt at my blackened feet and washed them with trembling hands. In a voice that cracked and broke as she spoke, she bestowed a blessing of long life upon me and the feet that would carry me through it.

The oil from her flask dribbled into the dirt as she anointed one foot and then the other, muttering about patience and zeal and health in every step. When she finished her blessing she peered up at me and said simply, "Wait for him."

She raised her arms like a child asking to be lifted up, and immediately two guards stepped forward to assist her. She clutched my hands in hers and repeated her advice, an old woman telling a young woman to take care of her husband.

"Wait for him," she pressed, and there was an urgency that belied her simple advice.

Wait for who? I asked, unable to help myself, even if she couldn't hear my question.

"The King, Milady," she answered instantly, and a smile broke across her face, creating a thousand creases to hide her secrets. And mine. I smiled back.

For how long?

"As long as it takes."

She inclined her head, a regal nod, and stepped back from me, letting the guards draw her away. I wished she would return and tell me more, tell me how to wait when I wanted only to run. I needed a mother, or at the very least a guide, and I had neither. I took a deep breath, filling my chest with the courage to move forward. Then I stepped into the cool darkness of the cathedral, the sinking sun at my back.

The horizontal rays pierced the stained glass on either side of the huge arched door and made kaleidoscope colors on the black stone aisle that led to the raised altar. Circular stone benches in ever-widening rings created a ripple effect from the center where I was to kneel with my back to the entrance, waiting for the king to arrive. He was not to see my face until he knelt across from me, and I was not to see his.

The benches were filled with the rich and well-connected from every province, the Council of Lords sitting on the first rows, Lady Firi and four others to my left, four to my right. The prior, a royal advisor appointed by the king to perform Jeruvian rituals and rites, stood at the altar, waiting for me to approach. His robes were black with an emerald undertone of Jeruvian green. He wore a tall, gold dome on his head, carved with the ancient symbols of Jeru. The mouth, the hand, the heart, and the eye—the Teller, the Spinner, the Healer, and the Changer.

The prior greeted me by name and bid me kneel as he touched my lips, my hand, my chest, and each closed lid, bestowing blessings on each, and lighting a candle over incense that made my temples throb and my throat itch.

Then he stood back and faced the entrance expectantly. The heads on every man and woman in attendance swiveled as well, watching eagerly, awaiting the king. Except my father. He did not turn his head. Neither did Lord Bin Dar or Lord Gaul. In fact, not a single member of the council turned toward the door. They all sat with their faces forward, waiting. A black knowledge sat on their features like ink, and I read it with growing alarm. They couldn't know for certain that Tiras would not arrive unless they knew the king's secret and had trapped him with it.

We waited in silence, the room a tomb of growing speculation. The questions of the congregation became so engorged, they burst the confines of private thought and pressed against me, stealing my space. Seconds became minutes, and minutes became an eternity. The curiosity in the cathedral reached its peak and started to wane, the burning query clearly answered. The king was not coming.

TWENTY-ONE

"Holy Prior, have mercy on the girl," my father said, rising. "Dismiss the gathering."

The prior nodded, his eyes wide beneath his domed hat. "Of course, Milord. As you wish."

He raised his hands, bidding the people to be useful and well, a Jeruvian blessing, and the congregation rose, almost as one.

I did not rise from the altar.

"Milady, are you well?"

I lifted my eyes to his and nodded once, slowly, precisely.

"Do you understand, Milady? The king is not coming."

I nodded again, in exactly the same manner, but I did not rise.

"Can you not even whisper?" the prior chided me.

I couldn't. My lips could form words, my tongue could move around the shapes and sounds, but I could not release them, not even on a whisper.

"Is she deaf as well as dumb?" the people murmured, and Lord Bilwick repeated the question, raising his voice so it bounced off the stone walls. A few people gasped and some laughed, stifling uncomfortable giggles into the palms of their hands.

"Lady Corvyn, the king is not coming. You will rise," Lord Bin Dar demanded.

I will wait.

He couldn't hear me, but the words gave me courage, and I said them again, making them a mantra.

I will wait.

"You have been dismissed," Lord Gaul insisted.

I will wait on the king, just as I was instructed.

"The law states the lady must reach the altar before the sun sets. But there is no law that dictates when the king shall arrive. Let her wait." It was Lady Firi, her voice rising above the fray, and for a moment the congregation was silent.

Boojohni spoke my name from a dark corner, his worry making the word fly like an arrow through the assembly and pierce my quaking heart, but I didn't turn toward him, though I took courage in his presence.

"Rise, daughter." My father gripped my arm, his fingers biting, attempting to force my withdrawal.

I heard the hushed grate of metal hissing against the leather of a sheath. Then another sword was drawn nearby, and another.

"The lady will wait as long as she wishes. I will stay with her," Kjell called out, and I could hear him approaching from the entrance where he'd stood to await the king.

"As will I," another warrior cried out.

"And I," Boojohni cried, moving toward the altar.

"Stupid girl." My father's desperate hiss was a sharp slap, far worse than his grip. He released my arm and stepped away. But he didn't leave.

No one left.

I bowed my head and closed my eyes, and the murmuring around me faded with my concentration. I'd called the Volgar birdmen. I could ask the birds of Jeru to help me save the king.

All the birds in Jeru come,
Sing a song of martyrdom.
Every cage and every tree,
Set the birds of Jeru free.
If the king among you flies,
If the king among you dies,
Lift him up and bring him here,
To claim his troth to every ear.

I don't know how long I sang the summons, the words pouring from my head, but when I felt the approaching wave, I raised my head, searching for Tiras among the throng. A sound, not unlike a sandstorm filled the cathedral, and within seconds became an ear-splitting cacophony of bird calls accompanied by the deafening clap of countless wings of every size and strength. Those in attendance began to rise in alarm or cower beneath their upraised arms. The door of the cathedral still stood wide, an invitation to an absent king, and with a whoosh and a roar, the cathedral was filled with birds moving in concert, the soaring ceilings obscured by a tornado of rushing wings. I searched for red tips and a silky white cap among the throng, praying for a miracle, my eyes clinging to the whirlwind spinning round and round over my head, but I could not make out one bird from the next, so great was the churning mass. A few of the onlookers ran from the church, screaming and fighting to get out the doors. Several of the lords pulled their cloaks over their heads and the guards raised their bows, letting arrows fly into the swarm. I searched for Kjell, anxious for him to call off the guard, but he was no-where to be found. I set up a spell, urging the birds to exit.

Birds of Jeru
Where's your king?
If he is here, then you must leave.

Like a flock of starlings, the birds began to dive and roll, a perfectly orchestrated finale, out the cathedral doors, until once again, the house of worship was an empty shell. Feathers fluttered through the air and clung to the altar before continuing to the floor.

"What in the world was that?" I heard someone say, and the prior muttered something about evil and the powers of darkness, as he lit another candle and waved incense through the air.

"This has gone on long enough," Bin Dar exclaimed, standing. Lord Gaul stood with him, and slowly the other lords rose as well.

"I agree." The king's voice rang out from the back of the church. "Let's proceed, shall we?"

A collective cry went up, Tiras's name on every tongue. The lords grew white and quiet, their eyes scurrying, their jaws slack, and I braced myself against the temptation to turn and verify the king's presence. But I knelt with my back stiff, eyes forward, waiting for him to come to the altar as Jeruvian custom demanded.

I counted his steps as they echoed through the hushed cathedral, slow and steady, my heart beating double time to their rhythm. Then Tiras was kneeling across from me, his eyes burning, his palms upon the altar, his posture submissive but his expression that of the conqueror.

I wanted to demand answers, to berate him, to send sharp words between us, but mostly, I was so overwhelmed to see him that I stayed still, my eyes clinging to his.

"You are still here, Lady Lark," Tiras murmured, his lips hardly moving as his eyes gleamed.

And you are still an ass, I answered, finding my voice, my relief making me weak, even as I fought to remain strong just a bit longer.

"Prior, please proceed," the king commanded.

"Where have you been, Majesty?" the prior stuttered, and the king's jaw clenched at his audacity.

"There are those who seek my life, Prior. Those who don't want me to take a queen or continue my rule over Jeru. Are you one of them?"

"No Majesty. Of course not. Thank the Gods you are here," he mumbled, performing the sign of the Creator in the air, as if seeking divine assistance. His gaze swung between the apoplectic lords and the kneeling king who waited impatiently for him to begin the ceremony. With another sign of the Creator, he squared his shoulders and began. He did not look at the lords again, nor did I.

My head was an ocean of words, my chest a storm of sensation, and I heard little of what transpired in the following moments. The prior spoke a blessing on the king, touching his eyelids, his temples, the lifelines on his hands, his wrists, and then performed the same blessing on me. I placed my hands over Tiras's when directed, the brush and slide of my palms against his making my bare toes curl and my breath grow shorter.

When the Prior asked me if I would give my life to Tiras of Degn, if I would honor him by taking his name as mine and taking his body into mine, I could only nod, though I gave the words to Tiras.

I will.

When the prior asked Tiras if he would give me his name and give me his seed, he too nodded, but his voice rang through the cathedral, loud and bold, and my toes curled again.

"I will."

The prior laid the Book of Jeru upon the altar, opening the pages to the list of kings, and handed me the quill.

I found the line next to Tiras's, an empty space I was expected to fill, and with a firm hand, signed my name. I heard my father sputter and protest.

"She cannot read or write," he argued. "She cannot even give her consent."

"She can," Tiras said, his gaze rising from my name and falling on my father. "And she has."

"What have you done?" my father moaned, echoing the question I had posed to him, even as the prior pricked our fingers and pressed our bleeding hands together, a symbol of the merging of lives and bloodlines.

"So it is written, so it is done on the first day of Priapus, the month of fertility. May the God of Words and Creation seal this union for the good of Jeru," the prior said, repeating the words of the crier when he read the bans. The prior placed a crown of Jeruvian ore on my head, a crown so heavy I could barely lift my chin.

"You may rise, Lark of Degn," the prior prodded.

I rose on legs I couldn't feel, willing the clothes on my body and the air around me to keep me upright.

"King of Jeru, behold your queen," the prior commanded, his voice rising with his relief that the ceremony was completed. For what felt like a small eternity, Tiras gazed up at me from where he still knelt beside the altar. Then he rose, his eyes still on mine, and took my hand. Turning, he presented me to the people assembled and to the lords who looked at me with green eyes and yellow hearts, their bitter thoughts tinging the air around them.

"People of Jeru, Council of Lords, behold your queen," the king proclaimed. The congregation dropped collectively to their knees, their eyes remaining lifted, as their king had instructed.

And it was done.

My head hurt and my back burned from holding my spine straight and my crown from falling, and when the wedding feast ended and the women retired, I walked up the winding staircase, a maid trailing behind me, my train gathered in her arms. It was not Pia this time, but a girl I didn't know, a girl with gentle fingers and a shy smile who carefully removed my crown and the jewels from my hair and brushed it with smooth strokes as my neck bowed in weary relief.

She washed my body, though I longed for my bed. I fell asleep with my head against the edge of the iron tub, but awoke as she urged me to step out, drying my body as I swayed and tottered like Boojohni when he'd had too much to drink. She rubbed oil into my skin, the scent not unlike the oil from the earlier anointing, reminding me of the old woman's counsel outside the cathedral.

Wait for him.

The words invoked an ache deep in my belly, an ache that felt like pleasure but lingered like pain. I *wanted* to wait for Tiras. I wanted to see if he would come to me again, if he would come without my beckoning, on two legs instead of red-tipped wings. He'd kept me close through the festivities, his hand on my elbow, his length at my side. I'd had so many questions and fears, but no chance to ask them.

When I'd commented on his clothing—the same clothes Kjell had been wearing when he escorted me to the castle gates—Tiras confessed. "Kjell is naked in the vestry. Better him than me. I sent a discreet member of the guard back with boots and a cloak."

I laughed silently, but Tiras's eyes were grave, even as his mouth twisted with mine.

"There was a trap set for me, Lark," he supplied quietly. "A trap you managed to spring. And there will be more." It was then that our careful conversation had been interrupted by merriment and a call for toasts, and I could only worry and wonder until I was too tired to do either and left his side for the relative safety of the royal chamber.

The maid helped me don a white nightgown of whisper-thin silk that felt like a caress, and I climbed on the bed, so weary I could only smile at her gratefully, relieved that the day had come to a close. She stoked the fire, though the room was plenty warm, and I didn't bother to crawl beneath the covers. Exhaustion made waiting impossible, and I fell asleep almost immediately.

I slept for a time, but came awake instantly when I heard a whisper and a soft touch against my face.

"What do you want, little Lark?"

I opened my eyes to find the king's face in the darkness where he loomed above me. The fire was smoldering but the moon was high, bathing the room in white and quiet. It took me a moment to disentangle myself from sleep, to make sense of his question and his presence beside me.

I was his queen. He was my king. And he was here with me in the dark. I was strangely at peace and unafraid of what this moment meant, and I stretched my limbs carefully, not wanting to pull away from his hand on my cheek. I liked when he touched me, and I didn't think he knew how much. I hoped he didn't.

What do I want? What do you want, husband?

He smiled as if the title pleased him, though the smile fled almost immediately. His countenance was shuttered and his voice bleak as he answered without hesitation.

"I want to know that my kingdom is safe," he whispered. "Our kingdom, Lark. That is why I chose you. You will protect her."

He was so morose, and I put my hand over his to comfort him, even as I inwardly retreated. I was chosen to protect. A weapon.

But you will keep her safe, I soothed, believing he would. His shoulders drooped, but he still held my gaze.

"A bird cannot wield a sword."

His words were so filled with pain that I had no response. My heart began to pound beneath the thin fabric at my breast, sympathetic and sad and suddenly frightened. As if he felt the change in me, Tiras pulled his hand from my face and slid it down my neck, across the pulse that fluttered there, and rested it, palm flattened, on my thundering heart.

"A bird cannot wield a sword, my queen. And before long, I will be nothing but a bird."

I shook my head, resisting his dour prediction, and his hand curled in my gown, desperate, as if he needed something to hold onto.

"But not tonight . . . tonight I am still a man. Still a king. And you are my wife."

His eyes grew fierce, and the hand at my breast flexed and flattened once more, as if he'd let go of his despair and traded it for desire.

I refused to look away from him, though my body said *flee,* and my heart begged for tenderness. I was not beautiful. I was not vivid or bold. I was small and scared, a wisp. Exactly as Kjell had once described—a tendril of pale smoke, hardly there at all. But the way Tiras was looking at me made me believe I was vibrant and brave. He made me feel powerful.

He loosened the tie between my breasts. I didn't flinch or pull away, but I didn't assist him in my disrobing. He opened my nightgown, unwrapping my body, and I felt the air whisper against my skin. Moonlight created a narrowing path from the window to the bed where I lay, and it continued up over the covers, across my newly-bared skin and up the wall, creating an outline of the king looming over me.

"Your skin is like ice," he observed.

I don't feel cold, I responded. My inner voice was calm. Level. I wanted to punch the air in triumph at my control. He would not know how much I wanted him, how much I longed for him. I would give him anything else. But not that.

He shook his head, arguing, and his hair swept his shoulders.

"No, it isn't cold like ice. It is translucent. You are silver from head to toe." He ran his flattened palm from my shoulders to my hips. I definitely wasn't cold. I was liquid heat. I was terror and curiosity and denial disguised as indifference.

"You glow, Lark." His hand climbed back up again and swept over my unbound hair. I swallowed, suddenly close to tears.

Then why does no one see me?

"I see you," he said.

And he did. I was at his mercy, naked and vulnerable. His eyes lingered over each trembling inch, taking me in. Seeing me.

I fought the urge to cover myself, to turn away, even to avert my eyes. He unbuttoned his shirt and threw it to the side. His breeches followed, and he covered me, skin on skin, his forearms bracketing my head, his lips hovering over mine. I sent up a grateful prayer to my mother and the God of Words that my lips could not whimper or beg. Because I would have done both.

"Let me in, Lark," he whispered.

I knew he didn't just refer to my body or my mouth, though the heavy press of his flesh urged surrender, and the wet heat of his lips pled submission. He wanted me to give him my words.

Body. Not soul, I told him, rebellious to the end.

"Both." His kiss seared his demand on my tongue, and for a moment I forgot to resist as our mouths moved and our bodies conversed, exchanging secrets without sound. My hands pulled him closer, and his fingers tangled in the length of my hair, wrapping the long strands around our bodies as he rolled to his back, taking my weight with him.

"Let me in," he demanded, and I could feel his yearning rise again, the yearning that had an origin separate from us. From me. From him.

Tiras. Tiras. Tiras.

It was the only thought in my head, and it seemed to satisfy him, though I felt sorrow rise from his skin, like a cloud had drifted across the moon.

TWENTY-TWO

When I awoke the next morning he was gone, and my body felt like a wanton stranger. I was sore in places I had never been sore and happy in ways I had never known before. The act of consummation, both strange and wonderful, had literally *consumed* me, and I was no longer myself.

The pain had made the pleasure all the greater, searing the moment into being, imprinting Tiras into my heart and onto my body. I had felt his desire to claim, even as he kissed me softly and swallowed my hurt, soothing it with gentle hands and tender words. The words had risen from his skin even when he wasn't speaking, and I had called them to me, collecting them like falling leaves, pressing them between the heavy pages of my memory so I could keep them.

My maids brought water for a bath, but after they filled the tub I turned them away, not wanting curious eyes on my skin. I felt different, as if I'd shed my old scales and was reborn, and I needed to be alone with this new me.

I braided my hair and pinned it around my head to keep it out of the water, and slid into the welcoming heat, closing my eyes and drifting off into the solitude behind my lids.

I didn't hear the door or the soft tread of his boots over the thick rugs, but I felt him when he drew near, and I opened my eyes to see Tiras watching me, his brows drawn in a perplexed V. He crouched down at the edge of the huge iron tub so our eyes were almost level, and he reached out and pressed a thumb to the bow of my top lip.

"You pout even when you smile," he commented softly. "It's this full top lip."

Does it not please you?

His own lips twitched, and his hand fell away, drifting across the point of my chin, down the long column of my neck to rest on the water lapping at my breasts.

"It pleases me," he whispered. "*You* please me. And you surprise me."

You are a fine teacher. I meant to mock, to protect my vulnerable heart with nettles and barbs, but it was the truth, and it rang as such. I swallowed and looked away, but his voice drew me back in.

"When I changed from bird to man yesterday morning, someone was waiting for me."

I stared at him, waiting. When he seemed lost in thought, I urged him on.

Who?

"I don't know." He shook his head, as if clearing it.

"As I shift I am unaware. I can't hear or see. It's as if I'm not present at all, caught somewhere between the two sides of myself. I flew to the balcony wall and through the doors and began to change. That is all I remember. When I woke, I was naked in the dungeon, my hands and feet in chains."

I could only gaze at him in horror, my mind tripping over who and how and most importantly, why?

"Someone knows about my gift. Someone knows when I am vulnerable. And someone knew where to wait for me," Tiras added gravely.

The ramifications of such knowledge rendered us both silent, our eyes sightless, our thoughts heavy. Then I began to shake my head, not able to make sense of it.

If my father knew you could change, he would have exposed you immediately. He wouldn't play these games.

"I know. The lords may have known something, but if they knew I was Gifted, they would not be wasting their time interfering with a wedding."

A treacherous thought wormed its way to my consciousness, and I shared it without considering how it might be interpreted.

Maybe Kjell was trying to protect you . . . from me. What better way than to make sure I can never be queen?

Tiras gazed at me in stunned horror then closed his eyes as if pained by the thought.

"Do you believe it was Kjell?" he asked, and his vulnerability suddenly matched my own. I thought about his brother, his only friend. Kjell didn't like me. But he loved Tiras. I had no doubt about that.

If it was Kjell . . . his motives are pure.

Swift relief rippled across the king's face before his jaw hardened and his eyes tightened.

"If it was Kjell, he will answer for it."

I hope it was him.

"Why?" Tiras gasped.

Because he would never harm you. If it was someone else . . .

"Our troubles are just beginning," he finished my thought.

I nodded.

"There is a small grate high on the wall that leads to the courtyard, and through the slats I could hear the trumpets signal the procession, but no one could hear me when I called out, and no one ever came all the hours I was locked away."

How did you escape?

"Every cage and every tree, set the birds of Jeru free," he quoted softly.

You heard me?

"At dusk, the grate suddenly sprang open, and I could hear the birds shrieking outside. So many birds. I changed into an eagle, and the manacles fell from my talons and my wings, far too large for a bird. I flew out through the grate and became one of a thousand birds descending on the cathedral, heeding your call. I thought I was too late."

I thought you couldn't change. So I decided to wait . . . until you could.

"Stubborn woman," he murmured, but the tightness in his features had eased, and his eyes were warm on my face.

I didn't know what else to do. The lords were angry. The people . . . mocked me, and I wished to be invisible, the way I usually am.

Tiras lifted his hand from the water and touched my jaw with the tips of his fingers.

"You *are* easy to overlook. Slim and pale and so quiet. But now that I've studied your soft grey eyes and traced the fine bones of your face, now that I've kissed your pale pink mouth, I don't want to look anywhere else. My gaze is continually drawn back to you."

Without hesitation I gave him another truth.

You . . . are . . . impossible . . . to overlook.

His breath caught, and for the first time, I was the one who leaned in, the one who pressed my lips to his, the one who cradled his face in my hands. He allowed me to lead for several long seconds, letting me taste him and test him. Then he rose and brought me with him, scooping me from the water like a nymph from the sea.

And I was consumed once more.

My father left Jeru City without a word. Maybe he was resigned to the fact that he would never be king, or maybe he simply went home to plot and plan beyond the king's easy reach.

The lords from Enoch, Janda, and Quondoon left two days after the wedding, but Lady Firi, Lord Gaul, and Lord Bin Dar remained in Jeru City for a week, making everyone uncomfortable and making Tiras take precautions with my safety and his own that he would not otherwise take.

Why must we tolerate them at all? I asked Tiras, sitting at his side, watching Jeruvians dance and minstrels perform the evening's entertainment, wishing I were free of my crown and the secret looks and the words that slid around the lords like snakes.

"They are members of the council. They are lords of Jeru. Lords of lands that have been passed down through their bloodlines since the children of the Creator came to be. Do you want me to murder them in their sleep, my bloodthirsty wench?" Tiras murmured with a smirk.

I thought of Tiras, chained and naked in the dungeon of his own castle, and was tempted. Tiras asked Kjell if he'd been the one to lock him in the dungeon on our wedding day. I was not present, but I'd felt Kjell's flood of betrayal and outrage rise up through the walls, even as he pledged his loyalty to his brother. Tiras believed him. I believed him. I wished I didn't.

They want to oust you.

"I am king, but I am subject to the support of the provinces. If the provinces rise against me, against Degn, then my kingdom ceases to be. They will put a puppet on the throne. Someone they can easily influence and control."

Like my father.

"I have a powerful army. I have loyal soldiers. But they come from every province, and they are sworn to protect all of Jeru, not just the king."

We were interrupted by Kjell, accompanied by the ambassador from Firi. She curtsied before the king then curtsied to me, giving us both a brief glimpse of her beautiful breasts. Kjell moved to Tiras's side, and the ambassador extended her hand to me.

"My queen, will you join me?"

I looked beyond Ariel Firi to the long line of ladies assembled to engage in a traditional dance, and immediately started to shake my head.

"It is custom," she said, dimpling prettily and grabbing my hand. "You must."

I don't know how, I pleaded with Tiras to intervene.

"You are Jeru's queen, of course you must participate in the dance," he said, his grin wicked. "Lady Firi will take good care of you."

Drawing more attention to myself with my hesitation than I would by simply going along and blending into the bright fabrics and spinning women, I stood and followed Lady Firi to the floor.

"Have you done the dance before, Majesty?" she asked innocently.

I shook my head.

"Follow me. It's quite simple."

The music began, a song I'd known once, long ago, a song my mother had sung, and her mother before her, and her mother before that. It was the maiden song of Jeru, a song of celebra-

tions and rituals. A song for women. But there'd been so few op-
portunities in my twenty summers to celebrate or sing, tucked
away from the world where I would not harm or be harmed, that
the song was like a long-lost sister—part of me, but a stranger
still.

I did my best to copy the graceful sway of hips and arms, the
steps and the turns, but my mind was captured by remembrance,
and as the words to the maiden song were sung, I knew them,
though I couldn't have pulled them forward on my own.

Daughter, daughter, Jeru's daughter,
He is coming, do not hide.
Daughter, daughter, Jeru's daughter,
Let the king make you his bride.

I heard the words in my mother's voice, lilting and sweet, as
if she sang my future from my past. I spun without knowing the
steps, and danced without knowing what came next. My eyes
found Tiras, visible in slivers and pieces as I whirled with Jeru's
daughters, and the voice in my head became a voice of warning.

Daughter, daughter, Jeru's daughter,
Wait for him, his heart is true.
Daughter, daughter, Jeru's daughter,
'Til the hour he comes for you.

It was a silly song, an ancient song, a song of being rescued
by a powerful man, of becoming a princess, as if a princess were
the only thing a Jeruvian daughter might want to be. But it disturbed me, as if my mother, a Teller of considerable power, had
made it all come to pass. She had sung me to sleep with that
song—*Daughter, daughter, Jeru's daughter, 'Til the hour he*
comes for you.

'Til the hour.

Curse not, cure not, 'til the hour.

'Til the hour he comes for you.

The maiden song and the curse my mother whispered in my ear the day she died became one in my head.

"Are you unwell, Highness?" Lady Firi touched my arm lightly. I realized I had stopped dancing, making the line bunch around me.

I fanned myself, signaling a need for water and air, and she nodded agreeably.

"Let's step into the garden, shall we?"

I followed her gratefully, keeping my chin high to keep my crown from sliding around my ears and over my eyes. I knew it made me look haughty, but haughtiness was preferable to bumbling.

The garden was fragrant with the last of the summer's blooms. The leaves were falling and the air was starting to grow crisp and cool. Jeru City didn't get much snow like Corvyn, or Kilmorda, or even Bilwick to the east, but the days were growing darker and shorter, the light fading faster, taking Tiras when it fled.

"You lied to me," Lady Firi said breezily. "You knew that dance, and you did it very well. The king was pleased."

Her choice of words made me flush. Pleasing the king brought to mind other things. I shrugged carefully and smiled a little, pleading innocence without a word.

"You are quite lovely. I didn't think so at first. I do now. Shall we be friends, Lady Lark? That is your name, isn't it?"

I wondered if I could trust Ariel of Firi. She had spoken up for me as I waited at the altar. She had stood with Tiras against the northern lords. Kjell seemed smitten, and I would love to have a friend. But her eyes often lingered on Tiras, and the silent words she exuded were guarded and stiff, as if she were wary of me too.

I nodded, allowing the use of my name, and she leaned in and whispered in my ear.

"I can hear you, you know."

I drew back as if she'd slapped me. She laughed, a lovely, tinkling sound that made the flowers tip their heads toward her.

"When you speak, I can hear you. Just a word . . . here and there. At the feast you asked me if I wanted more wine. You thought I didn't know it was you."

I stared at her blankly, revealing nothing, and she pressed a gentle finger against the thundering pulse on my neck.

"Don't worry. The Firi are descended from the Gifted too. I have my own shameful secrets. Your mother was a noblewoman from Enoch, yes?"

I confirmed nothing.

"All of Enoch is descended from the first Teller. Enoch and Janda. There were Gifted in Kilmorda, though many of them were destroyed by the Volgar. Some say the Volgar are descendants of the first Changer—though he was a wolf and the Volgar are . . . birds." Her voice was light, informational, but she didn't remove her hand from my neck. She held it there, softly, like a caress.

"And some say the Volgar were spun from vultures. I tend to believe that, having faced them in battle. The Bin Dar descend from the Spinners, the Quondoon as well. It is all part of our history," Tiras spoke up behind us. I hadn't heard or felt him approach with the blood roaring in my ears and Lady Firi's knowing fingers at my throat.

Lady Firi dropped her hand and turned with a demure smile and welcoming eyes. Kjell trailed after Tiras, a constant shadow since the king's wedding day abduction.

"The king speaks truth." Lady Firi inclined her head in agreement. "But the Corvyns and the Degn descend from the warrior who slayed the Dragon Changer. There is no Gifted in their blood, which is why the throne has remained in the Degn line for over a century, with a Corvyn always waiting in the wings. Pure blood. No taint." She looked at me and winked.

"But then we marry and mate. And things become messy. Don't you agree, Kjell?" The smile she tossed toward Kjell was flirtatious. Or provocative. I wasn't sure. She was friendly and relaxed, but the words she said and the words she hid were different. Something was bothering her. I had a feeling it was me.

"Indeed. But the king is of Degn. I am of Degn. We should both be without . . . taint," Kjell said with a hint of bite.

Lady Firi walked toward him, turning her back on me and the king, as if we were all old friends. When she drew near, she raised herself on her toes, letting her lips touch Kjell's ear. Maybe she didn't intend for me to hear, but the words found me anyway, the way they always did.

"But we all know differently, don't we?"

TWENTY-THREE

The lords and ladies eventually left, leaving relative peace in their wake, but in the days and weeks following our nuptials, the king was tireless, as if time was slipping from him. He slept very little and was almost always in motion, and when he wasn't, he was listening carefully, ruling judiciously, and instructing. Always instructing. He kept me by his side, demanding my attention and my focus, and when I grew weary or resistant, he would level his black eyes on me and remind me that I was now the queen, and I had "much to learn." He made me seethe even as I sought his approval.

There were nights he couldn't stay with me and long days when the paltry light of winter didn't make him a man again. I did my best to fill my time with reading and writing, but I missed him with an intensity that made his absence painful and his return a celebration. In the dark or the light, in the great hall or in our bedchamber, he was gruff but gentle, arrogant yet attentive, and he made love with a ferocity and focus that made it impossible not to bend myself to his will, even as I found ways to challenge and defy him.

Once a week, when the change didn't take him, I sat with Tiras during the hearings as he listened to one Jeruvian after another state his case, only to come to a swift decision before beckoning another forward. His subjects respected him, though there were a few who argued, and one who spit at his feet before being dragged away.

Two full moons after we were married, a young woman was brought before the king, her hands chained, her face and clothes filthy, as if she'd been dragged through the streets. A man stepped forward with her and accused her of being a Healer.

I looked at the chains around the woman's wrists and the defeat in her face and interrupted the questioning, pushing an order at Tiras with such adamancy that he winced.

Tell the man to let her go.

"What is your proof?" the king asked, ignoring me.

She heals? That's her crime? I raged. Tiras did not even turn his head. He listened patiently as the man described two different instances when the woman had lain her hands on dying children, and they were miraculously cured.

"Is this true?" Tiras asked the woman, who hardly raised her head.

"Yes," she answered wearily.

The man who held her chains dropped them at the foot of the dais.

"She has sorcery in her, Your Highness," he murmured fearfully. "I want nothing more to do with this."

"Where are the children now, the ones she healed?" Tiras asked.

The man pointed behind him, to a woman who stood with two children in the line waiting to be heard.

"They are *yours*? Why have you brought them here?" I could feel Tiras's incredulity, even as my anger began to tint the air around me. It was a wonder no one could see it.

"They were healed unnaturally. I want you to command her to remove the curse," the man insisted.

He wants his children to die? I asked, and Tiras shot me a look that demanded I be silent.

"I cannot do that. I heal. I don't harm. It is not in my power to make them sick again," the woman said, as if she'd said it a thousand times before.

"Why did you heal them if you know the law forbids it?" Tiras questioned her.

"Because I . . . can. It would be wrong to see suffering and not alleviate it if I have the power to do so, wouldn't it?" the healer pleaded.

"Bring the children forward." Tiras demanded.

The woman, who was clearly the mother, walked forward with trepidation, the children at her sides wide-eyed and clinging to her skirts.

"Are they completely healed?" Tiras asked the mother, who looked at her husband and then back at the king.

"Yes," she whispered.

"Do you want them to be sick again?" Tiras asked.

"No, Majesty. But I'm afraid," the mother answered.

"What are you afraid of?" Tiras pressed.

"That she took something from them," she replied.

"In exchange for her cure?"

She nodded.

"What do you think she took?" Tiras asked.

"Their souls," the mother whispered, and began to weep.

"Did you exact a price for your healing?" Tiras asked the healer, who was shaking her head in horror.

"No, sire. I only have the power to heal. I am not a teller. I cannot curse," she answered.

Tiras, let the woman go.

The healer's head jerked around, and her eyes grew wide. She had clearly heard me.

"What does justice demand?" the king asked the mother, even as he laid his hand on my arm, warning me again.

"She should be stoned!" the father cried, and the mother winced.

"Did you ask this woman to heal your children?" the king asked the trembling mother.

"Yes," she whispered.

The father moaned and began to implore the king with frenzied words. "She bewitched my wife! We were afraid. We thought the children would die."

"It is illegal to be a Healer . . . and it is illegal to seek their services," the king reminded him. "The punishment is the same."

The Great Hall grew quiet, and the man before the dais began to shake.

"What does justice demand?" Tiras asked again, and this time he addressed the father. "I will let you decide, but whatever punishment the healer receives, your wife will receive as well."

The man seemed stunned by the turn of events, and his eyes touched on his children and his penitent wife before glancing off the healer who was at his mercy.

"I . . . will . . . not seek . . . further retribution," the father babbled. "The Healer is free to go."

"As you wish," Tiras nodded. "Remove the chains."

The man did so, his eyes cast downward, and with several subservient bows, he ushered his family from the hall.

"Go now, Healer. And do no harm," Tiras cautioned, a common phrase, but his eyes found Kjell who stood at attention nearby and something passed between them. When the Healer left the hall, Kjell followed her.

That night, Tiras did not come to bed, and I lay in the darkness, my eyes focused inwardly. I knew where Kjell had gone. He'd gone to the Healer and offered her sanctuary and sustenance in the castle walls. At this moment, she could be tucked away in the tower room where I had learned to read and Tiras had drawn pictures on my walls.

Beneath her tattered clothing and the layer of grime, the Healer had been pretty. Maybe beautiful. Her hair had been long and dark, her skin a deep olive. Kjell had once taunted the king with mentions of both, as if Tiras preferred women who were nothing like me.

She would be of use to him. Perhaps she could heal Tiras where I could not. And maybe this time, the Healer *would* exact a price. Maybe instead of his soul she would demand his heart. I shot up from the bed and dressed, not caring that my hair was unbound and my emotions untidy. I commanded doors and lit sconces as I walked, flinging spells and searching even as I prayed that Tiras was in eagle form so that I wouldn't find him in the state I was in.

I found him in the library with Kjell, a room towering with books from every land, a room I had frequented often since becoming queen. It smelled of wisdom and words and Tiras, who greeted me with an outstretched hand. When I didn't move forward to take it, he withdrew it, and Kjell looked between us with an awareness I resented.

"Lower your gaze from my wife, Kjell," Tiras said suddenly, as if he resented it as well, as if my appearance was provocative. My rumpled hair tumbled down my back, and my feet were bare, but I was dressed. I would not be shamed and I would not apologize for the interruption, though out of courtesy, I shared my words with both of them.

If you seek the Healer, I want to be present.

"What are you talking about?" Tiras asked slowly.

The Healer . . . the one at the hearing today.

Tiras's brows rose as if I'd surprised him, and my heart twisted in my chest, interpreting his surprise as confirmation.

Kjell followed her from the hall.

Kjell cursed, and Tiras sat back in his chair, regarding me with hooded eyes.

Is she here? In the castle?

"No," Tiras admitted. "But we know where she is."

Kjell cursed again, and Tiras dismissed him with a terse command, his eyes never leaving mine. When the heavy door closed behind Kjell, I continued.

I will not be discarded.

"What?"

She might be able to heal you. I cannot. But I will not be cast aside.

"Is that what this is about, Lady Degn?"

She is of use to you. Have I outlived my usefulness?

"You are of great use to me. I will put a child in your belly. A son who will be king."

I hissed at his smirk, suddenly so angry I lost my ability to be coherent.

Arrogant . . . ass . . . impossible!

I couldn't get the words out fast enough, and I stood, clenching my fists, gritting my teeth, holding myself perfectly still so I wouldn't hurl myself at him.

Tiras laughed as he rose, and I knew he was intentionally provoking me.

"Look at you! Standing there like a bloody ice sculpture. But there is fire beneath that ice. I've felt it," he insisted. "You try so hard to be indifferent, but you are anything but indifferent."

I am not a weapon, and I am not a breeding mare! You want to use me? I won't let you.

He advanced on me, arrogant and all-knowing.

"You won't LET ME?"

I won't let you!

Tiras drew so close that I had to crank my head back to see his face. Our bodies did not align—I was too small for that—but his hips pressed high on my belly and my breasts were flattened against him. His hands stayed at his sides, but he was using his size to intimidate me, and that made me even angrier.

You think because you are bigger than I am that you can force yourself on me?

"I don't *have* to force myself. You know it, and I know it."

I am your wife, but I will do as I please, I raged, and the spell rose in my head without effort.

Belt that holds my husband's pants,
Loosen now and make him dance.

Tiras's belt flew from his breeches like a sea serpent, slithering through the air only to strike at him with its tail. He stepped back from me, his eyes growing wide as he gripped the gyrating length of leather, holding it at arm's length with one hand as he held up his pants with the other. But I wasn't finished.

Boots upon my husband's feet,
Kick him so he'll take a seat.

Tiras fell flat on his behind as his boots shimmied and wriggled free, throwing him off balance. His boots then proceeded to kick him on his back and his thighs as he yowled in stunned outrage. "Lark!"

Shirt upon my husband's chest,
Wrap yourself around his head.

His tunic promptly rose like Tiras was shrugging it off, only it wrapped itself around him, obscuring his angry face. I started to laugh then. I couldn't help it. He looked so ridiculous sitting on the floor of the library, his socks hanging from his feet, his breeches falling around his hips, his shirt over his head, and his boots and belt attacking him.

Tiras lashed out and grabbed my skirts, yanking me down beside him. "Call off the hounds, Lark!" he bellowed, and I laughed even harder, shaking with mirth even as he rolled himself on top of me and valiantly fought the tunic that kept wrapping itself around his face. The tunic was slightly dangerous, the boots weren't very accurate, and the tail end of the belt had made a welt across my cheek. I decided enough was enough.

I performed a sloppy rhyme, and Tiras let out a stream of profanities as the shirt ceased its murderous attempts and the belt and boots fell to the floor, inanimate once again.

Tiras's breathing was harsh and fast, his hair mussed and falling over his eyes as he braced his forearms on either side of my head. His big body pressed me into the floor, making it hard to draw breath. I was well and truly trapped, but I felt like the victor regardless.

Are you injured, husband?

He was glaring and angry for all of three seconds. Then the lines around his eyes deepened and a smile broke out across his face. He laughed with me, but he kept me pinned beneath him, his face inches from mine.

"You enjoyed that, didn't you?"

Immensely.

"Tell me this, wife. Is there a spell to quickly remove your dress?" he whispered, still smiling, his breath tickling my mouth.

I felt my face grow hot, and I closed my eyes, trying to retreat, even as I immediately considered a spell to render us both naked.

"I *will* put a baby in your belly," he promised, and the mirth was mixed with determination.

My eyes snapped open as he brushed his lips across mine, back and forth, like he was painting with his mouth. The sensation made the roof of my mouth tingle, the palms of my hands tickle, and the bottom of my stomach turn over. He didn't increase his tempo or his pressure, and he spoke even as his lips caressed mine.

"You have all this power—you heal, you convince, you persuade, you destroy—but you want me to believe you feel nothing," he murmured. "I know differently."

I have all the power, but you will destroy me.

"Only your walls, Lark." He deepened the kiss, licking into my mouth as if he knew he'd find me there hiding from him. My toes curled against the rug, and my body softened beneath his, wanting to accommodate him, even as I turned my head, denying him to prove I could. He moved his mouth to my neck, whispering as he kissed my throat.

"I said once that you are like ice. And you are. Silver and perfect . . . glistening. And hard. You're so hard, Lark. I want you to be soft sometimes. I need you to let me in." He was sweet and cajoling, but I knew he wasn't referring to lovemaking so much as he was referring to the walls I was constantly disappearing behind.

I shook my head.

If I let you in, I will have nothing left. If I am like ice it is because ice is impenetrable. Strong.

He opened his mouth against my breast and shifted his weight to the side, so one of the hands that bracketed my head was free to move down my body. I clenched my hands at my sides and tamped down the growing fire beneath my skin.

"Touch me, Lark," he commanded, picking up one clenched fist to bite playfully at my fingers.

When I touch you, I cease to be.

He groaned as if the confession only stoked his ardor, but he rolled off me suddenly, as if he were weary of the effort it took to get past my defenses. He reached for his shirt and his belt and sat forward to pull on his boots. "For God's sake, woman. You don't cease to be. You simply change."

I sat up too, missing him already and unable to figure out how to give him what he asked for without giving in. I touched tentative fingers to his cheek and he froze, as if my apologetic touch was the last thing he expected.

Why must I change, Tiras? Why do you want so badly to break me? I asked, the voice in my head small and scared.

"Because there is fire beneath the ice, Lark," he shot back. "And I like your fire." His intensity radiated from him in the form of heat. He burned so hot all the time, I could feel him re-shaping me, drip by drip.

I shook my head, suddenly close to tears, but refusing to let them rise.

No. Beneath the ice are all the words.

He looked at me, dumbfounded, one boot on, one boot off.

Have you ever thought that maybe it is better this way? That I can't speak? If I can wield words without making a sound, what could I do if they were set free? I scare myself, Tiras.

It was such a huge confession, such a monumental crack in my defenses, that I dropped my eyes and raised my hands to my face, needing a moment to regroup. Tiras wrapped his fingers around my wrists and pulled my hands from my eyes, making me look at him.

"You don't scare me," he whispered. "You frustrate me. You infuriate me. But you do not scare me."

Not now.

"Not ever. You are good to your core, Lady Degn. Maddening. But good." He released my wrists and rose to his feet, his shirt still hanging open, his belt in his hands. I wanted to scream in frustration, to pull him back down beside me. I was a terrible wife, a terrible queen. He wanted to give me a child, and I made it into an epic battle, when in truth, I would have liked nothing more than to make a child with him.

Tiras?

"Yes?" he sighed, his back to me, tucking his shirt into his breeches.

Will you kiss me again?

He looked down at me, and a smile that was almost tender lifted the corners of his mouth, and heat rose again in his eyes.

"You told me once you would never ask for a kiss."

I grimaced.

"Do you like it when I kiss you?"

Yes.

His smile deepened, but he waited, making me squirm, making me *ask*. I stared at him then bowed my head, surrendering.

If you kiss me slowly, for a long time, it is easier for me to . . .

"Let me in?" he finished for me.

Yes.

The word was a sigh and my cheeks were aflame, but he reached for me, pulling me from the floor and into his arms, enveloping me, making me feel full in a way I'd come to crave. I raised my face to his, closing my eyes and seeking his lips. And he kissed me for a long, long time.

TWENTY-FOUR

Tiras didn't suddenly become a bird at sundown. It was as if the night slowly pulled him away, leaching him, until resistance was futile. When the moon was fat and bright, he seemed more able to combat the pull, but even then he suffered to stay human, and sometimes daylight was not enough to restore him. I could ease his pain, giving him more stamina to combat the change on his own, but my words and his will proved increasingly insufficient to alter the course of his gift.

I would often wake alone in the hours before dawn, the darkness of our chamber making his absence heavier, harder, hopeless. I lived on a pendulum of extreme joy and great strain, waiting for him, welcoming him, and being left once more. The pendulum seemed to be gaining momentum instead of losing it, swinging higher and deeper even as he stayed away longer and longer, only to return for briefer and briefer periods of time.

The morning after the hearings, I awoke to sunlight and an eagle on my balcony wall. I approached him with longing and an outstretched hand, hoping the consciousness of the man was stronger than the wariness of the bird. He let me stroke his silky white head for a breath-stealing moment before turning his eyes toward the stretch of forest to the west. Then, with a swift unfurling of his wings, he left me, and I watched him fly away.

For three days I waited for the king to return, and when dawn broke on the fourth day, with no sign of Tiras, I went searching for Kjell, determined to seek out the Healer he'd followed from the castle after the hearing.

I dressed and braided my hair quickly, not bothering to wait for my ladies maid, eager to steal through the castle halls before everyone was stirring. Words slid from dreams and warmed the air, and I listened to each one before descending the stairs and following the thin thread of tension that seemed to cling to Kjell wherever he went. I found him in the stables, and he seemed almost relieved to be given some sort of task.

Kjell had discovered that the healer dwelled in the small settlement called Nivea that had sprung up around the ancient sea bed west of Jeru City. After the hearing, he'd trailed the young woman, keeping his distance. When she'd reached the western gates, she'd melded into the laborers and craftsman leaving the city and returning to their homes for the day, and he'd followed her to a humble dwelling surrounded by similar homes of artisans and jewelry makers, as well as stone cutters and masons who lived and labored outside the protection of the city walls.

We sought her out at sundown, clothing ourselves in peasant robes. I covered my face and hair with a plain veil and Boojohni balanced a basket on his little head and walked ahead of us, a perfect distraction. All eyes were drawn to him, a novelty in a city afraid of differences of any sort, and Kjell and I were able to blend into the crowd. It was easier leaving Jeru City than it would be to return. Once the gates were closed, Kjell would have to reveal himself to the watchman for re-entry, but we were more worried that the Healer would get word of our presence and hide.

"She was greeted and welcomed at every turn. She had been missed, and her family was overjoyed to see her," Kjell murmured, and I didn't comment on the sliver of regret I heard in his voice. "If word spreads that the queen is in Nivea, the villagers will assume the worst."

Kjell's fears were well-founded, for when we neared the Healer's cottage, nestled with dozens of others along the cliffs of the cavernous sea bed, alarm wailed in the air, as audible to me as a Volgar's shriek. We'd been spotted and identified.

She knows we are here.

Boojohni stayed with me as Kjell broke into a run, reaching the front door as a slim figure burst from the cottage, colliding with him, only to fight and scrabble, kicking and thrashing to get away.

Kjell cursed as she raked long nails across his cheek and she doubled her efforts.

"Shh, Lass," Boojohni soothed, his little hands raised in surrender.

Can you hear me, Healer? I asked her, my voice loud in my head.

She stilled instantly, and her eyes met mine, widening with horror, as if she'd managed to convince herself that my interference at her hearing was all in her head.

"Y-yes," she stammered. "You are the queen. You told the king to release me."

You did nothing wrong.

"You are the queen," she repeated, and the same surge of dismay that colored her words welled in my chest. I *was* the queen, and I had no idea what I was doing.

We mean you no harm. We need your help. Will you talk to me . . . inside?

We'd managed to draw the attention of a few onlookers, and we needed to take the conversation elsewhere. Kjell had not loosened his arms whatsoever, and she dangled from his embrace.

She nodded slowly, and I bid Kjell to let her go. He set her on her feet and moved between us, keeping her close. She led the way into the cottage, brushing Kjell as she passed, and with a brief hum and a soft touch, healed the bleeding wound she'd inflicted on his face. Kjell cursed like she'd run him through, his eyes spitting and his hand on his blade, but the Healer didn't give him a second glance. She'd demonstrated her power even as she extended mercy.

The stone cottage was small and neat, a room for sleeping, a room for eating, and not much else. None of us sat and Kjell remained near the door, as if to guard against a trap. The Healer's pale eyes clung to mine, as blue as Kjell's and startling against her black hair and olive skin. I felt colorless beside her, and a stab of insecurity found its mark before I shored up my icy walls and focused on the task at hand.

"Are you . . . like me?" she asked.

Gifted?

She gasped when I said the word, as if she'd spent her whole life avoiding it. But after a brief pause she nodded.

"Yes. Gifted."

I am.

"Majesty," Kjell growled, shaking his head, and Boojohni stiffened at my side.

It isn't something I can hide from her, Kjell.

Kjell's distrust rose and spilled over, mingling with his fear of what he'd been taught to hate. The Healer looked at him briefly and extended her hand toward him once more, as if to ease his discomfort. He glowered, and she withdrew her hand.

"I am a Healer. But . . . what are you?" she asked, her gaze returning to me.

A Teller, though I seem to be able to command healing, to some extent.

"A Teller who can't speak?"

I had no desire to share my story, and when I simply inclined my head, offering no explanation, her brow furrowed.

"Why are you here, Majesty? Am I to be arrested again?"

I wasn't sure of how to proceed, of what to share, and she pressed me again, "Why did you come to my home?"

The king is not well.

"And you cannot heal him?"

No. I can't. The truth weighed heavily on me, and she cocked her head, as if she heard my helplessness.

"You want me to heal him." It was not a question.

I nodded again. She pursed her lips, and her eyes moved from me to Kjell to Boojohni and back again.

"If I heal him, what will you give me?"

Kjell snorted as if she were a greedy money-changer. But I understood self-preservation.

What do you need?

"Sanctuary. Leniency. Not just for me. But for those like me. Like us."

She wanted me to save an entire community when I couldn't even save Tiras. But I didn't hesitate to promise, *I will do all in my power to make it so.*

It was the best I could do, and maybe she knew that, for she nodded and I began to breathe again.

"What ails the king?"

I hesitated again, afraid of revealing something I couldn't take back, of endangering Tiras, of endangering the young Healer with knowledge she shouldn't have.

The king is . . . like us.

She shook her head, confused. "I don't understand."

He is Gifted.

The girl raised incredulous eyes and shook her head in disbelief. "The son of King Zoltev is Gifted?" she marveled. Then she laughed, a great, shaking sound that held more grief than mirth.

"The Gods are just," she muttered, fire lighting her eyes. "May the late king burn in hell."

"The late king was my father. You would do well to remember that," Kjell said, baring his teeth.

The Healer turned steely eyes on him. "Somehow that does not surprise me."

King Tiras is not like his father, I contended desperately.

"No? I am not so sure." The Healer had not looked away from Kjell, as if his behavior made her doubt the nobility of his half-brother.

I had no response but the truth, and I gave it to her.

We are losing him to the change.

"Being Gifted is not an illness," she argued, her head swiveling towards me. I'd told Tiras the very same thing. *I can't fix what isn't broken.*

I only ask that you try, I pled, and she regarded me doubtfully.

"I will do what I can, Your Majesty."

The Healer's name was Shenna, and true to her word, she returned to Jeru City with Kjell four days later. Tiras had returned as well, but his eyes were different. His eyes had always been so brown they were black. Now a warm amber circle ringed his pupils. Eagle eyes.

"It was the same with my hair. I changed, but my hair did not. One day it was black. The next day as white as snow. As white as eagle feathers. Soon I will have talons instead of toes and wings instead of arms." His tone was wry but his golden eyes were bracketed with worry.

When the healer asked permission to touch him, he agreed, his eyes on mine. I didn't want her to touch him, and he knew it.

"Stubborn woman," he breathed, and the cage that surrounded my heart constricted until I couldn't breathe. The healer smoothed her hands down his arms and across his eyes, her face calm and her eyes closed. She hummed, a low mellow sound, never varying from a single note, a lute with only one string, plucking away.

"Why is she doing that?" Kjell murmured. Shenna's eyes snapped open, but continued humming for several more seconds as she moved her hands.

"It is the sound his body makes, the note he sings," she responded eventually, and though she'd ceased humming, I could hear the tone continuing, fixed in her head like a dominant word.

"It is the frequency with which his body heals itself, I am simply singing with him, strengthening his ability."

I reached out my hand. Tiras took it, and I closed my eyes as well, breathing my words into the note the healer sang, telling him to be whole.

"I cannot heal him," Shenna said, finally. Tiras sat motionless, Kjell paced, and I mourned.

Why? My voice was a cry, and Tiras winced.

"Because he isn't ill," she insisted. "His body sings with health and vigor . . . and strength."

"But he is becoming something else. It's happening more and more often," Kjell contended, anger masking his fear.

Shenna shook her head again. "I know many Changers. It is never like this. It is always a choice."

"You know many?" Tiras asked, raising his strange gold eyes to the healer.

"I know many," she breathed, trusting him. Trusting us.

"Bring them to me," Tiras commanded, and Shenna looked to me, pleading for reassurance.

I could only meet her gaze helplessly. I had no idea what he intended.

"No," she answered, shaking her head. "They would never come."

"Then take me to them," he said. "And I will show them that I am one of them."

"Why?" Kjell interrupted. "Why would you do that, Tiras? Why would you expose yourself in that way?"

"You will need allies when I'm gone," Tiras answered, and this time his eyes did not meet mine.

Resistance bubbled in me, denying, denying, denying.

TWENTY-FIVE

W e left the city at dawn the next day, disguised much like we'd been before, dressed like villagers and artisans, veiled and quiet, carrying baskets and avoiding eye contact. We walked to Nivea, to the cottage of Shenna the healer, who welcomed the men with wariness, but extended her hands and some warmth to me, as if my gift and my disability comforted her. Vulnerability invited trust, apparently.

"I have told the elders. They have circulated the news among the Gifted. Each will decide whether to show themselves or stay hidden. If they don't come here today, we must accept their choice. I will not reveal them to you," Shenna said firmly. Her parents were present, along with her great-grandfather, a man named Sorkin, who was so old he could stand next to the cliffs in Corvyn and blend into the lined, grey rock. But in Nivea, the rock was black and shimmering, like Tiras's eyes had been before the change made them gold.

Sorkin was a healer too, a man who'd lived through the reign of Tiras's great-grandfather, a king even more feared and hated than Zoltev. He watched us with careful eyes, exuding both caution and hope. When Tiras bowed to him, the old man's face softened the slightest bit. He reached out his hands and cupped Tiras's face, not asking for permission, and he began to hum, just like Shenna had done the day before. After a time, he stopped, his hands falling away, the note ringing through the cottage.

"There is no sickness in you, Majesty," he murmured, his brow furrowing with distrust.

"There is also very little . . . time," Tiras said, and Sorkin studied him intently, not confirming or denying what Tiras claimed.

Sorkin stepped away from the king, lifting his hands to my cheeks as well. "There is life in you, my queen." His eyes cut to Tiras. "I can hear the hum of two heartbeats."

My breath caught. I had suspected as much, but shared my suspicion with no one, wanting to wait a little longer, to be sure. Now I had no doubt.

"It is very soon, and the life is young. But there will be a child," he predicted with certainty.

I turned to Tiras, who took my hand and pressed a kiss on my palm where the prior had merged our blood months before. Joy trembled on his lips and took root in my breast. His pleasure was well noted by Shenna and the old healer, and their eyes warmed and their wariness ebbed.

"Thank the Gods," Tiras breathed, as if another bridge had been crossed, another battle won, and the roots of joy in my chest grew tiny thorns.

"Thank the Gods," the Healer repeated. "Now let us begin."

From the room beyond, a woman named Gwyn was summoned, a woman so ancient and so familiar, I could only stare. It was the old woman from the cathedral, the woman who had anointed my feet and had bade me wait on my wedding day. She bowed gingerly before me, and my spirits lifted with her smile.

"When we last met, you were not yet a queen."

I curtsied deeply, grateful to see her again.

"We meet again, and you are not yet a mother, though you will accomplish this too." Her eyes moved to Tiras, and she acknowledged him with a deferential nod of her silver head.

"Majesty, how can we serve you?" she asked him, though I suspected she already knew.

"What is your gift, Mother Gwyn?" Tiras asked, bestowing the title with obvious respect.

"I see things others cannot. I know things others do not. And I recognize the Gifted, Highness," she said without artifice.

You are a seer? I interrupted, surprised.

She smiled at me, as though my voice in her head was pleasing.

"My ears are not as sharp as they once were, but I hear you perfectly."

I bowed again. *It is good to be heard.*

"I am a Teller, as are you, my queen," Gwyn continued, answering my original question. "Though the things I see I cannot change. I can't command the wind or water. But I know when a storm is coming."

"What is the king's gift, Mother Gwyn?" Sorkin pressed her gently, steering the conversation to the matter of most importance. He wanted to know if Tiras was sincere.

She tipped her head and studied Tiras, taking note of his golden eyes and his pale hair. "His gift is strange," she reflected.

"Aren't they all?" Kjell cut in acerbically.

The old woman simply smiled and nodded at the bristling captain of the king's guard. "Indeed, good man. But your gift is not simply your ability to change, Majesty," she said, directing her words to Tiras once again. He raised his brows and glanced at me.

"Your gift is your will," she said. I could attest to that. "People obey you," she continued. "They yield to your demands. Even your brother, who bows to no one, would prostrate himself before you if you asked him."

Kjell scoffed but extended his hand, palm forward, as if to keep the woman at a distance. She closed her eyes briefly and almost sniffed the air, reminding me of Boojohni, before she opened her eyes and regarded Kjell patiently.

"The gift of the Healer is the easiest to deny, especially among those who are comfortable with war and suspicious of love. There is power in you, young man," she said softly, but she let Kjell be, and let us all make what we would of her words.

Throughout the long afternoon, the Gifted arrived in small groups, as if the parade was being carefully controlled. We didn't know where they came from. We didn't ask. No gift was an exact replica of another. Each was different, each unique.

And the display was truly staggering.

The Changers and the Spinners were most eager to share. Healing was a harder gift to demonstrate, and the Tellers impossible to verify. The future hadn't happened yet, and none seemed to be able to use their words the way I did.

A man the size of a boulder, who had to stoop to enter the house, spun stones into bread and fed us all. A child spun cotton into coal with a flick of his wrist. We watched a woman spin Kjell's sword into a length of rope, and a rope into a snake. I jumped back, startled.

"It is not a real snake," the Spinner laughed.

I watched it coil around itself and raised my eyebrows in question. It certainly looked real.

"I can turn one object into another. But I cannot create life where there is no life. It is simply the appearance of life."

"What do you mean?" Tiras asked, and Sorkin explained.

"Some say that the Volgar were created when a lonely spinner attempted to turn vultures into humans. It can't be done. The Volgar may have human parts, but they don't have human hearts. They have no souls or conscience. No ability to reason or love. There is no virtue. Only instinct. They simply became a different sort of beast."

"But the vultures are living things . . . unlike the rope," Kjell interjected.

Sorkin picked up the snake, and without warning, he pulled its head off. The frayed edges of the rope stuck out from the scaly body of the snake where the head had just been.

"It cannot strike. It does not eat. It does not sleep. It does not have the instincts or the inner workings of a snake. It is a rope, animated by a touch. A man can become a beast. But a beast cannot become a man."

The room grew silent, and Tiras turned his eagle eyes on me for a heartbeat. "What makes a man a beast?" he asked quietly, addressing Sorkin but still looking at me.

"His choices."

"Not his gift?" Kjell asked bitterly.

"Not his gift," Sorkin answered. "What a man does with his gift is the true measure."

Kjell had no response and the demonstrations continued. Lu, a little girl with green eyes and inky black hair became a kitten that scampered at my feet. A troll with a long, red beard became a goat that neighed incessantly and bit everything in sight. A boy named Hazael became a horse, all coltish legs and flowing mane, and a mother of three became whatever animal she wished, morphing from one to the other at the king's request.

They could all hear me—Spinners, Changers, Healers, and Gwyn, the only other Teller in the room.

For every person who shared their gift, I shared mine as well, spinning a rhyming spell that made the dishes wash themselves, a sock darn the hole in its toe, a fire start, and a turtle fly. They clapped and marveled and begged for more, and I acquiesced, hoping it would be enough to soothe fears and build trust. But Sorkin was not deterred. At the end of the day, he made his demand of the king.

"We have shown you our abilities. Now you must show us what you can do," the old Healer demanded, his voice soft but adamant.

I do not want him to change, I protested, raising my voice so all those present could hear me. The gathered Gifted looked at me in surprise.

Every time he changes, it is harder for him to return, I explained, and shocked murmurs and unspoken questions rose in the air like dusty moths. I brushed at them, denying them and wishing them away.

"Lark," Tiras murmured, and I knew before I looked at him that my protestations were useless.

"I've given my word," Tiras said.

"Perhaps when he changes, Sorkin and I will be able to better understand why there is pain," Shenna offered, reaching out her hand to the king. Sorkin moved close as well, and Tiras bowed his head, as if receiving a blessing instead of invoking a transformation. They began to hum together—Sorkin and Shenna—but the mellow, low vibration Tiras's body had emitted earlier in the day was now a high ringing. The Healers struggled to recreate it, straining for the pitch. Shenna started to shake her head helplessly, even as she breathed into the note, strengthening it, matching it.

Then Tiras roared, throwing back his head and howling like his heart was being pulled from his chest, fighting the pull, only to be dragged away. Like millions upon millions of dust particles gathering and bursting and rearranging themselves, he disintegrated and became something else. His white hair clung to his head and neck like a silken hood, obscuring a face that suddenly ceased to exist. Then wings unfurled, even as his body melded into the air.

It was glorious and ghastly, triumphant and tragic all at once. I fought the urge to weep and throw myself into the space where he had been that I might become what he was.

Shenna and the old Healer fell back, as if they too had never seen such a thing, and Kjell opened the cottage door.

Unlike the other Changers—the kitten, the horse, the goat, and the mother who changed effortlessly—my eagle king soared up into the cerulean sky, and he did not return.

Lost.

The eagle's word made me ache.

No. Not lost. I know who you are, I pressed, stroking the feathers on his breast.

Lark.

My name rose from him, and I knew he was telling me the same. He knew who I was too. He was still Tiras, beneath it all, and that was almost worse.

"The king is asking for you, Milady," Pia announced, popping into my chamber in the early afternoon a week later. My hands froze mid-air, the book I held slipping from my fingers. "He asked that you be present for a meeting with his advisors."

He is back? I pressed, but she didn't hear me, of course, and she continued bustling around my chamber as if the king's comings and goings were of little concern to either of us. I doubted she'd even noticed he was gone.

I tidied my appearance in a rush and flew down the corridors and the main staircase to the room I loved most in the entire castle. But there were others assembled, and as I neared, I modulated my pace and pulled on my composure. I could hear the rumble of voices, and my belly flipped in anticipation.

Tiras sat in the library, his brow furrowed, poring over records and ledgers, Kjell and two other members of the guard seated in front of him. When I slipped inside he greeted me, but didn't look up. Kjell and the other men rose and bowed before dismissing me as well. I sat in my customary seat, a quill in hand, making primitive notes—wholly insufficient and childlike—as if I understood any of it. He wore riding gloves and boots that rose above his knees, as if he'd come in straight from the stables and gotten to work. No one commented on it. His presence filled the space and demanded attention, and his height and breadth made the room seem smaller and the day so much longer.

We conducted the business of the kingdom for several hours, the stream of people in and out of the library making private conversation impossible, though I occasionally sent Tiras a humorous word or a thought, a bright butterfly to catch his attention. He didn't acknowledge them, though occasionally his lips twitched and he rolled his eyes, making me believe I'd accomplished my aim.

I exercised patience as he sought advisors, received updates, and worked with all the mania of a man on borrowed time. As yet another meeting drew to a close, Tiras referred to an inspection from the day before—a trip to the kingdom's vaults and Jeru's mines—and I sat up straighter, listening even as I grew more and more confused.

When did you return? I pressed, not caring one whit that he was speaking.

Tiras didn't answer immediately, and I bridled my words, allowing him to finish his instructions to the surveyor of the mines. When his instructions became a new topic altogether, I interrupted again.

"Tiras?"

His golden eyes shot to mine then fell immediately as if the work before him demanded his absolute attention.

When did you return? I asked again.

"I returned three days ago," he addressed me directly, though those present had not heard my question. "I visited the outposts and spent time on patrol. It had to be done."

Three days?

My face and chest stung like I'd been slapped repeatedly.

He'd been Tiras for three days. Not Tiras the bird. Tiras the man. Whole. Present. And I hadn't known.

"There is much to do," he said flatly, though his eyes narrowed in warning, as if he thought I might start mentally pulling books from the library shelves and winging them at his head. The king's advisors cleared their throats as if they'd suddenly realized there was a bit of a silent showdown underway.

I swallowed, keeping my words in my chest so they wouldn't flood my head and become angry spells, but they slithered and snapped, and I stood, unable to trust myself to contain them.

The king's advisors shot to their feet, parchment and scrolls falling to the floor. I acknowledged them, just a stiff jerk of my head, and moved swiftly toward the door.

"Lark," Tiras called after me. I ignored him.

TWENTY-SIX

donned my cloak and set out at a steady pace, making my way up the hill that led to the cathedral and beyond to the cliffs that guarded Jeru City. I didn't wait for an escort. I was not a prisoner anymore. I was partially hidden beneath the large cowl of my cloak, and if anyone noticed me, they kept their distance. I kept my eyes on my feet until I reached the bell tower atop the church then stopped to catch my breath, peering up at it and waiting for the knell of the hour, signaling all was well as the sun sank beyond the horizon.

The air was cold, and the bite against my cheeks matched the raw scrape of my breath. I'd noticed that when I walked briskly, my belly tightened as if to draw my child to me, to brace against the physical demands I was making on myself. It wasn't unpleasant or painful. But it made me aware. It demanded I pay attention and not ignore the life growing in me, early as it still was. Tiras had the same effect on my heart. It tightened whenever he was away, demanding I remember, that I think about him, that I wait.

Wait for him, the old Teller had said. Her words had been prophetic. I was always waiting.

I felt Shindoh, heard his excitement, his eager happiness at having his master on his back and fresh air in his lungs. I even knew the moment he sensed me and quickened his step toward me. But I didn't turn to greet him.

"Lark," Tiras called, the words he exuded very different from his faithful horse. *Stubborn* and *woman* were the most prominent ones. I stopped walking and turned on him, not even waiting for him to get abreast of me before I responded to his not-so-private opinion.

I may be a stubborn woman, but you are an insensitive ass.

"And you are the queen. You must think like one. You must act like one. You must do your duty even when you are angry with me."

You chose me, remember? Me. Lark of Corvyn. I am not a Changer. I cannot transform into a queen.

He ground his teeth. "And where is your guard? You must have a guard when you leave the castle!"

I have no need of a guard. You are just like my father. I will not be a prisoner.

"You also have to stop wandering around at night, Lark. It isn't safe. Especially when I am not here."

I turned away and began to walk, frustrated by his imperiousness. With a snarl and a spur of his horse, he was on me, swooping me up with one arm and placing me in front of him on Shindoh, exactly as he had done a lifetime ago.

His fingers spread on my lower belly, testing the way it swelled against his palm. I tossed my head, my hood sliding down my back, and his lips found my ear as if he couldn't decide whether to nuzzle my neck or berate me. He did both, running his rough cheek against my jaw and along my throat before he spoke again.

"You aren't invisible. I know you think you are. But someone could harm you." His tone was hushed but harsh. "Why do you do that?"

What? Get angry when you return and avoid me?

He was motionless, contemplating, and I waited for him to answer.

"No," he finally whispered, and I felt his remorse drip from the word. I stared blindly ahead, refusing to blink so the angry tears would not fall.

"No, not that. Why do you walk in the forest at night, all by yourself? I see you, even as an eagle. I watch you. And I am afraid for you." His voice was suddenly so gentle that my will crumbled like the dry leaves beneath Shindoh's feet.

I know you watch me. That's why I do it. I am looking for you.

His arm tightened around me and his lips found my ear again, but he didn't speak, and his yearning covered us both, obscuring everything else.

You have told me to let you in, Tiras. Begged me. And I have. I have opened my doors wide. Yet . . . you stayed away.

He cursed and gripped my jaw in his gloved hand, turning my face toward him so I could lift my eyes to his.

"Don't you understand? I would do anything to stay here with you. I am losing myself!"

I started to shake my head, pulling on his wrist and releasing myself from his grasp. *No.*

Indecision matched his yearning before he suddenly swept both away, and with a swift jerk, yanked the thick leather glove from his left hand with his teeth, revealing what was beneath. His hand was still that of a man, but as his fingers tapered at the tips, talons jutted from the very ends. My heart climbed my throat like a caged animal, and I could only stare, transfixed.

"I can't even touch you without a glove anymore, Lark," he groaned. "I will harm you."

Without a word I smoothed my fingers over the talons that had broken through the skin. They were twice the length of his natural nails, tubular and sharp. His fingers flexed like he wanted to pull them away, but he didn't.

I raised his palm to my lips and kissed it gently. Then I glided his hand over my jaw and held it against my face, welcoming his touch.

"I am losing myself. Piece by bloody piece," he whispered. "And you have to let me go. Jeru needs a queen. Someone who is strong and wise and powerful."

That is not me.

"Of course it is. I knew it the moment I met you."

No! It isn't. I have all this power, but I can't save you.

The ice that shielded me, that made me strong, began to drip, drip, drip and stream down my face, and Tiras laid his cheek against mine, pressing my head into his shoulder and holding me tight.

You chose me because I am of use. But I chose you because I wanted you. All I ever wanted was for you to love me in return.

He froze, and when he pulled away and peered down at me, it was all I could do not to open a hole in the earth and climb into it. His eyes gleamed in the gathering twilight, and he began to shake his head, rejecting my words.

He brushed the pad of his thumb against my cheek ever-so-softly then jerked his hand away, curling his talons against his palm. Without comment, he sheathed his hand in his glove once more and spurred Shindoh forward, as if words failed him. They had failed us both.

"I need to show you something up there." Tiras pointed up the narrowing road before us that led to the jutting cliffs and shallow caves that made up the eastern perimeter of Degn. No wall was required here. Jeru City nestled at the base of the hills, sitting on a huge plateau that dropped off again beyond the western wall before descending to sea level and the settlement of Nivea on the outskirts.

I eyed the cliffs and the steepness of the path. *It will be dark soon.*

"I won't leave you . . . not yet. And Shindoh knows the way."

He did, and he climbed steadily, impervious to our weight. Within a quarter of an hour, Tiras veered off the trail at a jutting overlook. The city lay below us, the shadows muting the colors, the wintery light softening the edges and the angles. The castle turrets and towers gleamed, the green flags echoing the color of the evergreen trees that crowded the wall like faithful sentinels.

He slid off Shindoh and pulled me down with him, tethering the horse to a nearby tree and finding a seat among the rocks that peppered the overlook.

"This was my father's favorite spot," Tiras said quietly, as we gazed at the shimmering city below us.

I stiffened beside him, not wanting to talk about King Zoltev. He brushed the back of his hand against my chest, as if to soothe my heart, to apologize for bringing his father's memory to my mind. But he didn't stop.

"He would sit right here and look down over his city and vow that no one would ever take it from him. That is what he feared the most. Everyone was a threat."

So he removed anyone with any power that might prove greater than his own.

"Yes," Tiras whispered. "He did."

You fear losing Jeru as well. My words were sharper than I intended.

"Not for the reasons you think," he murmured, taking no offense. "I don't fear someone will take Jeru from me. I worry that I won't protect her."

For a moment neither of us spoke, watching the shadows lengthen and connect as the day came to an end. The castle sconces were lit, and light began to flicker from homes and watch-towers, making the city glow.

"Do you know how he died, Lark?" Tiras asked.

I realized suddenly that I didn't. King Zoltev had killed my mother, and three years later he ceased to exist. I was only eight at the time, but Boojohni had taken my hand in his and told me the king was dead, that he couldn't hurt me anymore. I'd had ongoing nightmares about him, about his sword and my mother's blood, and his death was an enormous relief to the entire keep.

I'd gone to my mother's turret, closeting myself with her things. For the first time since her death, I'd made poppets and tried to will them to dance and climb and fly. I thought with the king's death, maybe my words would come back, that I would no longer have to be silent. But my poppets had remained as still and lifeless as my mother's body on the cobblestones, and my inability to speak had persisted.

No. I don't know how he died.

"He killed himself. Right here. Kjell was with him along with several members of the guard. They said he just . . . jumped. We never found his body."

You will trade your soul and lose your son to the sky.

My mother's words rose in my mind, and I knew Tiras heard them.

"What did he trade his soul for?" he whispered. "I've never understood why he killed himself when he never felt remorse or guilt. Everything my father has done—even his death—has filled me with guilt."

How are you responsible for his death?

"I thought perhaps my gift drove him to it." Tiras swung his gaze to mine, and he didn't look away. "I have spent the last fifteen years trying to be everything he was not. A good king. A fair ruler. A just man."

You are all those things.

Tiras shook his head, disagreeing with me, our eyes still clinging in the murky light.

"I am more like my father than I thought. He wronged you, and I have wronged you. I have taken you from your home. I have used your gifts. I have taken your will and spent myself in your body. I have given you worry and fear and responsibility. I have taken. Endlessly. And you have given endlessly. I only wanted to save my country. I told myself, 'I'm doing it for Jeru.' That's what my father always said when he did something terrible."

Bile rose in my throat, the taste of rejection, and I shot to my feet. I moved away from Tiras, from the rocky ledge, needing a moment to prepare myself for what he was surely building up to. But he followed me.

"You were not supposed to love me, Lark. I did not set out to make you love me. And I was not supposed to love you. But I do. And it is terrible."

I whirled, so surprised I would have fallen if Tiras hadn't been right on my heels. He caught me and set me back on my feet, his hands gripping my shoulders, his face raw, his despair billowing around him, making the darkness ripple like water.

I laughed.

It was soundless and dry and it hurt my chest. But I laughed. I knew exactly what Tiras meant. It *was* terrible. I laughed until I felt my face change, crumpling from mirth to grief, but Tiras was relentless.

"Every second I am a bird, I long to be a man. For you. For me. For the child I was so desperate to create. Not for Jeru. For us. You said I chose you because you are of use to me. And I did. But know this, Lark." Tiras's voice broke on my name, but he didn't pause. "I have loved you every moment of every day, and I will love you until I cease to be. Bird, man, or king, I love you, and I will *always* love you."

In the quiet of our chamber, Tiras's kisses were fevered but his caresses were careful, touching me with the backs of his hands, his fingers curled away from my skin. I welcomed him, feeling the battle within us both, the need to reconnect and disconnect simultaneously. He pulled me to him even as he tried to purge me from his pores, and I memorized every line and plane and sinew, afraid that each moment might be his last. We were urgent. We were slow. We were barreling toward the finish, even as we started all over again.

Tiras seemed loathe to release me, but in the quiet space after passion was spent and our skin cooled, he rolled away. I followed immediately and gathered him to me, my eyes almost as heavy as my heart.

"Stubborn woman. Sleep." Tenderness rang in the familiar command, and a smile touched my lips before his mouth found mine again.

I couldn't sleep. I wouldn't. I didn't. I squeezed every second from the time he had left, kissing his mouth and holding him close until he began to shudder, his eyes full of pain, his body arching from the bed. He was holding on for me, and I put my hands on his chest, willing him to stay, pressing words and spells into his skin. But he was now a part of me, and I could not cure myself.

Then he was gone, bursting from the room, becoming a bird before he reached the balcony wall, soaring up and away from me like he'd never been there at all.

TWENTY-SEVEN

For a solid month, Tiras didn't come home. He didn't change. He was an eagle by day and an eagle by night. Some nights he came to me as a bird, leaving me little things, a rose, a magnificent feather, a glittering, black rock as big as my fist. Each morning there was another gift, but no Tiras.

Then he stopped coming at all, though I watched for him wherever I went. I visited the mews daily, my eyes clinging to the rafters, pretending to be interested in the irritable falcons that bristled whenever I approached. Hashim, the Master of the Mews, didn't question my sudden interest in his birds or my frequent visits, but after several days, he greeted me with a careful suggestion.

"The king must have told you about my eagle friend," he murmured, not raising his eyes from the bell he was attaching to a falcon's hood.

My heart lurched but I didn't flinch, and I watched him warily, waiting for him to continue. He glanced up briefly, and his eyes were kind.

"He has not returned, my queen, not for a very long time. I watch for him too. If he does, I will send word immediately. Never fear."

I could only nod, fearful of revealing too much about myself and about the king, wondering if Hashim had known Tiras's secret all along.

Kjell was as drawn and quiet as I, and though there was little love lost between us, we'd formed an alliance, desperate to protect the king and the kingdom, though that was getting harder and harder to do. We'd spread rumors of his travels to shore up support in the provinces, though the guards must have wondered who accompanied him on these official royal visits.

Twenty-eight days into the king's absence, a message was received by carrier pigeon from Firi. Volgar sightings were increasing in the area, and nests near the shores of the Jyraen Sea were causing general unease. The Lord of Firi wasn't asking for reinforcements, but the news added to the bleak atmosphere in the castle.

What would Tiras want me to do? I asked Kjell, pacing from one end of the library to the other. *I need him to come home.*

"There may come a day when he won't return, Lark," Kjell said quietly. "We have to face that."

He will return. He always has.

"You have to start making decisions without him," Kjell urged. "It is what he has been preparing you for."

I can't rule alone.

"He was convinced you could." It was the kindest thing Kjell had ever said to me, and when he raised his blue eyes to mine, I saw something new there. A begrudging respect, a sliver of forgiveness . . . something. For the first time, I didn't feel any disdain or dismissal.

"You have to start somewhere. There hasn't been a hearing in a month. The people are afraid, crime is rising, and altercations abound. Our dungeon is full, and the guard doesn't know what to do with those they are holding. You have to take his place. You are the queen."

Will you help me? Will you speak for me?

It was Kjell's turn to balk.

How will I render judgments if I can't speak?

Kjell groaned and fisted his hands in his hair.

Sometimes Tiras and I pretend that I am whispering in his ear. That way it doesn't look so odd when we communicate in front of others.

Kjell looked as if he regretted his insistence on a hearing day, but he agreed, the word was spread, and the following morning I walked into the Great Hall amid confusion and wonder, chatter and whispers. I sat on the throne, and the guard, already briefed by Kjell, began to organize the line of hesitant subjects, who looked as dubious as I felt.

And it began.

One by one, the people approached, quickly stated their case, and a judgment was made. I listened more to what they weren't saying, just like I'd done before, terrified that I would make the wrong choice. Kjell would lean in, I would cup my hand over my mouth, pretending to speak privately, though my lips never moved, and I would tell him my judgment. He would repeat my verdict and we would move onto the next case. He never questioned me or raised a condescending eyebrow.

I grew more confident as the day progressed, relying almost entirely on my ability to hear what others couldn't. When I was unsure, I asked Kjell for guidance, and he would make a suggestion. But that happened less and less as the day wore on.

Toward the end of the day, a man came forward and laid a large satchel at the foot of the dais.

"Tell the queen your trouble," Kjell commanded impatiently.

"I caught a Changer," the man exclaimed excitedly. "I hunt them . . . for the good of Jeru, of course."

"Show me," Kjell commanded, sounding exactly like Tiras, and I heard the same apprehension in his voice that gripped my chest.

The man opened his satchel and pulled out a huge black bird with a glossy white head. He laid it out carefully and stepped back, puffing his chest and standing akimbo like he'd presented me with a chest of jewels.

The bird was limp and lifeless.

I rose from my throne, overcome with dread, and Kjell hissed beside me, telling the hunter to back away. I knelt beside the bird and raised his red-tipped wing. I started to shake, my vision blurring as Kjell pulled me away. The feathers were still warm, and bile rose dangerously in my throat. I collapsed in my throne, unable to stand.

"How do you know it was a Changer?" Kjell asked, his voice so cold the man shivered where he stood, sensing his offering had not been well-received.

"I saw her change," the man babbled. My heart stuttered and skipped, and guilt warred with the sliver of hope that made me ask, *Her?*

"Her?" Kjell repeated.

"She was a woman one moment . . . then she changed. She flew away. I set a snare . . . and I caught her when she returned."

"And you killed her?" Kjell asked.

"She is a Changer," the man repeated, as if that were explanation enough. I rose to my feet once more, outrage giving me mettle, and the man must have seen something in my face that alarmed him, for he began to back up.

"I didn't mean to kill it. It was alive in my snare. I covered it in the shroud and put it in the sack. There must not have been sufficient air."

The law says only the king can condemn the Gifted.

Kjell repeated what I'd said, and the man began to tremble.

"But . . . King Zoltev—" he stammered.

"Is no longer the king," Kjell finished. He turned and approached my throne so that I could pretend to confer with him.

He has lost the right to hunt. If he is caught hunting, he will be executed. Killing eagles—Changers or not—in Jeru is now prohibited. Let it be written, let it be done.

Kjell repeated my judgment.

"But . . . how will I live?" the man wailed.

Tell him he may trap rodents and snakes. Each week he may present his kill to Mistress Lorena in the courtyard of the castle, and she will pay him for his services to Jeru.

The man accepted the judgement with wide eyes and made to take the eagle.

Tell him to leave the bird.

Kjell did as I asked.

I want to know where he killed her.

"There's a cottage in the western wood, not far from the perimeter wall. She was there," the man answered Kjell without hesitation, eager to redeem himself.

My heart ceased beating once again.

When I couldn't continue with the hearings, Kjell told those waiting in the long line that we would resume first thing in the morning. I waited—sitting motionless on my throne—until the hall cleared and the guard moved to their exterior posts. Kjell waited with me, standing over the bird, his hands clenched and his eyes wet.

"I don't know what to do," he confessed. "I don't know what is right or wrong anymore. And I'm afraid I'll never see my brother again."

I went looking for Tiras. It wasn't the first time in the last twenty-eight days. I'd disregarded the king's wishes repeatedly, walking through the forest with Boojohni trundling behind me when I couldn't escape him. He had stayed close, sensitive to my emotions and to the ever-increasing absences of the king. But I had magic on my side, and that night I slipped away unnoticed.

I walked to the cottage in the western wood, the one where Tiras had shared his secret, the cottage so perfectly described by the huntsman. No eagle swooped down to greet me, to give me words and point me toward home, but there were signs that someone had been in the cottage. A dish, a comb, firewood on the hearth.

None of the items had been there before. I touched the comb in confusion and turned toward the bed where I'd spent a miserable night after escaping the castle, wondering where I would go and what I would do. Someone had slept in the bed since. The bed was not made. Had Tiras changed and simply stayed away? Had his Gift taken yet another piece of him, a piece that made him believe he could no longer return to the castle?

I slumped down on the bed, so weary I could no longer stand.

Tiras? I called. *Tiras, please don't hide from me.*

The shutters on the cottage banged against the stone, lifted by the wind, and I listened for an answering voice, a heartbeat, a flutter of wings, but heard nothing but my own trepidation. I bowed my head in dejection, my gaze falling to the hard-packed dirt floor.

A bit of white lace protruded from under the bed.

I leaned down and grasped it, only to find it caught on something heavy. Kneeling, I peered beneath the old frame and saw a valise, tipped on its side, garments spilling from the top. I tugged it out to examine it more closely, and fingered the lace in bewilderment, pulling it free from the valise. The lace was attached to the neckline of a voluminous gown, its light color indistinguishable in the darkness. A pair of dainty shoes, a size larger than my own, silk underthings, and another gown were folded beneath it, along with a fine, scarlet cloak.

Someone had made themselves at home in the king's cottage, but it was not Tiras.

I exhaled in painful relief, still shaking my head in bewilderment. I didn't know what to make of it, but I knew one thing. A woman had been there. A Changer. And now she was dead.

The bird the huntsman had presented to me the previous day had been removed from the Great Hall when I returned the next morning. The floors gleamed, and the room had been aired, and I mourned again over the bird that wasn't really a bird. Kjell was at my side again, my mouthpiece, and I resolved to question him over its whereabouts when the hearings were over. I doubted I would tell him about my discovery at the cottage; my late night wanderings would earn me an around-the-clock guard.

I greeted the line that had already formed with a tip of my head and a crook of my wrist, beckoning the first subjects to come forward. The guards kept things moving along in an orderly fashion and kept a measure of security between me and those who left the hearing unhappily or in chains. As the day wore on and the judgments commenced, one after the other, a murmur suddenly rippled through the crowd and a cry went up.

The guards immediately moved in front of me, concerned that a squabble had broken out in the line, or someone had grown violent. I felt his name swell from the throng, as if he'd suddenly become the focus of every thought. *King Tiras. King Tiras.* I stood, desperate to see over the guard that had closed ranks in front of my throne. Kjell rose with me, parting the guard and descending the dais with his hand on the hilt of his sword.

"Step back. Move back!" Kjell ordered, and I stretched to peer beyond the wall of protection around me. Then I heard his name again, spoken with exuberance and welcome by the men who stood between us.

"The king is returned! King Tiras is back!"

I don't remember standing or leaving the dais. I only knew I was moving through the crowd as Kjell and the guards I pushed past sought to create a path for me, their arms outstretched on either side to hold back the swell. But the crowd parted easily and without hesitation, a wave of deferential bows and bobs opening the way before me.

Then I saw him, standing at the rear of the hall, a full head taller than almost everyone around him, though those nearest him had fallen to one knee, baring him to my view. He was dressed for judgment day, except for the long black gauntlets that covered his hands and forearms, making him look like the warrior kings he'd descended from. A crown adorned his white head, and a cape of royal green swung around his shoulders. His mouth was unsmiling but his eyes clung to mine, warm and amber, and as familiar and welcome as my own heartbeat. Then I was running, my feet flying, and I was in his arms.

"You are not acting like a queen," he scolded as he lifted me off my feet and buried his face in my hair. "The people will think me soft." I couldn't answer, couldn't form words at all, and clung to him as he embraced me in return.

Without loosening his arms, he raised his face from my neck and dismissed the entire gathering with a simple, "Go now and do no harm."

No one muttered—or even thought—a word of complaint.

TWENTY-EIGHT

We had little time to celebrate or rejoice.

Late in the night, boots sounded in the corridor, and Kjell pounded on our chamber door.

"Tiras. We've a visitor. Come quickly."

We rose and dressed without question, rushing to the center courtyard where torches were blazing, making the shadows dance and climb, reaching toward the parapets that gaped like huge teeth above us. The captain of the watch had just begun briefing Kjell on the situation.

"She was at the city gates, demanding entrance. She says she's Lady Ariel of Firi. She's on foot, and she's by herself," the watch captain explained.

Kjell cursed and began striding for the gate that separated the inner bailey from the outer bailey.

"Where is she now?" Tiras demanded.

"The watchman told her she would have to wait until dawn, Majesty. Those are his orders."

"She's still outside the gates?" Kjell roared, spinning back toward the watchman.

"No, sir," the captain of the watch hurried to explain. "He woke me, afraid that she might actually be a noblewoman. I sent guards over the wall to see that it wasn't a trap. She was alone, sir. We lowered the gate, and she is being brought to the castle."

As if on cue, a trumpet sounded, and we rushed through the gates to the lower courtyard, watching as the portcullis was slowly raised. Two guards proceeded her entrance, then Lady Ariel of Firi took several weary steps and collapsed to her knees. Her hair hung in matted rows, coated with dust and trailing down a crimson cloak that was torn and splattered with gore. I recognized the scent that clung to her, the streaks of green and black that sullied the pale dress that showed beneath her cloak. Not human blood. Volgar. She clutched a dagger as if she'd gone to battle herself and barely survived.

Kjell was at her side immediately, swooping her up in his arms. Her dagger fell to the cobblestones, the clatter making her jerk. When Kjell didn't stoop to retrieve it, she reached for it desperately, as if an attack was forthcoming and she wanted to be prepared.

"Ariel. You're safe. Be still," he soothed, and her head bobbed against his shoulder, and her arms went limp in relief.

"There were so many," she whimpered. "The Volgar . . . there were so many."

"Are you alone?" Tiras asked, alarmed. "Where is your guard?"

"Scattered. Dead." Her head bobbed again, and her eyelids fluttered.

"Firi is three days away, on horseback. Did you come by yourself?" Tiras pressed.

She's exhausted, Tiras.

Tiras nodded, agreeing with me, but his brow was furrowed and his mouth drawn into a tight line.

"Take her inside, Kjell. Questions can come later, when she's had food and rest."

Lady Firi refused to sleep but allowed the maids to attend to her, washing and dressing her in borrowed robes before sitting her down to a pre-dawn supper at the king's table. After a stiff draught for warmth and courage, she told us what had brought her to Jeru City under such conditions.

"My father is ill. I don't know how much his heart can take. When we started getting word of Volgar along the seashore, he demanded I come here. He wanted me far away from any conflict, and I could not sway him."

"We received word of sightings from your father a few days ago," Kjell said, and Lady Firi nodded emphatically, looking between Kjell and the king as she continued.

"I started out with members of my father's guard, but we were attacked late on the second day. It was as if they followed us." She paused in the retelling, her hand trembling as she pressed it to her lips, and I remembered the journey from Corvyn to Jeru when I'd seen a birdman for the first time, leathery skin and enormous wings, plucking grown-men from their horses.

"We couldn't defend against them. They just kept dropping from the sky. My horse bolted into the trees. I kept going, afraid at what I would find if I went back."

"What happened to your horse?" Tiras questioned gently.

"He ran and he kept running. He was terrified," she whispered. "When he finally stopped, he wouldn't get up again. He was foaming at the mouth, and there was blood on his chest. He was injured in the attack, but I didn't know . . ."

"And you walked the rest of the way," Kjell finished for her.

"Yes." She raised piteous eyes to Kjell's, dark and luminous and so beautiful, my own breath caught. Kjell sighed and looked at Tiras.

"What are we going to do?"

You and I will go, I said, turning to Tiras. *Kjell should stay here with Lady Firi. Someone has to stay.*

"I'm the captain of the bloody guard, Lark!" Kjell inserted, tension radiating from every pore. Tiras shot a warning look at him, and Kjell threw up his hands and stalked from the room without another word.

Lady Firi watched him go with knowing eyes and stood as if to follow him.

"You must rest, Lady Firi. We will decide what should be done on the morrow," Tiras murmured, rising and extending a hand to me. "Mistress Lorena will see you to your quarters."

"King Tiras, have you ever acknowledged Kjell as your brother?" Lady Firi asked sharply, her brazen query making my eyes widen. She curtsied deeply, her head lowered, "Forgive me, Your Highness," she implored, her voice thick with remorse. "I am not myself after the events of the last days, and I care very deeply for Kjell. I spoke without thought."

Tiras regarded her thoughtfully, his mouth pursed, but I was not fooled. Her impudence bothered him. Her question bothered him more.

"I understand," he murmured, pardoning her. "Rest well."

But Lady Firi was not quite finished. With soft entreaty, she raised her hands and her gaze to mine.

"Majesty, please don't travel to Firi. If something were to happen to you or the child, I would not forgive myself," she said.

My hand found the slight swell beneath my gown, surprised that she knew. It was not visibly apparent. Perhaps word of my occasional morning sickness had started rumors among the servants. Perhaps they had let something slip to Lady Firi when they attended her.

She smiled at me kindly. "You have the look about you, my queen."

I inclined my head, not confirming or denying, and Tiras bowed slightly.

"All things will be considered. Goodnight, Milady." Tiras's voice was cold, and she heard his displeasure.

Mistress Lorena stepped forward and bid Lady Firi follow her. We were silent as we watched her retreat, and when their footsteps faded, I turned to him.

If something were to happen to me, and therefore my father, who would be next in line for the throne?

"If there is no Degn and no Corvyn—" Tiras began.

But there is a Degn, Tiras. Kjell is a Degn.

"Yes. He is. But Kjell was never recognized by my father. He is Kjell of Jeru. Not Kjell of Degn," Tiras explained.

But what if he is recognized by you? If you claim him as your brother?

"Kjell does not wish to be king. Despite what Lady Firi insinuated."

It matters little what we want, I quoted, remembering the words Tiras had said to me after the battle with the Volgar.

Tiras regarded me soberly, his mouth turned down.

If you recognize Kjell, then if something were to happen to me . . . and our child . . . Kjell would be the heir to the throne. One more layer of protection for Jeru.

"Yes. And Kjell would never forgive me."

I forgave you.

"Without desire, there is only duty," Tiras whispered, quoting me as I quoted him. "But sometimes our greatest desire is to do our duty." Then he closed his eyes, as if offering up a prayer for strength, though I heard only his yearning, and it made my heart tremble.

Tiras spent the following day closeted with maps and men, their hushed words wafting out from behind closed doors, words I could have easily drawn to me if I'd wanted to. I didn't. I'd awoken with a lurching stomach and a pounding head, and I kept to my chamber with dry toast, peppermint tea, and Boojohni to comfort me. I laid across my bed, my hair streaming over the side, and he brushed my locks gently, as if he'd been a lady's maid in another life and an exceptionally good one.

He was full of kitchen gossip, and I listened drowsily, floating in his affection, allowing myself to be coddled. When he ran out of juicy natter, he started to hum, and I joined in, allowing the voice in my head to lilt along with his.

Daughter, daughter, Jeru's daughter,
He is coming, do not hide.
Daughter, daughter, Jeru's daughter,
Let the king make you his bride.

Daughter, daughter, Jeru's daughter,
Wait for him, his heart is true.
Daughter, daughter, Jeru's daughter,
'Til the hour he comes for you.

Boojohni stopped suddenly, his brush stalling in my hair as if he'd found a knot. When he didn't continue singing or brushing after an inordinate amount of time, I opened my eyes and lifted my head. He was staring sightlessly at the silvery tumble of my hair, seeing something that wasn't there.

Boojohni? I prodded. What's wrong?

"Have you ever thought maybe it wasn't a curse, Bird, but a prophecy?" he said oddly, refocusing his gaze on mine.

What are you talking about?

"The day yer mother died. The words she told ye. The words she told yer father."

I swallowed, the memory making my throat close the way it always did.

"Maybe yer mother wasn't forbidding ye to speak," Boojohni hedged. "Perhaps she was just tellin' yer father ye wouldn't and tellin' him to protect ye. To keep ye safe."

I stared at him, dumbfounded.

"Meshara couldn't do what ye do, Lark. Her gift was different. Her gift was one of knowing, of seeing, of *warning*. Ye are the one who can command."

I shook my head, not understanding, but Boojohni only grew more adamant.

"That song . . . the maiden song. Yer mother used to sing it to ye. It reminded me of her, of the things she knew. The things she *knew*, Lark!" he repeated emphatically.

My mother was not the first to sing the maiden song, Boojohni. I felt dizzy again. I didn't want to talk about my mother or the day she died.

"No. That's not what I'm tellin' ye. The song just opened me eyes."

I waited, knowing he would explain.

"I heard the words yer mother spoke that terrible day. I was afraid the king would strike her again. I threw me-self over her." Boojohni's voice grew high pitched with suppressed grief, and emotion swelled in my chest.

"Do you remember what she said, Bird?"

She told me not to speak. Not to tell.

"Yes," he whispered, nodding. "She did. She knew your gift was dangerous. She told ye to wait until the hour was right."

When will the hour be right?

"Yer using yer gift now, Bird."

Then why can't I speak?

"Maybe ye . . . can." Boojohni was almost pleading with me, and I could only gaze at him in disbelief.

"Ye were a wee child. Ye saw something terrible."

I began to shake my head, but he didn't stop.

"Ye blamed yerself. Ye became afraid of yer words."

No! I can't speak, Boojohni. Don't you think I've tried? I can't speak!

"Shh, Bird!" he said, wincing and patting my cheek. "There, there. Yer gonna make my head explode."

I was going to make my own head explode. I laid it back down gingerly, focusing on slow, deep breaths, and after a moment, Boojohni resumed his gentle strokes with the brush, as if the conversation were over. I was too nauseated to pursue it, too troubled to dwell on it, and regardless of what Boojohni suggested, I still couldn't speak.

He started to hum again, but this time I didn't join him, letting the melody drift around me. Before long my stomach settled, and my drowsiness returned.

"What word did ye give the prince that day, Lark? I've always wanted to know," he muttered.

I was sure I hadn't heard him right, sure it was just the pull of dreamy sleep, but in my mind a memory swelled and kissed the backs of my lids, a memory of an enormous horse and a black-haired, dark-eyed prince.

TWENTY-NINE

I awoke to a different set of hands in my hair, hands that caressed with careful strokes and eyes that reminded me that time was fleeting.

"I should have let you sleep, but I missed you," Tiras whispered, apology written all over his face. I would have smiled at his sweet remorse, but he looked so desolate I reached for him instead, pulling his mouth to mine and relaxing his bleak expression with soft kisses. He returned them eagerly, and for a time we lost ourselves in the desperate reacquaintance of our mouths.

"There is much to do," he whispered finally, and I sighed against his lips, hating those words, hating even more that I could feel his anguish and his desire to remain exactly where he was, with me, lying in our shadowy chamber, hiding from everything but each other. There was much to do, and my king did not want to do it. Yet he did, and it was one of the reasons I loved him so desperately.

If there is much to do, then we must do it.

He pressed his forehead to mine, and his gratitude and relief billowed around me, making my eyes prick with tears.

"Thank you," he whispered.

When do we leave for Firi?

He stilled, raising his head slowly. His relief became trepidation once more.

"I cannot take you to Firi, Lark. I will not take you into battle again."

Tiras, you know you must.

"I won't," he shot back, adamant. "Do you really believe I would take you to Firi to face the Volgar? That I would let Lady Firi huddle in my castle whilst I sent my wife into battle?"

Yes.

"No, Lark."

We dressed for dinner in silence, and when we descended the stairs toward the Great Hall, he held me back and drew me close for the space of a heartbeat before letting me go again.

Kjell was waiting for us, pacing restlessly, and when we entered the hall and Tiras pulled the heavy doors closed behind us, Kjell glowered and folded his arms across his chest.

"What is the plan, Tiras? Firi is under attack, and we dress for dinner? We sleep yet another night in our own beds?"

"Quiet, brother," Tiras said without heat, and Kjell sighed heavily.

"I will go," Kjell said. "I will take two hundred of my best men. The Volgar cannot have recovered their numbers in so short a time. We will secure Lord Firi's fortress and gather what information we can on the Volgar's numbers. We will burn nests and destroy eggs. And you will stay in Jeru City with the queen. It makes the most sense," Kjell summarized neatly.

"I am going with you," Tiras said, and Kjell's eyebrows shot up in surprise. He eyed me speculatively then searched his brother's face once more.

"What if you don't come back?" Kjell asked softly. Tiras closed his eyes and bowed his head, as if searching for the courage to continue. Dread coated my hands in perspiration. When he opened his eyes, they were as blank and hard as gold coins.

"Tonight I will acknowledge you as my brother," he said to Kjell. "I will claim you. You will be Kjell of Degn, and as my brother, you will be in line for the throne."

There was a moment of blaring silence. Then Kjell began shaking his head, and he took a step back.

"I don't want to be king, Tiras. I won't do it."

"It is not about what we want, Kjell," Tiras exploded, his calm sizzling in the face of his desperation. "Bloody hell! Save us all from our desires! None of us here can have what we want. None of us! This is about the future of Jeru. Do you want Corvyn or Bin Dar or Gaul to get their bloody hands on the throne?"

"I don't care," Kjell snarled. "I have *never* cared. My loyalty is to you, brother."

"And my loyalty is to Jeru. I have sworn an oath to protect her. I can't protect you or Lark if I don't protect Jeru. I can't protect my child if I don't protect Jeru. Don't you understand?"

"You don't have to atone for your father's sins," Kjell said, pointing a shaking finger at his brother.

"Yes, I do!" Tiras answered. "Since I was thirteen years old my life has been about nothing but atonement."

"So you married a Teller. Put a child in her belly. Outmaneuvered Corvyn. And now you want to position me in the wings?" Kjell raged. His eyes shot to mine, and I read the apology even as I flinched, scalded by his fury.

"I don't want you in the wings. I want you at the helm. You and I will go to Firi to fight the Volgar. And I will meet my end," Tiras said evenly. "It is time."

Kjell and I both stared back at him in horror.

"What are you planning, brother?" Kjell gasped.

"I can't continue to disappear and reappear. You've said it yourself. The people will lose faith in me, and eventually— sooner rather than later if my hands are any indication—I am going to change and never come back again. What then?"

"Your queen will rule, just as you intended. And when your child is of age, he or she will rule," Kjell retorted.

"I have left Lark unprotected. I have left her vulnerable," Tiras said.

I began to shake my head. No. No. No. This is not what I'd intended at all.

"She can protect herself, Tiras. She brought down the Volgar with mere words," Kjell argued.

"She has no voice. You will give her one. And you will give her the protection of your presence. You will give my child a father."

"I don't understand you."

"You will be king. And she will be queen." Tiras didn't even look at me. My legs became liquid and my belly floated away. I wrapped my arms around the small mound of my abdomen, sheltering the life that grew in me, even as Tiras was being ripped from me.

"No. I won't," Kjell whispered, incredulous. "You can't do this, Tiras. You can't manipulate and maneuver and *will* me to comply."

My voice felt heavy and black, and it pulsed behind my eyes. *I have bowed to your will over and over again, Tiras. But I will not be passed to your brother like an inheritance. I am going to Firi.*

"No Lark. You aren't. Kjell and I will go."

We will all go! I've faced the Volgar. I will do it again.

"That was before."

Before what? Before you accomplished all your designs? The words sparked furiously in my head. *You need me.*

"Jeru needs you more. Our child needs you more! And it is not safe. You aren't a sword. You aren't a weapon. Remember? What if something happens to Kjell, and I'm a bloody bird? Will you lead the men into battle alone? You will stay here, and you will do as I say!" He was so adamant. So sure. So cold and hard. Telling me what to do. But I was a Teller. And I would not be told.

I flung out my arms angrily, splaying my fingers in time with the words that shrieked through my head.

Winds outside this castle come,
Sweep away the king's own throne.

The windows suddenly shrieked and shattered in the Great Hall, and wailing gusts filled the space, whipping my skirts and tangling in my hair. Tiras's throne toppled and crashed against the gleaming, black floor before flying across the space and smashing into the far wall, burying its two rear legs in the colorful fresco of Jeru's history.

"Lark! Enough!" Tiras bellowed, but I was far from finished. My agony howled in my chest like the winds I'd summoned, and the tears I rarely released flooded my throat and filled my head. I called down the water from the skies to wash them away.

Rain that gathers in the clouds,
Wrap me in your velvet shroud.

I was caught in a torrent, spun up like a sea God, and the tears from my eyes merged with the rain soaking my skin and drenching my robes. I was floating without sinking, without drowning, without being submerged at all. Even the walls wept, paint dripping in long sorrowful streaks, destroying what once was.

"Lark!" I heard Tiras again, only this time his arms coiled around me, anchors in the storm, and his lips were on mine, warm and insistent, coaxing the war from my words.

"Be still," he urged, and the shape of the plea made his mouth a weapon.

You cannot give me away!

"Forgive me," he entreated.

"By the gods, Lark!" Kjell shouted, his voice whipping in the gale. "Stop!"

I'd forgotten where I was. I'd forgotten *who* I was.

Wind and water, glass and tears
Leave us now, disappear.

All at once the room was still. Tranquil. Almost remorseful. But I was not.

The only sound in my head was my own ragged inhalations. My breath burned in my chest as if I'd run a great distance, chasing what I could never quite reach. I didn't raise my head. I didn't need to see my handiwork or survey the damage. Tiras was as silent and motionless as the air around us, his hands cradling my head, his mouth still pressed to the whorl of my ear. His clothing clung to his chest, and I could see the warmth of his skin through the fabric made sheer by water.

"For once I agree with the queen," Kjell muttered, and without another word he strode from the hall, his boots squelching with every step. The great oak doors moaned, opening then closing behind him, and I heard him reassuring a servant—or many—in the corridors beyond.

You cannot give me away, Tiras.

"I cannot keep you," he whispered, his voice as tortured as my breaths. "And I can't continue doing this to you."

My hands rose and fisted in his shirt, wanting to hurt him and heal him simultaneously. My nails scored his skin but he held me fiercely, his arms almost constricting, for the space of several heartbeats, pressing his mouth into my hair, and I beat my hands against his back, furious and heartbroken, even as I burrowed my face in his throat.

If you cannot keep me, let me go.

I felt his heart pounding against my cheek, but his arms fell to his sides, and he stepped back, as if he were truly mine to command.

"Where? Where do you want to go?" he asked, his voice so heavy I longed to call the wind again to lift us up and carry us away.

Wherever you are.

"I can't do that either," he whispered. "Where I'm going, you cannot follow."

I wanted to rage, to compel, to call down heaven and summon hell. But though the words trembled on my lips, I could not release them. I couldn't weave the spell that would give us a future or change the past.

Promise me you will remember and obey, my mother had whispered so long ago. *Promise me you will remember.*

I remembered.

I remembered the way the king's sword sliced the air. I remembered the heat of my mother's blood seeping through my dress. I remembered the words she pressed into my ear. I had never forgotten.

Swallow daughter, pull them in. Silence daughter, stay alive.

I took a step back from Tiras, then another, making myself let him go. He was right. He could not keep me. I could not keep him. My sopping dress wrapped around my limbs, slowing me, but I gathered it up in shaking hands and turned away from the king. I left him there, standing in the center of the Great Hall, the history of his kingdom streaming from the walls and puddling around him. It was a history I would do anything to forget.

At sundown, trumpets pierced the air, and the people stepped out of their homes and leaned out of upstairs windows, listening as the castle crier began to wail from atop the tower beside the castle gates.

"His Majesty, King Tiras of Jeru and Lord of Degn, has claimed the honorable Kjell of Jeru, Captain of the King's Guard and son of the late King Zoltev of Degn and Miriam of Jeru, as his brother in blood as well as in arms, from this day forward, henceforth and forever. What the king has sworn let no man dispute. What blood has joined let no man destroy."

I watched as Kjell assembled the king's guard—a thousand men—leaving two hundred behind to guard the castle and the city wall in his absence. Tiras was not with them, though Kjell had saddled Shindoh and kept her tethered to his own mount. I hadn't seen him since I'd left him in the hall. I hadn't said goodbye, he hadn't found me in the dark to press sorrowful kisses into my skin, and we hadn't bridged the gulf between what we wanted and what we had.

Lady Firi and I watched, side by side, until the gates were lifted, and we were the only two left in the courtyard.

"The king was not with them," she remarked curiously. Carefully. And I answered without hesitation.

He left at dawn with a dozen men. A scouting party. They will double back in shifts.

She nodded, accepting my explanation, and I wondered, not for the first time, if lying changed the way my voice sounded in her head.

"God-speed," she whispered, her eyes on the trail of dust that followed the warriors beyond the wall. The castle stood on a rise, and we could see beyond the wall of Jeru City into the land of Degn. The army would head north to Kilmorda and veer west toward Firi, just beyond the cluster of hills on the border.

A cry pierced the air, and an eagle swooped overhead, perching on the castle wall. He spread his wings, posturing, the blood-red tips of his feathers vivid in the sunshine. Light, both blinding and warm, beat down on our heads like hope and redemption, yet the king was still a bird.

I would not speak his name, even in my head, for fear Lady Ariel would hear. So I gazed up at him, refusing to blink, my eyes burning and my hands cold.

Lark.

I felt my name drift across the way and land on my chest, a feather from his breast, warm and soft. *Mine*, he said. Another feather.

Always, I answered. *Always.*

Lady Firi reached for my hand, as if my *always* were just a simple *amen* to her prayer of *God speed*, but I didn't let her take it. I needed both hands to hold the pieces of myself together.

Then Tiras flew, a swath of black against the blue, creating a hole in the sky that urged me to follow or fall in. Then I was. Falling, falling, falling.

"Highness?" Lady Firi asked, her voice a peal of distant bells ringing in alarm. The hole Tiras made became deep and black, without a sliver of blue, and I let it swallow me, pulling me down, down, down, to where my words lived.

THIRTY

or three days I existed in that hole. There was little sound, little light, and no warmth. I moved through my duties without knowing what I did. I slept without dreaming. I ate without remembering what I consumed. Boojohni slept on the floor by my bed, though I insisted he leave. He just looked at me with sympathy and made himself a nest of sorts. We didn't converse. Not because he didn't try, but because I struggled to find my words in all that black space. It took all my strength to keep my eyes from closing and the darkness from absorbing me. I had no hope. I felt no joy. I saw no future that didn't fill me with anguish, so I didn't think at all. I didn't make words or cast spells. I just was. And that was all I could manage.

On the morning of the fourth day, The Master of the Mews asked for an audience in the Great Hall. He bowed deeply, dropping on one knee, and for a long moment, he didn't raise his head.

I touched the arm of the guard who attended me, who then prodded Hashim to proceed.

"Sir?" he inquired. "Are you unwell?"

"We received word from Firi, my queen." Hashim's face was pale, and his hands trembled, making the small piece of parchment he clutched vibrate. He stood and extended it toward me. I didn't take it. I couldn't. His hand fell back to his side in surrender, and his shoulders collapsed.

"The message was brought by a carrier bird," Hashim whispered. "The king . . . is . . . dead."

The guards at my side gasped. I did not react at all. I sat with my hands in my lap, my face frozen, my heart silent, my mind as black as the hole I couldn't escape.

"I'm sure there will be an official messenger, and his body will be escorted back to Jeru City. I will relay any further communications I receive," Hashim said feebly. I reached out a hand to him, numbly, automatically. He took it, and I inclined my head, eerily poised, thanking him for his terrible words.

"Majesty?" A guard asked hesitantly. "What do . . . we do?"

"Do you have anyone who can speak for you, Majesty?" Hashim asked kindly. I wanted to reveal myself, to ask him if *he* would be my voice, but I hesitated, emptied of hope, not daring to trust. I reached for the bound book of blank parchment and the ink and quill I'd begun to keep on a small table near my throne. With hands that felt like a stranger's, I asked for the only person who might be able to assist me. Someone who already knew my secret.

I wrote her name on the page, my shaking hand leaving behind ill-formed letters and splotches of ink.

Get Lady Firi.

"We will send word to the Council of Lords," Lady Firi advised. Her manner was as closed as mine, her expressions unreadable.

If she felt surprise or grief, it did not show. I made no judgement—behind my own walls was scorched earth. We'd retired to the library and I sat at the king's desk, surrounded by his possessions but none of his confidence.

"The crier will make the announcement at sunset, and the city will begin Penthos, the period of mourning," Lady Firi continued.

I nodded dully and met the eyes of my personal guard, who had suddenly taken on the role of royal spokesperson and official messenger.

"I will make sure it is done. Shall I inform the king's advisors as well?" he inquired. I nodded again, resisting the helplessness that rose like smoke from my chest. Tiras had been so desperate to prepare me to be queen, but I was not equipped for this.

When the guard left the library, Lady Firi pulled up a chair and sat across the desk from me, her movements brisk, her tone measured.

"The lords will come to Jeru City, Majesty," Lady Firi warned. "They will seek to have you set aside. They will declare you unfit. You must consider how to proceed."

I had no immediate response, and she stared at me with guarded eyes, waiting. Knowing. My heart was a great mass of Jeruvian ore, black and solid, and so heavy my shoulders wanted to buckle, and my body wanted to slump, letting the weight of the rock pull me face first into the floor.

Kjell.

It was all I could think of, but Lady Firi nodded.

"The Lords may wait for the king to be laid to rest. But if the battle in Firi continues and Kjell is unable to accompany the king's body back to Jeru City, the funeral must take place without Kjell. There are precedents and rituals that must be followed."

There wouldn't be a body. Tiras was gone, but he wasn't dead. I had to believe that.

And if he doesn't . . . return?

Lady Firi eyed me sharply. "Kjell?"

I hadn't been talking about Kjell, but I nodded anyway, her suggestion turning my stony heart to molten fear. What if neither of them returned?

"Then you will have some decisions to make. Do you want to be queen?" she asked softly. "You are carrying the heir, but . . . perhaps the wisest thing to do is to let the lords have their way."

And what might that be? What do the lords want?

"Control. Power." She shrugged. "And Tiras has not been especially malleable."

If I am found unfit . . . who will replace me?

"The council might name your father regent. You would still be queen, but he would be the true ruler. Your child would still be heir when it comes of age. If it lives that long. Of course, you could take another husband . . . someone who could provide a buffer and a . . . voice." She spoke gently, but I heard a whisper of mockery, of doubt, escape her thoughts. I didn't know if the scorn was aimed at me or at the constraints placed on all women in Jeru.

What would you do, Lady Firi?

Her eyebrows rose in surprise. "Me?" She laughed and shook her head, but her eyes gleamed, and her mouth tightened briefly. When her eyes met mine again, they were flat and hard.

"I would resist them. Wait. Stall. And when the time is right . . . make your move."

When the trumpets sounded at sundown, I returned to my chambers and huddled in the king's wardrobe, pulling his clothes around me, drawing his scent into my lungs and holding him there. But the words still found me, and for two hours the royal crier threw his announcement into the sky, declaring the king's death to the citizens of Jeru.

"His Majesty, King Tiras of Jeru and Lord of Degn, is dead. King Tiras was mighty in battle and strong in both spirit and body. He was righteous and just. Jeru weeps and Degn mourns. Our lady queen has declared Penthos upon the city for seven days. In this time of mourning, there will be silence on the streets of Jeru. Citizens will return to your homes each day at sundown and there remain until sunrise," the crier bellowed. "On the seventh day, the king will be raised up, that all may publicly mourn his passing. May the God of Words and Creation welcome his soul and protect our lands."

As my father's keep in Corvyn was the closest lordship to Jeru City, he was the first lord to arrive at the castle. I received him in the library, poised, expressionless, and filled with dread. He strode in, cape flying, hands wringing, eyes conspiring. He didn't sit in the chair across the desk but waited for my guard to step outside and close the heavy door. I didn't fear for myself in my father's presence. My mother had given me that much.

"They will seek to kill you, Daughter," he said without preamble. He didn't specify who "they" were, but I knew. I indicated the chair with an open palm and waited until he tossed himself into it with restless elegance, sweeping his cape to the side so he wouldn't wrinkle it.

I knew he couldn't hear my voice, so I made no attempt to speak. Instead I scratched out a primitive message and placed it in front of him. It was odd to be communicating at all. He had

always treated me like an ugly but priceless heirloom—
something to be kept, preserved, and hidden in a corner.

I die, you die.

He read it and pushed it aside. "The council does not know.
They are disdainful of the Gifted. They would not believe
Meshara's prophecy, and if they did believe, the knowledge may
not deter them."

I despised my weakness in writing, my childish letters and
my simple words, but it was all I had. I used the paper once
more.

I am with child.

He stared at me with growing horror. "All the more reason
for them to kill you," he gasped. His thoughts screamed, "Stupid
girl. Stupid, stupid girl."

**Kjell of Jeru, the king's brother, is next in line for the
throne,** I wrote, my hand shaking, my eyes burning. It took me
so long to form the sentence that my father grew impatient and
yanked the paper from beneath the quill the moment I finished.

He read my words and scoffed. "I know nothing of this."

I took out a new piece of parchment and formed a response.

The king acknowledged him.

My father's jaw dropped, and for a moment he was silent,
words snapping around him like sparks before he ran a thin hand
over his face and slumped in his chair.

"The council will be livid."

I pulled the parchment close and painstakingly summarized
the situation. **I die, my child dies. I die, you die. I die, Kjell is
king.**

My father was quick to come to his conclusion. "You must
make me regent, Daughter. The lords will agree. You will be
safe. Your child will be safe."

I studied him quietly, my eyes on his, my mind full of questions, full of words it would take me a lifetime to write. I thought

about Corvyn and the forests I'd grown up in. I could go back. I could raise my child. I could give up all claim to the throne. I had no desire to rule, and without desire there was only . . . duty. I closed my eyes and dropped my chin to my chest. Then I dipped my quill and wrote out my simple confession.

I never wanted to be queen.

My father read my sentence and smiled at me. It beamed from his face, transforming him.

It was the only time he'd ever smiled at me.

"Then it's settled. When the lords arrive, we will tell them what's been decided," he said.

I shook my head slowly. No.

The smile faded from my father's face, and disappointment carved new lines around his mouth.

"There is no other course, Daughter."

The king chose me.

My father yanked the paper from beneath my quill and ripped it down the center. "He did not choose you! He wanted your gift. He wanted your power. He *used* you!" my father spit out, leaning across the desk so I could see the charcoal flecks in his pale grey eyes.

My breath stilled, my heart stopped, and I could not look away from him. He didn't retreat, but stayed crouched over the desk, his face almost touching mine.

"You don't think I know what you can do?" my father whispered, the sound grating and harsh, sand against stone. "You are like your mother . . . but a thousand times worse! You killed her, and you sentenced me to a lifetime of fear."

I rose on trembling legs.

Crown that sits beside my bed, find your way onto my head.

Within seconds the crown I rarely wore winged its way through the balcony doors of my chamber, over the courtyard, and through the library window. It hovered above me and descended with careful precision over my coiled braids. It was the only response I could think of that didn't require a single word.

My father cursed and stepped back.

"You . . . are a . . . child. A mute! You cannot rule Jeru. The lords will destroy you!" He'd given up whispering, and there was desperation in his voice. For a moment I let myself believe that his desperation was for me.

"If I could, I would kill you myself," he hissed, and the moment of hope was dashed.

With a quick flick of my words, the stiff-backed armchair he'd risen from scooped him off his feet and rose swiftly into the air. He cried out and tried to jump free, only to have the chair rear back like a wild stallion and race toward the library doors. They opened at my command.

I cannot speak, I cannot shout,
But I can still make you get out.

I instructed the chair to upend. I heard a bang and a crash, and the chair returned, empty. With a clap of my hands and a sharp spell, I slammed the doors shut and locked them.

THIRTY-ONE

heard Boojohni sniffing beyond the library doors and disengaged the lock with a weary word so he could enter.

"Bird?" he whispered from the doorway of the empty room.

I'm here, Boojohni.

"Where?"

Under the desk.

He didn't ask why I was hiding. He just shut the library door softly, trundled over, and peered around the chair I'd moved in front of the opening. He was small enough he only had to tip his head. He pulled the chair away and crawled in beside me, patting my upraised knees.

"Ye've been cryin'. . . . I'm glad. Grief is good. Ye can't heal if ye don't grieve."

My father is here.

"I know," he sighed.

I hate him.

"Ye can't heal if ye hate, either. So let him go, little Lark," Boojohni said, wiping at my tears with stubby fingers. I let him, needing to feel protected. In truth, I felt more vulnerable than I'd ever been in my whole life.

The lords are coming.

"Aye."

My father knows what I can do. Only his fear for himself has kept him quiet, but he's desperate. If he thinks he can expose me and have me removed from power without getting us both killed, he will. If he tells Lord Bin Dar or Lord Gaul, they will take the throne and the Gifted in Jeru will be rooted out and destroyed.

"Those who persecute the hardest usually have the most to hide," Boojohni said, and we sat in troubled contemplation, resisting the responsibilities being foisted upon us. But hiding for very long was impossible, and it just stoked my apprehension.

I could go to Nivea before the lords arrive and warn them. I'm certain they've heard of the king's . . . death.

Boojohni was shaking his head before I even finished speaking.

"No, Bird. Leaving the city right now would be almost impossible. The castle is filled with eyes, and everyone has a hidden agenda. I will find a way to warn the Healer; she will warn the rest."

I'm afraid, Boojohni. I can't fight the whole world by myself.

My dread grew with the admission, and Boojohni reached for my hand, taking it in both of his. After a long silence he spoke, his voice troubled.

"Ye need to get word to Kjell. Something's amiss, Bird. It's all happened too quickly."

Tiras told me he wasn't coming back. He told me it had to end.

"Aye," Boojohni repeated. "But not like this. Not with you alone in Jeru City and Kjell and the army in Firi. It doesn't make sense."

My feelings of abandonment had been overwhelmed by my sorrow, and I hadn't been able to separate one from the other. Boojohni's suspicion made me pause, and all at once, my fear became terror.

It only made sense if something had actually happened to the king.

A solution came to me as I lay in the darkness, my eyes riveted beyond the balcony doors to the low wall where Tiras had perched and left me things—little gifts that let me know he was nearby, messages from a king.

I shot up in bed.

Birds delivered messages.

I threw off my covers, pulled on my cloak and my thin slippers, and stole down the hallways, dropping spells of distraction and diversion to clear my way through the castle and across the middle and upper baileys. I didn't worry about being seen. I worried about being followed.

The mews were hushed and dim, the birds resting like pampered princesses on their little roosts. I took one step, then another, hoping Hashim hadn't gone to his quarters for the night. Then I heard him descending the stairs from the pigeon coops above, and I tensed, awkward and second-guessing my decision.

He jumped a foot in the air when he saw me.

"My queen!" His eyes shot to the rafters, checking for winged strangers. "What . . . are . . ." He caught himself. "How can I be of service?"

I took a deep breath.

Can you hear me, Hashim?

His face was perfectly placid, but his eyes flared impercep-
tibly. Triumph flooded my chest.

I need your help. I don't know where else to turn.

"Majesty?" he squeaked, his voice so tentative I flinched at
the position I was putting him in.

I nodded somberly. *Yes, Hashim.*

He took several steps closer, his mouth quivering, his eyes
glistening with awe.

"Yes, I can . . . hear you. How can I help you, my queen?"
he whispered. I extended my hand, and he took it without hesitation. The nerves in my belly eased slightly. I did not scare him.
I'd simply surprised him.

*I need to get an urgent message to the captain of the guard.
Can you send a carrier bird to Firi?*

"Yes, Majesty. But the birds can only fly to and from a set
location," Hashim began, hesitant. "If the king's army is camped
beyond Firi, and the city is under attack, my birds may reach the
mews in Firi, but the message may not be relayed to the captain
for some time, if at all."

My heart sank, and I dropped my eyes and released
Hashim's hand.

"What is the message, my queen?" he pressed gently.

I need to know from the captain himself if the king is dead.

Hashim's face brightened. "Is there reason to hope he is
not?" he asked.

*There is reason to hope and reason to fear. But the captain
needs to know what is happening in Jeru. The lords will seize the
throne.*

"I will go myself, Majesty. I will find the captain."

My jaw dropped. *But . . . it will take several days each way
on horseback, and it will be dangerous. You are needed here.*

His gaze was steady. Trusting. "It will not take me that long, my queen. And the mews will be in good hands. I have apprentices, and they are very able. I will go and be back in three days."

I don't understand.

"The king and I . . . we are the same," he whispered. "I will . . . fly . . . to Firi."

One by one the lords arrived, accompanied by small armies from every province, as if the king's death meant war. They commandeered wings of the castle and set up council in the Great Hall. I was commanded to attend then summarily ignored as the lords from Bin Dar, Gaul, and Bilwick raged and quarreled with the lords from Quondoon, Enoch and Janda. Lady Firi watched it all with narrowed eyes and folded hands, and I wondered if she wasn't taking her own advice, waiting until the time was right to make her move.

Tiras's acknowledgment of Kjell had enraged them all, including the ambivalent southern lords, but the king's advisors were quick to quote precedence and Jeruvian law. My father then proposed that the council appoint a regent and suggested, as father of the queen, that he be chosen. The king's advisors looked to each other nervously, well-aware that Tiras did not want Lord Corvyn on the throne under any circumstances.

"Has the queen requested a regent, Lord Corvyn?" Lady Firi asked mildly, drawing the attention of all seven of the bickering lords.

"The queen's wishes cannot be considered. She is unable to communicate and is therefore unfit to reign," my father retorted.

"That has not been established, Corvyn," Lord Janda boomed, and Lord Enoch, a cousin of my mother, concurred.

Then the arguing began again, tempers rising, opinions swirling, and no one attempted to consult me at all.

I took out my book of accounts and turned to a blank page. Very carefully, I composed a statement for the council, for my father, and for those who had any question about my willingness or ability to rule. I dusted it with sand as the men rambled, let it dry as the men aired out all their grievances, and when I finally stood, the lords rose as well, but their conversation barely stuttered and their eyes never left each other.

I walked to Lady Firi's side and extended the document I had painstakingly created.

Will you read this, please? I asked her. Her brows rose in surprise, but she immediately stood, taking it from my hands, then waited for me to return to my position at the table.

"The queen has prepared a statement and has asked me to read it to the council," Lady Firi projected her voice above the fray.

I waited until I had their suspicious attention and inclined my head, asking Lady Firi to begin.

"I am Lark of Corvyn, now of Degn. I was crowned Queen of Jeru in the presence of this assembly. I am a daughter of Jeru and of noble birth. I am sound of mind and body, and I carry the heir to Jeru's throne. I cannot speak, but I am able to read and write and communicate my wishes and instructions. My loyalty is to Jeru and to the late king. It was his wish that I reign. If a regent is to be appointed to assist me in matters of war and state, I would ask that Kjell of Degn, the king's brother, be appointed consort until the royal heir is of age."

My statement was met with silence and sidelong glances. Lady Firi had not raised her eyes from the parchment, and her stillness caused a pang of apprehension to curl in my belly. I needed one ally, one person with whom I could confer.

"I wonder . . . does the Lady Queen know the laws concerning the Gifted?" Lord Bin Dar queried. The sinister slide of his voice broke the silence. I was still standing, but I met his gaze, acknowledging him.

He continued easily. "I have eyes in Jeru City. Sources. Concerned citizens. There are rumors that our queen has been consorting with a Healer. Our late king refused to fully prosecute the Gifted. He has been lax in his duties and sadly, he has lost his life battling the Volgar, the very beasts his leniency created. Jeru is at war. We must destroy the Gifted, or they will destroy us."

I remembered Boojohni's words of days before. "He who persecutes the hardest has the most to hide." I wondered what Lord Bin Dar was hiding and what Lord Gaul and Lord Bilwick truly gained by supporting him.

"My question is this, Queen Lark." Bin Dar said my name with a lilting skip, as if it sounded silly to him. "What are your opinions on the Gifted? Your mother was a Teller. Will you allow them to live and breed and infect Jeru? Or will you have the courage to root them out?"

He knew I couldn't answer aloud. They all did. I looked from one to the next, the corpulent and the thin, the sweating and the pale, the conspiring and the weary. Bilwick and the lords from the south looked on, but their minds were on their stomachs. We'd been sequestered all afternoon. Lord Gaul and Lady Firi observed, offering nothing. My father glared, praying I wouldn't upend chairs, and Lord Bin Dar waited, spinning a quill in his skeletal hand.

As my gaze narrowed on the pale feather twitching between his finger and thumb, I saw it shift. For a millisecond, the white quill became a long-stemmed glass, as if his desire for wine had gotten the better of him. I blinked, and the glass was a feather once more, spinning, spinning, spinning.

My eyes shot upward, his narrowed, and I had my answer. I picked up my own quill and dipped it into my inkwell, forming the letters on a blank sheet of parchment in large, bold print, so he and the rest of the council could plainly read my response.

Shall I start with you, Milord?

At sundown on the seventh day of Penthos, I dressed in black from head to toe, and I climbed the hill to the cathedral, just like I'd done on my wedding day. The bells rang in intervals of seven, tolling mournfully over the city. I don't know how the sound had changed so much since that day, becoming dreary instead of bright, ominous instead of optimistic, but it had. Maybe it wasn't the bells. Maybe it was me—my ears, my heart, my hope. Maybe I was different—a Changer after all.

The people did not throw flowers this time. They stood silently and watched my procession, some weeping, some stoic, dressed in their own varying shades of grey, brown, and black.

It was not uncommon in times of conflict for a fallen monarch to be memorialized on the battlefield where he met his end, and sometimes, as with King Zoltev, there were no remains to honor. If Tiras were brought back, his body would be placed on a pyre overlooking the city for another seven days. At the end of that time, the pyre would be lit, reducing the king's body to dust and to the earth from whence it came.

But Tiras's body would not be brought back to Jeru. His remains would not be turned to ash. We'd been sent no further word about the details of his "death," no glorious accounts of his valor or updates on the war effort against the relentless Volgar. Hashim had not returned. A monument for Tiras would be erected next to the monument for his father, and his father before him.

The hill beyond the cathedral was littered with dozens of statues raised for warrior kings of Jeru.

The lords walked behind me to the cathedral, appropriately grim-faced and sober, and I did my best to pay them no heed, though their thoughts and concerns brushed at my set shoulders and my stiff back. Lord Bin Dar had called the proceedings to a halt after I'd challenged him, and they'd not been taken up again.

I had little doubt I would be set aside. The council had convened, but there had been a great deal of conversation and collusion, bargaining and coercion in private quarters all over the castle. I'd heard my name bandied about and my life bartered with countless times. Lords Enoch, Janda and Quondoon were in favor of letting me remain in my position as queen, but felt no fealty to me or residual sentimentality for Tiras. They simply wished for Jeru to be governed ably and for their own provinces not to suffer any ill-effects from its poor management.

Bilwick, Gaul and Bin Dar wanted me gone.

My father and Lady Firi stood on the outside, each for their own reasons, and watched with apprehension. My father argued for my life—and his—though that usually included placing himself in a position of power to protect it. Lady Firi kept her own company, and I could never snatch her words or her thoughts from the air the way I could with most of the other lords. I suspected her mixed feelings had a great deal to do with Kjell and his eventual return; she stiffened when his name was tied with mine in any way.

A stalemate had been reached, and all parties seemed to agree that until Penthos had passed and the king's brother had returned, no final decisions would be made. So I climbed the tall hill, dressed in black, a widow instead of a bride, and begged Tiras to rise again.

THIRTY-TWO

That very night, like an answer to my Penthos prayer, my eagle sat, perched on the garden wall beyond the Great Hall, silhouetted in moonlight that suddenly felt warm, golden, and impossibly bright, melting the ore around my heart, making it liquid and soft.

He spread his great wings and beat the air, and I followed him, just like I'd done before.

I didn't wait for Boojohni or summon a guard. There wasn't time, and I couldn't risk an audience if he managed to change.

Tiras?

Come, the bird urged, flying from branch to branch, wall to wall, making sure I kept up. I obeyed, practically running through the forest, mindless with joy, with brilliant hope, watching his wings flex and fold as he led me deeper. Before long the cottage beckoned, quietly peaceful beneath the bows of sheltering trees, and my heart was an eager drum, pounding in anticipation, needing to believe that Tiras would be able to change for me, that I would soon see him again.

The cottage was dark, and the shutters gaped wide, pressed against the stone walls instead of folded inward to keep the forest at bay. The eagle was nowhere in sight, and I stopped, suddenly afraid, suddenly wondering if, in my desire, I'd simply imagined the bird was an eagle. I called his name, sending the word into the night, and the call went unanswered. Even the creatures that usually hummed and scurried were silent.

Then a light flickered in the cottage, a lamp being lit inside the tiny space, reassuring me like a mother's voice. I ran, clutching my skirts in my hands, a sob in my chest. I pushed through the door, Tiras on my lips, and drew up short.

She wore the dress edged in lace that I'd discovered beneath the bed, the garment I had assumed belonged to the Changer who'd been captured and killed and brought before my throne on hearing day.

Lady Firi?

She laughed, fastening the ties at her throat. "I told you my family had Gifted blood. Did you simply assume it was a mild strain?"

You are an eagle?

"I am whatever animal I wish to be. A little mouse in the corner listening to the king make all his plans. A tiny bird on the sill gathering information like crumbs. A cat lurking in the shadows. A carrier pigeon delivering messages from Firi."

Alarm coiled in my belly.

Are you the Changer the hunter saw?

Her smile was smug, and she inclined her head, as if she were receiving applause.

But . . . you were . . . dead!

She waved her hand in the air. "I was pretending. No one expects a bird to play dead." She smiled—a kind, regretful twist of her lips that made the hairs rise on my neck. "I waited until the room cleared, until you left, and I flew away. Kjell watched me go. Did he not tell you?"

I shook my head. He hadn't. But one thing was clear. Lady Firi knew everyone's secrets.

You wanted me to believe you were the king.

"Yes."

Why?

"Because I knew you would follow me here. I failed that night. The timing was off. Then the king returned. I had to change my strategy."

I stared at her, not wholly comprehending. *But . . . why?*

"I want Jeru. In order to have Jeru, I must marry a king, but Tiras has taken care of that, hasn't he? He has made Kjell his successor. I didn't anticipate that, though I hoped. I thought I was going to have to take Jeru by cunning. Now I can just take it by marriage. The way *you* did."

I never wanted to be queen.

"Every girl wants to be queen," she snarled, her expression shifting so quickly I saw a glimmer of beast. "I can be a lion, a snake, a bird, even a dragon. Why not a queen?"

She shrugged, but there was anger beneath her nonchalance. "There have been so many things I couldn't have predicted. You, for one. I didn't even know you existed, and suddenly you were Queen of Jeru, snatching it away from me."

You were the one who kidnapped the king on our wedding day.

"I'm a Changer. I knew when the king would be most vulnerable. I knew his pattern. It wasn't difficult. My guards took care of the heavy lifting."

And the lords? My father?

"I told them the king wouldn't arrive. Promised them."

But he did.

"Yes. Another thing I couldn't predict." She tilted her head, considering me. "Did you have something to do with that?"

I didn't answer, forcing blankness to my face. Had she not heard me? Had only the birds been privy to my call?

"The king will not arrive this time, will he? He's not coming back. And Kjell will return, heir to the throne. So you have to die."

And the attacks in Firi? What if Kjell is killed?

"The Volgar are not in Firi. I lied. They are here."

I rushed to the door, and Lady Firi didn't even try to stop me, but her words were like knives in my fleeing back.

"Liege wanted you. I want Jeru. We have an arrangement."

I ran, pushing the words upward, needing to warn whoever could hear that death was descending from overhead.

All of Jeru, hear my cry,
Turn your faces toward the sky.

I heard and felt the dip and dive of wings above my head, but the wings above me were not those of an eagle. I'd heard the sound before. Talons pierced the layers of my cloak and my dress, grazing the flesh of my back and encircling my ribs like an infant clutches her mother's breast. I screamed soundlessly as my feet left the ground, crying for Tiras, for Jeru, for my child. Wind whipped at my face and pulled at my hair, as the ground grew farther and farther away. I expected to be released any moment, to plummet to my death, only to have the Volgar beast follow me back to earth to eat from my broken flesh. But the beast who held me firmly in his clutches flew without ceasing, his wings beating the air in a steady rhythm. Flap, flap, flap, soar. Flap, flap, flap, soar.

I could not compel him. I pushed and begged, straining to see him as I dangled from his claws, peppering him with spells that had no more effect on him than wishful thoughts. The beast continued to fly, ambivalent to every word I wielded.

He was not like other birdmen. His spiked, serpentine head sat on a man's shoulders, arms, and chest, the entirety covered in silvery scales, while his lower body was that of a bird. The underside of his black wings were shot with green and blue, like peacock feathers. Horrific and oddly beautiful, he was a conglomeration of man, bird, and reptile—a dragon—and I'd never seen anything like him.

Higher and higher we rose, the mountains east of Jeru City rising like a jagged fortress before my eyes, cliffs and crags jeering like sharp teeth from the shadows. The creature began to circle and slow, letting the currents sweep him downward, using his wings to slow our descent, until his great, feathered haunches grasped the earth. With a flutter and a thrust, he entered a gaping cave carved into the side of the mountain and dropped me unceremoniously.

Disoriented and dizzy, my head spun and my stomach revolted, my intense relief warring with a paralyzing fear of what was to come. I panted, pulling my cloak around me, wincing as the wounds on my back made themselves known. I struggled to rise and swayed against the wall of the cave, clinging to the rocks as I waited for the world to settle.

The beast watched my attempts to calm and comfort myself with strange fascination, his dragon head tipped at an angle, waiting for me to demand answers. It was dark in the cave, the full moon beyond the wide opening insufficient to light the deep corners. I crept along the wall, not foolish enough to think he would let me flee, but hopeful I could get closer to the entrance, closer to the light.

I didn't want to die in the dark.

He stalked me, allowing the few steps it took to bathe us both in moonlight, and then he spoke.

Do you know who I am, little queen? The words came from his mind, not his mouth. I shivered, hating the way they felt inside my head, intrusive and heavy, leaving no space for my own thoughts. It was the way I communicated, and I suddenly understood why Kjell resented it.

No. I made my voice a spear and flung it outward. He hissed, and steam curled from his narrow snout. He loomed over me, herding me to the cliff's edge.

I turned away from him, averting my face so he wouldn't see my fear. He crept closer, so close that my toes kissed the edge and his presence warmed my back.

"But I know who you are," he whispered, using his voice to show he could. His forked tongue darted between his teeth, and his scalding hot breath tickled the exposed skin below my ear, searing my flesh. I clenched my jaw, refusing to cry out, even with my thoughts, and I considered falling.

"You are Meshara's daughter."

I stiffened, hating the way he crooned my mother's name like a man savoring his wine. He touched the blistering skin on my neck with a scaled knuckle, and I felt a wet pop and a flash of pain.

"I've burned you. Forgive me. I forget how fragile a woman's skin can be. You are quite beautiful, really. Deceptively so. Like moonlight. Pale. Slender. One almost looks right through you before he catches his breath and looks back."

Tiras had said the same thing.

The beast stepped back, as if truly apologetic that he had blistered my flesh, and I eased away from the ledge, my eyes still glued to the cavernous darkness below.

"You are Meshara's daughter, Queen of Jeru, Lark of Corvyn."

My breath stalled, and I found his eyes in the wan light, waiting.

"My son made you queen. How clever of him."

My throat throbbed and my ears burned, and I touched tentative fingers to one lobe, uncertain I'd heard him clearly.

Your son?

"The king. Tiras," he whispered, and the S hissed between us. "I am Liege. But I am also . . . Zoltev. Do you remember me, Lark of Corvyn?"

I shook my head, adamant, resistant. Terrified. *You are Volgar.*

"No. They are animals. I am a man. With wings. And claws." I heard his smile, though I didn't see it.

Zoltev was a . . . man, and you are a beast.

"But if I want to be a man, I am a man."

I watched, unable to help myself, and true to his words, with an undulating twist, he stood before me, devoid of wings and claws, feathers and scales.

He looked like Tiras.

The arrogant set of his chin and his unapologetic stance made my heart shudder with recognition. His hair had greyed, his body had aged, and the eyes that looked out at me were Kjell's. But I knew him.

He laughed when my legs gave way beneath me. I teetered, catching myself at the last moment and slicing my hand on a sharp edge. Blood welled, crimson and warm, and dripped against the rocks beneath my fingers. My mother's blood had spilled over stones. It had pooled beneath our bodies and congealed in my hair.

The beast king crouched over me, dipping his finger into the blood on my palm.

"But why would I want to be a man when I can be Liege?" he said simply, drawing his finger into his mouth, tasting me.

He contorted and shook, and his lower body was once again clothed in feathers, his legs and feet resembling those of a bird. He rose, throwing back his head, and his wings tumbled down his back like a flag unfurled.

"I prefer to be something in between." He remained a man from the waist up, but talons shot out from his hands, neatly breaking through the skin on the tips of his fingers like a cat flexing his claws.

"I can be anything I want to be. I'm a Changer and a Spinner."

Not a Healer?

"It is the one gift I have no need of. There's no one in all of Jeru I want to heal."

Of course not. Healing required love.

"I've spun vultures into warriors, into an entire army. I started with a few and bade them attack. We left bodies to rot in the sun, and more vultures came. I spun them into Volgar, and one by one, I built an army. I tell them what to do. They are easy to control . . . aren't they? You destroyed so many of my creations, little queen. I should destroy you."

I struggled to stand, not wanting to cower at his feet, and he watched me rise, as if I amused him.

"I should destroy you, but you might be of use to me."

I flinched, and his black-winged eyebrows rose. "The beasts obey me because I am their creator. But I am not a Teller. I can't compel them with mere words. But you can."

I could feel them even now, the words that animated their huge, avian bodies and their simple minds. I could hear their hunger and their bloodlust, and I repelled them, flinging spells to keep them away. I couldn't see them, but they were near.

"I can hear you. You fear them. But they aren't coming for you."

Why are you doing this? You left. You made your sons, your subjects, all of Jeru believe you were dead.

"I jumped from the cliff, and I changed into a bird."

Why?

"Meshara said I would become everything I feared—a monster—and I did. Meshara knew what I was becoming. I might have spared her, but she knew. So I had to kill her."

He'd killed her because she *knew*. Boojohni was right. My mother had seen what was to come. It was not a curse but a prophecy. The realization swept through me with sudden clarity.

"I'd already begun to lose control. But after Meshara died, it became worse. I was changing without warning, entering the stables and shifting into a horse. Taking a bath and becoming a great, flopping fish. Turning everything I touched into something I didn't want. Gold into rocks and rocks into water, bread into sand and my sword into straw. I woke up one morning and the sheet on my bed had become a boa constrictor." He stared at me with pursed lips. "I was afraid of what would happen if my secret was discovered."

You left Jeru because you were afraid. But you aren't afraid anymore?

"I became everything I feared. Now I *am* fear. And no one can stop me."

He stared down at Jeru City and flexed his huge wings.

"My son . . . he is a Changer too. An eagle. But he can't control the change. Now he is gone, Jeru needs a king, and you are alone. I will let you live if you do as I say."

And what of Lady Firi? She thinks she's going to be queen.

He cackled. "She will make a good pet."

For a moment all was quiet in the city below, the distance creating an illusion of serenity. Then flames begin to gyrate and lick the sky, and Jeru came alive. The stench of pitch and smoke rose in the wind, and screams and shouts began to swell and find me across the distance. *Hide*, the people said. *Run*, the women screamed. *Volgar*, the men shouted. The word *mother* pierced the air along with the others, and I covered my ears in horror, not wanting to hear, not able to prevent it. *The birdmen are here. The Volgar are here. Run. Hide. Help me.* The words trembled and burst, only to swell again like the blisters the Volgar Liege had raised on my skin.

Tiras, I cried, *Tiras, your city. Your city is burning.*

"Call him, Lark of Corvyn. Call your eagle king. Call my son, so he will know his father has returned. The birdmen will kill and feed, and when the people are begging for mercy, I will extend it. I will call them off. And I will take what's mine."

Fire burning Jeru's streets,
Find the birdmen, make them flee.
Arrows in the archer's bow,
Find the birdmen, e'er they go.

Zoltev laughed, incredulous. "The city burns, and you spin rhymes?"

Volgar birdmen, hear my cry,
Jeru's burning, you will die.
Close your wings and bow your heads,
Every living birdman, dead.

"Do you really think they can hear you? That your words are so powerful across such a distance?" Zoltev mocked.

Rocks upon which Zoltev stands,
Tumble now beneath the man.
Open up and swallow him,
That Jeru will be safe again.

Zoltev bared his teeth and swung his arm, striking me across the face. For a heartbeat I was weightless, teetering between falling and flailing, my arms wide, searching for something to hold on to. Then I was part of the sky, a fluttering poppet in the wind, words rushing through my head.

I was falling.

THIRTY-THREE

t sounded like an eagle's cry, piercing and long, vibrating in my head even as the wind tore at my hair and cloak, grasping hands that dragged me toward the earth. But I felt sound leave my throat, felt it stream behind me as I plummeted. Then the greedy hands of gravity became powerful arms, the roar of the wind morphed into the clapping of wings, and I was snatched from the air by the Volgar King.

My body bucked, and my cloak came loose, continuing the path of my descent, flapping like a crimson bird caught in a gale. For a moment we spun wildly, wings and arms and bodies colliding in mid-air, careening toward the ground, and I closed my eyes so I wouldn't see the end. Then the wings that carried me caught the wind and tamed it, pounding it into submission, and we rose again, climbing the sky, seeking the moonlight and the stars, leaving death behind.

I screamed again, the cry billowing from my throat and into the night, and the king pressed his lips to my ear and spoke my name.

"Shh, my queen. It is me."

And I realized that the arms that wrapped around me were not scaled. The wings above me were not shot with green, and the man who'd plucked me from the air was not a beast.

Tiras.

Tiras?

I began to weep, locked in his impossible embrace, crying in horror and hope, disbelief and elation, watching the world stream below us, magical and hushed, a piece of a dream. I wanted to keep flying and never return, but the voices of Jeru rose from the ground.

Smoke and ash and billowing flames began to dot the landscape in every direction, and suddenly we were surrounded by a flock of Volgar beasts, screeching and diving in chaotic frenzy. They paid us no heed; Tiras was simply one of them, a birdman claiming his spoils, and I began to chant and cast my spells.

Spun from vultures, made to kill.
Volgar birdmen, stripped of will.
Born of fear and hate and shame,
Return to hell from whence ye came.

"It must end," Tiras spoke into my ear. "Jeru burns, my father lives, and this all must end."

The Volgar had to die. I couldn't send them away, couldn't urge them to fly. I had to destroy them, or it would continue.

In the sky and on the ground,
Volgar hearts will cease to pound.
Slower, slower, heed my cry,
One by one, you all must die.

Like flies, the birdmen began to fall, their wings stuttering, their bodies writhing. We fell with them, breaching the city walls and drawing the arrows of desperate men who couldn't differentiate between the Volgar swarm and a winged king. I abandoned the Volgar spells and hurled words of protection around us as Tiras circled the castle and came to graceful rest on the roof of the palace, folding his wings and releasing me only to bellow instructions at the open-mouthed archers.

"Majesty?" one shouted, and another lowered his bow and rubbed his hand across his eyes. Tiras wore breeches and boots but his upper body was bare, accommodating the wings. They protruded from his back, black as soot and tinged in red—identical to his eagle wings, but much bigger. The rounded tops eclipsed his broad shoulders, and the tips reached his heels. Hair, eyes, talons, and now . . . wings.

"Find me a sword!" Tiras roared, and he leaped over the edge, half-jumping, half-flying to the parapets below, running with his wings extended, shouting to his men and refocusing their attention to the task at hand.

Two guards lay in the bailey below, swords still clutched in their hands, their bellies laid open by Volgar talons. I didn't hesitate, calling on the weapons to rise and find the king.

One for his left hand, one for his right,
The king has need of you tonight.

I heard the marvel and the fear of the warriors watching as the swords levitated and flew toward the king. I called to him in warning, and he turned and swept them up, his teeth flashing and his newly-acquired swords clashing. Then he took to the air like an avenging angel.

He flew to the crier's tower overlooking the city square, and he called out to the people below.

"Women and children inside the keep!" Tiras roared. "Drop the bridge!" The guards along the entrance parapets rushed to obey, and the gates were lowered and the portcullis raised, allowing the Jeruvians outside the castle walls to find shelter within. They ran, hundreds of them, children clinging to their hands, eyes on the heavens, waiting for an attack that didn't come.

For a moment, the skies were clear, the last wave of birdmen decimated by failing hearts and slings and arrows. A wave of hope washed over the castle—a lull in the storm—and the people looked from one to the other, wide-eyed and expectant, even as they rushed for cover.

"Are they gone?" The murmur swept over the ramparts and the parapets. "Is it over?" the king's guard dared suggest.

The air was murky, the smoke obscuring the sky, and the darkness merciful. Hope became listening ears and bated breath, and atop the wall, Tiras's voice rang out again. His people turned their faces from the sky to the winged king standing above them, seeing what he'd been so desperate to hide. He was glorious and terrifying—black wings beating, white hair flying—causing awe and a strange reverence to ripple over the shell-shocked crowd.

"Citizens of Jeru, for too long we have persecuted those among us with gifts. Healers, Changers, Spinners and Tellers have hidden themselves in our midst, fearful of what would happen if their abilities were discovered.

"I stand before you, King of Jeru, one who has lived with the very same burden and the very same fear, and I ask you to come forward, out of the shadows, all who are Gifted, all who are not, and fight for your families. Fight for your city. For each other. The battle is just beginning. The Volgar King will destroy Jeru. He will set his beasts upon you, and there will be no distinction between those who are Gifted and those who are not. We will all die or be enslaved."

The courtyard was hushed for a heartbeat, then excited chatter and fearful questions filled the air. But there was little time for talk.

"Women and children, old and infirm, inside the keep," Tiras shouted. "All who are Gifted or skilled, lend your talents this night, and you will be welcomed and protected in Jeru from this day on by order of your king."

"They come, Majesty! The sky is filled with Volgar!" the watchman shouted.

Tiras abandoned the crier's turret and flew toward me, tossing one sword aside as he touched down on the roof of the keep, and with one arm swept me up against him, lifting off once more.

Take me to the watchtower.

He ignored my command, his eyes on the flustered guard and the panicked citizens that raced toward the keep in droves. He took me to the entrance of the keep instead.

"Stay with them. Keep them safe . . . Keep yourself safe within the castle," he instructed. His mouth took mine, hard and fast, and he was gone again, taking three running steps across the bailey before he was airborne once more. Closing my eyes, I called the Gifted, asking them to trust and obey. I'd seen the Volgar Liege. The battle was just beginning, and Jeru wouldn't survive him without help.

*Gifted men and women come
To the aid of Jeru's throne.*

The women and children crowded into the Great Hall, the windows shuttered and the doors barred to keep the birdmen from preying on them. I saw my father huddled with the other lords, eyes manic, calling for his attendants, who were nowhere to be found. I hoped they were on the wall with the rest of Jeru's men.

The glass on the long rectangular windows shattered, spraying the crowd below, and an enormous ball of fire pirouetted through the air. My mind stuttered, conjuring words to change its trajectory, but I was too slow. Lord Bin Dar, his cape and his terror billowing around him, flung out his hands. The fire met his palms and became water, drenching everyone around him.

A momentous silence swept the room, and Lord Bin Dar stumbled back, aghast. Exposed.

"He's a Spinner," someone cried.

"Praise the Creator," a woman added. "We are wet instead of dead."

One by one, the Gifted began to reveal themselves. Mistress Lorena spun spoons into swords and the bristles from her broom into hundreds of arrows. A child commanded the broken glass to be whole, and it rose in a million jagged pieces fitting itself together until the windows were covered once more. An old man became an elephant dragging the heavy thrones in front of the garden doors to reinforce them from outside attack, and a heavy-set woman became a dainty bird, flitting in and out of the castle, updating the huddled townspeople on the battle beyond the keep.

The wounded were dragged from the courtyard into the castle's entrance hall, and women scurried between the broken bodies of the guard stemming blood and separating the living from the dead. Lord Quondoon was among the caregivers, and as I watched he began pressing his hands to wounded limbs and torsos, humming as he moved in and out of the suffering soldiers.

I positioned myself at the entrance to the keep with a thin view of the bailey beyond and did my best to cast words without standing out in the open. There was no safety in the courtyard. The castle walls were high and strong, but the Volgar flew over them, dropping and devouring the outnumbered guard, talons dripping and wings flapping, and for every spell I wrung from my weary mind, another swell would come.

The words seemed to settle on some of the Volgar beasts and glance off others, as if the cacophony of swords and shrieks, of wailing and warrior death, created walls my words had to penetrate. We'd fought the Volgar in open fields, man against beast, but the castle keep and the towering walls put us at a disadvantage. The skies above were filled with smoke, and we couldn't see what was coming until a wave descended upon us.

"Kjell is at the gates of the city with two-hundred men." The cry rose, tinging the air with relief as if salvation had arrived, but judging by the number of wounded and dead in the hall, I could not remain where I was, throwing words through the cracks in the doors and the fissures in the walls. I had to get out in the open.

I ducked out the entrance hall and ran through the courtyard toward the upper bailey, hugging the walls until I reached the stairs that led to the siege tower above the town gate. The siege tower was the highest point on the castle's south wall, and once there, I would have a clear view of the battle and the skies.

Tiras was everywhere at once, a warrior turned lethal weapon. Ferocious and fleet-footed, his wings gave him lift as he scaled walls and flew from one battle to the next, thrusting and swinging, slaying one birdman after another, until his bare chest was coated in Volgar blood.

"Lark!" I heard my name slice through the air like a whip. I turned, still wielding words, and saw my father reach the top of the turret stairs that led to the siege tower, breathless and staggering, dragging a sword that I was certain he didn't know how to use.

He had followed me, and Lady Firi had followed him.

He said my name again, but my gaze was riveted on the woman moving toward me, her eyes flat and her jaw tight. She didn't greet me, didn't speak, and there was no question as to her intentions. One moment she was a woman in a blood-spattered

303

dress, the next she was a black panther on the parapets, sleek and muscular, stalking me on silent paws.

My father cried out in shock, and the sword he carried clattered to the ground.

"Meshara. Oh, Meshara . . . help us," he gasped.

I could command beasts, but I could not compel the Gifted. In a battle of words versus might, Lady Firi would be the victor. I commanded the parapet to tumble, but she easily avoided falling, leaping from section to section, trusting that I wouldn't demolish the entire wall. Then there was nowhere to turn, my back against the turret, the stairs beyond reach. She swiped at me, her claws raking my side and leaving a trail of fire in their wake. From the corner of my eye, I saw my father clutch his abdomen and fall to his knees.

An arrow sliced the air, a deadly whisper, and sank into the cat's side. A young archer stood on the parapets, his eyes enormous, his bow still drawn. The panther yowled, and the air shimmered, the black cat blurring and blending into something new.

The arrow clattered to the stones, expunged, and I began to run, my hand pressed to my side, taking the only opportunity I might get. I took three steps before I was plucked off my feet and drawn up into the sky, rescued from the clutches of one beast by the hands of another.

Liege had entered the fray.

THIRTY-FOUR

Nothing remained of the man. He was all beast—scales and feathers, talons and wings—breathing fire and sweeping his spiked tail behind him, impaling anyone who came within striking distance.

"Tiras!" The word boomed and echoed, a lion's roar, released from the cavernous chest cavity of a monster. It undulated in the air, and for a moment the battle around us ceased, the birdmen rose, and all heads turned.

Tiras rose into the air, wings caressing the sky, a sword in each hand, and Zoltev's scaled arm tightened around my ribs. He didn't retreat or dart away, but allowed Tiras to take a parallel position, a stand-off above the earth, birds and men, kings and conquerors.

"My son, I have your queen," Zoltev bellowed. "She bleeds, and I am not a Healer. Join me, and I will let you keep her."

Tiras's eyes shot to mine, and his regret was eclipsed only by his resolve. "Even you do not have that power, father," he murmured.

"But I do! We can have anything we want. We are Gifted. We are kings. You are exactly like me," Zoltev urged.

"You are a beast. And I have spent my whole life trying to be a man," Tiras said.

"Then you have failed. You are a bird. Your kingdom conspires against you, your city burns, and your queen . . . bleeds," Zoltev hissed, and he flung me aside. He shot upward, wings spread, even as Tiras swooped, catching me up against him.

"I build my own armies, I don't need lords and councils. I don't need knights and guards," Zoltev bellowed, commanding the attention of every man, woman, and child. With infinite care, Tiras descended and laid me on the cobblestones, shouting for Boojohni and retrieving his swords, preparing for battle as Zoltev called down his minions.

The Volgar Liege extended his arms, and his creations swarmed around him, falling from the haze and the darkness like he was the God of Words. Zoltev had not stopped with vultures. These new creatures had wings, but they were various shapes and sizes with differing colors and characteristics. Some breathed fire and others sprayed venom, some were the size of small children, others as large as three men, as if Zoltev had attempted to turn flying lizards and poisonous serpents into giants.

I closed my eyes and bid them adieu.

Zoltev roared in stunned outrage, and I clamped my hands over my ears, gasping in pain at the head-splitting volume, as the creatures began to writhe and die, falling to the courtyard like overripe fruit and spilling their juices over the cobblestones.

Tiras shot from the ground, swords drawn back, and thrust upward into Zoltev's belly. Zoltev's wings jerked and seized in stunned agony, and he dropped from the sky, hitting the ground with a sickening thud. In an instant he shifted, becoming Zoltev the man before transforming into the Volgar Liege once again, healed.

The king's guard ran toward him, lances raised, only to be swept off their feet by the dragon's spiked tail or engulfed in flame. Tiras rose above the beast, wings extended, drawing Zoltev into the sky. I willed the arrows of the archers to bury themselves in his scaly skin, but the dragon was wily, his hide was thick, and he rose above the smoke, beyond the view of the king's men, and we could only watch the haze in trepidation, eyes peeled, necks craned, listening to the battle of wings and wills above us.

Then through the hovering smoke, the Volgar Liege hurtled, wings pinned back, Tiras clinging to the hilt of the sword that protruded from Zoltev's reptilian chest. The dragon roared, shooting flames that engulfed Tiras's wing. With an inhuman cry, Tiras swung his right hand upward, thrusting his second sword through Zoltev's dragon-like snout, pinning his mouth closed and trapping the flames inside him. They collided with the cobblestones, the dragon king taking the brunt of the fall, wings twisted and trapped beneath him, Tiras still clinging to the hilts of both swords.

Warriors pounced from every direction, running their swords through Zoltev's body, ensuring he wouldn't change and rise again.

But the king didn't rise either.

The two lay motionless, a crumpled heap of limbs and wings, man and beast, and I heard a cry echoing across the courtyard, keening and sharp, reverberating down my throat and into my belly, lodging around my heart.

Screaming. I was screaming, just like before, the sound breaking through the rust in my throat and the walls of my mind. Then I was running and falling and running again, reaching Tiras's body as he was rolled from the beast onto his back, victorious yet overcome.

"Tiras." His name felt bigger than life on my tongue, and it rolled through my mouth like a growing storm. I realized his name wasn't just in my head but in my throat and on my lips. It sprang forth and rang in my ears.

"Tiras," I said again, calling him back with my will and my voice, demanding he answer. But he didn't open his eyes, and his breath whistled from his lips, wispy and faint. The left side of his body was charred and black, his left wing a shriveled mass of melted feathers and exposed cartilage.

I placed my hands above his heart, avoiding the wounded flesh and the seared skin.

Wounded flesh beneath my hands,
Be new again as I demand.
Wing that withers, singed and shorn,
Heal thyself, be whole once more.

His blackened skin began to pink, and his feathers unfurled, but my body quaked, and my sight began to fail. There was blood seeping through my gown, and pain radiated deep in my belly.

I lay beside him, my head on his heart, listening to the dreadful slog, heavy and slow. If he could change, he could heal.

"His gift is strange," the old Teller had said.

"He was not born this way," Kjell had argued.

But my mother had prophesied his change. She'd pressed words into the air, promising fate. And on the night she died, King Zoltev had begun to lose his soul and his son to the sky.

Realization flooded me.

I could not heal what wasn't broken. I could not alter Tiras's gift. But if the change was not his gift, if it was not something woven into his cells and sinews, then I could take it away. I could take my mother's words away. It was the first thing my mother had taught me. *Take the word away, Lark.*

I closed my eyes and focused on the day when I'd swallowed the words back into myself, just as I'd been commanded. The words on my lips, the shape of them, the weight of them, the rumble of the sound releasing from my throat as they came into being. I'd done as I was told. I'd remembered and obeyed. I'd swallowed every word, every syllable.

Curse not, cure not, 'til the hour.

That hour was at hand. The most important hour of my life. Dawn was nearing and Tiras would not live to see it. Not as a bird or a man. The hour was at hand, and I could not afford to be silent anymore.

I pressed my mouth to Tiras's chest and moved my lips around the shape of the word he'd become, taking it from him.

"Elgae."

His breast was warm, and his life force lingered, but his spirit wanted to fly, fly, fly. It was the only word left, and it resisted me even as I called it back and took it away, just like I'd done to the poppet clenched in my mother's fist the day it all began.

"Ylf."

As I moved my lips against his chest, pulling the word into myself, I felt the smallest crack, a fissure, and wind whistled through my lips. Just like the poppet, Tiras was quiet, a shell of something that no longer stirred.

I'd taken his word, his final word, and drawn it into myself.

And still he lay motionless, wings fluttering in the pre-dawn darkness, eyes closed, not an eagle, not a man.

"Tiras." I spoke against his lips, desperate to give him a new word, new life. "Tiras," I said again, straining against the rust in my throat, wanting to speak his name into being, but there was no change in him.

I threw back my head in rage and sorrow, the fissure in my throat widening, even as I tried to reclaim Tiras from the sky, taking away my mother's words.

Yks eht morf! I mourned, *Yks eht morf!*

But there was no answer from the sky. I had lost him. It was foretold, and it had come to pass.

I felt a hand on my arm and heard my name being spoken, but I would not lift my head from the king.

"Yer wounded, Lark. Yer bleeding." Boojohni tried to pull me away.

I can't heal him, Boojohni. I tried to make him change so he could heal himself. But he's not a man or a bird . . . He's both.

"What word did ye give him, Lark?" Boojohni asked urgently.

I moaned, trying to speak out loud and failing, the words like rocks against my teeth, awkward and sharp.

"The day yer mother died, ye kissed his hand. I saw ye! And ye whispered something. What word did ye give him?"

I could only stare in despair, shaking my head. *I didn't give him a word.*

"Ye did," Boojohni argued.

I couldn't remember. I remembered my mother and Zoltev's sword. I remembered her telling me to be silent.

"Do ye remember Tiras at all? He was just a boy. A boy on a big, black horse."

I closed my eyes, making myself go back to that day.

"Ye have to remember," Boojohni pled, his voice hoarse. "He talked to you."

He'd talked to me.

And he'd been . . . kind.

He'd smiled.

And he'd told me his horse's name.

I remembered.

It was the biggest, blackest, horse I'd ever seen—but I wasn't afraid. I was never afraid of the animals. Their words were so simple and easy to understand. This horse wanted to run. He didn't want to stand in the courtyard and hold still, but he did. He knew his duty. The prince wanted to run too. He was bored, and he wanted to be free of the guard around him and the fear of the people that bowed and kneeled whenever he was introduced. His father enjoyed seeing people bow. He didn't. He wanted to run. To fly.

The prince's eyes caught on something overhead, and his yearning was instantaneous and bright.

He wished he could trade places with the bird.

Then he looked down at me and smiled, releasing the yearning that made me hurt for him. He slid down from his mount and held out his hand to me. I took it without hesitation. He ran his other hand down the horse's long nose.

"His name is Mikiya." His voice was already husky and low, like a man's voice, though he wasn't yet a man.

I repeated the name on a whisper. Mikiya. It was a funny name, but I liked the way the word felt in my mouth.

"It means eagle," he added. "Because he wants to fly."

I still held his hand in mine, and my mother stepped forward to draw me back, away from the prince and his horse.

I kissed his hand, and I gave the prince a word so that he could fly away if he wanted to . . .

Mikiya.

"Mikiya," I said, the word sloppy and awkward in my mouth. My tongue was unaccustomed to speech. I looked up at Boojohni, desperate to say it correctly.

"Mikiya," I repeated. "Eagle."

"Take it away, Bird," Boojohni urged. I pressed my lips to Tiras's breast once more and withdrew the word I'd inadvertently cursed him with.

"*Ayikim*," I breathed. "*Ayikim*."

"Lark . . . look!" Boojohni crowed softly. "Look!"

The roots of Tiras's hair became inky and rich, the color spilling from his scalp and rippling down the white locks that brushed his shoulders, until his hair was completely black once more. The broken wings that jutted out of his back began to shiver and curl into themselves like parchment engulfed in flame, disintegrating into nothing more substantial than ash. We watched, awestruck, as the ash held the shape of wings for a single heartbeat, then whirled up and away, erased from existence.

Tiras's right hand lay against his chest, the talons chipped and encrusted with blood. Suddenly the talons were gone, swallowed back into the pads of his fingers, leaving them perfectly rounded and whole once more.

"Tiras," I croaked, begging him to open his eyes, wanting to see if the restoration was complete. But he didn't move. He didn't even stir.

I had taken away the word, but he was not healed.

I smoothed his chest with shaking hands, streaking it with the blood that wept from my side. I breathed a spell of healing—ill-formed words from my unpracticed tongue—calling on my mother who had loved me, on a God of Words who had given me my gift, and on Tiras himself who had flown beyond my reach.

"Close the gates of heaven and hell,
Turn him back and make him well.
Do not fly away, my king.
Jeru weeps beside your queen."

"Bird . . ." Boojohni said, his face contorting in helplessness. "Maybe it's too late."

"Do not fly away, my king. Do not fly away from me," I chanted, refusing to listen, pushing life through my hands and into the heart that no longer beat inside Tiras's chest. Then Boojohni left me, running for help or running for cover, I didn't know. My eyes were closed, my hands numb, and I continued to plead.

Seconds later I was swept up, embraced like a long-lost child, rescued temporarily from despair, but when I raised my eyes to the man who held me, I saw Kjell, his weary face lined with grief, his blue eyes nothing like the once-black gaze of the man I longed for. I turned my face and saw that Tiras still lay on the ground. The king had not been released from the sky.

"Let me go," I said, the words almost unintelligible. "I took the word away, but I can't call Tiras back."

"She's lost so much blood, Captain. She won't leave him. I'm afraid we're going to lose her too." Boojohni was crying.

Kjell crouched beside the king, releasing me as he touched his brother's face.

"He's gone, Lark." Kjell's voice was grief-stricken, and truth rose around him.

"No," I whispered. "He's not. I can still feel him."

Kjell shook his head, his throat working, his eyes bleak.

"Help me, Kjell. I am not a Healer. But you are. *You* are."

"No," Kjell whispered. "I'm not . . . I can't."

"Help him, and I will help you," I said, repeating the words Kjell had said to me a lifetime ago when he believed I could save his brother. My vision was starting to swim, and I didn't have the strength to move my lips, but he knelt beside me and put his hands where mine had been.

Listen to him.

"I can't . . ." Kjell protested, even as he grimaced, listening. Prayer and pleading oozed from his pores.

I put a hand over his and strained to hear the song of Tiras's soul, the frequency that would call him back and heal his broken body.

Listen, I begged.

I knew the moment he heard the tone—a tone so faint it was almost a vibration—because it began to pulse like a heartbeat, low and thready, swelling then fading as Kjell locked onto it and began to hum. His voice was gravely, untrained, and hesitant, but it was perfectly pitched.

I wrapped my mind and what was left of my strength around the timber of Kjell's voice. I pulled the note into my head and my throat, into my chest and my limbs, swimming in the sound. I pled for health and hope and second chances, my hands pressed over Kjell's.

When Tiras opened his eyes, eyes as deep and black as the night sky above us, I closed mine.

THIRTY-FIVE

awoke alone to light, warm and bright, streaming in from the open balcony doors to my chamber. The room was neat and quiet, the day beyond the palace walls serene. I listened for chaos, for the daily cacophony of life in the castle, and though I heard movement and industry, it was subdued, the thoughts and words wafting in with the sunlight reflective and soft.

My gown was gone. I stretched naked limbs and touched my side, feeling smooth skin and little else. I trailed my hands to my abdomen, to the small swell between my hip bones, and rested them there. I felt a quivering sensation—life and movement—and held my breath, wanting to hear as badly as I wanted to feel. The sensation came again—a brush, a caress, the whisper of water against the shore.

Safe.

The word fluttered in my chest. I was safe. My child was safe, and I was healed.

Safe.

But not whole.

I sat up gingerly and rose from the bed, pulling a dressing gown around my body. My hair fell in rumpled waves down my back and over my eyes, and I focused on the distraction of taming it. I swept it back carefully, tucking it behind my ears, my movements slow and precise, my eyes focused inward, my mind blank, and my heart . . . racing.

If I didn't look too closely, I wouldn't see that Tiras wasn't there. If I didn't breathe too deeply, I wouldn't feel the hollow echo in my empty chest. If I didn't move too quickly, I wouldn't reach any painful conclusions. And if I didn't listen, I wouldn't hear the silence he always left behind.

The light flickered at the corner of my eye, drawing my reluctant gaze back to the balcony, and my racing heart tripped and fell. He was there beyond the fluttering drapes, perched on the low wall, his wings extended like he'd just come to rest, the red tips and shimmering undertones catching the light.

My throat burned and my gaze blurred.

"Tiras?" I whispered, his name finding my lips like he'd never been lost. I said his name again, and it trembled there before slipping silently past my chin with the tears streaming from my eyes and scurrying down my cheeks.

The eagle stretched, spreading his wings like he meant to fly, and hovered momentarily above his perch. Then he shifted, slipping between the layers of the sky in stained glass shards of light before streaming out again, transformed. Whole. Safe and whole.

He saw me and stilled—dark hair and warm skin, gleaming eyes and a softly smiling mouth—and I gloried in him, even as I grieved. He crossed the space between us and touched my face with perfect fingers.

"You're crying," he whispered.

"You're . . . s-still a . . . bird," I stuttered.

His smile grew, creasing his cheeks. His joy confused me. "You're speaking," he marveled.

"You're still a bird," I repeated, undeterred.

His eyes clung to my mouth, his thumb tracing the swell of my lower lip.

"I am," he whispered, nodding.

My eyebrows lowered in confusion, and my lips pursed in question, inviting a kiss. Tiras took it, raising my face and ducking his head, kissing me with all the impatience of long separation and the devotion of long suffering.

"Tiras," I murmured, and his kiss deepened as if he liked the whisper of his name in my mouth. For a moment there was only relief and reunion between us, though I wept even as I welcomed him home.

"I took the word away," I cried against his lips. "But you're still a bird."

"Yes," he whispered, cradling my face in his hands and brushing away my tears.

"I was the one who made you an eagle. I didn't mean to. But I did. It was me." I stumbled through my confession, wanting to kneel at his feet and beg for forgiveness, to prostrate myself on the floor in front of him.

"Mikiya," he said gently. "I know. Boojohni told me."

"You wanted to fly . . . I didn't mean to hurt you. I didn't know what would happen."

"I still want to fly," he said with a rueful smile. "I can't imagine never being a bird again. But you didn't make me an eagle, Lark. You just made it impossible for me to be anything else." He met my gaze. "You took the word away, and now . . . I can change."

He backed away, his hand out-stretched, bidding me stay.

"Watch."

With a shimmer and a shift, Tiras became a huge black wolf, tongue lolling to the side like he'd run a dozen miles.

I clapped a hand over my mouth, capturing the cry that rose in my throat.

The wolf sauntered forward, raised an enormous paw, and rested it against my belly, extending the hand of friendship. I giggled and gasped, and the wolf immediately shifted into a slithering snake with golden stripes on ebony scales.

I fought the urge to bolt to the bed and climb up on it, protecting my feet. But the snake became an ape with great sad eyes, the ape became a swan with a graceful neck, and the swan became a sloth with long shaggy arms and a shy demeanor. When Tiras morphed into a braying ass, I began to laugh, recognizing his jest.

Tiras became one creature after another with no more effort or pain than it took for me to spin a spell or wield a word. When he stood before me once again, a dark-haired king with human eyes and hands, bearing no resemblance to the animals he'd been, I finally understood.

"My father was right about one thing," he said.

I tipped my head, waiting.

"He said that I am like him."

I began to protest, but he stopped my lips with a gentle touch.

"I have his Gift. I can change at will. But I don't want to be like him."

"So what are you going to be? It's up to you," I said softly, kissing the fingers that still hovered near my mouth.

"I want to be a good man. A just king. I want to be your husband, Kjell's brother, and our child's father. Beyond that, I will be whatever you want me to be," Tiras promised, and his voice echoed with sincerity.

"Then I think I will keep you," I whispered.

Boojohni said if you hate you can't heal, and Jeru had a great deal of healing to do. Jeru knew how to hate. It was something that had been taught and fostered. It was tradition and history, and it would take some time to change.

Spinners, Healers, Changers, and Tellers began to crop up in ever-growing numbers, emboldened by a new acceptance, and many people were afraid. Zoltev, with all his wondrous gifts, had given Jeru every reason to fear and revile the Gifted. He'd used his power to harm and destroy, and in the wrong hands, the Gifts of the Creator could be terrifying.

But the power to choose had been given to all of the Creator's children, whatever their gifts. As Sorkin said, what a man chose to do with his gift was the true measure, and Tiras and I passed laws to hold Jeruvians accountable for their actions instead of their abilities.

Kjell grieved. He grieved even as he tried to let go of hate, and neither came easy to him. He'd saved Tiras and he'd healed me, but he'd denied his gift for so long that learning to accept it was harder than hiding it. And he didn't trust his instincts. He'd been betrayed and rescued too many times by people he'd misjudged.

Lady Firi had disappeared, changing into yet another version of herself, slipping away to somewhere new. Her father passed away shortly after the attacks on Jeru City. She hadn't lied about everything. The Volgar had attacked a group of the lord's guard, but no one knew whether Lady Firi had orchestrated it all. No one knew how she'd struck her bargain with the Volgar Liege. We only knew she had, and nothing had turned out the way she'd hoped. Still we watched for her, comforted only by the knowledge that she couldn't change her face even though she changed her form.

Her days as Lady Firi were finished.

The lordship in Firi passed to the late lord's only living relative—a sister—and the Council of Lords worried and wrung their hands at the thought of a female ruling the province. But their protestations were hollow and their words weak, and they scurried back to their strongholds and fortresses, pretending control they no longer had. My father went back to Corvyn, having suffered no permanent damage from my pain.

I let him go.

Boojohni said I must.

I let hate go, I let him go, and I began to heal.

My limbs were tired, my back stiff, my steps slow. It wouldn't be long now. The tightness in my belly was almost constant, my girth almost comical, and sleep almost impossible. As Jeru slept, I waited, standing on my balcony overlooking the city square. The night was filled with gentle words, bedtime stories, and soft goodnights.

The breeze stirred my hair, and a piece of a familiar song wafted around me. A woman's voice, urging her daughter to sleep, sang the words of the maiden song like she'd sung it a thousand times.

Daughter, daughter, Jeru's daughter,
He is coming, do not hide.
Daughter, daughter, Jeru's daughter,
Let the king make you his bride.

I was careful with my words. I guarded them, used them prudently, and withheld them wisely. When I kissed Tiras and pressed my lips to his skin, I never marked him or left a wish behind. I'd learned how lethal a word could be. But tonight I sang the maiden song, liking the way the words fell from my mouth like tiny, white pebbles into the well of the world below me. My own daughter was coming soon. Gwyn, the old Teller, had predicted a girl. Tiras had sighed and muttered something about stubborn women, but joy limned his face, and his thoughts were ebullient.

Daughter, daughter, Jeru's daughter,
Wait for him, his heart is true.
Daughter, daughter, Jeru's daughter,
'Til the hour he comes for you.

The hour was nigh, and yet I waited for a restless king who still loved to fly. The shadows moved and shimmered, and from above the homes and trees to the east, I saw him coming, soaring, pale head and sooty wings barely discernible in the starlight. Then he was circling and descending, finally coming to rest on the low wall with a satisfied flutter. He didn't change immediately, but folded his wings and drew close to me, tucking his beak like he was ashamed.

I brushed gentle fingers across his tufted breast and over his downy head, forgiving him. From his heart I heard a word, and it made me smile.

Home.

EPILOGUE

She was so small. The only thing large about her were her eyes, and they filled her face, dark and solemn, like the midnight sky. Little bones, small features, a pointy chin, and elfin ears made her appear delicate, almost fragile, like a tiny bird. Her black hair—the same shade as her father's—was silky and fine and felt like feathers brushing my face when I held her close, furthering the comparison.

She was my little Wren. The name had entered my mind the moment I held her in my arms, and I accepted it, acknowledging it from the Father of all Words, trusting the name was meant for her.

"What are you doing, Wren?"

"I'm making poppets," she answered. Her little tongue peeked between her teeth, which happened whenever she attempted something difficult. She had a pile of ill-formed poppets beside her on the floor, and she wrapped a long piece of string around another one, creating a head, a torso, and four misshapen limbs. I crouched down beside her and picked one up.

"Tell me about them," I urged.

"This one loves to sing." She pointed at the lumpy doll in my hand. "And this one loves to dance—"

"Like a certain little Wren I know," I interrupted tenderly.

"Yes. Like me. And this one loves to run." She held up the smallest one.

"And this one?" I pointed to the poppet she'd just finished.

"This one is a prince."

"Oh?"

"Yes. The Prince of Poppets. And he can fly . . . like Daddy."

"Without wings?"

"Yes. You don't need wings to fly," she chirped.

"What do you need, Daughter?" I asked softly.

She looked up at me, her big, black eyes alight with knowledge, and she smiled.

"Words."

OTHER TITLES

Young Adult and Paranormal Romance

Slow Dance in Purgatory

Prom Night in Purgatory

Inspirational Romance

A Different Blue

Running Barefoot

Making Faces

Infinity + One

The Law of Moses

The Song of David

Historical Fiction

From Sand and Ash

Now available for pre-order

ACKNOWLEDGMENTS

I hate writing these things, not because I don't like to say thank you or because I don't have a million people to be grateful for, but because I'm certain I won't adequately express how very blessed I am and how humbled I am by the love and support in my life.

First, I must thank my assistant, Tamara Debbaut. I truly don't think I would have made it through this book without her. She's tireless, enthusiastic, unbelievably capable, and irreplaceable. Thank you, my friend. I will never be able to pay you what your worth.

Second, my editor Karey White deserves praise and presents for this one. She worked on a hairy, odd, erratic timeline, and all the odd hairiness was mine. I'm turning into a true artist. I'm completely nuts.

Third—my family deserves thanks and love and compassion. I suffer for my art, and my family suffers too, though they smile kindly and tell me they aren't in pain. I have four great kids and a pretty amazing husband, as well as parents and siblings and in-laws that love me and put up with me. I don't deserve them and they definitely don't deserve me.

Fourth—and these are in no particular order—I have to thank Jane Dystel and the whole team at Dystel and Goderich. They make me feel safe and sane. Hang Le for the amazing cover. To JT Formatting for the interior files—Julie always takes such good care of me. To the talented Maxime Plasse for his beautiful map of Jeru. To Mandy Lawler of Lawler Literary services, you do good work, lady.

Sixth, big thanks to great bloggers, my fellow authors, and my loyal readers. I am awed by their support. The world is a good place. Thank you, HARMONIES. Thank you, Tarryn Fisher, Penny Reid, Colleen Hoover, Jessica Park, Rebecca Donovan Elizabeth Hunter, K.A. Tucker, Alison Bailey, Jamie McGuire, Willow Aster, Leylah Attar, Debbie Macomber, Katy Regnery, Mia Sheridan, Karina Halle, A.L. Jackson, Eden Butler, Claire Contreras, Renee Carlino, Rachel Hollis, Stacey Grice, Beth Ehemenn, and so many others. Thank you for being kind.

Finally, I'm just really grateful for Diet Pepsi and Jesus. I know that isn't eloquent, but it's true. Now I'm going to go pop a cold one and say my prayers.

Thank you for reading! Now go and do no harm.

ABOUT THE AUTHOR

Amy Harmon is a *Wall Street Journal, USA Today*, and *New York Times* Bestselling author. Amy knew at an early age that writing was something she wanted to do, and she divided her time between writing songs and stories as she grew. Having grown up in the middle of wheat fields without a television, with only her books and her siblings to entertain her, she developed a strong sense of what made a good story. Her books are now being published in twelve countries, truly a dream come true for a little country girl from Levan, Utah.

Amy Harmon has written ten novels - the *USA Today* Bestsellers, *Making Faces* and *Running Barefoot*, as well as *The Bird and The Sword, The Law of Moses, The Song of David, Infinity + One, Slow Dance in Purgatory, Prom Night in Purgatory*, and the *New York Times* Bestseller, *A Different Blue*. Her next novel, *From Sand and Ash* will be released in October of 2016, via Lake Union Publishing.

Website:
http://www.authoramyharmon.com/

Facebook:
https://www.facebook.com/authoramyharmon

Twitter:
https://twitter.com/aharmon_author

Instagram:
https://www.instagram.com/amy.harmon2/

Newsletter:
http://eepurl.com/46ciz

Pinterest:
https://pinterest.com/authoramyharmon/

BookBub:
https://www.bookbub.com/authors/amy-harmon

CPSIA information can be obtained
at www.ICGtesting.com
Printed in the USA
LVOW13s1655180117

521395LV00014B/1327/P